THE RIDDLE OF THE SEER

THE RIDDLE OF THE SEER

A complete story, this is the first book in The Power of Pain series

ACM PRIOR

GA Roberts Illustrator

Langdown Press

The Dragon Chest

Jebbin heaved at the trapdoor into the attic until it thudded back against a pile of relics. Dust trickled into his eyes as he glared upwards. He wobbled on the stool, slopping oil from his lantern. Looking up cautiously, Jebbin pushed the lantern ahead of him and scrabbled up after it.

Rain rattled on the tiles and cuffed the rooflight, which dribbled cold paleness through its dirt-dimmed glass. The glow from the lantern thickened the shadows behind worm-chewed rafters. Jebbin swept nervously at festoons of cobwebs, drooping with dust. Spiders scuttled for the shadows or drew in hairy legs and dared him to come closer. Jebbin shuddered and peered about in the gloom.

There were stacks of boxes, sprinkled with bat droppings and stuffed with clothes, tools and wooden toys. There was his first shepherd's crook, once Marl's; Marl's first jigball stick, passed down to Jebbin - just like his leather breeches, his tunic and everything else. Jebbin scowled.

The Dragon Chest, as they had called it, stood alone. What a disappointment that had been! Jebbin and Marl had found the chest wedged in an attic corner, half-buried in barrel staves. The weight of its pitted wood fought them as they dragged it out, squealing as iron bands gouged runnels in the floor. How they had marvelled over the dragon head carved in proud relief over the catch. Ignoring the tooth-spiked gullet and the malignant stare from its iron eyes, they had heaved open the heavy lid. Folded neatly inside was babies' linen; clean and smelling of camphor. Nothing more. Careering downstairs, they had demanded to know the history of their momentous discovery. Their parents had exchanged a look but as their father, Tagg, stood morose and brooding, it was their mother, Lin, who had shrugged and said, "That's been around for years. It makes a useful laundry trunk. Look, I've got fresh honeycomb." And their attention had been diverted.

Now a rain-sodden easterly excused Jebbin from the chores that waited outside on any farm. He had been settling down in the log shed with a story when his father stumbled across him. The story had been copied out onto paper scraps by the scribe's son in the nearest town. It told of dashing heroes who plied swords for hire over lands leagues away from little Dorning. Jebbin thought it as exciting as Carrafon Dulene's tales. Tagg had snatched the pages from him and hurled them away as though they had been scorpions.

"How many times I got to tell you?" Tagg began an old and bitter ritual, pulling off his belt. "You're not to do it. No lettering."

"They're only words. They can't hurt."

"They can. They do." The blows from the belt fell with more sting. "They can leach the soul from your body. You've learnt them despite me; you'll not use them."

Jebbin blinked ferociously trying to keep the tears back, holding himself stiffly against the whistle and whack of the leather. When it was done, Jebbin tried to glower into his father's scarred face but dropped his eyes. Those scars were proof enough his father cared for him. Once Jebbin had surprised a bear and it had swatted him into unconsciousness with a single blow, half severing his arm. He remembered nothing more than waking in his cot, his arm bandaged with his mother's cross-over knotting. His father had attacked the enraged bear with a mattock and driven it off. Tagg's scars were far worse than his.

"Clear the lumber of your childhood from the attic so I can store apples there." Tagg's voice had held the same anger with which he must have faced the bear.

Jebbin picked up a castle of mould-softened paper and wood. Tagg was right. That castle had figured in a hundred stories of valour; stout defences, furious assaults and miraculous rescues, but it had always been made of adamantine stone and now it had shrunk with age. He tossed it down.

Everything had changed since he played up here with Marl. Jebbin rubbed his smarting backside and wondered whether the place had been swept out then or whether they had not minded the spiders. They had dreamed of becoming knights or wandering freebooters like Lord Carrafon. Now Marl would marry and settle over the orchards like a broody hen on eggs; the future held even less promise for Jebbin.

Carrafon had told his stories of bravado to the children of Dorning and never lacked for willing ears. He talked of dragons, giants and magicians who drank pain and vomited fire. He was a hero from legend to them with his jewelled rapier, silken clothes and ready money. Jebbin chuckled. Yes, Carrafon seemed free with his coin, tossing a gold ryal to the barman and giving a Trivan testoon to Elya when she refused to believe he had travelled so far. Then, just as the week was up, he absconded in the early morning and never settled his account. All his lavished money would scarcely have paid his slate from one boisterous evening. The landlord wailed; village greybeards sat on benches like stone oracles and told each other how they had predicted villainy. The children reckoned Carrafon a wily rascal and were thrilled when the militia thundered through Dorning after him.

Carrafon had cut a grand figure, vibrant and colourful. How they had shrieked when he attacked a scarecrow, leaping and slashing, posing with rapier a-quiver, then whirling again, shouting and stabbing until tufts of straw fled on the wind.

Jebbin snatched up a cane and struck one of Carrafon's poses. He saw his shadow in the lantern light: a giant with a magical rapier. Spinning about, he hacked the ramparts from the paper castle.

"Fly villains! Jebbin is upon you," he cried, whacking and slicing while the lantern recorded his actions in shadow writing on the wall. "Die, Dragon! I claim your treasure!"

As Jebbin lunged, everything happened with dreamlike slowness. His arm drove forward with the silly cane pointing at the dragon's mouth. He watched the point spear into the hollow gullet, sliding down as slowly and powerfully as an avalanche. Blue fire flickered along the cane and back to the dragon's head. Then the iron jaws clashed shut and quietness waited, poised.

Jebbin was still for a moment, feeling weak and drained but suddenly aware that the stinging pain of his beating had faded to a numbed ache. Catching sight of the broken cane, he forgot his weariness. He stared at the end in fascination. It was sheared off as cleanly as though his father had struck it with his felling axe. Jebbin sensed the hairs on the back of his neck lifting as he looked at the dragon's head. The jaws were clamped shut. With trembling hands, he lifted the Dragon Chest's lid, heavy no longer. The top now revealed a secret compartment housing a leather and copper-bound book, a black lacquered box and a tightly furled scroll, all carefully immobilised with strapping. Set into the lid's base was a short lever.

Shaking and sweating, Jebbin lowered the lid. With sudden energy, he attacked the piles of rubbish and began throwing his once cherished possessions down the hatchway with methodical detachment. All the while, the book seared his mind.

Assaulted with such vigour, the jumbled assortment soon took order; the pleadings of favourite toys leaving him unmoved as they teetered on the edge of the hatch and plummeted to oblivion. The moment the job was done, he quietly closed the trapdoor and returned to the chest.

Jebbin unrolled the scroll. Instead of the stiff, age-crackled parchment he expected, it was smooth and pliable like fresh hide. But it was blank. There were dots and swirls of colour in yellow and tan but nothing that could represent a hidden code. Jebbin re-rolled the silky material, strapped it away and took out the box. There was an S on the lid, looking uncomfortably snake-like. Inside there was a tiny measure and a drift of grey powder. He fingered it suspiciously, swirling runes in the coarse grains as he checked for anything hidden. Finally. he turned to the book. Nothing again, just a mess of spots, deepening in places to orange and charcoal. But not one word.

Jebbin's disappointment was so extreme that he slumped to the floor with the useless book on his lap, its water-spotted pages mocking his anguish. In despair, his unfocused eyes gazed right through it. As he did so, words loomed up through the page like rising fish. Jebbin almost yelped in shock and focused on the page again. It was as blank as ever, no matter how hard he stared and willed the words to reappear. He tried looking through it and suddenly there they were again, as though they floated an arm's length behind the book. He discovered that with great concentration he could hold them steady and read, which he did with mounting fascination. The tome was entitled The Practice of Magic with Annotated Spell Lists. Inside the cover was a name: Dewlin Voryllion, mage of the fifteenth rank. The book began with a short test.

'You who read these lines for the first time have satisfied your tutors with your skill - but the Practice of Magic is a dangerous art. You must *assay this task and, should you fail, put away this book and with it all thoughts of sorcery and the Web of Power. Live life without pain.*

Sear is the gateway to magic and the road to pain. When you are ready, inhale one minim of sear. Control yourself silently with the Mantra of Pain. Place the end of your staff in the palm of your hand. Focus the pain as you have been taught and release the syllables Dollor Commuto, Feeaht Lukkx. If you cannot create this light, your career as a magician is over. Leave this art while you may still practise another.'

Jebbin tried to push weariness from his watering eyes with his palms. Almost in disbelief, he stared again through the page to check the words were still there and that he had memorised the syllables correctly.

Jebbin had fantasized what he could do as a magician: pleasant images of boys from a neighbouring farm exploding into flame after ragging him, overbearing merchants turning into willing zombies to cook and play at his command. But this was different, something altogether more serious. A self-styled magician had visited Dorning once. He had tossed balls in the air and produced a piglet from a surprising pocket. But his magic had no connection with this book either.

Jebbin leapt up to show the book to someone, then stopped. Marl would snatch it away, dancing and scoffing, and it wouldn't be his anymore. His father would toss it on the fire, saying, "No letters. Flights of fancy pick no apples." There was a phrase he had heard for as many of his thirteen harvests as he could remember. In any case, there couldn't really be magic here, could there? He felt the solemn weight of the book in his hands and read the no nonsense text again. Supposing it did work? It could do no harm to try. The warning words loomed before him and he knew it could harm, oh yes. But only if it worked.

Jebbin returned to the lacquered box. He traced the S, wondering about *sear* and the ominous mantra of pain. Could he really cast a spell? How much would it hurt? He rubbed his numb bottom and his lips tightened in a feral grin. The pain would only last a moment. He teased out a single grain of the powder. Its bland greyness was frightening. Jebbin carefully twisted a scrap of cloth round the grain and stuffed it in his pocket. Then he strapped tome and box back into the lid and closed it, having reset the catch with the lever to hide his discovery. The jaws of the dragon sprang apart again and he drew out the end section of his cane. He flicked it aside and slid through the trapdoor, dangling until his toes touched the stool.

Mechanically, he crammed the rubbish into a sack to be burnt. Jebbin felt that the syllables churning in his head must be visible to anyone and he longed to attempt the spell but he gritted his teeth and determined to wait until dark when the least luminescence would be most easily visible.

That night, Jebbin stayed by the fire when the rest of his family retired to bed. He awoke clenched in an eerie chill. The fire had died to fluffy ashes and no light crept past the fastened shutters over the window. Excitement welled up, rolling back the vestiges of sleep. He knelt on the floor and tried to compose himself into what he hoped would be the right frame of mind.

He shook the grain of *sear* into his palm. With a snap of determination, he bent and snuffed it into his nose. His head banged back as though a hot pitchfork had been thrust up his nostril. His eyes bulged and breath whistled between his gritted teeth but he stifled the natural outcry. Long stoicism before his father's beatings and an older brother whose idea of teaching sword fighting revolved round hitting him with a jigball stick had taught him that much.

Having no staff, he crushed his palms together as he fought for control. Calm blossomed within him and he unleashed the words, almost spat them from him with the pain. As the syllables fled from his tongue, he tried to hold them in his cupped hands. Moving his thumbs apart he was amazed to see a small, iridescent ball flickering above his hands; the beautiful child born of his pain. With wonder in his heart, he watched the glowing colours dart and gleam and burst into darkness.

Next day, Jebbin was soon back in the attic. He hurried to the chest, picked up a piece of cane and prodded it through the dragon's jaws. There was no response, just like all the other times when he and Marl had fiddled with it before. In vain he poked, twisted and rattled the stick. He could find no catch and the secret lid remained hidden. He moved back and lunged forward rapier-fashion as he had done the previous day. It took a couple of attempts to spear the cane exactly down the throat. That elicited no response from the chest and a squawk from him as he skewered a splinter into his hand.

Jebbin was about to kick the chest in vexation when the answer came to him with shocking clarity. He had opened the chest with a spell. Without his father's beating to provide the pain, nothing would have happened. He cleared his throat nervously.

"Dragon," he croaked, "yield your treasure." The jaws yawned impassively. With a sudden fury, Jebbin jabbed the splinter into his palm and beat his bloodied hand on the chest. "Yield, dragon!"

Instantly the jaws snapped together. Breathing hard, Jebbin sucked his numbed hand and grinned. He opened the chest and took out the tome, still scarcely able to believe that magic was within his grasp. Here was a task he would not shirk; to become one of the legendary magicians that had always stalked his dreams. The pain did not yet seem so important.

* * *

Four more harvests had gone by with storerooms crammed or tight belts, as farming vagaries happened. His daydreams of what to do with magic had changed into more inventive reprisals for boys; girls playing a more disturbing role. But the reality of what a magician should do remained a mystery.

Jebbin closed the book with a determined snap. There was a thud as he dropped it into the secret compartment for the last time. A small cloud of dust puffed up and caught the sunlight, glowing like an echo of the ball of magical light. He used to summon that to remind himself that he really could cast spells, just to stare at it like a child with a perfect birthday present. Not any more. It was neither Dewlin's warnings about the unforeseeable effects spells could have nor the risk of failure. Magic hurt.

Leaving the book was easy. He knew all the spells by heart and it was safe in the chest. The scroll was harder to abandon. Jebbin was sure it held text like the book but whenever letters seemed about to appear, the dots slid and wafted like snowflakes and for all his efforts they still entwined themselves into knots beyond his unravelling. He shrugged and slammed the lid shut.

He swung down into the hatch, hanging by one arm as he lowered the trapdoor, then dropped. It was time to leave the farm despite regrets for family ties, friends, food and, greatest of all, Sola. He could not help smiling as he thought of her. He had shown the ball of light only to her. The reflection in her luminous eyes had carried him through years of hard study.

But nobody else; he could not suddenly announce he was a magician to folk who had last seen him wailing round Dorning market in his mother's footsteps. He would feel like a child caught trying on his father's coat. Demonstrations of power to prove himself were too painful. Nor were errors impossible and the thought of locals sharing ribald tales of his ineptitude made his ears burn. He had once failed a spell and the pain had lasted until he was able to control himself to cast a different spell. He had almost given up then. Now he feared to use the *sear* powder. But he also ached to use it. He had the power to use magic and he would do something real with it. He gave a grin his brother would not have recognised. The grin faded as he thought of one instruction - "Take nine minims of *Sear*..." Nine!

The pain of a single grain was like breathing steam. But he could cast magic. Squaring his shoulders resolutely, he marched downstairs.

Saying goodbye was harder than he had imagined. His parents listened in silence to his halting words as he said he could use magic, really cast spells and he had to leave them to learn what to do with it. His father looked troubled and spoke dispiritedly after three false starts,

"You shouldn't leave us. Don't walk the way of the sorcerer, son."

"Shouldn't you have a staff or something, dear?" his mother enquired gently.

"I'm a magician, not a village entertainer. I can do it. I must." Jebbin had predicted that his parents would be dumbfounded by the arrival of a sorcerer in their midst. He had steeled himself for rancour or refusals but their impenetrability disturbed him. He would have been hurt had he not been so buoyed with anticipation of a new life. He thought his father was mostly concerned at the loss of a pair of hands on the farm.

Eventually Tagg roused from his taciturn tangle. "Change your mind, son. Magicians become other than human; they grow away, get isolated. You don't want to spend your life twisting a knife in your own guts for some dream of power."

"It's not like that," said Jebbin. "There's a powder. I've learned to make my own *sear* with simple ingredients and a tiny spell..."

"Pain comes from many sources," said his mother quietly.

Jebbin thought she meant that his leaving would hurt them. "You don't understand about sorcery. I can actually do magic. I can't ignore it."

"Stay, boy," said Tagg. "To be a free farmer in Marigor is a good row to hoe. Magic and peace are no bedfellows. Your phantom treasures will already be seized by the ambitions of kings or the greed of dragons."

"Kings and dragons? That's what I want! Have you ever seen such things?"

"No, not I," said Tagg at last, glaring at the table from beneath beetling brows. "Already you have fallen into the secretive and deceitful ways of the magician, poring over that evil book when you could have lifted your eyes and seen the bright world outside."

"But it is into that bright world I need to go."

"Always the clever, twisting words."

"I'm not trying to be clever. I just want to go with your blessing."

"Then it's best you go. And will you become a travelling man? Have no hearth, no home field? Spend your time running from commitment in a foolish search for adventure?" Tagg turned in bitterness from his own soft questions, no longer seeking answers.

Jebbin remained adamant. They drank cider in a strained atmosphere, his mother offering common sense advice for his travels; Tagg glowering silently and chewing his afternoon hunk of bread with more force than necessary.

Standing in relief as soon as they finished, Jebbin collected his pack and started a few awkward sentences, which ran dry between the wells of hope and regret. He walked from his dearly familiar home and turned to say goodbye. His mother kissed him, sad yet strangely yearning, then thrust a parcel of rations into his pack of jumbled clothes. His father held him closely but there was a look in his eye Jebbin could not decipher.

Jebbin looked back often, having promised himself that he would not and saw his parents talking animatedly, perhaps arguing. Just before the house disappeared from view he saw them clasping each other, as though in another farewell, before his father trudged back indoors. The remaining figure looked tiny and Jebbin was almost hidden beneath a hemlock tree but he waved uncertainly at his home. For a fleeting moment it appeared that there was an answering wave but then he could see the small shape no more, only an early owl rising slowly out of the dell where his home lay. He shrugged and pressed on eagerly.

A couple of hours walking took him over Tumblehill, where they had the barrel-rolling contest after harvest, and down the sheep-nibbled slopes towards Sidea. As the ground flattened into the valley, alders marked the inquisitive windings of a stream. The light faded into yellow as he strolled into lines of aged pear trees. There was a cottage at the far end of the orchard. He saw Sola move past the window, preparing supper. As he approached, she swept a fat little hen out of the door. It clucked indignantly. A moment later, Sola threw out a handful of crumbs. The hen scratched and pecked a couple of times, then hopped back inside.

Beside the cottage, a sinewy man was splitting lengths of hazel with a billhook. Uprights of ash were mounted in a frame and a few completed hurdles rested against the wall.

"Hello, Bodd. They look good," said Jebbin.

"Almost as easy to make a good hurdle as a bad 'un and it's a tiring job fetching the sheep if they stray." Bodd looked up briefly and registered Jebbin's pack "You're really off?"

Jebbin nodded and slipped in to see Sola. Herby smells steamed from a pot of rabbit and vegetables. A loaf, a pat of goat's butter and a bowl of pear and fennel chutney waited on a table. Clacking down wooden platters, Sola smiled at him and blew him a kiss.

"Nearly ready. Talk to Dad a moment. I've got a present for you later."

Feeling like the hen, Jebbin rejoined Bodd and stood awkwardly.

"Where're you headed then?" said Bodd.

Jebbin never knew what the old peasant thought of him; anything between a legendary wizard wandering in his orchards and a play actor trying to impress his daughter. He guessed Bodd was pleased he was leaving and talked to fill the gap before supper.

"When I was hedging three years back, a witch-woman rode past, slouched astride a decrepit nag. She threatened to curse me if I didn't fetch bread and beer. So I did, then asked her to tell my fortune for me.

"She looked at me slyly while eating and said: 'Fortune telling, eh? My particular speciality! There's a lucky omen for you already, so who knows what wonders the stars hold for your future? But it costs, you know. It's hard work, telling. The more you pay, the more accurate it'll be. What can you afford, laddie? A fistful of golden ryals and your life will be mapped before you, a capful more and I'll show you every nuance of the future, each difficulty confounded with the perfect solution for your personal profit and aggrandisement.'

"Whatever that meant, she was obviously wise, so I offered her a helm. She just spat and made to rise. I said I had a crown in the house.

"She said; 'Perhaps that might suffice. An utterance of inestimable value for a crown and a measly helm. Gather coins while I prepare myself.'

"When I returned, the woman was rocking to and fro on her heels before some squiggles in the dust. Her grimy hand was outstretched and my money vanished too fast to get dirty. She motioned me down and gripped my hands between hers. With a series of moans that made my scalp prickle, she muttered words spiced with shrieking gibberish, mostly unintelligible, but I picked out several clear phrases:

" 'You shall see the towers of Triva ....Beware the city of Arin-Orca... Greater now shall be the son, greater than the father truly....You shall rise to wealth and power, taking lands to rule them wisely But remember Death awaits you, in the land of ....' and then she had faded off into racking coughs.

" 'Well then, did you hear what you wanted?' she asked me, regaining her equanimity with remarkable speed. So of course, I wanted to know this land where death awaits me, but she'd only say, 'No good asking me now! I don't know what I say when I'm telling. It's a trance, see? If you get another crown, I'll do what I can for you.' But I had no more crowns and she departed, chuckling like knucklebones.

"Of course I didn't mention it to Tagg, especially the bit about the son being greater than the father. Perhaps even he once dreamed of being more than a farmer." Realising he had said the wrong thing Jebbin continued hastily. "Probably rubbish, but I need some goal and there's no harm in heading for Triva."

"Hmf. Better stay at home if Death's a-waiting elsewhere. Still, Sidea's but a few hours' walk for one long of leg - unless you plan to conjure a winged chariot? No? At Sidea's inn, you may dine like King Orthogon and sleep on feathers for but a few golden ryals. Nothing for a magician, I'm sure, but if our gruel is enough for you, I see it's ready."

Sola's smile made up for Bodd's gruffness and after the meal Bodd went to bed, caustically pointing out that some people had work to do in the morning and could not summon demons to do it at the flick of a finger.

Sola presented a bundle to Jebbin. He shook out a cloak, midnight blue on the outside, azure on the inside, shot through with silver runes.

"It's marvellous. How did you do it?"

"I think it's perfect for a magician on his way to fame and glory. The material cost me all my savings. Now you'll have a bit of me to remember always."

Jebbin slipped the cloak round his shoulders and they walked together under the pear trees and said their goodbyes. Holding her close, her head beneath his chin, Jebbin breathed her scent, looking up through the branches.

"They should have been in blossom," he said.

After a while, Sola asked dreamily, "You'll be back for Apple Home?"

"In six days? I don't expect to be home in sixty days. I don't know what a magician does, but I know nobody in Dorning can tell me."

"We had a magician here once."

"Sola, pretending to find a toad in Elya's ear is clever, not magic. If it had been Marl's ear, it wouldn't even have been surprising. This is different. I can cast spells, just like in stories. I've never met anyone like that."

"Don't you go dragging a toad out of my ear." She wasn't listening. For her, hearth and orchard were enough. He held her close, aching with the realisation that even she did not understand that magic demanded a wider canvas and he had to go.

They kissed and parted at dawn, Sola tripping into the cottage with dew darkening the hem of her skirt. Jebbin shook creases from the cloak and strode south with the intention of reaching the Billyrillin river and drifting west until he came across the Golden Road. Even in Dorning all knew of that highway, running uncounted leagues from Merrin, Marigor's capital, to the age-hardened fortress-city of Jerondst in Azria. Few even of the great caravans rolled from one city all the way to the other and none of those mighty merchant trains came anywhere near Dorning. The Golden Road passed through Triva and Jebbin had a mind to make the first part of the witch's prophesy come true by visiting the towers of Triva even if the wealth and lands to rule did not follow along handily. However, opportunities must abound for a man of wit and power before then.

A short cut of his own devising and he missed Sidea altogether. Nevertheless, the weather was kind and his first night was spent comfortably curled under his cloak in a holm-oak brake. After his packed breakfast, he drank from a rivulet where he performed some perfunctory ablutions. Jebbin lay full length and let the morning sun soak into him. At last he could relax without the threat of his father sending him off on seventeen errands, all to be done at once. The life of a strolling magician seemed infinitely better than toiling in the orchards and vegetable plots around Dorning.

By the following afternoon, he was less sure. Lunch had been meagre, supper would be leaner yet; a condition he seemed destined to share. The tussocky downs were stretched about him, flickering with butterflies and pearled with tiny, pink flowers but offering neither food nor water. In vexation, he kicked a thistle head, which exploded in a scintillating cloud of seeds and butterflies.

At the sound, a sheep rose from behind a gorse clump, bleated accusingly and trotted off to join others he had not seen. Deducing that tended sheep meant shepherd, Jebbin followed them as meekly as a lamb and soon came to a track down to a village.

Whistling happily, he left the village with provisions bulging his pack and still coins in his purse. An old man travelled ahead of him with a laboured stride, aided by a long stick. Jebbin soon overtook him and asked what lay on the road ahead. The wayfarer, who introduced himself as Dordo, had little of value to relate but chatted with wry humour and Jebbin felt that in his company the leagues might fall behind more slowly in fact but quicker in seeming.

A while later, the two turned a corner in a wood to see a wagon over-turned, the occupants apparently slain. Four men were busy looting, one hooting with mirth as he tossed cloth from a broken crate, another yanking a ring from a pale hand. Jebbin motioned Dordo back and fumbled in his pockets for *sear*, so awash with fear and excitement he could barely remember a spell. He picked out a grain and pushed it into his nose. For the first time, the pain sawing at his nerves meant something; it hurt just as much but it had a flavour of its own. It wasn't just pain, it was a weapon, power, magic. He turned to see Dordo, shaking his stick fiercely, doddering down upon the attackers. Even as Jebbin leapt forward, one of the robbers callously felled the aged man with a blow from a hammer. As Dordo fell back and lay twitching, Jebbin charged forward, marshalling the syllables of a spell. Pain from the *sear* flamed up his nose and curdled into words he hurled at Dordo's attacker who slowly crumpled against the wagon wheel, swatting feebly at imagined lights. Jebbin thought of more *sear* but he was untutored and just one grain took him too close to being Numbed. He leapt forward. His cape billowed and flashed its own runes as Jebbin flung his arms wide and bellowed at the remaining brigands.

"Fly, villains! The power of the gods lies unleashed in my mind. Fly or perish!" For a moment, Jebbin thought they would run, a visible frisson of fear wriggling over them.

Then a bearded man shouted, "There's naught but trickery here. At him, lads!" With a dextrous flick, he sent a hammer spinning at Jebbin, catching him on the knee.

The pain came as a wave of nausea quite unlike the bright pain of *sear*. He tried to use it for a spell but it was a bloated, amorphous blob beyond his shaping. All the pain-power roared out of him in a thin sheet of white flame, dizzying against the sky. Even as he tried to blink the grogginess from his brain, three men were on him and there was nothing for it but to fight. He blocked the first blow at his head just as Marl had taught him and swung his clenched fist into the man's midriff, knocking the wind out of him with a satisfactory whistle. Then another kicked Jebbin's feet from under him, somebody's knee caught him on the chin and they piled on top of him in a whirlwind of fists and boots which greyed into nothingness.

Eventually Jebbin recovered, an event he viewed with mixed feelings. He was surprised to be alive but with consciousness came a flood of complaints from all parts of his battered body.

"Sweet Lessan! Now I know how the grass feels after the clog dance."

He peered about and saw the four bandits lying still near the wrecked wagon. His own head and left leg had been bandaged with cross-over knotting and his cape lay folded nearby. Dordo, showing little sign of his brief battle, was sitting with his back against a tree, sipping from a flask and staring blankly over the dismal scene. Jebbin struggled to his feet and hobbled to the wagon. The victims were laid in a dignified line, their paltry goods and coins stacked beside them. The brigands were also dead, raised welts round their necks suggesting they had been strangled.

"Dordo? How can this be? What happened?"

"I cannot say. I lost my struggle with one of them and anyway, it seems we were too late to help these poor travellers."

"Some struggle."

Dordo ignored him. "Perhaps the Sidea militia, armed with whips and lariats, rescued us in the nick of time."

"And ride off with this carnage on the road? Unlikely."

Jebbin limped to the robbers' bodies. Faces once bestial in rage were now accusingly flaccid and forlorn. Death he had seen before; villagers slain by accident, age or disease, but this deliberate killing brought the realisation that he could have been lying so pallid and empty. Avoiding touching them, he lifted a hefty leather bag from the bearded man's belt. Jebbin's knees began to wobble. Swallowing hard, he returned to Dordo. Opening the drawstring, he poured coins into his palm.

"What do we do with all this money?"

"Those poor folk. I must report to the nearest militia. Perhaps they had family to claim their effects. You can keep the robbers' gold. I want no share. Maybe you killed them."

"Perhaps," said Jebbin, slightly startled. "I am a magician, you know."

"I guessed from the cloak. But you have no staff."

"Well, you have a stick and all you did was batter one with your head," Jebbin said, feeling the old man should be more impressed.

"I downed one. Perhaps my second spell summoned energies greater than I knew to slay them all."

They sat for a while letting the sun ease their aches. Jebbin spotted the draft horse snorting nervously nearby. He managed to quieten it, removed the broken traces and tied it to a tree. Returning to the old man, he asked,

"Do you know Bodd and Sola from near Sidea?"

Dordo nodded once.

"I have just come from there. They..." Jebbin paused uncertainly, clinking gold ryals and angels in his hands. "I would like to prove something to them. To myself, really. You said you were going back to the militia. Could you take some of this back to Sola?"

Dordo shot Jebbin a calculating look. "I didn't say I was going *back*."

"Please?"

Dordo's reply was so long coming, Jebbin thought he had been refused, but at last Dordo murmured to himself, "Meet a boy pretending to be a mage though he hasn't even got a staff. He finds a pile of gold and can't wait to give it away. How can I refuse?" He held his hand out for the bag. "Good luck to you, son."

Jail

When Jebbin regained muzzy consciousness, he found himself moving along a corridor. His head hanging low, he watched his feet and knees bumping along the stone floor and was faintly glad he could not feel them. With an effort, he looked ahead and tried to focus his eyes. Corridor. There was nothing else to do so he closed his eyes again. They descended a cold stone stairway, the steps dished from long use. Jebbin could certainly feel his knees now and wished he could not. Trying to voice a firm complaint, he heard somebody groan at the same time and wondered who it might have been. The guards dragging him along were holding a conversation over his lolling head and their words were becoming comprehensible.

"Very likely swing for it. I mean, if he's as useless as you say, it's hardly worth putting him in the Death Squad. What else can you do with an assassin?"

"Can't quite believe he is an assassin, though."

"No? And it was you he was trying to stick on that little pin of a knife! Look at it this way: someone comes sneaking up in the brush beside the road, prinkles over to the gate and tries to shove a blade into the guard. What's that sound like, Fitch? Someone selling flowers?"

"I know. But he was so appallingly bad at it! I was thinking about the next fencing match when I had this queer sensation, felt all tired and feeble."

"Feeble-minded, more like. Sounds normal to me."

"Anyway, then he hops towards me. Did he think I hadn't seen him, for Nakki's sake?"

Jebbin groaned again. Now he remembered casting a spell to send the guard to sleep. Optimistically assuming that Fitch had been asleep on his feet, he had taken his knife out in case of emergencies and crept forward. Then Fitch's sword had sizzled out like a falcon strike and Jebbin's knife had spiralled over his head with a clink. Just as his eyes and mouth had gaped open in surprise, Fitch's sword had come whistling back to strike his temple with the pommel and he had collapsed.

"A bad assassin'll hang as high as a good 'un," continued the second guard cheerfully.

"I wish I hadn't hit him so hard. He looked so, well, sort of surprised. I honestly don't think he expected me to do anything at all. Perhaps I shouldn't have - at least we'd know what he was up to."

"What he was up to was no good, that's what. Let him go trogging past you out of mild curiosity and when he yerks Lord Tremenion, awkward questions get asked. You did right, Fitch."

"I'd like to know all the same. Don't seem quite right. Still, orders... Hey jailer! Bung him in number four."

"And quick about it. We're late for supper!"

Large keys clanked and Jebbin was propelled through an iron door which closed with a thud that echoed with finality.

He had expected to find himself alone in a small cell and was briefly relieved to be wrong. Then Jebbin assessed the inmates as the most brutal, filthy and mean-looking cutthroats he had ever seen and felt this was a bad time to be introduced to such dregs. The floor on which he was sprawled was a hand-span deep in stinking watery slime. He staggered to his feet, wiping at the gunge. The other oc-

cupants sat upon a bench running round the circumference of the
cell. There was no obvious gap for him and when he moved towards
a small nook, his fellow prisoners expanded themselves to make it
clear that further cluttering of their section of the bench was un-
desirable. Looking round in despair, Jebbin saw none he felt up to
tackling physically in his present state.

"Look at that pretty cloak! Surely not another magician in our
midst. Bow, everyone!"

Jebbin glared at the speaker, a buck-toothed man sitting with his
arms folded. "Please make a space." When the man just sneered at
him, Jebbin continued grimly, "Or learn what a magician can do."

A roar of laughter greeted this comment but amidst the hoots a
lean man forced a space and supple fingers motioned for Jebbin to
join him. "Come and sit. There'll be space a-plenty tomorrow."

Others were less disposed to let the matter rest and there was a
crackle of heckling.

"Mighty magician? Looks more like a drowned mouse!"

"What do you want him next to you for, Hiraeth? Fancy a
catamite?"

"Another pain-burner, no thanks! You're all cripples and
masochists. We've got one already and without a staff none of you
are more'n a bag of foul wind."

"I am a magician and I don't need a staff," Jebbin fired back.

Amid more derisory laughter, a tall man with black hair, seeming
isolated even on the packed bench, spoke definitively. "Then you're
a double liar. All magicians require a focus. We Gesgarians have developed the art until we can use a sword as that focus..."

"But it's back to the bag of wind when you've lost it, eh Orrolui?"
snorted another, although his laughter stopped abruptly under Orrolui's venomous glare.

"Leave the boy alone," said Hiraeth. "Sit down, lad, and stop
making a fool of yourself."

"I have my mage's powers and had I my *sear*..." said Jebbin obstinately.

"More lies," said Orrolui. "All magicians keep *sear* about them; under their nails, in their hair, sewn into every item of clothing. But without the focus, magic is impossible."

"And even if they have no *sear*, some twist their own broken fingers..."

"Or break their own teeth..."

"Or leave skewers in their flesh so they've got the power."

"Here's what you've got," yelled someone, flinging a handful of slop at Jebbin's head. "Sit in that, whippersnapper!"

Ignoring the jailer banging on the door for silence, the buck-toothed man shouted over the din, "Hey, I've an idea. He wants *sear*, let him have it. Give me some, Gesgarian."

Orrolui contemptuously opened his curled fingers. A greasy grain of *sear* lay on his palm. The buck-toothed man snatched it up. With two others, he pounced on Jebbin and thrust the ball into his mouth.

In the bedlam that had the jailer thumping the door and yelling threats to deny them rations tomorrow, Hiraeth leapt up to pull Jebbin to the bench but with startling speed a massively-built man burst forward, a casual shove sending Hiraeth reeling back to his place. The buck-toothed man received a blow that laid him flat in the floor filth. His cronies were hurled off Jebbin. "Balgrim's beard, enough!"

An awkward silence fell, punctured by the drip of slime from Jebbin's clothes. Ignoring moans from the buck-toothed man as he hauled himself towards the bench, the thickset man eyed Jebbin quietly. Although short and naked to the waist, he was almost square with hard muscle and the hair that was absent from his head sprouted freely elsewhere. Huge hands were balled into gristly lumps like old bones and his eyes glittered with annoyance.

"Everyone knows sorcerers can't cast spells without a focus; staff or sword. You know different. You've made me, Bolan, get wet feet and lost everyone food. Don't like that and don't care for folk talking big. So prove what you say. There's enough pain in here."

"Yes, and magicians can burn everyone else's pain, too!"

"Superstitious nonsense," said Orrolui. "We're hearing all the fairy tales today. We use our own pain for power."

"What do you cause so much pain for, then?"

"Quiet," growled Bolan. "So do it," he said to Jebbin.

But fire was screaming round Jebbin's mouth. Acid dissolved his teeth and bit at the bare roots. He was failing to hammer the pain into control and feared the wrestler was about to give him more. Jebbin's mind went as blank as a slate dipped in a stream. He found himself staring fixedly at the hairs on the wrestler's belly as Bolan shrugged his arms wide. With a cry, Jebbin dragged all the pain resonating through the web of power into a single drop and spat it towards the wrestler. A tiny flake of white energy blazed through the dungeon like a sunbeam in a nightmare and ploughed into Bolan's chest.

Blood splattered up into Bolan's face. He clutched a vast hand over the hole in his flesh as though trying to hide a gem but blood leaked rapidly between fingers scarred with simple steel and dripped down in a red parody of the water from Jebbin. Without speaking, the wrestler plodded back to his bench where he leant against the wall, pressing his hand to the injury, and watched Jebbin impassively.

Standing with his back against the door, Jebbin's face was white with effort and fear. If there had been silence when Bolan intervened, now there was an utter stillness that went beyond mere absence of noise.

Jebbin's pulse stuttered red at the edge of his vision. Swaying and light-headed, he pushed himself away from the door and sailed through the slime to the space beside Hiraeth, which grew as he neared it until he fell onto the bench. Blurred faces swam round him in the grey fog of his exhaustion, pierced only by the avidity of Orrolui's stare.

The night growled with muttered conversations. Nobody spoke to Jebbin but many darted him dark, surreptitious glances as they gnawed suspicions and whispers flickered from side to side. No sorcerer could cast a spell without a focus. What wight or demon is this?

Jebbin spoke only once to thank Hiraeth for his lone stand and great kindness in a place that saw little. Hiraeth made no reply but his hand squeezed Jebbin's arm. Jebbin felt warmth flood through him and could have cried on Hiraeth's shoulder. Instead, he swallowed a lump in his throat and collapsed into sleep.

He was woken by the door banging wide. A guard passed a scroll to a swarthy man in a plumed helmet, addressing him as Captain Gorve. The Captain read from the scroll.

"The wondrous Talnavor jigball team. Perhaps we'll ease back on the celebrations next time - unusual though a win for the Tigers may be." Everyone from one side bench trooped out together, many clutching their heads. Jebbin noticed that each wore an orange striped jerkin, in various states of filth and disrepair.

Captain Gorve read out names. Bolan was one of those escorted out, still clasping his injury of the previous night and leaving a dark stain on the bench. Before trudging off with the others, Bolan gave Jebbin a long look and a nod. It seemed a gesture of respect, even approval, rather than the animosity Jebbin had feared. Jebbin assumed those called were to be released rather than redistributed amongst other cells or even executed but nobody said.

The remaining residents now had room to spare. Jebbin would have liked to talk to Hiraeth but the lean man was suffering from the careless whack the wrestler had given him. Jebbin had no healing to offer and left Hiraeth alone while he pondered his position. It was not long before Orrolui paddled across to join him. When Jebbin looked up to acknowledge his presence, Orrolui thrust out a long and sinewy hand.

"I am Orrolui of Gesgary and I would be your friend."

Jebbin looked up suspiciously, remembering Orrolui tossing *sear* with a callous flick, those black eyes coolly assessing him. But Orrolui's hand was out-stretched in a friendless place and the Gesgarian was prepared to talk while others shunned him. Jebbin, who had been longing for congenial company, pumped the proffered hand in a foreign curled-finger grip, without considering how this association would further alienate the others.

Orrolui sat down, shaking his head ruefully and his feet delicately to flick away the slime. "You made me look a fool," he whispered wryly. "I've hardly finished saying it's impossible before spells are flying and Bolan blasted. Bolan too, a real celebrity! A simple light spell cast without a focus would have done it. Just between us, how did you do it? You must have some new miniature focus."

"No, I haven't. I don't use one."

"Oh, well, it's a bit stand-offish between fellow magicians but if you really don't want to tell me..." Orrolui paused, eyebrows raised hopefully.

"Honestly, I don't need one. I didn't even know anyone else did."

"Nonsense! In the history of sorcery, every single mage has required a focus. You know how spells are cast - it is obviously essential to use a focus. Who were your tutors? Didn't you notice any long sticks they waved about?"

"Orrolui, believe me, I had no tutors either," said Jebbin in a small voice that ignored Orrolui's sarcasm. "Wizards are rare as hen's teeth. I learned from a book. There was a test that mentioned a staff but since I didn't have one I went on without and it worked. I've never had any sort of focus."

"Teltazzar! This is incredible," breathed Orrolui after a pause, his blazing eyes irradiating Jebbin greedily. "You can really cast spells without any kind of focus? And you had no tutors? Teltazzar!" There was silence as both wrestled with indigestible information.

"Jebbin, isn't it? Yes, Jebbin, I am Gesgarian. You know what that means? No? Of course, no tutors. And you've not travelled far either?"

"More or less directly from home to dungeon with little pause in between and not much of that very comfortable," admitted Jebbin with a grimace.

"I see. Well, our customs are different." The nearest prisoner evidently overheard and spat into the scum but Orrolui continued unheedingly. "We use a sword as a focus and our magic system is different."

"How so?"

"First tell me of your adventures. I'll assess your capabilities and gauge how best to proceed. Leave out nothing."

"Oh. Well, I walked south from Dorning onto a barren downland. I missed Sidea and never learnt the name of the next place but there I fell in with an old fellow called Dordo. We chanced upon a wrecked carriage being looted by robbers. Dordo went tottering at them, shaking his stick and was immediately felled. I downed one robber with a spell but the others didn't believe my threats of violence and set upon me, too swiftly for me to defend myself knowingly and I received a beating."

"Defend yourself knowingly? Explain."

"I recovered to find the brigands all dead with welts round their necks as though strangled. Dordo suggested it was the local militia or my power that slew them all.

"Anyway, with some of their loot, I stayed at a variety of inns, ordering the best as befitted a magician. But no one believed me and I was overcharged for everything. I remember one proprietor show-

ing me the room she reserved for her special visitors and telling me
it had last been slept in by the Duchess of Wethrin. It was so cold
and damp that I wondered if the Duchess was still wedged between
the clammy sheets. However, I could hardly go from town to town,
massacring anyone who sniggered at my claims, though the idea did
not lack appeal.

"By the time I reached Talnavor, I decided to take service with
some lord, who would doubtless be keen to offer food, apparel and
accommodation for the honour of housing a sorcerer who might
cure his warts or cast some pox upon his foes. I called in at the
first prestigious manse I found. The interview did not go well." Jebbin recalled a miserable night huddled under his cloak trying to
find a position to ease his bruises. Before the jeers of a couple of
loutish guards, his attempt to produce an amazing fireball had gone
awry. While he reeled under the undischarged *sear* pain, they had
pinched his purse, thrashed him soundly when he objected with a
modest threat - something about blasting their miserable bodies
into a vapour – and thrown him out.

"I was then desperate. With no money I was on the verge of
crawling home in failure. I needed to force people to believe I'm a
powerful sorcerer with endless spells at my command. I decided to
use my powers to send the next castle's guards to sleep, and creep
into the lord's bedchamber. I would wake him in the night with a
magical light. He would assume I had teleported in and employ me
as a defensive mage. Guards would never mention they had slept on
duty and my future would be assured."

"Had that plan - for want of a better word - worked, your future
would have been exceedingly brief. Nobody would believe anything
unless you held a staff. What went wrong?"

"My spell against the gate-guard evidently failed and he, er, spotted me trying to get past him and thought I was trying to kill him.

Now, I don't know what this place is or where I am, only that I'm likely to be hanged as an assassin."

"This castle, a relic of the Cusantic heresies, is owned by Lord Tremenion who is unlikely to forgive an assassin. Now, were those really all your spells?"

"I know the formulae for many more that are too... the pain..."

The Gesgarian drummed his fingers, calculating. Jebbin had pretended to no great power but Orrolui was plainly intrigued by the dead brigands. Equally clearly, he thought the whole tale was a charade designed to gain his help. But then Orrolui's gaze slid over the stain where Bolan had sat. That spell at least had been cast without a focus.

"They will suffice to illustrate the point. In your system, each spell has a discrete level and operates identically every time, though some will resist the effects and others not, depending on their strength and training." Jebbin nodded and Orrolui continued. "Not so with us. We use a harmonic structure with relatively few spells but each basic spell may be cast at higher harmonics, having greater effect but needing more strength to control higher levels of pain. Our spells and how we achieve this is the greatest secret that any Gesgarian carries with him, but you carry a greater one yet. Now I offer you a bargain." Orrolui spoke softly but with needlepointed vehemence, his normally pale face throbbing pink with passion. He gripped Jebbin's arm with incisor fingers and stabbed the air in emphasis.

"I will be your missing tutor. I will lead you in the esoteric art of the Isles of Gesgary; teach you the secret system woven from the Web of Power by generations of Archmagi of the Isles; all the spells you will ever want: summonings, alterations, abjurations - YOURS! But," he dropped his voice to a whisper which quivered with emotion, "you have a prize still greater; freedom from the artefact, power within the self! Jebbin, give me that gift, I beg you."

At that moment, the cell door crashed open and armed men peeped through, wrinkling their noses against the sour reek within. Captain Gorve consulted his scroll briefly and called into the cell. "Hiraeth and Meerwyn. Hurry up, unless you're keen to stay at our little inn?"

A girl scampered up the steps, followed more slowly by Hiraeth who turned to speak to Jebbin as he passed but the Captain forestalled him.

"No gabbing! One word and you stay."

Hiraeth shrugged, winked and climbed the steps where the door erased him from the world of the cell.

Jebbin looked towards Orrolui who had not moved during the exchange. "Why are you here?"

"What? Why?"

"It may have escaped your attention but I stand accused of attempted assassination and it appears that I will end my magical career along with any other I might have considered at the end of a rope. This makes any bargain a little hollow."

"Teltazzar's teeth, no! You must not let your talent die."

"I'm not keen myself since it has unfortunate side effects upon my person."

Orrolui's eyes narrowed suddenly. "You're calm. A mage with your powers - you cannot be waiting like a cow for slaughter! You have some scheme for our release."

"No, the full realization just hasn't dawned on me yet. But why are you here?"

"Bah. A trifling misunderstanding, blown out of all proportion because of my race." Orrolui's eyes glinted sideways towards the nearest prisoner and his voice lowered further. "In a nasty fit, Tremenion confined me here until a solitary cell was available and decreed that my release depended upon his personal decision. An outrageous version of justice! Since I am allowed no representation during my incarceration, I doubt my name will occur to him with a kind thought about freedom. Jebbin, if you're to be hanged and I'm to be jailed in solitude for an indefinite period then we must exchange information. If I had my powers to unleash on the unsuspecting guards... We must!"

"In the circumstances, you may get the best of the deal but I accept. However, as I know nothing of your magic, or any spells with a focus, I don't know how to teach you different."

With that, the two magi, already shunned by the other inmates, retreated further into isolation, curtained off behind the foul vapours and the murmurings of conversation. Eventually, Jebbin taught Orrolui the simple testing spell he had found in the tome from the Dragon Chest. Orrolui sucked a grain of *sear* into his nose, tasting the pain like a connoisseur with a rare vintage. Then he bent keenly and cupped his hands together. Closing his eyes, he intoned the syllables precisely but they fell as lifeless pebbles from his lips and they both knew even before he opened his hands that there would be no pearl of light. After a still second, Orrolui clamped his hands together savagely, teeth bared in a rictus and eyeballs bulging, he hissed the first syllables and roared the last, banging his hands down as he completed the spell. Not the least evanescent flicker of magical flame rewarded him and he glared up at Jebbin balefully.

"I cannot cast the pain. You mock me with this futility. Nothing can work without a focus. It's all lies and trickery and vainglorious mouthings!"

Jebbin made no reply except to inhale another of Orrolui's grains, close his eyes and softly expel the syllables, "Dollor Commuto, Feeaht Lukkx."

As the ball of light wafted in the air, there was a low sound of wonder from the other prisoners as if from one throat and Orrolui subsided, astonished. The light burst into spangles. Orrolui thrust the heels of his hands against his nose, then stammered apologies but Jebbin cut him short.

"Tell me of your system. It may help." Jebbin watched the Gesgarian narrowly. He knew the pain that must be flaming through Orrolui's nose, but Orrolui was ignoring it. His control was superb.

"Jebbin, I must gain that ability. Hear me now, whatever gods or demons are passing, I will have that power or die in the attempt! Listen then. Our harmonic spells: take the staffstamp, our simple defensive spell, excelling by its speed of operation. The focus is planted on the ground and the spell cast. The first harmonic produces an Orgen wall before the caster; at the second, an Orgen cylinder surrounds the mage; at the third, an Argen wall is created and so on. The six harmonic produces a Ulargen cylinder twenty paces across."

"Orgen? Argen? Ulargen?"

"The Orgen wall is proof against small animals, thrown knives and the like but is disrupted by magic. The Argen wall is twice as strong and will resist minor magic. The Ulargen wall will repulse most material attacks short of an avalanche and magic of less than the fifth circle."

"It's confusing but I see what you mean about the different systems. You must teach me the spell."

"But it's hopeless. The very name is the staffstamp - and you have no staff. Understand?"

"Yet you cast the staffstamp with a sword? Teach me all you can and if I fail we're no worse off."

Orrolui taught him the words so casually Jebbin was sure there should have been something more. Jebbin knew that once released, a magical discharge will have some effect and if he failed to control that effect the consequences could be embarrassing, painful or even fatal. He tried asking details but the Gesgarian said that further theorizing was pointless and while others watched in disinterested suspicion, they decided to try the spell. Ensuring that the spell should work on wood, Jebbin stood on the bench while Orrolui cautioned him to concentrate as never before and cast the spell at the highest resonance he could manage. After a curt nod, Jebbin inhaled a minim of *sear*. For a moment, he almost relished the pain, the portent of power. Then he reached high with his hands, fingers stretched to the ceiling, thumbs touching like a shadow puppeteer and then brought them swooping down as he thrust his foot firmly onto the bench and delivered the spell. Orrolui immediately swung his fist at Jebbin's kneecap but his blow rebounded from solid air. Sagging in amazement, Orrolui's second hit degenerated into a soft slap on the back of Jebbin's knee. Jebbin let the spell slide down like a wet sheet into the muck on the floor.

"Phew!" he said, squatting down. "Disappointing. All that effort and only the first harmonic. Still, I can learn from that and next time..."

Without turning, Orrolui flicked words at him in pizzicato vexation. "You don't have the least inkling of what you've done." Suddenly he spun about, rigid fingers clutched round the hollow air. "It takes an apprentice YEARS to learn a major spell like staffstamp. You complain it's cast at a low level! Teltazzar!"

Orrolui threw himself back on the bench in a rage, like one that teases a dog by holding a morsel out of reach and then finds it eaten at a swallow.

The door opened for the delivery of their supper. Although fresh water was always available from a ewer by the door, their diet depended on what was left over from the garrison. Tonight each inmate was allocated a wrinkly apple and a round loaf with a wedge of overripe cheese jammed into it. The only sanitation was provided by sudden surges in the water level which washed some of the scum away through a grating but did little to improve the odour. When practicable, the guards would often toss bundles of food to the prisoners to prevent anyone having to slog through the filth and they did so tonight. Their throws were generally good and only Gorp dropped his. When it came to Orrolui's turn, the guard ostentatiously pocketed the apple before contemptuously dropping the loaf in the floor slime and spitting towards it.

"Enjoy your last meal, Gesgarian, specially seasoned for you!"

Without complaint, Orrolui ignored the laughter about him and retrieved his bread, blandly wiping away the foulest adherents with a stained sleeve. Only Jebbin was close enough to see the balled knot of his jaw muscles promising vitriolic revenge if the opportunity arose.

When they had eaten, Orrolui spoke again. "That's it then. Tomorrow it must be, or I shall be locked away alone and you will swing. You must learn to blast those guards in an instant. If I only had my scimitar!"

"It sounded as though you were also for the rope."

"Well, what difference?" Orrolui went on too quickly. "I don't fancy rotting down here for eternity. Now, how much pain can you control? Five minims, six?"

"One - usually."

"One? You're no mage, barely a pathetic apprentice!" Orrolui turned away, then back, contempt for a novice warring with awe for one who could learn spells of a different system in a day and then cast them with no focus. Jebbin interrupted his vacillation.

"Why did the guard pick on you so?"

"I'm Gesgarian; that alone is enough for vilification. They call my homeland the Dark Isles because they fear us. But to show them they're right in that at least, there's a spell to blast these guards - though Teltazzar knows how you can learn it by tomorrow, let alone gain the strength to control the pain," whispered Orrolui, rubbing his nose which still roared with a minim of *sear*.

"Even if we could incapacitate all the guards, we cannot trust..."

Jebbin paused and rolled his eyes round the cell, "and that would leave us still in the dungeon, alarms tolling, the stairs locked and warded against us."

"Dead guards raise no alarms," Orrolui cut in. "We'll be out of here at least. If I can just get to the guardroom and my sword, these worms will pay! But above all, you have to get me out of here first and you have to do it tomorrow."

"If it takes longer to learn your spell, I can rescue you from your next cell, surely."

"No, that adds too many unknowns." Orrolui hesitated, then hurried on, "I'm not sure what my fate is to be and later may be too late in truth." When Jebbin made no immediate reply, Orrolui's whisper became desperate. "Jebbin, I'm working on a riddle to a fortune. Get me out of here tomorrow and I swear by all the gods that we shall tackle it together and share whatever rewards there are."

"What riddle?" asked Jebbin, startled by Orrolui's vehemence but intrigued.

"I have a page from Echoheniel's Enchiridion," breathed Orrolui, barely audibly.

"Yes? What's that?" asked Jebbin keenly. It was Orrolui's turn to look surprised.

"You have much to learn. I swear I will teach you all I can but for now you must learn spells. And you'll have to concentrate much harder. Nothing will suffice at the piffling first harmonic."

"Orrolui, after the staffstamp at first harmonic, I would not have wanted more *sear*. Go through your spells once more, I've a better idea than getting Numbed by excessive pain."

Orrolui listed spells and listened to Jebbin's plan with poor grace. Considering Jebbin's lack of power, he eventually acceded, only remarking bitterly, "My hope of survival seems slim. If we meet Fitch, this precious guard whose face you know, act very fast."

The magicians were sitting far apart when Orrolui gave a tiny nod and Jebbin buried his face in his hands, sniffed *sear* and fought the pain.

Gorp was the only prisoner who habitually sat with his feet in the ooze. Round-shouldered and flabby, his cumbersome movements made him seem heavier than he was. Soft, thinning hair crept down almost to his shoulders before dying of boredom. His eyes stared across the cell while he outlasted his sentence with inanimate indifference. Gorp slumped vacantly, his mouth hanging open. With a sudden spark of interest, he looked down at his feet, brow winkled. He peered vaguely from side to side, then jerked his feet up with a shout, showering slime over his neighbours.

"What are you doing, you maggot-brained clod?" roared the nearest.

"Something moved!"

"Your toes falling off, I hope."

"No," said Gorp after inspecting his feet. "Something...Look, there!" he cried. There was a hush as the prisoners studied the area around Gorp. Across the cell, near Orrolui, there was a dull glop as a hole puckered the surface of the slime briefly and faded. No-one had seen him flick a loose flake of masonry and the quiet deepened to a nervous silence.

"Over there!" someone shouted, pointing beneath Jebbin where a vile insect-like creature surfaced momentarily and subsided. Another boil in the fluid near Orrolui indicated that several creatures might lurk in the mire.

"What in Lessan's name? Some chimera of spider and crayfish?"

"They look like chorints," said Orrolui. "Creatures from the Kermion marshes. Beware, their bite is deadly poisonous!"

Even as the key clanked in the lock to signify the guards bringing the morning meal, a chorint propelled itself from the scum onto Orrolui's leg, biting instantly. Orrolui howled in panic, flailing frantic blows at it. As the door opened, foam flecked Orrolui's lips as he fell forward into the muck, thrashing wildly as other chorints rolled over him in a mad wave. The guards stood transfixed in fascinated disgust, then leapt back as a volley of the horrid creatures vaulted towards them. More piled onto the benches round the cell which exploded into pandemonium. Uttering wild cries, most of the prisoners stampeded towards the door, leaving Orrolui wallowing helplessly. Powerless to stop the charge, the guards fled for reinforcements, abandoning the escapees to scatter through the dungeon.

Jebbin lifted his head from his hands with a groan and stood up slowly, breathing deeply.

Orrolui too rolled to his feet. "Teltazzar, what a stench! The things I have to do to support your paltry illusions." He stopped suddenly as he realised that a prisoner with curly grey-speckled hair was still sitting unperturbed on the bench.

"Don't mind me. Terribly impressive, but I've seen magical tricks before. Excuse me if I decline to get my feet wet. I'm out tomorrow and see no need to make matters worse."

Orrolui and Jebbin glanced at one another, shrugged and trotted out, the former complaining bitterly about the discomfort of his fouled clothing. They had not gone far before the remaining prisoner yelled, "Quick! It's an illusion. Get that Gesgarian!"

Orrolui stopped rigid in the passage. "The fool changes prison for death."

Jebbin was quicker. Running back to the cell, he slammed the heavy door and locked man and cries inside. On a sudden impulse, he dragged the keys from the lock and rushed the wrong way up the corridor, ignoring Orrolui's impatient calls. He unbolted the next door, opened the grilled hatchway and tossed the keys through before racing back to Orrolui.

"That illusion was the second harmonic. I daren't risk the second spell."

Orrolui grabbed Jebbin's shirt and shook him violently. "This is not a game," he spat and thrust *sear* at him.

Jebbin shrank back from it. "That's two minims, again. I'll be Numbed, or worse."

The Gesgarian's dark, red-rimmed eyes bored into Jebbin's blue. "If you fail now, we both die. By the fangs of the Yellow Demon, I am not going to die here. Concentrate now, blast you, take the pain!"

Pinned by steel fingers and blazing glare, Jebbin gave a great cry, spreading his arms in agony, immolated by the *sear*. Intoning the spell, he threw his head back and clutched his hands over his face. Snarling with effort, he drew his hands down, his features and shape blurring and wavering. With a final shout, he flicked his fingers downward and stood in the guise of the gate guard, Fitch. His legs quivered and the features began to blur again. Then he became aware of Orrolui's fiery spirit supporting him just as the Gesgarian's arms held him up.

"Come on, hold it. You've done it. Hold on, Jebbin, hold on!"

Gritting his teeth, Jebbin cudgelled his unpractised brain until his outline firmed and solidified while he gasped on Orrolui's hard shoulder. Behind them they heard a muffled but triumphant bawl as someone found the keys Jebbin had hurled into the muck of the second cell.

"Well done, my friend, but there's no time to pause. We must go," urged Orrolui and led Jebbin up the steps. When they reached the upper dungeon door they found it blocked by two guards with halberds.

"No more spells. I'm Numb for now. This has to work," Jebbin whispered to Orrolui. "'Ware prisoner! Off to the guardroom for special attention," he called with a nasty guffaw. The first guard laughed and sidestepped but the other paused.

"What's going on, Fitch? And how could you get there without me knowing?"

"Fat lot you ever know! Budge over quickly now."

Unsatisfied, the guard's eyes narrowed but just as he framed another question, three more prisoners began pounding up the stairs behind Jebbin.

"Nakki's sake!" cried Jebbin. "Let me through, you fool."

Instinctively the guards let them pass and then resumed their positions. As the magi hurried away they heard thuds and cries from behind them. Glancing round, Jebbin saw the guards using the butts of their halberds to great effect. They did not look hard pressed.

"Where's the guardroom?" hissed Jebbin. Orrolui made no reply but signalled that Jebbin should follow. They were fortunate in not being questioned until they reached their destination; most of the men-at-arms on duty were hurrying to quell the prison disturbance. Jebbin opened the door and shoved Orrolui inside. The Gesgarian took a histrionic leap and landed on his knees, much to the surprise of the two men-at-arms in residence.

"Relax, it's me," drawled Jebbin, still disguised as Fitch. "I've brought this scum from the dungeon on his last trip."

"What have you dragged him in here for?"

"Ha! Caught him trying to use a magical medallion to whisk him back to the Dark Isles, I should not wonder."

"Real magic?" one of them whistled in amazement. "Let me see it, hey?"

"Why not, providing he doesn't get it - and careful how you touch it! It has to go in the locker with the other things. Open up while I fish it out, then."

To Jebbin's immense relief, the guard was sufficiently intrigued to open a hidden locker without demurring. Jebbin called to the other guard to keep an eye on Orrolui and inspected the locker.

There were racks of weaponry. "I suppose this is the slug worshipper's sword, eh?" he asked tentatively, pointing at a black, bastard sword with death runes on the scabbard.

"If you must know, it's the golden scimitar," put in Orrolui quickly.

"Hoi! Stop him, Garn. Fitch should know that better than anyone. He's spellbound!"

But the warning came too late. Jebbin snatched out the scimitar and hurled it in a glittering arc to Orrolui, who caught it and swept the blade from its sheath in one motion. With a cry of pure delight he sang a spell and a gout of clinging fire wrapped lasciviously round the charging guardsman and detonated implosively, the sudden inrush of energy bursting internal organs and rupturing blood vessels.

Dealing Jebbin a blow that sent him sprawling, his accustomed features washing back over him, Garn darted for the alarm cord, but Orrolui's scimitar was singing back to its master and the steel sliced ravenously. When Jebbin scrabbled to his feet, a grinning Orrolui was clutching his sword in the tight embrace of a lover.

"Let's go," the Gesgarian cried and danced towards the great gate, ready to blast any opposition, Jebbin running at his heels.

As bells jangled forlornly behind them, the two sorcerers hurried down the road away from the castle, snapping their fingers and making rude gesticulations at the scene of their incarceration. There were barely a quarter of a league away on the Dadacombe road when a group of a dozen riders under Captain Gorve came galloping round the castle in pursuit. Far too late to avoid observation, the magicians scuttled for the thin shelter of a tree. As they tried to hide themselves, Gorve reined in his mount.

"Right, men. It's our duty to recapture two powerful magicians. These legends of olden days have passed through rock to escape our dungeons and slain several of our colleagues without sustaining injury. Before such baleful strength, rather than divide our force, I propose we guess in which direction the miscreants have fled: right to Talnavor, or left to Dadacombe." Here he paused and looked significantly left towards their poorly concealed quarry. "My own view is that Talnavor is more likely, does anyone concur?"

There was much nodding of heads and sage agreement. "Yes, Talnavor it'd be." "Must be, surely." "Well, I'd go to Talnavor."

"Right! Courage all of you and we may see our families again. Now ride!" bellowed the magnificent Gorve, whirling his sword aloft on his prancing steed, his white plume dancing. With a last flourish of the blade and a final caracole from the horse, he led the party thundering down the road to Talnavor. Orrolui and Jebbin watched them go in amazement, then clapped each other on the shoulder and continued on their way to Dadacombe.

A Thievish Entanglement

The room bristled with tension, menace and swords. Impassive as granite, Bolan sat in a carved wooden chair, face set in stony obduracy, his arms pinioned with leather straps. Men with drawn daggers stood by each shoulder. Bolan noted that one was trembling and the other had perspiration sliding down his temples.

Rapiers at the ready, another couple warded the door, still more thieves lined one wall. The focus of attention was a broad desk before Bolan, behind which three men were ranged; one sitting in comfort and beaming happily, one standing fidgeting and a striking-looking man with a sepia face surrounded by a mane of yellow hair perching easily upon the desk, one booted foot swinging and scraping at the polished wood.

"News travels fast," said Bolan, breaking a silence.

"There are ways of impelling such travel," murmured the cheery man. He was plump, with the smiling face of a genial uncle but when his pudgy, be-ringed fingers beat a tattoo, those about him marched in step with alacrity, for Guthreg was a full Guild Master. Bolan doubted that one of his rank had been seen in Dadacombe since the place was built and the local thieves were jittery.

"Time you released me," said Bolan, voice as harsh as a rock fall.

"Yes, yes," smiled Guthreg, "all in good time. We will apologise for the unfortunate manner of your travel here and we'll say no more of the accidental death of Rathu, who was doubtless inept as well as rude - isn't that so, Ansin?" He directed a notably un-smiling glance at the local thief captain standing on his right, who wilted visibly.

"Now!" said Bolan. "Or you scum will join Rathu inside a dog's belly."

"Ah, not wise at all. Worry these heroes with such threats and they might find a way to prevent you exacting them while you're still in their power. Hm?"

Bolan glowered for a moment, then his head snapped back. "Kill me? Bolan? Name must mean something to you, unless thieves have grown deaf. If anything happens to me, even in this benighted area, you vermin will be exterminated the moment the news gets out."

A glimpse of Ansin's face confirmed that he had calculated something similar but Guthreg merely chortled happily as though trading jests with some court gallant.

"Dear me. But you would be dead! And I assure you that news can be impelled or impeded with equal ease. Long might it be before any heard of your demise and, maybe, it might even ap-pear that your old friends were guilty of your assassination in a fit of jealousy! Hush now. Ansin will set you free soon enough and there will be neither reparations nor repercussions, eh?"

"Forgive me, Master," broke in Ansin, "but why is all this nec-essary?"

"Well, my dear Ansin, we can see that nasty wound in our friend's chest for ourselves now you have invited him here. What wholly devilish weapon could create such a devil of a hole? You don't know? More to the point, neither do I. So, impossible though it seems, we must believe this tale of a magician operating without a staff; all is corroborated. Now, Ansin, would you roll a magician for his purse?" Guthreg enquired in his most avuncular fashion. Ansin shook his head in horror but did not reply.

"If a mage exists who can cast spells without a staff, how shall we recognise him? We risk grave personal injury! Even if successful, rob or kill some of the few wizards remaining and the displeasure of powerful patrons will marshal forces against us that will make our humble profession unprofitable. No, this one baby sorcerer presents a major threat; perhaps he could pass on his talent, as he seems prepared to do, and precipitate a breakdown of the whole system. That, dear Ansin, would never do, would it?" He beamed round at the assembled thieves.

"Wizards from the Dark Isles need no staff. What of one more?" asked Bolan.

"Penetrating wit! Such acuity," said Guthreg, giggling with delight. "Tell me, great gladiator, why do you call them the Dark Isles? What do you know of these Gesgarians?"

"They're evil." Bolan paused uncertainly. "Eat children; sacrifice women in fire. Worship the slug god and.... well."

"Marvellous!" said Guthreg, clapping his hands in glee. "Too kind. Such a compliment to our propaganda. You met one of these terrible Gesgarians in your little cell. Did he bite the heads off cockroaches and rats? Perform foul rites in worship of the worm god - oh, sorry, the slug god, wasn't it? No? Extraordinary! Still, if a loathsome Gesgarian raised the Hue and Cry you wouldn't take part, would you? Of course not, though you might kick him for disturbing you. Just so! And you've never heard of any lord employing a Gesgarian."

"No slug god?"

"I thought our fine rumourmongers had gone too far with that one. People are so keen to believe any gossip. No, we have controlled the magicians of the Dark Isles in our own way. It has become the finest self-fulfilling slander. This Jebbin requires different handling."

With a sudden shake of his butter-bright locks, the man sitting on the desk kicked it in decision. "Seems simple enough to me. You want this apprentice mage dead before he grows in power or forms alliance with some noble; we of the Militant Arm perform the deed. It might have been tricky were he still in the castle but since his escape today I see no need to call upon the expensive aid of the assassins." He emphasized the last word as though he wished to plant it in Ansin's mind but the effect was marred by Bolan.

"Escaped? How?" said Bolan, his sudden movement causing the chair to creak and his guards to thrust their knives forward warningly but he was otherwise ignored.

"Bravely spoken, Balvak!" said Guthreg. "However, moving in over their heads would be discourteous to our local branch. Ansin, you have two days to bring this matter to a conclusion. I assume that is sufficient?"

"Yes assuredly," said Ansin. "Journeying with one of the Dark Islanders makes him easier to locate and..."

"Quite, quite. Well, that's splendid. Now you may show us out through your minions and release this good pugilist later. We will await at Dadacombe's least awful inn and expect good news shortly. Oh Ansin, our fledgling sorcerer Jebbin is coming this way so if you hasten I'm sure your redoubtable heroes can arrange a suitable reception before he reaches Dadacombe, hm?"

Ansin bowed and the thieves, whispering like schoolboys, filed out behind their august visitors. The two door-wards remained to guard Bolan but they relaxed at the culmination of the meeting and tucked away their weapons.

"Remind you that Guthreg himself ordered my release," Bolan ground out without bothering to face the two guards.

"True. He also said later and we don't want trouble, so sit."

Bolan sighed. He breathed deeply twice and then rocked forward onto his toes. With an explosive grunt, he straightened his powerful legs and brought his fists up against his shoulders. The leather straps withstood him, but the arms ripped from the chair and the seat skittered backwards into the wall. With speed astonishing in one of his bulk, he leapt towards the horrified guards, reaching the first before his sword had cleared his belt. Brushing the weapon aside, Bolan punched the man in the throat and spun to face his second adversary, knowing the first would pose no further threat.

"One sound from you will be your last," he hissed.

The remaining thief was terrified. She held her rapier forward, its sparse garnets underlining her low status; but its point quivered as much as her chin and watching with round eyes as her friend flopped to the floor with a crushed larynx did nothing to bolster her morale. In that moment of inattention, Bolan's arm lashed out again, the chair arm hit her on the side of the head and she fell flat on the matting with a look of relief on her face. Bolan opened the window. As he expected in the Thieves Guild headquarters, it was designed for a quick getaway. Then he crept to the door and glanced down the stairs.

Ansin, bowing and bobbing like a waiter, waved Guthreg and Balvak from the guild house with a few awkward compliments and wishes for a pleasant stay in Dadacombe. Ansin's one ear burned a telltale red of rage, undermining the sincerity of his performance. The other ear had been sliced off long ago and the amateur surgery had done little to improve his looks. Firmly closing the door, Ansin turned towards the anxious gathering of thieves. His fixed smile fell away like a lead weight as his lips resumed their customary sneer. His triangular head moved from side to side like an insect's as he favoured his band of robbers with an unflattering inspection.

"In order to expedite the rapid and keenly anticipated departure of our grinning Guild Master, all matters currently under operation are hereby suspended until the completion of this assignment. No individual action of any kind will be tolerated until further notice.

"However, I'm sure we've all learnt something from our superior. News of death can be impeded, eh? I dare not free Bolan; the man's a homicidal demigod with an unforgiving nature and Guthreg's a fool if he thinks otherwise."

Upstairs, Bolan's smile was colder than winter. He backed into a different room and glanced round. Brass-bound chests were stacked along one wall, a tool rack of magnifying lenses, scales and gem cutters stood near the door. A desk was covered with a worn cloth of gold that reached to the floor. It was strewn with papers, clumps of them held down by an unlit lamp, a dagger and a purple weight. Bolan slipped under the desk. He could still hear Ansin.

"Urma! Take three, no four men, get up there and kill him. Get rid of the body in absolute secrecy. No news of this gets out. Ever. Understand that for your lives. Now go. Gafeluc?

"Over here, Ansin."

"This trainee pain-burner Jebbin: who do you need to be certain, and by Balgrim I mean certain, of him?"

"Ha, no-one. But if he has the Gesgarian with him, I'd better have someone along to keep the worm-lover occupied."

"You've never faced a magician, however weak. Take two others, use surprise to get the job done and hurry back here as soon as possible. Take Yokk too, he needs combat experience. Remember, throwing hammers and coshes only. Pain gives them power. Get going. Payl, did Rathu have any dependents?"

"He lived with a woman down Arbour Street but they didn't have no littl'uns." It sounded like an older man's voice.

"That's something. See to Rathu's burial and give her the usual dispensation. All right, Urma?"

"No," Urma's voice was matter-of-fact. "The window's open. Bolan's gone."

"What? Out of my way, you clods," roared Ansin, his feet thumping up the stairs. There was some muffled cursing, then Ansin called from the head of the stairs, "The Guild House goes on defensive alert as from now. See to it."

A few moments later Bolan heard Ansin speaking with quiet authority, "Payl, you'd better contact the Assassins' Guild immediately."

"Surely our own..."

"The Militant Arm is not open to us for reasons that should be obvious even to your addled brain, so unless you fancy tackling Bolan with a dagger, arrange contact with the assassins forthwith."

"For Bolan, the cost will be exorbitant!" gasped Payl.

"Then it is indeed fortunate we are the Thieves' Guild," said Ansin. "We have no choice and money is of little consequence to the dead. Nakki preserve us from that meddling Guthreg."

He came into the office and paced up and down, muttering. Bolan heard him pick up a pile of papers and start rustling through them irritably.

Shortly afterwards, there was a knock on the door and Payl was called inside.

"Ansin, I think we're in trouble. No, hear me out, there's something else."

Ansin bit back a sharp retort, clicking his tongue with irritation and listened to his subordinate.

"I think it's Toomsly," said Payl.

"Toomsly? What's that cur got to do with this fiasco?"

"His guild branch runs three towns now. Dadacombe would make the fourth and best."

"I know but he can't move in over our heads. He tried once and we were too strong for him."

"He started in one town. Talnavor and Poxall 'ad their own branches then. And we knew he 'ad guests staying but not who they was. D'you wonder how Guthreg and his thug got here so quickly?"

"Guthreg staying with Toomsly? Guild Masters aren't permitted to involve themselves with branch wrangles!" said Ansin.

"No but I bet they've bought his help somehow. Guthreg set it so if we don't succeed in this killing he can take Guild action against us for incompetence, even close us down, leaving the way clear for Toomsly. He deliberately arranged Bolan's presence here to reduce our effectiveness. We can't buy Guthreg off and pay the assassins as well. I'm not sure we could out-pay Toomsly anyway."

"What do you suggest? A pre-emptive strike against Toomsly?"

"And play straight into their 'ands if we fail? We must succeed against Jebbin. I just wonder if there's more what we don't know."

"You think this whole Jebbin affair is a set-up then?"

"Probably just a useful coincidence but it don't matter. We're too late to dodge the trap and the only way out is to kill 'im."

"Gafeluc will do it - unless foiled by more of Guthreg's blasted trickery."

"We're ambushing him on the road because Guthreg told us

to, instead of waiting for a nice alley in town. We should send more lads to bolster Gafeluc."

"No. We must not weaken the Guild House; Balgrim knows what Bolan will do. In any case, they'd probably arrive just in time to spoil the ambush. You're right in this. It all fits. I couldn't see why Guthreg insisted we pull in Bolan and then demanded his release. It puts a lot of pressure on us and we were too stupid to see it coming. I don't like depending on the assassins but this time we must." Ansin sighed but spoke with decision. "Send Urma to the ambush point but tell her to make certain she's seen by no-one. Whatever happens, she must not interfere but report back here. We need more information. Damn that Guthreg."

Ansin hurled the papers back on the desk and stabbed the dagger right through them. He hurried out with Payl. Frowning, Bolan emerged from beneath the draped table and softly moved to the window.

* * *

At the start of their flight, Jebbin and Orrolui had made slow progress, cautiously avoiding other travellers and frequently stopping altogether as they talked over spells and systems and pain. Always, how to control the pain.

Towards noon, they passed an oak spreading a blanket of shade over a patch of soft grass beside a twinkling stream. Orrolui spied a satchel beneath the tree. An inspection revealed a stack of hard biscuits, a round of goat's cheese, an apple and a flagon of cider. They washed their filthy clothes and spread them in the sunshine before settling themselves against the tree and munching happily on biscuits.

The cider had all gone and Orrolui was just slicing the apple when a jingle alerted them to the approach of a horse. A farmer, who had spent the morning stumping after a plough and now anticipated a cooling draught of cider, rounded the trees alongside the road and spotted them at their illicit meal. He hefted an iron plough paddle with a few trial swings and advanced towards them with a purposeful stride.

"I believe my legs will carry me faster than his and this seems like a good moment to put that boast to the test," said Jebbin.

"The retreat would lack dignity. This lump only exists to supply us with provisions. Perhaps he will also suffice for a demonstration: behold the stasis spell at the third harmonic. Attend."

Jebbin shifted nervously while Orrolui counted grains of *sear* and the muscular farmer closed with them, the heavy paddle twirled with alarming ease in his hands. Suddenly the ploughman stopped with a puzzled expression on his seamed face, straining his legs with little effect.

"Notice that any effort to move one muscle excites the antagonistic muscle to an equal extent, thus effecting a stasis. Since some muscles are more powerful than others, movement may occur but in a disordered fashion," said Orrolui as the farmer toppled to the ground, locked in a struggling tetany, and lay jerking in spasms, his bowels voiding themselves involuntarily. The horse stamped and snorted in unease but remained where it had been left.

"If too great an effort is made, ligaments and tendons may be damaged. Observe that the peasant can still breathe. The next harmonic of the spell includes the intercostals, thus permitting diaphragmatic breathing only. The untrained, flapping about like a fish out of water, will swiftly lapse into a faint. I see no need to waste such power on this fool. Advanced techniques in control permit the diaphragm to be stilled even with no antagonistic muscle to work on. The ultimate masters of this spell perform the full Hearthammer. They reach inside their subject, grasp the heart and - so! - stop it. I have not yet faced that amount of pain," continued Orrolui, heedless of the terror twisting the farmer's face as he felt the Gesgarian's uncertain mental fingers groping in his entrails. "But it's time to be on our way; the earth-grubber will bother us no more. Great magi take what they will from lesser mortals." He gave the soiled form a look of contempt. "Very much lesser in some cases."

Jebbin looked back uneasily to see the farmer rolling up onto his hands and knees, groaning quietly, then glanced sidelong at Orrolui swaggering along beside him. The incident cast a shadow on his euphoria.

Later, they decided that pursuit was unlikely and ceased hiding when anyone rode past. Eventually they even hitched a ride on a cart carrying sacks of flour from a mill to the baker in Dadacombe. A squall ran in from the north and hurled hard-boiled drops of cold rain at them while they huddled together beneath Jebbin's cloak. Neither the miller nor his stolid beast seemed greatly perturbed and soon the squall tired, the rain fading to a steady drizzle as evening and Dadacombe grew closer. Drained by action, spells and elation and perched atop the canvas covering the sacks of flour, the two magicians should have been easy targets for an ambush as they gazed vacantly ahead.

Orrolui noticed it first. He nudged Jebbin gently and glanced significantly forward. A hand from an unseen body was waving a red scrap of cloth to and fro. The hidden signaller held up three fingers and pointed to their left a short way in front of him, then one finger and pointed to the right. They caught a flash of bright yellow hair before greenery swallowed the hand.

"What...?" began Jebbin in a whisper.

"Hush! Three on the left, one right. When I say, jump right and..."

"It could be a trap!"

"Then why warn us? We were straw targets. Get ready," Orrolui paused, "now!"

They vaulted simultaneously from the cart into the shrubbery and ran towards a squawked curse. Too late, hammers whistled tunelessly to themselves as they whirled from the trees on the left. Spotting a sudden agitation in a dense clump of foliage, Orrolui and Jebbin crashed through the undergrowth towards it. A small, bearded man coalesced from the leaves before them, a hammer in his hand. Too keen to draw his rapier before the magicians reached him, his hasty shot missed Jebbin and the hammer buried itself shamefully amid the flour sacks. Orrolui swept his scimitar down in a deadly arc but the blade jammed in an overhead branch and the thief's rapier flashed forwards. Jebbin was still rushing full tilt and his flying leap took the bearded man in the side before the rapier reached its target. As Orrolui wrenched his sword free, Jebbin's fist slammed under the thief's chin. The jaw clacked audibly and the thief collapsed.

Jebbin leapt up to see the remainder of Gafeluc's force charging across the road. The miller was waving a mace and roaring defiance at the thieves as Jebbin and Orrolui crushed *sear* into their noses and generated the Gesgarian Blast spell in unison. Jebbin aimed his spell at the head of the nearest thief but missed him completely and was barely able to defend himself as the man jumped for him, the two crashing down together. The massive power of Orrolui's projection demolished Gafeluc, striking his belly with such force that his body broke in two, legs and arms strewn in a heap, twitching grotesquely. Ignoring his embattled companion, Yokk took one look at the Gesgarian and his eager scimitar and fled down the road.

Jebbin was getting much the worst of the melee on the ground. As he leapt, the thief had drawn a dagger and in trying to avoid it, Jebbin was providing an easy target for his aggressor's fist, knees and feet. A deft and callous thrust of Orrolui's scimitar ended life and struggle though Jebbin thrashed on wildly before he realised it was over. Blood ran freely from a long cut in his forearm. He tried to stem the bleeding with the end of his shirt. Orrolui was unsympathetic and waved away Jebbin's thanks with irritation.

"Always aim for the thickest part of your opponent with a spell like that. A miss can kill you. If we're fighting back to back, it could kill me too. But how in Teltazzar's name did you learn to cast it?" Orrolui returned to the miller who was bellowing exultant abuse after Yokk.

"I'm right grateful to you two gen'lemen, foreign or no," he declared after a final curse. "I never seen anyone move so fast in all my life and that spell," his gaze slid squeamishly over the mess that had been Gafeluc, "well, I never did! Just wait 'til I tell 'em in the Oak an' the wife'll never believe me neither. Magicians on my cart! We showed 'em what for, by Balgrim! They 'adn't even got the brains to try for the money on me way 'ome. I never seen the likes of it, never knowed nothing about it afore you went a-flying off the wagon. If you'll 'ave a drink with me, I'll be in the Oak when I've sold me flour. Hop up now and let's get moving. Not hurt, are you lad?"

"I'm all right," said Jebbin trying to smile bravely although his shirtsleeve was soaked with blood. A little sympathy would have been much appreciated for he was dizzy, bruised all over and his arm was throbbing painfully.

"Jolly good. Look sharp then," said the miller, clacking the reins to his stoical horse. "Come up here and join me, sir," he added to Orrolui, "It's more comfortable."

"Another time, don't just bleed like a sheep, use a cut like that for power," Orrolui said to Jebbin as he climbed past. "Fools should know better than to use sharp edges but, in a crisis, they all fall back on the weapons they're best with."

Jebbin glared balefully at the pair of them before trying to find a comfortable nook. He rubbed his numbed nose and wondered how much pain it was worth suffering to avoid other pain. Cold, wet and aching, he longed for a bath, a good meal and a soft bed. Unfortunately, he had no money to pay for such luxuries and no strength left to fight for them. After a last thought that Orrolui would come up with something, he fell into a wretched doze.

He only woke when the miller left them at the sign of the White Mace, where Orrolui had been staying before his unexpected sojourn in Tremenion's castle. Orrolui explained to the innkeeper, that he had no funds with him at present since he had lodged all he had with the notary before leaving on business. It was too late to collect money this evening but if they could be accommodated overnight he would fetch it first thing in the morning. Although the innkeeper was a fawning individual with a breathy, simpering voice, he proved surprisingly adamant and even after much coercing, Orrolui could only reserve a poky little room with two bunks on the understanding that he paid in advance before supper. If that meant turning the notary out at this late hour, so be it.

As a Gesgarian, Orrolui was accustomed to such treatment and drowned his pride with bile. They trudged off to find the notary, Orrolui telling a limping Jebbin that he had deposited not only coinage with that worthy but also Echoheniel's riddle.

"Might the notary not be tempted to pilfer valuables or even steal the riddle?"

"Notaries are gentlemen of established probity and repute," reproved Orrolui.

"I'm surprised you're so trusting," said Jebbin, then winced at the ghastly bitterness of Orrolui's laugh.

"Since Gesgarians are legitimate targets? Well, for reasons

that will become apparent, I will trust no tampering has occurred."

Orrolui rapped with a gleaming copper knocker on the door of the notary's house and waited, a faint curl twisting his lip. The door opened after a moment and a portly woman peered out, her puffy cheeks adorned with a large wart. After a second, her eyes widened in recognition.

"You!" she spat.

Jebbin stepped back smartly, never having heard such venom loaded onto a single syllable but Orrolui gave a minuscule bow and stepped onto the threshold.

"Dear Madam, perhaps you would be kind enough to fetch the notary. I have important business."

"Out or I summon the watch. My husband is indisposed."

"How tragic. A fire, possibly?" The curl in Orrolui's lip grew larger.

Nonplussed, the notary's wife glared at him in silence. Orrolui continued with an unctuous smile,

"I daresay the details of the fire are not entirely in the public domain; no doubt it's best left that way. Perhaps you could fetch my box if I described it?"

The woman eyed him speculatively through narrowed eyes before turning on her heel in decision, calling over her ample shoulder.

"I know your filthy box well enough. Do not take one step into my house." She returned shortly and gingerly held out an unremarkable box of lacquered wood with dim runes painted upon it. Orrolui inspected these briefly and blew out his cheeks.

"Nasty burns, I imagine. I sincerely hope he recovers shortly and may his good name last forever. My thanks, dear lady." As the door was savagely slammed, he continued in the same tone, "Or more specifically, may the the flesh-eating pox gnaw his rotting carcase for eternity." Orrolui turned to where Jebbin stood, blood now staining his breeches. "The runes must be touched in the right order to prevent a fire flash. Since the power has been lost from three runes, the notary's burns will be severe though the documents will be unharmed. And now, a visit to the apothecary to get your arm bandaged, I suppose."

They were ushered into a treatment room with a huge desk and a long low table of dark wood. The room was completely lined with shelves of the same wood. Glass bottles and jars were sorted by size; raw ingredients on one side, finished preparations on the other.

"Looks like the inside of a coffin," said Orrolui as the apothecary came in.

The apothecary sniffed. He brushed crumbs from his supper off his black coat into the unlit fireplace and smoothed his enormous whiskers. Speaking in short, precise sentences, he told Jebbin to lie on the table. He cut away Jebbin's sleeve, making little disapproving 'ah' noises.

"Have to be stitched." He inspected the swollen edges of the wound, blood still oozing onto the table. Clicking his tongue, he pored over the shelves and collected a white jar with a broad cork top. "This cream will take the sting out of it for a while."

Just as he was loosening the top, the Gesgarian's long finger pressed it down.

"We do not require extra treatments. Just stitch it."

The apothecary looked uncertainly at the wound, and then at Orrolui's unwavering stare. "Very well. There will be discomfort." He turned up the wick on the lamp and poked thread at the eye of a needle, occasionally glancing sideways at Orrolui.

Jebbin looked at the cold curiosity in Orrolui's face, then focused on the wall as the apothecary's needle dug into his raw flesh. When the last stitch was pronounced done and the cut bandaged, he stood up. The apothecary looked terrified. Orrolui's expression was unchanged. Jebbin raised sweaty hands to his lips and blew through them. White flames roared in the empty grate; a wave of light and heat swept over them, causing the apothecary to leap back in fright.

"Now it is Numbed." He smiled grimly at the amazement on Orrolui's face and left the Gesgarian to pay the apothecary, who was quivering in the far corner.

They returned in silence to the White Mace where the innkeeper rushed over to meet them, more effusive and grovelling than before.

"Have trouble keeping our lodgings, did you?" asked Orrolui, his voice dangerously even. "A booking error, perhaps?"

"No, good sirs, by no means, ha ha, and indeed yes. A booking error, just so, but I find I have more space than I thought. My best rooms, poor as they are, lie at your disposal. Good fortune attends you. Ha ha, yes. I'll send the boy for your luggage."

"We have none. The old room will suffice if you will light the way. In truth our funds are scanty."

"No, no, I cannot hear of such a thing!" The innkeeper seemed panic-struck. "The finest chambers unused while you wrestle bedbugs the size of badgers at the back? Never! The price is the same. Come upstairs, I beg you."

Jebbin followed immediately; Orrolui climbed more slowly, muttering that altruism was rarely bestowed on Gesgarians. They now had a room apiece, each airy and well-appointed with soft beds and lavender-scented linen. Located on opposite sides of a landing, both had large windows overlooking the street. With a shrug, Orrolui pronounced the rooms adequate and suggested to Jebbin that they collect their free drink from the miller at the Oak and listen for any interesting conversations.

When they found him, the miller had already consumed more than his usual quota and pounded them both on the back with such gusto that Jebbin could hardly breathe and Orrolui's hand clenched over the pommel of his scimitar. Good as his word, the miller bought them a jug of beer but after regaling anyone who would still listen with yet another embellished rendering of the afternoon's battle, he regretted that it was time he was heading home. No-one objected so he stood and gave Jebbin another elephantine massage. Orrolui pressed his own back against the wall and expressed the hope that the miller should have a quieter journey home, though doubtless the mace would quell any argument at need.

"True, by Balgrim! One look at it and they wouldn't come near me before," roared the broad-shouldered miller. Cackling with laughter, he strode from the inn, whirling his right arm in mock fighting.

The two magicians sighed in relief and settled back in their corner. Side by side, they savoured their beer in silence awhile. With the miller gone and little hope of further spectacle, the remaining patrons returned to their usual companions and the air filled with laconic opinions of the attack thwarted by, of all things, a Gesgarian. The conversational buzz lulled Jebbin until a sudden thought struck him. He leaned towards Orrolui and spoke quietly. "Tell me about this riddle then. Who is Echoheniel?"

"Echoheniel's Enchiridion is the handbook of a seer who lived some six hundred years ago. The folios from the handbook were dispersed individually over the Belmenian Empire and stored in places of safety. A mere fifty years of political upheaval were sufficient to lose most of those priceless pages. However, each single folio seems to reappear in the time to which the prophecy on that page relates - cynics suggest that they can be interpreted to bear on any situation with hindsight. Nevertheless, Echoheniel's verses have had profound effects on many campaigns and lost treasures have been unearthed by her accurate instructions."

"You said we were dealing with a riddle."

"So we are and that's why it's the Enchiridion. You'll understand when you see it."

Having grown accustomed to the isolation generated by the company of the Gesgarian, Jebbin was surprised when a man asked to join them.

"Hiraeth!" he cried. "Sit, pour yourself a beer. How are you?"

"Well enough, thanks, but amazed to see you two here."

"We were released shortly after you, and I left chattels in Dadacombe," broke in Orrolui quickly.

"Ah. Yes, I heard of your daring escape. All the more reason for you not to be seen here. I won't give you away but the miller's story has flown on loud wings. Very public spirited of you to intervene on his behalf but it has drawn attention. After your performance to date, I don't see the Dadacombe watch trying to take you in but by tomorrow a detachment will be sent from Tremenion's. You should lay low for a few days lest they find you on the road. I have other company tonight but if you want to vanish in my house tomorrow then you're welcome."

"Hiraeth, once again I owe you a debt and we gratefully accept both advice and lodgings," said Jebbin, forestalling Orrolui's ingrained suspicions.

"Think nothing of it," smiled Hiraeth. "How's your arm? Looks bad."

"Spell Numbed at the moment. No more than an ache."

Hiraeth looked at him oddly. "Feeling pain is part of being human, you know. Still, I suppose you haven't any healing spells for that blow Bolan dealt me? Not that the great ox meant any harm, he just thinks everyone's as iron-hard as he is. Oh yes, that's another funny thing. Did you know that Bolan was temporarily abducted by the Thieves' Guild? Lessan knows what they were doing, but the news that he was lifted was noised abroad even before he escaped, snorting fire and brimstone."

"They're a lax lot to let that news slip out," chuckled Jebbin.

"Slipshod indeed," said Hiraeth, then the conversation foundered in a sudden chill. Orrolui's mobile features had set as though frost had sealed them beneath a skin of ice.

"Before? Are you sure the news was bruited abroad *before* he was released?"

"Yes, quite sure. Which is strange because there were no witnesses to his kidnapping."

"That's one oddity too many." The Gesgarian tipped beer on the table into a wide puddle, then dragged *sear* into his nose. Fist on his scimitar, he spoke a spell and softly jarred the table. Vibrations rippled the surface of the beer. As they faded, Orrolui could see Urma's pale and pinched face. She was talking furtively and sipping occasionally at a mug.

"So I told him they got wind of the ambush and evaded it, killing three of ours. Yokk ran away, again, but was shot in the back by a dart. Ansin doesn't think that could've been the pain-burners and thinks whoever killed Yokk warned them about the ambush. As Yokk was neither poisoned nor robbed, he reckons it was our own Militant Arm but he didn't say why. Ansin sat there, drumming his fingers on the table, then he says to me, 'Urma, Jebbin must die today or we're all in grave danger. I have another plan for you and one other but be very careful and trust nobody else. Where the force Guthreg tricked us into has failed, we must employ the best thievish subtlety.' So we've got some job later."

"What have you seen?" asked Jebbin as the spell vanished.

"Someone I saw watching this afternoon. See you." With a curt nod, Orrolui slipped from the Oak, his eyes alight with inner fire, leaving the other two to shake heads over his departure and talk into the night.

* * *

In a dingy bar at the poorest end of the Merchant's Quarter, a man hunched over a grimy table and stared into his untasted glass of wine, biting his lip blankly. Beside him, his wife drained the last of her drink and placed the glass beside an empty pewter mug on the table, wiping away another ring mark with an unconscious gesture. Her eyes were red and moist but she smiled bravely.

"Chin up, Trincol. At least we know the worst now. He only confirmed what we suspected: we've lost the lot. It's not your fault. Nobody could've predicted this new religion sweeping around Rulion. We built up from nothing and, by Nakki, we can do it again! We're older but perhaps wiser too, eh? And Tavi's old enough to help. I'll hurry home to the children; we'll see you when you've finished your wine. There's bread for tonight and who knows what tomorrow may bring?" She patted his shoulder affectionately and gained a wan smile in return as Trincol stroked her hand.

His wine finished with a shuddering gulp, Trincol sighed, then pushed himself back in his chair and slapped his hands on his thighs with determination. He was about to rise when a tall man with dark hair and a thin face sat down opposite him and slid a full glass of the inn's finest, such as it was, towards him. Trincol remained stationary and viewed the newcomer askance, his eyebrows raised in question. The stranger grinned and lifted his own glass in silent toast. Trincol left his new wine untouched.

"Sudden gifts are like puppets," he said. "They have strings attached."

The tall man's grin grew wider still. "The price of that wine is enough of your time to listen to me. If you give me your time, then the wine is free."

Trincol shrugged, unable to turn down any patron, even a

Gesgarian. He sipped the wine and motioned for his benefactor to continue.

"I'm a merchant from Tu-Tanai, a stranger in Dadacombe. You don't appear busy and I hope to offer you a small commission if we can agree suitable terms."

Trincol remained silent, looking through narrowed eyes over the rim of his glass, but his agile eyebrows asked the necessary questions.

"A ryal for an hour of your time to help me play a prank. I've concluded much profitable business with a couple of chaps at the White Mace who used to deal with my archrival Jebbin, who resembles you. To get the business with me, they've had to abandon an arrangement with Jebbin.

"Jebbin was defrauding them but they're terrified of the crotchety devil. It would be hilarious if you turned up there tonight and pretended to be Jebbin. It'd frighten them to death! Say yes and I'll pay three ryals. One now and two later if all goes well. Deal?"

Trincol still made no vocal reply but the way his eyebrows shot up underneath his fringe suggested that his decision was made.

"Just put on this cloak, march into the room I'll indicate, announce yourself as Jebbin and call the lads frightful villains. Don't worry if they're hiding. Just ham it up and that'll be splendid. I'll be next door to clear things up if they should happen to see through you but in their nervousness I'm sure they won't." He pushed two silver crowns across the table. "We should go right away as I'm late for my appointment. If there is any trouble just call for me and I'll explain everything."

Trincol mused for a moment but his need outweighed any caution. With the middle finger of his right hand, he flicked the crowns into his left palm.

"Very well. But what is your name?"

"My name?" said the tall man. "My name is Orrolui."

* * *

When Jebbin rolled back to his room, having consumed rather too much ale, he was carrying a rush-light to ward off the weight of the night. Heading for the room's lantern, he tripped over a bundle on the floor and fell into the table, rocking the lantern. His attempt to steady it sent it flying to the floor. Giggling, he picked up the lantern and lit it from the rush-light, slopping hot wax over the table. He rested on the bed for a moment and watched the whirling antics of the ceiling. If he concentrated, he could stop it moving and that made him feel more comfortable. Unfortunately, every time he closed his eyes he knew it was sneakily spinning again and he had to glare at it once more to keep it still. With a groan he decided he needed fresh air.

He caught his feet in something on his way to the window and crashed into it, knocking the shutters banging into the wall from which they rebounded and nearly hit him on the head.

"Well that's how we go if we can't pay the bill," he said and roared with laughter which broke up into snuffles as he remembered to be quiet. Feeling a little better after some deep breaths he reversed towards the bed, trapped his heels against the bundle and landed flat on his back.

"Ozcuttocks," he said after a long pause. Wiping his hands on his shirt to clean away some sticky slime from the floor, he began to prod the pile in an effort to determine its nature, talking to it the while.

"Look here, this won't do. Upsetting guests in the middle of the night! What are you? You look like a man except you have no head. How carel..."

The drunkenness vanished from his veins like smoke in the

wind. He turned from the body in horror and spewed on the floor. "Sweet Lady Lessan," he whispered, retching again as his eyes lingered on the weeping neck. "Orrolui!" he shouted and fled the room.

When Orrolui had calmed Jebbin, he left him in the other room while he made an unnecessary check on Trincol's corpse, recovered his crowns and returned, pausing only to summon the night porter.

"Nakki's sake, Orrolui, they'll lock me up again. They'll think I did it. Why d'you call them?"

"Because most of the people in the Mace will have heard your silent entry and that poor fellow has been dead for an hour at least. In the morning the difference will be less conspicuous."

"But they'll be suspicious, get the watch to keep vigil overnight so they can investigate in the morning and then they'll have us when Tremenion's men arrive tomorrow. Had you thought of that?"

"Yes, naturally. Stop snivelling and listen. That's twice someone's tried to kill us. Yes, the watch will be called and they will keep a very close eye on the Mace tonight. Their protection should keep us alive. Whoever organised this will be watching and I don't want to walk out into a strange town in the dark where unknown killers hunt me. Given our current reputation, courtesy of that idiot miller, plus the fact that you are clearly an innocent party in this murder, we can walk away from here first thing in the morning, long before Tremenion's henchmen roll up. Then we vanish with your friend Hiraeth and quit Dadacombe as soon as possible after that. Leave everything to me."

Orrolui closed the door and pacified the innkeeper who was hopping up and down, loudly lamenting his reputation and wringing his hands as the large, muddy boots of the watch stumped through the inn. As expected, Orrolui was cautioned that he and Jebbin should remain lodged at the White Mace until investigations were complete but the deferential manner adopted by the captain and the outright wonder shown by the members of the watch reinforced his view that none would interfere with their departure. The fracas in the company of the miller now stood them in very good stead. Only the notion that they had foiled a robbery, and the rumour of the power of his spell against Gafeluc, prevented Orrolui, as a Gesgarian, from being swiftly incarcerated.

Riddles

Hiraeth turned at the door, cramming a woollen hat down over his ears and huddling into his cloak. "You should be safe here, but for your sake and mine, keep well hidden. I have a commission, but I'll be back around noon." He forced his way out into a barrage of wet leaves from the autumn wind that had been banging its damp nose against the window.

Orrolui's suspicious eyes had narrowed further at the mention of the commission and he watched Hiraeth as he passed the window, cloak flapping like a storm crow.

"To business then," cried Jebbin impatiently, trying to ward off his memories of the previous night and the pain coming back into his arm with a show of exuberance. "Show me this riddle-meree of yours."

"Very well. The question is, can you read it?" Orrolui opened his casket and withdrew a kelpy scroll, similar to the one in the Dragon Chest. He held it tightly for a moment but shrugged and passed it over to Jebbin with a wry smile.

"One day, perhaps, I'll tell you what I underwent to obtain this folio. It is beyond value. Now, can you make it out?"

Confidently, Jebbin unrolled the paper and stared through

the maze of dots until he caught the hidden letters. "Ha, yes, easy enough," he said and began to read.

A minacious bloncket fortress inexpugnable rears on a ponent salebrous paramo.

The gerent a nocent angekkok, a flagitious tregetour with engoument for niffled bibelots.

Beware the goustrous jotun of fabulous procerity, lethiferous goliard prolling excubant below.

Behind morne infare and heaumed guards, for jeremiad or epinikion,

Be not quayd at this proairesis. Take viretot down louche atramental khud

Or aby eviternal ultion for acedia. Vital now is schetic docimasy!

"Yes and no! I can read it but it doesn't mean anything!"

"Exactly. Yes and no, priceless and worthless. Quite a conundrum." Orrolui lapsed into an introspective trance so Jebbin returned to the scroll.

Turneth ever towards the brooling fragor.

In epifocal chamber sinical strepent borborygmic dirdum

Be not poupt by the proceleusmatic portal that may illaqueate.

Seek oppilated, procryptic adit ere taigling causes labefaction.

Excind fallal lilin, muquixis, a xoanon for puja, under intrados or soffit at kerf.

"Sweet Lady Lessan! One odd word and I could deduce the meaning from the context but one just rolls directly into the next. I recognise this word; perhaps I could guess at the next but put the two together and the sense of it wavers and vanishes. It's like trying to hold a wet icicle in numb hands." Jebbin shook his head and slowly spelt out the rest of the riddle.

Take aperient cavin detruding to froughy utricle where abides the leal and impavid sempect,

Existence prorogued by hormic ideopraxism.

At anagnorisis with hakam yeve obsecration Hanjar! And join ces-
tui in one nisus.

Divellicate aumbry on the berm. Don yataghan, averruncating
artefact balsamic of marasmus
And guarish Hanjar's puisne opinicus.
Take the jussive jymold weapon, jee thyselves, be hend and doughty,
Be enfeloned. Pyrotic accablation, ustulation to Garwaf's kwankot!
In this epexegetic emplasy, I, Echoheniel, refute parablepsis - this
will be so.

"I'm lost. Can you explain?"

"Echoheniel was a seer who helped righteous causes. In revenge, an 'evil potency cursed her with acatalepsy through an-
fractuosity and synchysis.'"

"What?" blinked Jebbin.

"Her words, quoted in Clearmont's Lives of the Great."

"Indeed, but what does it mean?"

"The results are before you. She could peer into the swirling
fog of the future but she made enemies and was cursed to prevent
her from communicating her foreknowledge."

"So how does this enigma help us?"

"Because," cried Orrolui at his most intense, "the facts are
there! The expressions are obscure, the words may have their
most elusive meanings but it will be accurate and it must be true.
There will be treasure and look here; at least one artefact. An
artefact, Jebbin! Real power! Teltazzar, this is the key to a fortune if we can only find the lock. And we're moderately lucky."

"How so?" enquired Jebbin suspiciously.

"This was written in her middle phase. Immediately after her
cursing, things were relatively straightforward - if never easy.
Knowing her words were misinterpreted, Echoheniel tried various methods to render herself more comprehensible. Such was
the nature of her curse that every method she tried left her work

more abstruse than before. At the very end she employed ken-
nings, that's like calling the sun Lessan's lamp, only she used
complex terms, of course, and those visions remain totally inex-
plicable."

Orrolui fell silent until Jebbin prompted him with a gesture
towards the scroll. "And this stage?"

"Clearmont mentioned this epexegesis," said Orrolui. "Apparently she adds words trying to make the sense clearer. However,
if you slightly misinterpret the first word or get the wrong emphasis on the second, you don't realise they refer to the same
thing at all. Misleading unto confusion."

Jebbin pondered the curse; the seer desperate to convey her
foreknowledge and her despair and rising insanity in the face of
evident failure.

"Couldn't the curse have been lifted?" he whispered.

"Possibly, perhaps at the cost of her gift. Who can tell now? I
can't imagine how these verses turn up at apposite moments but
I'll use it. There's an artefact in this trove and a weapon, a jussive
jymold weapon - and they will be ours! Whatever it takes, whatever the cost, I swear they will be ours!"

"You should learn the price before you swear to pay it."

"What a mealy-mouthed attitude! When I commit myself to
a project, I will achieve the end I set myself. For these two things;
spells without a focus and the treasure of Echoheniel, I will not
count the cost. If there is suffering, I will suffer. By Teltazzar,
I may die in the struggle but my resolve will not be broken.
Never!"

"That makes you a fanatic. Don't magicians value reason?"

"Pah! There is no high destiny, no preordained fate of power
and lands to rule. I carve my own future from whatsoever and
whosoever stands in my way and that will be my monument. I'll
forge my own fate - whatever the cost." The Gesgarian bit off the

syllables and spat them at Jebbin but Jebbin did not quail and met those saw-toothed eyes without flinching.

Eventually Jebbin returned to the study of the parchment while Orrolui fruitlessly assayed the tiny light spell without his scimitar. Engrossed in such fascinations, they forgot their irritations and fell to discussing spells and possible meanings of phrases within the verse. When Hiraeth returned he found two close comrades and the fire burned out. Admonishing them gleefully, he unpacked hot confections of spicy meat and pastry and spilled tomatoes about them, fencing them in with a loaf of bread. He disappeared into the small larder to draw off a jug of beer and the three of them lunched in style.

Later Hiraeth fetched a well-worn lute and played with startling brilliance, his fingers moving with languid grace and precision, now flickering into a blur of melody while the rain pelted an accompaniment on the windows. Jebbin stretched out in contentment, drawing deep the scents of the room; hints of dampness from the outer air, the tang of spices from their meal, logs crying aromatic tears over long-felled forests, a yeasty spark of ale and underneath it all, the soft bite of wood-smoke. Hiraeth sang a crooning air in a wonderfully warm, deep voice that seemed to stroke the bones and then a livelier country ballad.

"By the Lady," cried Jebbin at the end, clapping in spontaneous appreciation, "you should do that for a living."

"But I do," said Hiraeth with a grin. He bounced to his feet and swept off an imaginary hat. "Hiraeth, bard of Merrin at your service!"

"Anyone can play a tune. How do we know you're a bard?" said Orrolui, his voice low.

Hiraeth looked at Orrolui sadly. He spoke the ancient words in a gentle voice and began a new song.

"Listen then, and see...

"Asharne grinned with fierce joy as he caught another glimpse of the Rokepike's proud bulk high above him, lust for possession written on his flat Aelan face. Marking the end of the Hithrogael Spikes, Rokepike castle dominated all routes to the mines and pastures of the western Aelan Plain.

He rode past hairpin corners warded by squat and doorless towers, streaked with arrow-slits like birdlime. Asharne squinted up through the snow-gleam at the towered walls and louring keep; soaring spires reflecting the surrounding peaks.

As prince of the Condor tribe, Asharne commanded all Condor raiding parties. Once ensconced in the Rokepike what raiding there would be! The whole power balance of Western Ael would change at his touch. Asharne mused over friends and foes amid the feuding tribes of Ael, sifting new alliances.

He kicked his horse past a gully without sparing a glance for a merchant slumped in dejection beside a plundered wagon. Swelling with elation, he entered the Rokepike. He tossed his piebald's reins to a Bear groom and laughed aloud as the horse bit and lunged. Shrugging his heavy fur cloak to the floor in the strange heat of the Rokepike, the Condor prince stared about him. A rustle of brilliant silks flashing azure, gold and carmine drew his gaze to a balcony where a group of Bear women had gathered to watch his arrival. Away from the heated warmth of the Rokepike, such clothes were denied Aelan women save for the brief weeks of the mountain summer. Asharne snorted and looked away disdainfully.

Ahead were huge doors opening into the great yard. Beside them gaped a black passage, its lintel carved with demonic faces lapped with flame. Wide corridors led left and right, guardrooms and sentries with the giant helmets of the Bear were posted just right. Battle honours and tapestries blazoned colour across the yellow stone right up to the vaulted ceiling. Above the doors hung a Condor battle standard, wrested in blood from Asharne's own tribe. It was old, for the Rokepike had slumbered for a generation, aloof from Aelan politics since the lords of the Bear had ceded stewardship of the

Rokepike to some wizard of the lowlands. Now that wizard spoke of moving and the Condor would displace the Bear from the Rokepike in a lasting victory. Nevertheless, so poignant a reminder of a Condor defeat jarred Asharne's mood. He scowled at the battle standard as though it were a deliberate slight. He hurled his helmet at a guard, who fumbled the catch and gashed his hand on the sharpened spike.

"Sloppy. Instruct the castellan of the Rokepike himself to bring brandy."

Asharne fidgeted in a waiting room with no fire and no draughts whipping his knees. He spoke aloud, "These walls will be defended by Condor warriors, carvings polished by Condor serfs, chambers graced by Condor women. They will." He was running his hands over the scalloped edge of a stone gaming table when a man entered and set a salver on the table beside him.

"I am Kistmaen, castellan of the Rokepike."

Asharne looked up sharply. Kistmaen was his height but much broader. Rather than the ceremonial robes Asharne expected, Kistmaen was wearing a woollen tunic and trousers, moss-green and unadorned but for an opal carved into white lightning. The stone drew his gaze like a lantern in the night: it was the levin of Ael, symbolising snowy, jagged peaks, the storms that played upon them and the fierce spirit of the mountain people of Ael. Asharne jabbed a finger towards it.

"You're Aelan - how could you leave such a fortress dormant? By the Levin, how can you accept the overlordship of a foreigner?"

"Even a bear can be chained," Kistmaen said flatly.

Asharne sneered, "How will it feel to be castellan without a castle?"

"That I hope never to learn."

Asharne frowned uncertainly, then glared into his goblet. "I said brandy, not this lowland lily-water!" he roared, dashing purple wine into the castellan's face. "You'll keep no keys for me when I hold the towers of Rokepike. No true son of the mountains would knuckle under to a flat-lander, sorcerer or not."

"Time to meet him then," said Kistmaen stolidly, heedless of the wine soaking his tunic.

"Now - and if his offer proves less than he promised to lure me here, you'll both suffer for it!" Asharne stepped back, smoothing his moustache in a show of hauteur to match the burly castellan's composure. His irritation was overgrown by his desire for the castle as they walked through broad flagged passages and out into the great yard; past the flicker of the armourer's forge, creaking from the well as chattering women drew water, a scullion scampering by with a basket of loaves, hunting dogs tussling noisily over nothing; the bright pulse of the castle's life but all arranged so nothing would hinder the defence. Asharne was in an avaricious dream as he followed Kistmaen into the enveloping warmth of the mighty keep and wound his way up into one of the Rokepike's towers.

Asharne swaggered into the presence of the master of the castle but his insouciance was punctured by Kistmaen's venomous smile as the castellan closed the door. There was something horribly knowing about that smile. Asharne glared at the bland face of Lykos, the master of Rokepike. The threat of trickery yawned like a pit - but who would dare molest the prince of the Condor?

"Surrender the keys to the castle."

"Never."

"You promised it to me and I will not be cheated."

"I offered you a chance to lead the tribes of Ael," said Lykos quietly, his fingers drifting over a pierced porphyry globe like a blind man's.

"You said there would be movement from the Rokepike; that the Condor could be the foremost tribe of Ael." When Lykos paid him no heed, confusion stiffened his ire and Asharne blundered on. "You wish to leave Ael and with the gift of the Rokepike buy Condor protection for your baggage. Here the Condor shall be pre-eminent!"

"I have languished too long without power," said Lykos softly, waggling his fingers through the naked flame of a lamp burning oil from a crystal sphere. "Watching those with authority squander it in meretricious posturings like the catoptric vanities of a courtesan. Like children, they must accept my rod of governance and, yes, my chastisement for their own good."

As Asharne stared in bewilderment, Lykos continued. "I first chose the warrior monks of Saint Sipahni as my instrument, honouring them beyond their worth. With Fist and Mind, they could have enforced my peace and justice over the lands, instituted my new spiritual order. We would have dissolved national boundaries and united warring people under my laws, good and just.

"Too weak to grasp my vision, they spurned me. A cabal of monks of the Fist rose against me. Betrayed by those I called my own!" Lykos clutched his nightwood staff, knuckles white as bone. "The mastery was mine but their treachery was cunning and I was Numbed and only barely limped here with the few remaining loyal monks, led by Rhabdos whose hazel staff has supported the impotent nightwood.

"There are no monks of Sipahni now and the Blessed Sipahni lies rotted and forgotten: thus is my revenge. Now my power will rise anew, not with some limp quasi-religion but through fire and strength of conquest. You are tools apt for this task. Your Condor shall be eminent, as you will be first, but not to squabble in the mountains. The many tribes of Ael shall be as one and I shall lead them."

"Mad," drawled Asharne. "Too long closeted in your tower, you have learnt nothing of Ael. The tribes are held apart by centuries of feuding that shall end in hot blood and blubbered guts, not soft words. When tribes band together, they will be led by such as I. I am Aelan, a son of the mountains! You are a mere foreigner."

"But I have the Rokepike."

Asharne paused, eyes narrowed to invisibility. How indeed had the flat-lander come to rule over the Bear in the Rokepike, one of the mightiest fortresses of many-castled Ael? "I heard you were nothing but a failed pain-burner, Numbed years back. The Rokepike lies wasted."

"Now it moves again. I had powers to crush armies!"

"Impotent? Had?" scoffed Asharne and spat on the floor. He turned to leave, saying, "I assume immediate control of the castle. Had is dead."

"I had them," whispered Lykos to the retreating form, holding his hand still in the flame of the lamp, "and now I have them BACK." He smacked his ebon staff down and violet-tinged force ballooned about him, sending furniture hurtling, bursting the door open and flinging Asharne into the wall. The room was silent but for Lykos' measured tread as he moved to stand over the dazed Aelan. He bent down, stared into Asharne's face and touched the blood that ran from his nose. There was a faint stench of burned flesh.

"The Rokepike awakens and shall lead all Ael into unity, then conquest of the lowlands from Belmenia to Marigor. I grant you this one chance to make the Condor a foremost tribe, for I require Aelans beneath me to lead the tribes of Ael. Your old alliances are nothing. All you have is allegiance to me. The consequence of rejection is the obliteration of the Condor. Kistmaen! Take this fool away."

Ignoring Asharne crawling towards the buckled door, Lykos moved to the window, toying with a little, agate figurine of the infant Baelar wrenching wide the jaws of the wolf that sought to devour him. He gazed from the tower, over broad battlements and tumbled rocks to the crumpled plain of Ael stretching eastward below him, the shadow of the Rokepike stealing softly across it.

"Now there is substance in this shadow," he murmured, pale lips barely moving. "The coadunation of Ael is begun. And nothing will be left to chance. Nothing."

"Sweet Lady Lessan! I saw everything as though I sat on Asharne's shoulder!"

"So you are a bard. Why that story? And how d'you get it?" grunted Orrolui.

"The spirit of the bard suggests you're involved in that story. It's the Song of the Wolf. And Lykos wants it known."

"I know nothing of tyrants in Ael and don't want to meet that one. And aren't bards supposed to wander the country in poverty, not loll luxuriously in their own homes," said Jebbin.

"Aha! Lute and flute I have played over half the world and this place is not mine. I own no dwelling and yet have houses everywhere," said Hiraeth, delighted with the surprise hollowing Jebbin's mouth. "These places, known to the minstrelsy, stocked by some notable amongst the townsfolk and supposedly for bards alone, remain inviolate in the same way that bards themselves can walk unscathed in places others wisely shun, although I've been asked to prove myself before and played for some outlandish rogues. In fact I've had some splendid evenings in such company but it does little to fill the wallet."

"The townsfolk here are most solicitous for their bards."

"Certainly, we are precious commodites! Naturally they have their own interests at heart: bards bring information and news, generate business, raise the town's reputation in general and the patron's in particular - I'll expect to play for him soon."

"Hope it isn't the notary. He didn't seem the solicitous type."

"If you think they really care for our well-being, take a closer look at this rack of medicines." Hiraeth reached down a selection from a row of bottles and jars with spidery labels. "An infusion of whortleberries and gold of pleasure with honey for sore throats. A decoction of elecampane roots to aid coughs and shortness of breath. This, a seething of pennyroyal and dropwort for hoarseness. Here's tincture of groundsel for arthritic and swollen fingers. Everything to ensure I can work but neither help nor remedy should I be expiring of the black jaundice!"

Jebbin laughed, then asked, "If this place is for bards alone, are you taking a risk in permitting us to lie up here?"

"Only a small one if you stay low and no other bard visits Dadacombe."

"Did you play for Lord Tremenion?"

"Naturally. An error, in retrospect. I have this notion that a bard should sing of the vicissitudes of the people and so call them to the attention of their lord with suggestions on how matters might be improved, always couched in jocular terms. Tremenion was proof against my humour but not insensible to my jibes, it seems, and I was summarily consigned to jail as a disturbing influence - only for a couple of days, of course."

"I'll bet you've made up a good rhyme about him for that!"

"No, I can see his point. I'll warn other bards, though. Now, you fellows should be safe here. The rain's eased so I'm off for a nose about town to see what's happening and whether you've been forgotten. I may end up working for a while so expect me when you see me. If another bard does come in, tell him you're with me and beg him to say nothing. Whatever else you say or do, never offer him violence." This last said with a pointed look at the Gesgarian, who equally pointedly ignored it.

Hiraeth tucked his lute into an oilskin bag and saluted them farewell, leaving the magicians to their teaching of spells and worrying of riddles. Well versed in the rhythms of towns, Hiraeth knew where to see the thieves and their channels of communication. Today he noted desperation on a few faces. He remembered the attack on the miller's cart that had ignored the miller himself, dim figures in Jebbin's room at the White Mace and the death of poor Trincol, pretending to be Jebbin. He did some quiet guessing and shook his head over the Gesgarian's unscrupulous methods.

Strolling round the market area, Hiraeth watched a tall man talking to a ragged urchin. The man had a bright dagger at his hip and the faint line of a second in a sheath at the back of his neck. Hiraeth was close when the man lifted the urchin clear of the ground and shook him violently.

"I don't care what it costs you. We'll talk gold when you've found him. Fail and you get nothing - only your life if you're lucky. Now run!"

The lanky thief tossed the child aside and strode away, muttering to himself, too preoccupied to notice the bard casually following. At length he stopped and dropped a silver leopard into the bowl of a huddled beggar. The mendicant swept the coin to his teeth before beckoning the thief down to his level. Hiraeth could hear nothing of their conversation except that the pitch of it rose somewhat. Suddenly the thief's hand flew to his hip dagger but before he could draw it, he leapt backwards, coughing and spluttering. After a while he was able to stand straight again and wipe tears from his eyes.

"Balgrim curse this poxy mess!" he shouted and booted the beggar's copper bowl down the street. "And you, get that information, or else."

Hiraeth eyed the retreating form with a faint smile. Not all beggars were paupers and if they didn't keep a few tricks up their sleeves then theirs would be lean pickings indeed. The bowl tinkled towards his feet, rolled upright and mutely importuned him. He wiped it clean and returned it to the beggar, who viewed him quizzically.

"Business seems up and down today?" ventured Hiraeth.

The beggar looked ostentatiously into his empty bowl and turned it upside down to emphasize the point.

Grinning, Hiraeth quoted from the beggar's charter, "The more who seek information, the more information there is to impart, more gold is offered to those dispensing news and more snippets are accorded to the seekers."

"An excellent system! The lives of all are thus enriched."

"But if I were willing to pay for news, I should become another item for sale."

"If you want no news, then I beg for alms," said the beggar.

"What size donation ensures that it's purely a gift and I'm in no wise concerned with information?"

"Though naturally you might like to ease your bones against this dry wall and idle away a wearied hour in gossip and badinage with one of an intellectual mien?"

"Your perceptions are acute."

"It's refreshing to talk with one versed in such arts," chuckled the beggar. "All brute force and blabber, these locals."

"I could sing 'The Beggar King's Revenge' wherever he drinks."

"Perfect! Do that for me and you are a cousin from Tu-Hridi, finding better times."

The bard sat beside the beggar and the two chatted on all manner of subjects, ranging from the raids from Tachenland to the rumbling rumours of chaos round Rulion. A sudden squall of hail stampeded over them and was gone. As the drifts of ice faded, Hiraeth learned that Jebbin was indeed to target of the thieves, who seemed under great time pressure.

* * *

Bolan had lodged in the Warrior's Enclave in a house assigned to any of the great names when they visited. There two women served him when necessary but he could also find solitude as required. Today he waited in the garden, neither strolling by the lilied pond nor relaxing amid the scented herbs and conifers but hidden in a marshy patch of ferns, from which vantage he could watch the door to his lodgings. He wanted his pack but would not risk the assassins finding him unawares.

It was a long wait but Bolan was patient, remembering the words of one of his tutors, "The rash do not necessarily die young, nor do the prudent always grow old but that's the way the odds run." There was a diversion when an itinerant weapon-smith called at the house. A maker could gain much kudos from the approbation of a celebrity like Bolan and the wrestler had occasionally been approached. Top gladiators rarely purchased their own equipment. The smith lowered his handcart of wares and waited a long time by the door for one of the women to answer, fiddling nervously. When the door finally opened he spent futile moments trying to demonstrate his weaponry to the girl before she apparently convinced him that Bolan was absent and he left dejectedly, shoulders more bent under the burden of failure than when he had approached with a sprightly step and merely the weight of his handcart. Shortly after he left, the girl departed by the back entrance on her own business, leaving the house deserted.

At last, two dark-clad figures sidled up to the house in the last of the light. They paused, one pressing his ear to the door while the other darted furtive glances over his shoulders. The listener eased the latch open. Jerking his hand back suddenly, he looked critically at his finger, sucked it a couple of times, then scuttled in behind his fellow, shaking his hand absently.

Bolan paused for a moment, wondering whether stalking two suspected assassins might be short of prudent. He shrugged, muttered, "Any action is better than none," and crept to the door, left ajar for a hasty exit. The men had split up. Upstairs, one was softly padding from room to room. His accomplice was crawling slowly towards the door, gasping wretchedly and dragging one arm behind him. Bolan squinted down suspiciously but the upturned face held no threat. The eyes were dull and unseeing, foamy spittle bubbled around blue lips. Ignoring him, Bolan silently closed the door, slid the bolt home and glided up the stairs.

The intruder emerged from a bedroom as Bolan neared the top. Even as Bolan lunged at him, a throwing dagger blossomed into the thief's hand and whirred forwards, forcing Bolan to roll sideways. The intruder raced for the stairs but the wrestler had merely substituted one form of attack for another; Bolan's foot struck the man's knee and sent him careering into the wall. The intruder jerked himself backward rather than scrabbling on for the stairs. The wrestler's boot cracked the plaster just where he would have been.

"Capathon, help!" the intruder shrilled to his comrade as he turned to face the wrestler, whipping a second dagger from his belt. He rushed forward and sent his last blade whistling at the broad chest of the fighter. As Bolan ducked, the thief leapt in the air on a clear path for the stairs but Bolan straightened and flicked the hapless man higher. The intruder's face struck the lintel above the stairs and he spun over to land with his head on the edge of a tread and tumbled to a slack heap at the foot of the stairs.

As his last foe looked in no condition to give him any information, Bolan returned to Capathon, who now lay prone, twitching slightly. Capathon gurgled horribly as a shuddering fit wracked him, then choked on his last breath in a flabby rattle. Bolan turned him over with one foot, touched an eyeball to ensure he was dead, then bent to inspect the useless arm. The hand was puffy and dark, a small scratch on the index finger marked by a drop of black blood. Bolan recalled Capathon jerking his hand from the door catch and sucking it. Brow creased, he stepped ponderously to the door. Carefully unbolting it, he inched it open and studied the latch on the outside. A tiny device of wire held a little pin pointing down, hidden by the latch itself, to just where a hand would rest as it opened the door. Above the pin, a sac was empty, having been compressed by the wire when the catch was operated.

"Assassin's work!" Bolan breathed into the night air. "Thought these were the assassins and proof the Guild had paid them. But these are Guild members!" He kicked the door shut with sudden rage as he realised how he had actually watched the assassin fitting the deadly device and suspected nothing. Had it not been for the thieves' timely intervention, he would now have been lying where Capathon stretched so stiffly. But why had the thieves come at all? They certainly weren't looking for him.

However, the assassins had evidently taken their payment and would not rest until he was dead or forced to flee. The choice was simple to Bolan and retribution seemed to be falling on the Thieves' Guild for their kidnapping without effort from him.

Bolan moved to the bedroom and thrust his few belongings into a large pack. He collected two purses of coins, tossed one into the pack and tied the other to his belt. It was a swift search indeed from a thief to leave those behind. He straightened suddenly.

"Jebbin! Missed him on the road and if they're looking here then they're checking his cellmates, so getting desperate," he mused aloud. "If he is with any of them, it'll be that bard." He tightened the drawstring on his pack with the snap of decision and hoisted it easily. As Bolan passed, he noticed that the thief at the bottom of the stairs was stirring, blood running freely from his head. Bolan shrugged. That would be more bad news on the way to the Guild House. Leaving the mess for the quartermaster, he strode from the building without a backward glance. "If the assassins are watching, be lucky to lose them - but any action is better than none."

* * *

"Orrolui, you have forbidden any transcription of this scroll and I am wearing myself to a nubbin reading it. I'll cope - but there's something else."

"Yes," drawled Orrolui from his somnolent position by the fire.

"This is a vital enterprise, you say, and I'm doing my utmost to help solve it but you're dozing like a grandmother and show precious little interest in my offerings. Why is that?"

"You need the practice."

"Practice! I'm practically exhausted and that's all you have to say?"

"That's why you need the practice." Orrolui swung himself into an upright posture and continued. "You wouldn't expect to run five leagues quicker than an Aelan hill runner, he practises every day to become stronger. Similarly, you must exercise your mind and soon you will be able to read these scripts without tiring. It's just the same change of focus to read them that you need to stand between the world and the Web of Power to practise magic. Nothing is achieved without effort and pain."

"Hm. But that wasn't the question. Why aren't you fascinated by my bejewelled suggestions?"

"Because," said Orrolui, grinning like a crocodile, "the riddle is as good as solved."

Orrolui gave a staccato laugh at Jebbin's look of slack-jawed amazement.

"Yes, you join this quest near its ending. After a fruitless period gnawing at that scroll, I concluded there must be a better way, one, indeed, that would allow some progress. There's a sage in Shekkem who holds a copy of Telmarion's Compendium of Artefacts. While not able to remove it altogether, I was able to peruse it while he was, ah, unaccountably distracted and I found the reference I sought to the Staff of Sumos: an artefact conferring the ability to understand unknown scripts and languages. Failing, I confess, to unravel the page from Echoheniel's Enchiridion myself, I committed a rite a short while later and communed with the demon Zaeboth." Orrolui licked thin lips slowly and continued in a stony voice. "Through him I learned the location of the staff. No intercourse with demons, however, is truly satisfactory and that information was also concealed in a rhyme, formed at the time in letters of blood from erstwhile supplicants - that matter need not concern us now. This rhyme, fortunately, proved more comprehensible than that offered by Echoheniel." Orrolui reopened his casket and tossed the last scroll, an ordinary one penned in a neat hand, to Jebbin. "Thus you find me on my way west to Tuli's tower in Triva where I shall collect the staff and solve the larger riddle."

"One of the towers of Triva? Fascinating!" said Jebbin, reaching for the paper.

The Staff of Sumos nearby lies.
From the Foamfin's furthest reaches,
To the foggy, claggy ground
Where curséd Kimbril crushed the Kalcos
Turned the course of campaigns round.
Hie thee west - and hasten hardily
For the sought seeks not the seeker,
Nought greets tracker coming tardily -
To the tower where Tuli tarried,
By humans harmed and harsh hounds harried.
Then Do-ael's Drop, dank and dreary.
Heedful be of ghostly cries
This points the place but be you wary
The Staff of Sumos nearby lies.

Jebbin pushed the scroll forward and snorted, disliking Orrolui's smug air. "Intriguing. And you understand this appalling poetry from the demon Zaeboth?"

"I have information on all salient aspects. Permit me to elucidate." Orrolui ticked off points on his fingers. "Foamfin, a river merging with the Oropin in Gelavien. Kimbril: a successful Belmenian general during their most expansionist period - he destroyed a nest of demon-worshippers which would explain why Zaeboth calls him accursed. Kalcos: the dominant Family of Shekkem who had long held out against the Belmenians. Retreating when their long-beleaguered capital of Tu-Tanai fell, they were forced eastward until Kimbril crushed them in a famous battle at Manugee where the fogs and mires of Shekkem failed to help them at the last. Tuli: one of the great princesses of Shekkem who was once travelling on the Golden Road in a caravan that was attacked and despoiled by bandits in Triva. Tuli escaped and fled south, alone but for a manservant. The raiders heard of her value from a prisoner and set their savage hunting dogs on her trail. However, Tuli and her servant reached a tower just ahead of their pursuers and there they barricaded themselves against attack for three days after which they were rescued by a patrol of Algolian soldiery tracking the reavers. Finally, Do-ael's Drop is the only waterfall, and that a small one, in the length of the Do-ael, the river bounding the eastern edge of the Kermion marshes. A place of scummy pools and slippery rocks and little else so this staff must be at Tuli's tower." Orrolui performed a flowery bow at the end of his recitation. "I trust you are impressed?"

"No. There's something far wrong here."

"And that is, pray? I had not realised you were so learned in demon lore."

"The idea's to solve this conundrum, not argue over who's done it. You dismiss Do-ael's Drop. That may be right but what of the source of the Foamfin or this Manugee place? You're ignoring them altogether."

"Well," frowned Orrolui, taken aback, "you have to walk west from Shekkem to reach Tuli's tower. Had I been granted the rhyme in Kashatar and walked west I should have become lost in the wastes of Malistan. It's necessary information."

"And the Foamfin?"

"Well obviously, I, er, I'm not sure. I had…There was some reason, I can't remember. There's no point in galloping round in a square, is there?"

"But you aren't galloping at all! It says you get nothing if you don't arrive soon."

"Yes, but that's merely poetic expression surely." Orrolui sounded suddenly crestfallen.

"And talking of expressions, there's one that worries me even more than the rest: the Staff of Sumos nearby lies. It's the title and last line. You can take it two ways; either the staff is lying about nearby, or the staff nearby does not tell the truth."

There was a long pause while Orrolui glared at his feet as though they had caused him some mortal hurt and Jebbin studied the paper, ignoring him.

"Teltazzar curse all pox-ridden demons to the nether planes that spawned them!" exploded Orrolui in a fit. "I've been mazed, ensorcelled with a blindness. By the seven bells of Athrogem, Zaeboth will pay for this trickery! And you," he snarled at Jebbin, "do you have some constructive points to make, having destroyed my paltry maunderings?"

"As a matter of fact, if it's not too late and if the staff is worth going for anyway, yes, I do have an idea. Hiraeth has travelled widely but we really need a cartographer."

"But I've told you all about the rhyme, what more do you want?"

"Wait until Hiraeth gets back," smiled Jebbin in revenge for Orrolui's earlier attitude. "In the meantime," he relented, watching the rage build brick by brick in Orrolui's face, "we might assail that light spell together. If you try to meld with me and follow it through, you may be able to see what it is that I do that you don't."

Orrolui mastered his emotions with difficulty and dropped himself into a chair by the table. He rolled a grain of *sear* to Jebbin and inhaled one himself. He breathed deeply twice, sharply expelled the air, then cupped his hands on the table before him. Jebbin took the opposite seat, surrounded Orrolui's hands with his own and gazed into the Gesgarian's eyes, the pupils like black rods of massive cold. Staring into that void, Jebbin concentrated on blankness and felt the familiar sensation of vertigo as the world closed in, the room spinning into nothingness, only Orrolui's eyes remained, looming impossibly large. He sensed Orrolui's questing mind, the banked fires of his powerful brain, lidded and controlled in black iron lockers but seething and bubbling with excitement. As the bright spark of pain rose to touch the web of power, Jebbin supported it with the first syllables of the spell and moved it across the immeasurable gulf that was no distance at all to Orrolui's waiting hands. He ignited it with the final phoneme.

There was a violent, blinding flash that stunned both of them with its actinic intensity and sent them sprawling backwards, Orrolui's chair tipping right over and landing him flat on his back, sightless eyes aimed at the ceiling. Jebbin dragged his hands from his own eyes and blinked. The fire alone was visible as a dull glow. As his vision gradually recuperated, he looked down at the recumbent Gesgarian who was whispering in awed tones, "I see, I see," while his hand crawled round to collect his scimitar and hold it tightly, pulsing echoes of light along its edge.

"I believe I could do it! To build power," Orrolui shook his head wonderingly, "will take time. But I could do it."

Jebbin watched Orrolui's lips curling back in elation and the increasing speed of the flickering glimmer on the blade hinting at a forthcoming ecstatic eruption of power. With a glance at the darkened sky outside, he ran forward and grabbed Orrolui's wrist.

"No!" he yelled, "No more. We're in hiding, have you forgotten? Orrolui, we must not call attention to ourselves!"

Even as he shouted, the door smashed open and two figures rushed through. "Too late, fools," bawled the hindmost, slamming the door behind him.

In an instant, Orrolui rolled to his knees, thrust more *sear* into his mouth and brought his scimitar swinging round, rippling with energy but Jebbin dived at him and bore him down, crackling with undischarged power. The foremost of the intruders fell headlong under the table and lay motionless. The magicians slowly rose to see Bolan shuttering the windows.

"Choose swiftly, fight or flight? If that worm," the wrestler indicated the thief sprawled on the floor with a jerk of his head, "found you then your hiding place is divined. Indeed, found it myself," he added with considerable pride.

"Wait," cried Orrolui, clutching his *sear*-flamed jaw. "You're going too fast. Why is it so desperate for the thieves to find us? If we're cornered here, we can't fight off the entire Guild. If we fly, we'll surely meet patrols on the road; we can't outdistance them. If we take to the fields and are spotted, we risk being stalked by stealth and dying without the chance to strike back. Our choices are fraught!"

"Bolan, he's right. Neither flight nor fight will serve us now. Why are you... I mean, you've done much to help us already, for which many thanks." Embarrassment burned his cheeks as he saw the edge of a bandage under Bolan's shirt. He tried to continue brightly. "This matter requires guile. Where did you collect this fellow?"

"After incidents in my quarters, time to quit Dadacombe.

You're both bound up in this matter and unfairly set upon, even the Gesgarian, it seems. Guessed where to find you and to spite the thieves came to warn you of their interest. Spotted a flash of light and then him peering through the casement, so grabbed him and tossed him inside."

"Is he still alive?"

"Currently. But even if we kill him, when he fails to report back, truth will be deduced."

"Then he must report back. But he must report that we are not here and we shall thus gain a respite."

"No blandishments or threats from us will prove sufficient for him to lie to his Guild Master's face," growled Bolan.

"Excellent idea, Jebbin!" said Orrolui, smacking the table. "Don't worry about that, Bolan, leave it to me. He'll tell what he believes he saw but it won't be strictly the truth - and I need to use a spell."

Kneeling down, Orrolui cradled the head of the thief and opened his eyes. He muttered for some time and touched the man on the forehead with the point of his scimitar. The three of them then sat back against the wall and waited in tense silence for the thief to rouse. When he eventually did so, with much groaning, it took him a long while to struggle to his feet. That task achieved, he recovered swiftly. Looking carefully round the room without appearing to notice that he had company, still as waxworks but for glittering eyes and droplets gliding down Bolan's forehead, the thief then tiptoed round the house. In the larder, they heard the familiar trickle from the beer barrel as the interloper sampled the contents, then an appreciative belch. His search completed, the thief eased the door open, peeked furtively into the street and vanished into the night. At exactly the same moment, all three began to talk again;

"Well, that's that," said Orrolui contentedly.

"Now we'll just have to wait and hope..." began Jebbin.

"If he was listening and shamming, we're in trouble," said Bolan, looking as though he had just completed an arduous bout but then the tension dissolved in the liquid of Orrolui's conviction and they laughed together in their shared victory.

Later Hiraeth returned and told them of his day. He added that he had spent part of his evening playing at one of the largest inns. Chief amongst the revellers there had been Captain Gorve and his men. Rumbustious with ale, they had taken to asking any newcomers whether they were magicians, because if so they were about to be arrested. This sally bemused most customers but afforded the group enormous hilarity. Hiraeth suggested that Gorve was not over-dedicated to his task and they had little to fear from that direction.

"Is there a cartographer in Dadacome?" asked Jebbin. Hiraeth nodded. "Then as soon as I have consulted him we should leave swiftly, for this quest brooks no delay and we have dawdled enough."

The minstrel's house was equipped for neither defence nor protection against burglary; the bars on the shutters were designed to ward against gales, not thieves, so the company decided to take turns on watch. They passed an uneventful night, entertaining themselves with speculations of Ansin running short of sleep and hair in the Guild House.

In the morning, the four were facing their dilemma which Orrolui was expounding. "We're safe enough here for the time being as that poor fool obviously reported this place deserted but with every thief on the lookout for us, the Guild calling in all its markers and the assassins Bolan has brought on our heads searching for us too, the minute we step outside they'll be on to us. If we stay here, it's only a matter of time before they find us. We mustn't underestimate the power of the Guild in a place as big as Dadacombe. In any case, we're in a hurry and cannot afford to hide until the search is abandoned."

"Surely, we have two magicians here. Can you not magically teleport away?"

"I would need the contents of an archmage's workroom to do that. And Jebbin, no."

"What about some spell or illusion to change your appearance?"

"It may come to that but the maintenance of such a transformation is tiring and it's a long way out of Dadacombe and its patrols. Worse, there are Lookers who can see through the finest illusions and to whom the use of magic would shine like a beacon in the night; the Guild will certainly station their Lookers on the road. Then if we're revealed without knowing it or your magi are tired beyond spelling, we'd have no chance at all."

"Also, I must visit this cartographer," said Jebbin.

"I'm not implicated and can do that without suspicion," said Hiraeth.

"You may not be hunted but you will be suspect and mustn't do anything out of the ordinary," said Orrolui.

"I'm a bard! I travel constantly and what would be more natural than consulting a cartographer for the best route?"

"When did you last visit one?" asked Bolan.

"Not recently; I'm not a caravan master. Still, it would be reasonable."

"That still leaves us with the main difficulty. Since we cannot avail ourselves of horses, for all ostlers and wranglers will be doubly watched, our departure will perforce be slow. It must, therefore, be totally unsuspected."

"Disguise!" said Bolan triumphantly. "Swathe ourselves in habits and cowls and pass as priests of Nakki or some deity from Shekkem."

"And stand out like goats in a nunnery. A few improvised blankets are not going to suffice and we have neither time, skill nor materials for precision."

"Could we sneak away through the sewers beneath this place until we are beyond the town limits?"

"Not far, I regret. The sewer ends in a cess pit."

"With a blast of power, I could start a fire or two, even set the Guild House ablaze, then in the noise and confusion while the thieves rush to protect their property and the militia try to extinguish all the fires..."

"...Except the Guild House because they loathe the thieves..."

"...We could make a break for it, perhaps even snatch horses and ride pell-mell out of here. What about that?"

"Such fires could get out of control! A large part of the militia will have camped at Egsbury Hill last night and tonight for their monthly training. We don't actually want to burn the town to the ground," murmured Hiraeth.

"We may have to try it but Ansin's no fool. The moment magical fires burst out, he'll guess the sorcerers he seeks are creating a diversion and redouble his road defences whatever the cost."

There was a pause after this furious discussion while Bolan screwed his face up and scratched his head. Suddenly Jebbin leant forward.

"I think we have it, if we put all these ideas together."

"Oh excellent, I would hate to miss out on the cess pit" said Hiraeth, arching his eyebrows

Jebbin failed to notice the bard's humour and continued. "No, but the fires, Bolan's disguise and so on. First, we find some way to fire the Guild Headquarters and as much else as we can in the way of uninhabited buildings and warehouses and get them well alight. The thieves will have their work cut out trying to put out the Guild House and stop the roads as well. The militia will be called out to deal with the blazes but there are few of them because most are at Egsbury Hill and if we've done our work well they won't be able to douse them. In the time it takes the rest of the militia to gallop back from Egsbury, the fires will have taken hold and the barracks will be emptied as all available personnel are drafted in the emergency. We make use of the confusion, not to escape as expected, but to steal militia uniforms from the barracks and then, when order is restored and the thieves think they must have missed us despite their best efforts, we turn Orrolui's hair grey with the tincture of groundsel and dirty our uniforms, ideally by taking a turn at real fire-fighting, and trudge away with the returning militia to Egsbury, perhaps even borrowing a mount or two then. Hm?"

"Far too complicated. It could go wrong at a hundred points!"

"Perhaps, but the chances of any part of it miscarrying seem remote. Providing we can fire isolated buildings so homes and lives are safe then I vote for the plan," said Hiraeth. "It might even make a good song."

"Cunning as a ferret," chuckled Bolan. "'With you, young fellow."

All eyes turned to Orrolui, who gazed at the table through narrowed lids for a moment, then banished anxiety with a wave.

"Pah, why not?" He grinned wolfishly. "And you can rely on me for the fire-raising. There'll be no sneaking about with flasks of oil and tinderboxes. We can all stay tucked up in here, assuming you can indicate the relevant buildings somehow. But I will require a few spell components and positively no interference."

"Agreed!" cried Hiraeth. "Then if Jebbin will supply me with his questions for the cartographer and Orrolui with a list of whatever he needs which isn't in the house already, I'll be off. But first, let's drink to the venture." He danced to his feet and scurried off to the larder where the beer barrel was beginning to look seriously undernourished. When the vintner supplying the house made his regular visit, Hiraeth was going to acquire a reputation as a fearsome tippler.

* * *

The bard pushed into the dim, little shop underneath a faded sign that read, 'Erridarch, geographer to the Emperor'. The dry smell of a scriptorium tickled his nose as he struck a copper pipe with a leather mallet to summon the cartographer. He examined his cramped surroundings while waiting. Maps were stuffed into earthenware pots; charts and scrolls littered every available surface and competed for space on the walls. A large, metal copying frame tilted dangerously in one corner. Above it, racks of shelves overflowed with pencils, dividers, rulers, gadgets and books. A huge lodestone was suspended over the main desk, upon which a giant sheet of partially inscribed vellum was held down by a motley assortment of jars of coloured inks, stands for various nibs and quills and an empty pewter pot smelling of wine. Hiraeth was just bending over it when a small man with mouse-coloured hair came hopping into view on lamed legs.

"Yes, yes, yes?" he chirped, peering up at Hiraeth with bulbous eyes. "A bard, eh? Off on some mysterious commission for a bag of gold in an unknown town? It's happened before, you know. The whole world laid out before me and what am I asked? Where is Stethime? No idea what country, of course, just expects me to know off the top of my head! Ridiculous, you might think, but it didn't take me long. I don't suppose you want to find Stethime, do you? Quite nice, I'm told. Well, speak up, don't be shy."

"I'll try to keep my courage up," Hiraeth smiled down at the little man. "Now, we're going to need a big map."

"Big?" said Erridarch indignantly, turning up the wick of a filigreed brass lantern. "A big map? Come now, what do you know? A carpet-sized map of a garden, the world on a fingernail - big doesn't mean anything. You tell me what you want and I'll pick map and scale. Each to his own now, I shall not sing a song, you let me say how big maps should be."

"Right. Do you know the Foamfin river?"

"Know it? Of course I know it? I know every river from the Kleocarrin to our own Chucklin, from the Oropin to the Feluga, no, to the Dekalioka even!" cried the little man, tapping his forehead with his fingertips. "Just tell me what you want to know, then I can ask the questions, should any be necessary."

"Right. I want a map that covers everything from the source of the Foamfin to Manugee in Shekkem and running from Doael's Drop in the north to Tuli's tower in Triva."

Erridarch paused, staring at Hiraeth with his swollen eyes wider than ever, then snapped his mouth shut and flicked expressive hands skywards.

"And that's all? Three quarters of the known world on one map and you cover the whole thing in a quick sentence? Have you no sense of distances? The massive mountains that thwart any road or the endless plains, the great cities of Belmenia, the trackless Kermion marshes?"

"Well, if you can't do it..." Hiraeth interrupted the course of geographical instruction.

"Can't?" spluttered the cartographer, "Who said can't? I'm just trying to inject a little sense of occasion; the dignity of leagues, I call it. Folk are always in such a hurry these days, wanting to travel the length of the Golden Road in the time it takes to move a finger, and usually a grubby finger at that, along the line on my map. Still, still, still I suppose we must hurry, hurry, hurry." Erridarch pattered on, dragging his unresponsive feet to a huge, old wine jar and rootling in it amongst the largest scrolls, his birdlike hands fluttering through the crackling paper with practised speed.

"Yes, here it... no, this one. But why? Where are you going that you need such a chart?"

"That's what I need you to tell me."

"You don't know where you are going? Ah, my poor friend, there are many who don't know where they are going but at least they know whither they are bound. What do you want my maps for? To pick a faraway place with a strange name that appeals to you? Stethime not good enough?"

"I want you to draw a line from the source of the Foamfin to Manugee battlefield and then another from Tuli's tower to the falls of the Do-ael. There must be something where the lines cross and that will be my destination," Hiraeth said, referring to the paper Jebbin had given him.

"You're quite mad, of course, but I'm used to that. And what does it matter? First, four angels for the consultation," said Erridarch, clutching the vast map to his narrow chest. When Hiraeth had counted coins onto the table, the geographer dutifully pocketed them before shuffling the apparatus about the table until the new map was pinned and lighted to his satisfaction. Hiraeth watched as nimble fingers whisked frames and pins and rulers to and fro until the cotton threads designed a cross. The bard craned forward and looked at the juncture.

"Nothing!" he exclaimed in dismay.

"And what did you expect? The capital of the world?" Erridarch blinked owlishly at him. "Don't look so despondent, the world is full of wonders." He stroked the contours of the map as though he could bring them within the range of his crippled legs.

"But the only wonder I wanted was the one at that point."

"The men of today, so easily dejected. We have but begun, now we must close in upon that region until we view it from but a stone's throw away, as though we might look up through this window and espy the very land you seek." Erridarch spoke wistfully and gazed longingly towards the cobwebbed window, but even at such a modest distance, all views were a blur to him and the visions that were unveiled before his misty eyes were hidden to Hiraeth. Then he busied himself with measurements and angles and compasses, seeming to forget his client altogether as he scuttled from map to map, absorbed in his work.

After much precise shifting of maps, frames and pins, he straightened and pensively regarded the results, his lower lip stuck out like a beak. He glanced across at the bard and cleared his throat to gain his attention. "It looks as though you're right."

"Right?" said Hiraeth, who had been humming over recently learned lyrics in a reverie that had developed as his fascination with the cartographer's meticulous measurements dwindled. "What do you mean?"

"Attend, regard," Erridarch gestured towards his last map.

Hiraeth was startled to see a map marked not with mountain ranges and cities but crisscrossed with thin red cart tracks and azure brooks, dotted with spinneys and ponds, a noteworthy estate delineated in straw-yellow ink, two tiny hamlets and a village named in black. Two threads crossed to the north of the village. Hiraeth looked up with shining eyes.

"Farralei!" he breathed.

"The lines, you will observe, are not bisected precisely in the village. Nonetheless, considering the starting scale, I think this is within an acceptable margin of error. I have done my best."

"Magnificent!" Hiraeth applauded, beaming at the little man. "A stupendous effort that leaves me amazed, truly. And worth far more than four angels. Please accept another."

"No, no. Four angels is the fee; I am not poor and my wants are few."

"Is there nothing else I could give you?"

"Oh, surely yes," sighed the geographer. "Come back. Return

and sing to me of what it's really like, sing of the ice-torn mountains, vast forests and mighty rivers; towered cities of exotic peoples with strange customs; sulphurous fire-lakes and volcanoes; the steppes and high plateaux..." his voice faded into the realms of imagination and his hands, which had gripped Hiraeth's arm fiercely, fell away like autumn leaves in the island forests of Torl.

Unhesitating, Hiraeth plucked a silver ocarina from his pocket and began to play. In a voice enriched with compassion, he sang the sad, sweet song of the Ailya river, its giant swirls and ponderous breathing as it waxed brown and heavy with the soils of Belmenia until finally it died in the ocean, giving birth to the huge silt banks that threatened the great port of Tarass. All the while Erridarch stood enraptured, lips slightly parted, his eyes again on the grimy window but seeing the liquid ebb and flow that dropped from Hiraeth's words until at last the song ended with the haunting mewl of the plaintive gulls diving over the sand bars. The ensuing image-laden silence was finally broken by Hiraeth, sounding suddenly hoarse.

"I will come back."

Erridarch smiled slightly and nodded before he tottered away on maimed legs.

"Erridarch, one thing more." Hiraeth referred to Jebbin's scrap of paper, remembering the mage had stressed that he mention this last to none but the geographer. When Erridarch stopped and half turned, he asked, "Where, and what, is a ponent salebrous paramo?"

Erridarch's eyebrows raised in surprise, then he sighed and rubbed his glaucomatous eyes gently before labouring back to the desk. Without speaking, he shuffled the stack of maps until the first one topped the pile again and ran the very ends of his fingertips over its coloured surface as though he sensed its contours. Appearing tired, he looked up at Hiraeth and shrugged.

"It's difficult to say one place. A paramo is a high plain set above the norm, scant vegetation blasted by gales; these are esoteric terms for the public. There are, I suppose, three such areas. The most typical would be the centre of the mountains of Ael but also there are the highlands of the Sultanate of O-Ram where springs the Xar and perhaps the high hills far to the west of Yriallin. The first of these would also be the most salebrous, or rugged, but the last is the most ponent, western. If that is where you seek you will not return and sing to me, for it lies as far north of Jerondst as it is west of Yriallin and its terrors still conceal the source of the river Feor which feeds the Felugan Sea. But perhaps you want the western end of the salebrous paramo of Ael? It could be so, I cannot tell."

"Ael again," said Hiraeth softly. "Then no further shall I go and I will return." He slipped from the shop while Erridarch's head was still held high.

Feeling subdued, Hiraeth returned to the others with the items required by Orrolui and the news that the magi's next destination was Farralei, to the north of Lana.

"Ho! Not impossibly far, eh?" exulted Orrolui. "We'll be there soon enough to satisfy the cry for haste, Jebbin. The staff is almost ours, I feel it in my bones. But how did you solve the demon's riddle?"

"Time for such questions later," Hiraeth said. "Farralei lies in the empty region between Ael, Marigor and Tachenland. Travel there is perilous and we are few, even if I travel so far with you."

"Faugh!" spat Orrolui darkly. "Let me perform this conjuration and you shall judge what we have to fear from tribesmen, be they mountain goats from Ael or monkeys from Tachenland. The time is at hand: unpack my adjuncts, build up the fire. Now you shall witness such a training of the strands from the web of power that Dadacombe shall not forget for many a year."

"Remember, the Guild Hall and warehouses only."

"Where exactly are these buildings, then?" asked Orrolui over his shoulder, busy mixing powders in a mortar while Jebbin rigged an iron cauldron over a stacked fire.

"Well," began Hiraeth uncertainly, "if we are, say, here, this street runs so." He made a dot on the table and a line with spilt beer. Orrolui watched with quick eyes as the map grew, nodding in understanding until Hiraeth had finished and then turned back to the cauldron. He tossed in his concoction, plucked the cork from a polished flask and swiftly added a thick, dark liquid with a nettlesome reek of brimstone, burnt copper and child-hood fears. He drew in *sear* and cast a spell over the cauldron, his face twisted with pain.

"Don't like this mummery," muttered Bolan. He turned to Jebbin. "Sure you want to do this to yourself?"

"The pain is just a path, it goes." said Jebbin, feeling unclean. "You get hurt in your profession too."

"Don't do it to yourself though."

"I've never seen anything like this," said Hiraeth in horrified fascination. "I thought it would be one wave of the sword accom-panied by a quick word."

"Teltazzar!" growled Orrolui, glaring at them from under knotted brows. "Will you stop twittering? Hiraeth, you sing a perfectly good song but play lute or flute to augment the effect. Bolan, you can kill a man with your bare hands but find it easier with a sword. I can flay a man's skin with excoriating magic but I too have ways of bolstering the power so I don't have to flay my own skin for the pain to do it. Keep silent until this is over."

Having inhaled enough *sear* to make Jebbin's eyes water in sympathy and Hiraeth to groan in disgust, Orrolui's breath hissed through his teeth as he struggled to control the pain. He began a soft chant as the fluid in the cauldron began to bubble and smoke, holding his scimitar before him in both hands and swaying from side to side before the flaring light like some monstrous cobra. Slowly the cauldron's contents frothed and grew, spitting tiny drops that flickered huge in the firelight. Then a runnel overflowed the cauldron's lip and dribbled down the side, pausing and swelling at the base before sagging into the blaze below. Immediately a gout of lurid yellow flame belched upward and with a cry of power that twisted the air, Orrolui darted forward and sliced it through with his scimitar. Snagged by the insidious chant, the dissected flame contracted but stabilized and became brighter yet until it floated about Orrolui's head as a marble of intense light, an image of the sun. Another gobbet fell, another plume of fire billowed and again Orrolui clove it with his sword and a syllable of magic bound it to shrink and circle him with its brother. Once more and again and thrice more Orrolui shouted and struck until moisture gleamed on his pallid skin and his dark eyes writhed in the glare of the globes. He knocked the cauldron to tip the remaining mixture into the blaze and gleaned the last of the fiery sprites. Ridged and corded, he turned to the table, teeth bared in a feral grin, and slashed downward with the scimitar, the point stabbing at each of the places indicated by Hiraeth. Each time the tip speared down, a fireball streaked away to challenge the sun with a crackling explosion in the distance. As the last departed, Orrolui fell back into a chair, panting. His breathless chuckle developed into a braying laugh until he struck at the air with his fist.

"Ha! What about that? Teltazzar, that was good. Hark!" he said, cupping his hand round his ear in an exaggerated pose as the clank of alarm bells began to call a doleful message to the militia. "That'll keep them busy enough, I know. Now you lot had better fetch those uniforms. Go, go!"

As the others roused themselves from their amazement, Bolan dropped his heavy hand on Hiraeth's shoulder.

"Stay. Done more than your share already and with no call to flee."

"You think not? When the thieves and assassins discover where you've all been concealed, my stay in Dadacombe would become exceedingly uncomfortable. This leave-taking is too much fun to miss."

"Nevertheless, this is down to me and the youngster. We'll let things hot up first. If we bump into thieves taking up stations on the road or returning to the Guild House then all this goes for nothing."

So it was that much later, when the fires had finally been doused by the militia now returning to their training fields, four weary fire-fighters plodded from the gates of Dadacombe. Other groups dotted the way back to Egsbury Hill, all walking with that silent, companionable gait that comes from hard toil in a common cause. The horses had been taken back ahead of them, away from the terrifying fires and smokes of Dadacombe. A man leaned against an aged tree, his doeskin breeches and soft, olive tunic unstained by smoke. One foot was hitched up behind his backside, his knee thrust out. Across his lap lay a rapier. The man was offering up a small yellow stone against the hilt but glancing up frequently to view the departing folk. Suddenly he frowned at the four of them, then pushed himself upright, the rapier swinging to his side.

"Don't look at him. Keep walking," muttered Orrolui.

Just then, a girl with shrewd eyes and a lithe body scampered forwards. "I think you're looking for two men," she said, eyeing the man speculatively.

"I may well be, what of it?" The thief was still looking at them over her shoulder, moving sideways to keep them in view.

"What'll you pay?"

"Nothing for nothing." His eyes flicked to the girl, then he looked at her more appreciatively.

"A ryal for their direction and another for when they left."

"A crown in all and only if you're right," offered the thief, glancing once again at the fire-fighters. Jebbin had stopped. Orrolui covered this by brushing soot from his uniform and pushed him on.

"A helm now and an angel if you find them, don't haggle further. You can find me at the Griffin." She looked at the man sidelong through lowered lids and added in a coquettish voice, "If you want to."

The thief leered at her for a moment, then flicked her a silver helm and raised his eyebrows in question.

"Two men sneaked away just after the fires started, going due south straight over the fields into Fletcher's Copse. On foot. And one was a filthy Gesgarian."

"You sure about the direction?"

"For my angel, I'm sure. It's not my fault if they evade you. See you in the Griffin anyway, maybe?" She slipped away from him and danced off into the town while he watched her retreating form, sucking his teeth in pleasurable anticipation, before trotting off towards the Guild House.

"Strange," said Hiraeth. "Was that a chat-up line or someone using wit to make a quick helm?"

"No," said Jebbin. "I can't place her but she was familiar, or she reminded me of someone. Maybe this old guy I met, Dordo."

"I don't trust coincidence or unknown purposes. Head for that horse-pond. I need to know more." Orrolui rolled *sear* into his hand.

The Gesgarian intoned his skrying spell and thrust his scimitar into the water. As he withdrew the blade, ripples wobbled into a view of the Guild House. A thin smoke still trickled upward from the western quoin where the outer wall had fallen away. Props and stays supported sagging joists within while blackened furnishings peeped shyly at the world without. The thief was slouching towards the main door when he stopped at the sight of the door wardens.

"Oops, new guys," he muttered to himself. He scratched a bristly chin ruminatively. "Looks like problems have come to a head. Maybe a change round at the top. If I have to pick sides, I might get it wrong. Or I could have a beer." The thief set off in the direction of the Griffin.

The view drifted to an upstairs room of the eastern wing, where Ansin, white-faced with eyes bloodshot from smoke and sleeplessness, was confronted by Guthreg, who was shaking his head sadly.

"Dear me! Two whole days and nothing to show for it but one decapitated innocent. I'm sure I made myself clear. I can scarcely credit that two strangers, even a Gesgarian, lie low in your own town and you, a captain of thieves, cannot find them! And just look at you, scorched and singed with the Guild House wrecked." Guthreg tutted and lifted pudgy hands in despair. "Really, such a bad reflection on our honoured institution. While I extend my personal sympathies, I'm afraid that for the good of the Guild...."

"Master," broke in Ansin, "we can pay."

"What with, pray? The sum in your coffers is known to me and astonishingly meagre it seems. Perhaps you've not been operating as you should of late - or have you been embezzling Guild funds?" Guthreg smiled curiously.

"Never! I... but," Ansin's jaw clenched in rage as Guthreg's traps caught him. He could hardly admit to paying the assassins to kill someone a Guild Master had ordered released unharmed.

In desperation, he tried to attack. "Master, you are forbidden to interfere in the rivalries of Guild factions."

"If you have allegations of impropriety, you are entitled to bring your slanders before the Militant Arm. Happily, Balvak is here and he is a zealous seeker after truth. No? I suspected not. I'm merely acting, according to charter, in the best interests of the Guild. You've been foolish and must be replaced."

Wild-eyed, Ansin ripped out a rapier encrusted with rubies and sapphires and faced the Guild Master. "Very well, I accept I've played this badly but I'll step down in favour of one of my own men."

"Oh, I have no objection in theory." Guthreg patted a thespian yawn and ignored the rapier. "But unfortunately none of your subordinates have sufficient experience for the post."

"Payl has more experience than that Toomsly viper!" spat Ansin.

"But none of leadership."

"Neither had I when I came to office!"

"Quite. Hardly a recommendation. But your fraternal promotion of Toomsly has merit."

"Never. My thieves would refuse to serve under him," said Ansin, the sparkling rapier dangling from his blistered hands.

"They will be given that choice, of course," Guthreg smiled directly at Ansin.

"You giggling glutton, I cannot impeach you but I can kill you. Laugh now!" So shouting, Ansin darted forward with a lunge at Guthreg but met nothing more than a sudden spray of acid. He had dropped the rapier even before the crossbow bolt hit him in the small of his back and he crumpled to the floor.

"Thank you, Balvak. Why do they never go gracefully? Ah well, send in Toomsly."

There was a flicker of yellow hair as Ansin was tossed against the wall. Unmoving, he watched over a widening slick of his blood as Balvak shepherded Toomsly and his two lieutenants before Guthreg.

"Great Guild Master," gushed Toomsly, his glance sliding over the previous incumbent of the post of Dadacombe captain, "this is a wonderful day. Here's the promised item plus five hundred ryals of gol..." He stopped suddenly seeing the expression of horror of Guthreg's face.

"Balvak!" cried the Guild Master, "Take those items into custody immediately as evidence. Toomsly, I cannot believe that you, whom I trusted with this onerous and elevated position, should instantly repay me with an attempted bribe before witnesses. Such a sorry affair. Still, perhaps I'm being over hasty over a tragic lapse. I shall keep the matter in abeyance for now and whether I take further action will depend upon your future performance. I'm sure I can depend upon your untiring zeal, Toomsly. Come, Balvak. Good day, gentlethieves." He turned at the door, "And Toomsly, that matter of Jebbin is now in your hands. Do not fail me nor the Guild."

Leaving a tableau of faces frozen in shock, Guthreg waved a cheery farewell and they could dimly hear his high-pitched mirth as he descended the stairs with Balvak. Ansin, too, gave a tiny laugh that seeped out of him in dribbling bubbles, then he died.

Journey to Farralei

Mindful of Guild spies from Dadacombe, Hiraeth alone would slip into sleepily suspicious villages for flour or beans and dark gritty bread while Bolan kept unblinking watch and the magicians continued their discussions of spells, magical methodology and the ability of the mind to control pain.

As one day's sun sank into misted blue hills, they camped beneath an old tree, far from noisy dogs or prying eyes. The top of the tree had been killed when some animal had ring-barked it with the scoring of powerful claws. It remained defiantly upright, an outstretched hand in rigor mortis; lesser branches and bark all sloughed away. Bolan inspected the timber and selected a straight, knob-ended section, a head taller than himself. He trimmed the thin end until it was rounded and free from cracks, then wielded it as a quarterstaff with slashing strokes and jabs. The wood was hard and smooth as polished bone and in his hands it became an awesome weapon.

"Most impressive, but will it really supersede the sword?" asked Jebbin.

"For you. Has some advantages; reach for one. Here, have at me with my sword."

When Jebbin waggled the sword at Bolan, the right-hand end

of the staff swept the blade aside and, as part of the same movement, the left-hand end swung round and whacked him in the ribs.

"Move faster. Similarly when the staff attacks..."

Jebbin was just in time to parry the staff but again the other end caught him.

"Oof. Yes, I see, but I can't use it like you and if we do meet trouble, I'd be better using magic."

"Exactly. We're four unremarkable travellers, safe from the rabble of Dadacombe. Soon as you use magic without a staff, we become news again. Might stir up the same trouble afresh. Now you have a staff and if you use magic, the only surprise will be in meeting a magician." Bolan scratched his bulbous nose reflectively. "And if your opponent's expecting a spell, a clout round the ear with that may produce gratifying results, however ineptly you swing it."

"Thank you. I should've thought of that. Show me how to use it again."

Bolan brightened and enthusiastically demonstrated the new weapon until Jebbin was more likely to hit someone rather than fall over it himself.

After a meal of wheat cakes and a bottle of amber Amasca wine, a bed in the yellowed bracken seemed comfortable enough, warmed by a fire built from the tree's last bounty. They smiled up at the stars pin-holing the silent black and listened to Hiraeth's crooning voice in the breathless night. But when all was quiet and they were stilled in sleep, the cold painted them in delicate patterns of rime, then crept in to shake their bones with frozen fingers. They rose before dawn, chilled and stiff with cramped muscles, every noise and groan they made amplified in the hollow hall of the night. Bolan alone was unaffected and dozed on while a shivering Orrolui poked ashes with a stick clutched in shaking fingers and eventually blew the fire back to life. He huddled before its radiance like a lizard while Jebbin prepared more wheatmeal for breakfast. When handed a mug of tea, Orrolui clutched it under his chin with both hands and remained motionless, vulture-like, until it was cool enough to drink. When it was half-gone, he spoke.

"Tomorrow, we sleep inside. One thief, a whole Guild of thieves, and I'll fry them all. Better yet, freeze them," he croaked to nobody in particular, tilting his head back to stare at the dwindling stars. "Expose them to those black gulfs where no man sails. What winds blow there? And how are those empty silences filled? When I gain the power, I'll ride those dark lanes and plumb those endless depths, remote and alone." His voice faded away but he still stared up with unblinking gaze into the limitless realms above, his thin, pinched face lit from beneath by the refulgent fire.

Over breakfast they agreed with Orrolui. However long the reach of the Dadacombe thieves, nights were not safe even in Marigor and some perils were worse than either cold or whatever beast had barked the tree. Jebbin alone had spoken against the plan but, when pressed, had revealed in a shamed voice,

"I have no money. Bolan and Orrolui have their stores, Hiraeth can earn his living in any inn from here to Kathos but I have not a copper piece and no wish to batten on my friends. Neither will our adventure permit further delay while I seek employment."

He was halted by Bolan's kindly laughter. "Well said, lad, but if you become a burden, we'll tell you. Four can live as cheaply as three and you're not beholden."

Facing northwest, they left the tree stiffly enduring another sunrise with branches braced against decay, standing guard over a shoot from still vigorous roots. Soon they must cross the Billyrillin as Orrolui and Jebbin pressed on for Farralei. Then they would reach the Golden Road and if thoughts of wayfarers and tales intruiged Bolan, they sang in Hiraeth's soul.

During the afternoon, Hiraeth and Orrolui were walking some distance behind Bolan and Jebbin, who was striding along with his new staff. They watched as the broad wrestler regaled his keen listener with tales, occasionally borrowing the staff for ferocious gesticulations. Orrolui gave his head a tiny shake as he considered Jebbin.

"What's amiss?" asked Hiraeth immediately.

"He is," Orrolui jabbed a finger at Jebbin. Just for once, all guile and confidence fell away and his voice had a querulous edge. "Look, imagine you were a top bard, praised by your mentors as having exceptional ability and then along comes an untrained novice, plays your instruments like toys, learns your secret songs in moments and even has the gall to suggest improvements - and they are improvements, by Teltazzar. On top of that, he has some new capability like, oh, singing through his ears and thinks nothing of it. Well, it's like that."

"He's that good then?" prompted Hiraeth, who would have been delighted to meet such a novice.

"No, he's better. You remember that magic that struck Bolan back in the dungeon? It was no spell."

"I don't understand."

"Jebbin didn't know a spell that could do anything like that. I revealed one to him later and the only time he used it, he missed! But he was too terrified to think straight and would probably have forgotten a spell had he known it. But he didn't. So as a natural reflex, he launched a droplet of raw pain, the very stuff of magic but totally unfettered. I know it's impossible but he doesn't. Ah, Teltazzar, if I've not mastered his skill soon...." He left the comment ominously unfinished.

Hiraeth squinted sidelong at the Gesgarian but the shield was raised anew, the expression guarded. "Orrolui, he's no threat to you," the bard said quickly.

"Of course not," Orrolui smiled at him, sounding surprised. "We're all friends here."

Hiraeth frowned into the studied blankness of Orrolui's eyes but at that moment Jebbin called for them to hurry; there was a town ahead and Bolan was buying the first round.

Even on foot, they frequently passed hamlets strung between the larger villages. Here farms were small but thickly spread on the fertile ground and roads were stippled with merchants, trading through many little towns to build up shipments bound for the Golden Road to anywhere.

As they walked through the rich water-meadows banking the Bululu, a broad, slow tributary of the Billyrillin, they met farmers, toiling in the fields and orchards or preparing for winter in vineyards on the lighter ground where the smokes from bonfires of damp prunings clung to the earth like uneasy spirits. Fishermen too, wading in the muddy waters with lines and nets, were always willing to share a fish luncheon, their glistening bodies as natural as the willows and alders that sprawled along the banks, sipping the fading sunlight and fanning themselves with ever-moving leaves.

Then the weather broke. One afternoon the wind leapt out from bulging clouds and started shoving the walkers. They hurried towards Felice and the comforts of an inn. By the time they reached it, a fine rain was blowing horizontally to draw a lacy curtain across the distance. With Bolan's fist pounding the Apple Tree's door, they were soon admitted to the flickering dance of the common-room fire. Hiraeth ascertained that there were rooms available while the others steamed before the blaze, puffing and wiping their faces. The bard offered to perform for the company that evening, much to the delight of the proprietor, who called himself Tubbs. No bard had been seen in Felice for many a long year and Tubbs knew he had a profitable night in prospect. A potboy too slow to duck from sight was sent into the dripping village to spread the news that there would be rare entertainment in the Apple Tree that evening.

Tubbs offered them the finest supper the inn could boast on the house, providing they took it early before he was too busy. Clearly, the sooner Hiraeth was replete, the sooner he could start work and the more Tubbs would gain from his unexpected visitor. Tubbs showed them their rooms himself, then ushered them into the bathrooms where two women were busy heating water and filling a giant tub. Tubbs' wife, Utha, broad and cheerful, bade them welcome and promised a vigorous rubdown after their bath. This, she assured them, would leave them feeling fit to walk to Merrin in a day. Jebbin earnestly hoped that his massage would be administered by the other present, Lyria, a wispy girl with huge eyes in a pallid face and a slender, graceful figure.

When they had bathed, Utha and Lyria approached the tub together. Jebbin smiled winningly at Lyria but she ignored him and took Hiraeth's hand instead. Jebbin felt himself bodily hauled from the steaming bath and flopped onto a wooden slab. Utha's capable hands swept over his body, thumping and kneading until he doubted he could walk as far as the common-room in the evening. With a cheery slap, Utha pronounced him finished and moved on to Orrolui while he hobbled away to get dressed. From the door, he glanced back to watch Hiraeth receiving Lyria's slow and delicate ministrations. Wrapping himself in a scratchy towel he made a rueful grimace to the squirming Gesgarian and headed for the bedroom. Not long afterwards he was joined by Orrolui who was complaining about the treatment the other two were getting.

"Hiraeth is being practically drowned in aromatic oils, a few drops of which might have eased our torment and as for Utha going after Bolan - she tossed me aside like an old dish-clout and galloped off to get her prize like a mastiff after a rabbit! 'Oh, I left you to last, sir, a real man if I may say so, sir,'" he mimicked in an entirely unnecessary falsetto.

"Yes, well, I think brevity was the sole advantage of her massage. Bolan's welcome but I can't say the same about Hiraeth. I doubt Lyria could pummel the wings off a butterfly. Still, after the heat of that bath I could do with a drink. Coming?"

They sat to one side of a fire, sipping a thin red wine with a disagreeable oily bitterness. Orrolui said that if it were a mark of the finest the Apple Tree could provide rather than just another insult to Gesgarians, he intended to find supper elsewhere. Left to themselves, they fell to their usual topic of the practice of magic and Orrolui vehemently maintaining that at last he would be able to perform the light spell without a focus. Jebbin listened quietly and, when Orrolui paused, asked him to explain an anomaly in the fourth harmonic of the True Sight spell.

"No!" cried Orrolui sharply, smacking the flat of his hand on the table and jingling the glasses. "There has to be an end. I will not be leached to a husk while forever groping after your forbidden fruit. This was to be a sharing, not the free donation of a thousand years of secret research in the Isles you dare to revile and call Dark."

"I have never so called them and you were just saying you understood the new technique now. If you have the one spell, you can surely build upon it. You so nearly grasped it in Dadacombe."

"So tonight's the test. I thought I had it back then but there was a block. Will there be another? Will I truly build upon the one spell or will learning the next be just as hard? You cannot answer me." Suddenly Orrolui's face lightened with a grin just a little too wide. "Ah, forgive me Jebbin. I mean nothing by it, just tied in knots by that Utha. And perhaps a little disappointed by continued failure. Look, here comes the missing duo, at very long last. Utha took her time working over you, Bolan!"

The latecomers ignored jibes and led the magicians into a small dining area where a superior wine was arrayed. They settled down to a crock of pheasant breasts in lentils and spices with dishes of cardoons and plump radishes. Even Orrolui admitted that they dined well, though he added that if the earlier wine were anything to go by, a Gesgarian dining here alone would be lucky to get a boiled rat. Before they had done justice to the fruit bowl, Tubbs came sidling in to ask whether they were comfortable and had eaten sufficient. He was careful to leave the door ajar so Hiraeth could see the crowd gathered in the common-room and more folk hurrying through the door, cringing beneath the thrashing rain and calling for mulled ale or spiced wines, ruddy faces wet and glittering in the firelight. Hiraeth thanked Tubbs and said he was just about to fetch his lute. The relieved landlord backed out hastily and rushed away to attend his customers.

Hiraeth was in his element and worked the Felicans up to rousing choruses or held them spellbound in silence at his will, swapping from the ludicrous jig about the farmer from Torl trying to sell a pig as a monster goose to current affairs or songs of the great heroes from the ancient epics; the swan-queen Ioleni or the mighty Baelar of Carnen and his flying steed and if the deeds and stature of the legendary giant grew together, his audience revelled all the more. So much was their attention centred on the bard that none noticed the background noise level rising as the evening wore on: coughs and ratchet breathing from elderly fishermen, the tapping of feet, clicking of beads and shells about women's necks, clinking of glasses, windows clattering in the wind and the boom and crack of the storm.

While Hiraeth gulped beer in a pause, Jebbin glanced up suddenly to the window, feeling a strange inner twinge, then looked round the company cramming the inn from side to side, all happy and laughing with faces flushed from the ale and the warmth of the room. Taking advantage of the lull, beards wagged furiously in shouted conversations or bellowed orders to Tubbs and his overworked minions. Calloused hands passed trays of foaming mugs since none could push through the crowd. When a notorious skinflint complained that his drink, bought and paid for, had failed to arrive, everyone laughed all the more.

"If that's true, someone's had a drink out of you for the first time since your mother married!" roared a fishwife, joyfully clouting him between the shoulder blades. "Do it again, it won't kill you."

Everyone refreshed, the Felicans settled expectantly as Hiraeth began to strum a curious stringed instrument Utha had found and Jebbin wondered at his sureness of touch with an unfamiliar device. He turned to comment to Orrolui and frowned, his first empty syllable floating unfinished on the thick air. He leaned over to Bolan and asked, "Where's Orrolui? When did he go?"

The wrestler shrugged. "Don't know. Been gone sometime."

Jebbin sat as though listening to noises far from the sweet sounds of the common-room, then slipped away. The bedrooms were empty but away from Hiraeth's lulling spell Jebbin felt gripped by a strange uneasiness. He stared out into the storm, absently rubbing the scabbed cut the thief had given him as the lightning slashed jagged wounds in the clouds and the thunder groaned in protest. With sudden determination, he wrapped his cloak about his shoulders and hurried outside.

The storm battered at him the moment the door was open, icy pins of rain stabbing him while the excessive lightning sizzled and cracked ever more furiously. Hardly able to see through the pelting drops even when the flaring light split the gloom, Jebbin staggered up the slight hill out of the town, leaving the quaking houses to rattle behind him. Despite the cold dragging at him with the sodden weight of his clothes, Jebbin sweated with effort as he fought his way into the gale, his cloak whipping behind him like a scorpion's tail. His feet slipped on the wet trail and gusts left him weaving like a drunkard. Gasping for breath as the merciless wind tried to snatch it from him, he battled to the top of the hill.

Then he heard it. A braying howling laugh almost lost in the roar of the storm like a tin bell beside a waterfall. Blinking furiously and squinting into the rain, Orrolui's stark silhouette was suddenly etched on his retina, standing, fists raised and scimitar on high, facing the storm's wrath. The lightning flickered yet again and as the thunder stammered its response the Gesgarian sent his own bolt of power soaring into the soft belly of the clouds which roiled in torment and spat volleying shivers of light. Scant strides away, a tree shattered into dull flame and the earth itself bucked and tingled.

"Orrolui!" Jebbin bellowed into the shrieking gale, holding his hand before his eyes in a feeble shield.

The Gesgarian turned, still laughing, and, as one might toss a ball to a child in play, lobbed a bolt at Jebbin. Magic fire ballooned round him and detonated inward with massive force. Jebbin's eyes bulged as he fought to control the hammering blast, but as soon as the pain started crushing his body he mentally shifted to channel and deflect the power and a beam of force swept skyward to be lost in the inconceivable energies snapping above. For an instant Orrolui's eyes showed dispassionate assess-

ment but then he was roaring with manic laughter again, haul-
ing in *sear* and turning to scream defiance into the bloated night.
Again he whirled his scimitar and sent a spell writhing up to
challenge the awesome might of the heavens. They replied with a
flash that seared human eyes and a bang that so far surpassed all
comparison in grandeur that any but Orrolui would have been
humbled. Laughing all the more, Orrolui hurled yet another gout
of power upwards, tottering in the wind. Finally Jebbin grasped
him by the shoulders.

"Orrolui," he yelled, "no more! You're calling the storm. It'll
kill us both!"

"I did it!" Orrolui shouted back. "I don't need you. No focus.
Power within the self!" His hair was nailed to his forehead by
the rain but whipped from his neck like striking snakes. His eyes
sparked fiercely in exultation.

"I know. Come back now. There's death on the wind."

"You're too tame. You cannot understand."

"Understand what?" cried Jebbin, shaking the Gesgarian and
watching his staring eyes lose focus. He had to strain to catch the
answer as Orrolui sank lower, beginning to shiver with cold and
exhaustion.

"The desire to bawl power on power into the tempest. The
power and the pain! Teltazzar, the wild joy of the pain and the
power."

Jebbin threw one of Orrolui's arms about his neck and half-
carried him back down the hill, the wind slamming into their
backs and twice hurling them to the ground, slithering and
thrashing. He weighed the Gesgarian's words; the sucking thrill
of wild magic balanced by Dewlin's caution of madness. The
madness of the pain, the thrill of the power. But where was the
balance?

Orrolui's incoherent mumblings had faded before they

reached the Apple Tree and he was virtually unconscious when Jebbin dragged him into the dining room and dropped him before the small fire. Since nobody else would leave the common-room and the bard for a Gesgarian, Jebbin fetched towels, built up the fire and administered brandy to his fellow mage. He stripped the bedraggled Gesgarian and wrapped him in a dry cloak. Orrolui uttered no word and Jebbin left him gazing blankly into the fire with a mug of brandy in his hand while he changed his own clothes. Later, Jebbin helped Orrolui to bed. For an instant, he thought he caught Orrolui's eyes studying him, but then the Gesgarian seemed to collapse. Jebbin listened carefully as the Gesgarian muttered through the words of a spell of transmutation over and over again before fading into sleep.

The storm had raced away before Hiraeth finished, to be followed by sharp squalls that trailed in its wake like crows after an army, and such members of the audience that staggered away from the Apple Tree in the early hours of the morning made it home dry-backed.

Bolan rose in the morning to find Tubbs already up and in a fine humour, evidently considering the music to have been a fair accompaniment to the clinking of coins and glasses. When Jebbin and Hiraeth came down, he pressed them all to an enormous breakfast and said he could not allow them to travel today.

"Bards are precious folk and travel in these conditions would be hazardous." He opened the door and ostentatiously tapped a slippered foot in the puddle outside. "Mudslides, you know. Terrible. Perhaps you could play tonight?"

But he needn't have bothered with his warning. Orrolui was sleeping heavily after his strange exertions and could not be woken, so travel was perforce delayed.

Bolan enquired whether there was a weapon-smith of note in Felice. He was not pleased to be referred to the blacksmith but

went to visit him anyway, muttering that it was a forsaken, barbarous country and, furthermore, remarkably flat to be so prone
to mudslides. Hiraeth disappeared quietly with Lyria. Giving a
dismissive wave Jebbin concluded that she was too vapid for him
and thought wistfully of Sola. Left to his own devices, he took his
new staff and strolled alone, mulling over the spells Orrolui had
revealed in his murmurings last night. Wandering back, surprisingly damp from the fine rain drifting down, he met Bolan just
outside the Apple Tree. To his amazement, the wrestler exploded
into angry expostulations.

"Balgrim's beard! Where've you been hiding?"

"I?" Jebbin replied faintly, "I ambled up the road a step and
returned."

"Nonsense. Checked that way myself. Nothing but the odd
tree." He turned and called into the inn. "He's here, Hiraeth.
Slack-witted, but unharmed."

"What's the fuss?"

"Ha. Since you make enemies wherever you go, when you
missed lunch, vanishing without word or trace, we naturally assumed..."

"Missed lunch?" broke in Jebbin, frowning in disbelief.

"Hear me? Boy's brains are scrambled," snorted Bolan as Hiraeth emerged from the inn.

"I smell a wonder. Come inside, Jebbin. Tubbs can doubtless
be prevailed upon to fetch more food and you can tell us all."

"I'm not hungry, thanks. We've only just had breakfast."

Bolan groaned, raising his eyes to the heavens and strode off
to the dining room where he leant against the mantelpiece and
viewed the other two askance. Hiraeth and Jebbin followed more
slowly and sat either side of the table.

"Right. Tell us what you think happened."

"Well," began Jebbin haltingly, "I was thinking about a spell

Orrolui alluded to last night. I didn't think I had it all but perhaps..." He paused, his eyes faraway, then continued in a quiet, detached monotone.

"I went to look at the tree burnt in the storm last night, pulling the stitches from my arm. Standing on the hill, I held the top of my staff and rested my chin on my hands, adopting a tripod stance. I closed my eyes, thinking of the Gesgarian spell. I remember mouthing what I knew and pausing dreamily. I grew still and shut and the world about me withdrew. I could still smell the ash and brimstone from last night together with the soft scent of wet earth and hear, with startling clarity, the calls of cock pheasants and a robin; the gentle misting noise of the rain and the steady drip from the trees; the chewing of a goat not far away and even the gurgling of its stomach; a dog barking twice away down the hill and briefly the sound of talking from fields away. I could feel myself cooling and let cold permeate me, rejecting animal warmth for passive acceptance.

Then the tendrils of cold probed no deeper and I seemed inviolable. The world had retreated and left me isolated and remote even from the gentle breeze that rocked me, eddies pushing me this way and that, yet without effort I swayed upright and felt it only as the wind in the needles of my hair and the tiny droplets of rain collecting and dripping down me as over the rough bark of the pine. My conscious thought seemed to have ceased, slowed to immeasurability in that arboreal state, when to thrust out a finger-like twig might take a year. Indeed, I had no fingers but only was. A corporate whole, not seeing with eyes or hearing with ears but sensing as one.

"Visions I had; the incredible joy of unknowing, the release of just being, living through the slow roll of years, uncounting and uncaring. I saw a single treetop waving in a wild wind, pine branches thrashing against a black, starlit sky. But then there was a hint of falsity, as if this were not to be, not yet, or perhaps it was too long past, and my eyes opened. I was amazed to find it a grey day, raining gently and not the black night I had just left. Yet I could not move, still filled with the taste of the soil, and my eyes watched dully, automatic and unblinking. A tear, woken by the searching airs, trickled down my cheek, becoming one with the drops of rain.

"At last I began to open my fingers, each movement the suicidal breaking of lignin bonds, as I became reanimated. Finally I moved off, at first with creaking, stilted steps, becoming more fluid until once again I was returned and the time I had spent contracted to an unguessable unit. Thinking nothing more of my pause on the hill, I meandered back here and found this furore." Towards the end, Jebbin's droning voice took on vitality once more and he seemed his old self when he was finished.

"I suppose we can guess the nature of the spell and that it worked, but I have never heard the like of it," mused Hiraeth, mentally drafting lyrics.

"Don't know," Bolan said pensively, "sensing as one, neither hearing nor sight but a mixture of all senses. Some masters of martial disciplines speak of this. Perhaps you have the wrong calling!"

"I'm lucky to still have any calling. That spell has insidious dangers and without knowing them, I was fortunate to break out at all. Perhaps it was unlucky that I should have tried that particular spell but it did make a fine trap for a novice mage, one that nearly caught me."

"Jebbin, one word of advice. Don't mention this to Orrolui," said Hiraeth.

An uncomfortable silence fell on the trio. Upstairs, Orrolui writhed in dreams and visions of his own and was perhaps unaware of all else.

They were ready to travel on the following morning and, quailing before Bolan's glare, Tubbs had not demurred. Indeed, he seemed well satisfied and made them an excellent packed lunch. They stopped off at the blacksmith's where Bolan collected a pair of iron wrist guards, cushioned with leather. He clashed them together experimentally and then, agreeably surprised, paid the smith and thanked him heartily.

Orrolui was now the keenest to press ahead but he had become capricious, by turns aloof and surly and then effusively friendly. He was forever scanning the road for fellow journeyers and eagerly accosted any they met, assuming a bluff, genial manner and wheedling for details of where they had come from and whither they were bound. The others could not imagine what he sought and watched his agitation with vague apprehension. It was only when they neared the Golden Road itself that Orrolui found what he needed.

They were idly debating where to take their midday meal. Bare of traffic, the road rolled over rocky slopes of patchy grass and thyme into dank valleys of overhanging trees. With no signs of a village, there would only be stale bread, goat's cheese maturing beyond edibility and water for lunch. Ahead of them, the path forked, the main track winding up another hill, an offshoot turning into a wooded dell, dense with sallow and willow. A stream sparkled silver as it cascaded over rocks into the dell, marking a watering hole used by drovers and traders travelling east from the Golden Road. It seemed a providential site.

However, when they made to turn down the side road towards the dell, a rider moved nonchalantly into the track before them. A large man with a broad, weather-beaten face carried an air of authority with the same ease as the heavy spear that lay crooked in his arm. He looked bored but smiled and bade them good morning.

"I am Watchwarden Herrar from Valletha away over the hill," he gestured vaguely beyond the stream. "I regret this pool is polluted at present and not safe to drink. A sheep drowned in it, remaining undiscovered for some time. Until the infection has cleared, it's my trying lot to ward travellers from its waters. Since the odour is repugnant you would be wise to continue on the main road."

"Our thanks and may the hours pass swiftly," said Jebbin, turning back to the other track.

Hiraeth frowned as though Herrar had uttered an oath, then shrugged. "We have little for our own repast but you're welcome to share what we have and we are all eager for news of the region."

"I appreciate your kindness," replied Herrar, "but noxious vapours still swirl about here at times and would impair the flavour of your sustenance. I urge you to hasten on your way."

Jebbin and the bard duly walked on but Bolan's face was rapt and he appeared oblivious to the rider. In stark contrast, Orrolui was staring at the Watchwarden fixedly, eyes bright, a slight smile quivering about his lips.

"Come now," urged Herrar, "a pestilence may lurk in the degeneration and we cannot have travellers ailing! Move along there."

With staggering speed, Orrolui snatched his scimitar from its scabbard and hurled a spell at the watchwarden. Fire bawled over him, tightening Herrar's smile into the rictus of death. As Jebbin and Hiraeth spun round in astonishment to see Herrar topple from his stampeding horse, there was a muffled curse and a frantic rustling behind a leafy screen of bushes. Bolan snapped into action, rolling across the road and diving into the cover. There was a brief tussle and two solid thuds before the bushes parted again as a man flew backwards to land on his shoulders with his feet in the air. He collapsed flat with a groan, twitched once and lay still, his bow broken beneath him and spilt arrows marking the trail of his flight.

"Have you both gone mad?" gasped Jebbin.

"What is this belligerence?" demanded Hiraeth at the same time.

"Fighting in the dell," said Bolan.

"You should've used True Sight, Jebbin - no need now," Orrolui went on too hastily. "These are bandits, more evidently assail some party under the trees. We must render aid."

Jebbin looked at him in wonder for his unusual charity and then again in greater surprise. "You cast that without a focus!"

Orrolui nodded gravely. "I did that." Then a grin split his face and he roared, "Are we waiting until that merchant is quite dead? Let's go!" With loping strides, he set off down the track into the dell with Bolan beside him.

"I'm a bard!" shouted Hiraeth indignantly. "I can't start wars all over the place. Bards must be sacrosanct."

Jebbin looked blankly at him for a second, shrugged and sprinted after the others, leaving the bard muttering about madness.

The grassy track turned a slow bend, then ran gently down to a green pool. Here three wagons were drawn up, draft mules partly unhitched. Two muleteers lay unmoving beside them, pierced with arrows, but though the robbers had used the advantage of the willows for cover, the surprise had evidently been less than they had hoped and an effective defence had been mounted. Most of the waggoners had successfully taken cover and one at least was armed with a heavy crossbow and occasionally directed bolts at movements under the trees. One of the bandits was yelling demands,

"Throw out half your goods and we'll let you go. Delay and we'll shoot the mules and leave you stranded. You cannot survive for long! We control the ways in here and there's no help coming."

"Boil yourself in oil! Anyone moves and I'll shove his teeth out the back of his head with a bolt!" roared a defiant voice.

Jebbin grinned mirthlessly as he ran. The merchant wasn't fool enough to think the bandits would be content with half the goods, particularly those chosen by him. Furthermore, they would be unlikely to shoot the mules which were a significant and saleable booty.

Just then, the crossbow twanged again. The bolt pierced a cloak tossed over a bush and was answered by half a dozen arrows. Then the bandits leapt from their hiding places to charge the wagons. With no time to re-load, the merchant tossed the bow aside with a curse, his hands spotted with blood from a cut opened on one cheek. He snatched up a heavy mace, grabbed his shield and jumped down to meet his attackers, calling his men to battle. Jebbin wondered what he made of the ill-assorted shapes of stocky Bolan and lanky Orrolui pounding down the track on the bandits' flank, or his own form with the cloak billowing behind him, flashing its own runes.

The merchant roared wordlessly and put all the strength of his thickset frame behind a ringing blow with the mace. His opponent took the stroke awkwardly on the edge of his shield and howled as his arm snapped. Suddenly all his efforts were to ward off the wagon-master long enough for him to escape.

The battle rapidly degenerated into a series of individual combats and Jebbin slowed his headlong rush in admiration as his two friends smashed into the robbers. Bolan was straightforward and uncompromising, fighting with a detachment that belied his speed and power and calling to the brigands to lay down their arms. Orrolui could hardly have been more different, distracting and terrifying with displays and cavortings that seemed designed to call attention to him but, in his own way, operating effectively to keep himself safe while he killed with the most economical expenditure of physical energy and magical power.

As he faced a bandit, Orrolui threw both arms to the skies and bellowed to Teltazzar for aid. As he swept his arms down again, his opponent darted back into a defensive crouch but Orrolui spun away from him altogether. The robber, thrown by this tactic, was slow to attack as Orrolui's back was turned and before he had finished his stroke, Orrolui had whirled right round in a complete circle and delivered a furious slash. Hastily swapping from attack to defence, the robber was too slow to more than half-parry the attack and suffered a slicing wound in the shoulder. However, he was a practised swordsman and, while Orrolui was off balance, he forced Orrolui's blade down to leave the Gesgarian open to the counter-stroke. Ignoring his peril, Orrolui let his scimitar sink deep into the earth where he released it and stepped back. Momentarily confused, the bandit then gave a triumphant cry and drilled a savage blow at Orrolui, who stood still with his palms forward as though embracing the deadly arc. The sword shivered against the iron spell of the mage and, as the bemused bandit staggered, Orrolui thrust a finger in his eye, calmly collected his sword and sliced open the howling man's belly. Orrolui lifted his scimitar with a straight arm and looked along its shining, blood-smeared length to the next man running towards him. The result of his eccentric technique was immediately apparent as the man ducked and veered away to join another charging Jebbin and the lethal Gesgarian was left unmolested as he inhaled more *sear*.

Settling himself with *sear*, Jebbin almost welcomed the stinging fire that ripped at his face and gave him power. He moulded the pain with a syllable and spat the blast spell at the first aggressor and when he crumpled, turned confidently to the next. Then a tingling crepitation resonated inside his brain and the *sear* pain shattered into sparkling fragments, his words of power diminishing into a roaring jargon. It was as though all his magic were leaking out of his boots and he found himself mentally floundering, trying to plug a gap he could not find. He was aware of the man before him, tall and broad-shouldered with a stoat-like face surrounded by stiff, ginger-dark hair, initially cowering back, awed by the magic he had witnessed but then, noticing Jebbin's strange discomfiture, straightening and sweeping forward. Lost in himself, powerless and confused, Jebbin could only watch in dislocated horror as the robber's sword arm swung back for a brutal stroke. With the whirr of a stooping falcon, a blade came spinning from the melee below, chopping deeply into the bandit's upper arm and spraying blood upwards.

"Fight, boy! Fight!" Jebbin heard Bolan's voice bellowing over the din of the battle below and cutting through his eldritch torpor. Uttering a wild cry, Jebbin swung his staff and struck the bandit on his wounded arm. The sword fell away to bounce uselessly on the stones but the light of battle now blazed in the ginger-haired man's eyes. He drew a dagger with his left hand and lunged forward. Jebbin darted backwards and struck out again, beating the injured shoulder. The dagger swept back but Jebbin parried desperately and lashed out at the bandit's head. Still the bandit came forward, slashing awkwardly with the dagger in his wrong hand and trying to close with Jebbin while the mage whirled and thrust with the staff, again and again, frantic to keep the tall robber from him.

The bandit seemed preternaturally immune to the bludgeoning blows of the staff and followed Jebbin step by relentless step. Even with one eye blinded with blood and his right arm broken and pulped, he pressed inexorably after the magician, clutching the knife and grunting with each lunge or slicing stroke. Slowly,

Jebbin was tiring. Time and again he nearly tripped backwards or he jerked away from the remorseless dagger with failing reactions. He felt the strength ebbing from his arms, his breath coming in great, ragged sobs that caught in his throat, his own blows becoming weaker, less accurate, less frequent and still the robber clasped his dagger in bloody fingers and tottered after him, right arm dangling like an empty sleeve, his face and hair all bloody and matted like an apparition from a nightmare.

Jebbin became aware that Hiraeth was striding up and down in the middle of the battle near the pool, heedless of the danger, blasting out a high, strident tune on a little horn, the clarion notes cutting clear through the racket of screaming men, clashing weapons and braying mules.

"Fool," gasped Jebbin, "what's that going to achieve? Why doesn't he help?"

In spite of himself, the thought of the bard playing in the midst of the fight supported him, the ringing horn call suffusing him with new strength. His head lolled from side to side as, with a mighty shout, he dragged the staff right back and sent it flailing forward to land with a solid thwack just below the bandit's ear. Halted at last, the robber stood swaying, head down but still peering up at Jebbin with his good eye, his mouth open, broken teeth bared as he panted for breath. Drooling blood but driven by a fatal compulsion, he lifted the quivering dagger again as Jebbin stood gasping before him. Jebbin heaved the staff back once more and with all his remaining might, delivered a crunching blow that sent the bandit sailing sideways as though struck by a battering ram. Jebbin fell to his knees beside his motionless foe, collapsed onto his back and lay groaning.

When he was able to rise, the battle was over, the last of the attackers dead, fled or surrendered. Jebbin wobbled over on jellied legs to join the others and was amazed to find none of them injured.

"You could have helped me rather than practise for your next concert," he complained to Hiraeth.

The bard smiled and said, "Saved your life, didn't I?"

Jebbin chuckled. "You probably did at that," he admitted and threw an arm round Hiraeth's shoulders. "You certainly saved me," he said to Bolan. "I don't know how to thank you. How could you notice what was happening and then disarm yourself to help me?"

Bolan shrugged. "Didn't bother me much. Next chappie didn't have much use for his sword. Borrowed that for a while. What happened to you anyway?"

"I honestly don't know. I was using magic but suddenly everything just drifted away and left me high and dry. I was frozen."

"You fell victim to a spell," said Orrolui. "There is no other explanation."

"I sense you're right but surely the only sorcerers here were you and me?"

"Perhaps someone held an artefact and employed its power. I also sensed the touch of a spell. As a stronger magician, I ignored it."

Hiraeth looked quizzically at the Gesgarian, as though listening to the impure tone of a cracked bell, but before he could speak or Jebbin could mention his opponent's inhuman tenacity they were interrupted by the merchant limping up to them, a crude bandage wrapped about his thigh and dried blood smeared over his face beneath a crusted cut. He was a bullish man with prominent teeth and a receding chin who introduced himself as Chun. He thanked them all, demanding they rest and eat with his group.

They had accepted readily and as soon as the wounded had

been tended, the debris of battle cleared and all had washed away the blood and sweat in the stream that swirled down from the pool, they settled to a late meal; Chun bringing out the finest from his stock of salted roe, preserved meats, dried fruits and wines to grace the caravan's normal fare of onions, cheese and hard biscuits. Chun seemed overawed by Bolan's performance.

"You, sir, are the greatest warrior I have witnessed. You strode amidst them like a tiger among goats! Never have I seen the like. Might I know your name?"

"Bolan."

"Bolan? The incomparable gladiator of Mellu? Errela! What company to find on the road! Truly the gods have smiled on me today."

Chun prattled on, flattered them all mercilessly until Bolan was incoherent with embarrassment. Then talk turned to more serious matters as they discussed the news and doings of the world. Here Chun had much to tell them. News travels fast amongst merchants; often of great value, it is sometimes jealously hoarded and sometimes traded as a commodity but when non-competitive merchants met they talked freely, for events often overtook their sluggish wagons, rendering goods valueless in one location and occasionally priceless elsewhere. The principal issue now was the disruption to traffic on the Golden Road itself caused by proselytes of the new religion exploding outward from Rulion in Belmenia.

"A dark business it is too, by all accounts," growled the trader. "Folk surrendering will, life and possessions to some evil deity - or its priests more likely. Beatings, robberies and deaths a-plenty. Apparently no crime against a non-believer is considered as such. If that gets out of hand, no-one will be safe. Crowds of people, barely fed, partly clothed, mainly armed and totally brainless - I tell you someone should stamp that lot out straightaway. Trading's virtually impossible. Unless you're so heavily guarded it's un-economic, you're apt to lose your life if you fight and all your goods if you don't. Even then, you have to pretend to be a convert. When it all began there was good money for anyone getting goods into Rulion but now no money would be enough."

Chun spat in distaste and moved to other issues. The commander of the armies in O-Ram had revolted against the Sultan and looked set to depose him. The Sultan was trapped in Xaran and that, swelled with refugees, could not long be defended. Only his personal regiment, the Steel Warriors, remained loyal. Chun considered they should use the Steel Warrior's fearsome reputation to buy reasonable surrender terms for the Sultan without bloodshed but he admitted this was a merchant's view.

"Of course, all this instability in the west will add to the congestion of traders heading for the rich pickings of Lana fair."

Only Jebbin was unmoved by this remark; Orrolui looking up sharply, Bolan exclaiming in delight and Hiraeth spilling his wine.

"Great Lana Fair? This year?" demanded the bard.

"Indeed," said Chun, startled by their reaction. "I'm surprised this is news. Of all fairs it's the largest, most...."

"Yes, we know. But there was no clue it would come this year."

"You may know absolutely everything," said Jebbin peevishly, "but I've never heard of it. What is this Lana fair?"

Hiraeth replied, "Great Lana fair is held rarely and irregularly at times determined by the tribesmen of Ael. When they become deficient in foreign goods..."

"When their pestilential raiding has not gone well," broke in Chun bitterly.

"...And they have built up stocks of their own surplus items, they declare a Great Fair and a truce to all their depredations..."

"Which they mostly ignore..."

"...So all may approach and trade without fear. They fund the ground, marquees and booths and as it's the only time that there's access to the fabulous tapestries, leather goods and metal-work of the Aelan mountains, merchants flock to the fair. With such a congregation, many other shows and entertainments develop with generous prizes mostly provided by the Aelans. There we will find the Contest of the Bards...

"Gladiators, wrestlers, bouts in all the major disciplines..."

"Magical feats, fire-breathers flaunting their arts while surreptitious pickpockets practise theirs."

"I see. All things for all people. Well, tell all. When does this paragon of entertainment start, how long does it go on and when was the last?"

"I imagine the lesser stalls and booths will already be catering for those setting up the larger affairs. How long it lasts is governed to some extent by the time it takes the Aelans to do all the trading - or plundering - they require. Never less than a couple of months and usually longer. The last was eight, nine years back, I suppose. I have an order to fulfil some way to the east but I will be buying as I go and hurrying back after. I assume you four will visit the fair?"

They exchanged brief glances before Hiraeth spoke, "I think we may part at the Golden Road since my two sorcerous friends must attend to another matter but Bolan and I shall head directly for the fair. I hope we'll all meet there."

"We may all be there but meeting will remain chancy."

The meal over, they sat sipping liqueurs and nibbling sordida, a rare delicacy of candied fungi from the Kermion marshes. Chun sent two of his unscathed stalwarts to watch over the surrendered bandits as they dug graves for the fallen well back under the willows. He turned to his guests.

"I wonder what would have happened had you not happened

by when you did. Could we have held them off, outnumbered as we were? Pah, do not answer. It matters little, for either many of us would have died or all and in either case my little caravan would have been over. Nothing after six years of trading and growing, growing and trading. I owe you a great debt which I cannot pay but I must press you to accept a tiny token of my appreciation."

So saying, the merchant held out a bag of coins but Orrolui forestalled him.

"The size of the gift greatly honours the giver and I'm sure we are all overwhelmed by your generosity. Nevertheless, we could not think of accepting." Here the others looked in surprise but Orrolui rolled on smoothly. "Indeed, we count ourselves fortunate in having had the opportunity to extend the hand of friendship to men from other lands and are thusly richer already. To take gold would reduce our altruism to the merely mercenary."

Even Chun seemed taken aback. "I've never heard a Ges... so expressive a refusal," he said dubiously. "Surely I am permitted to offer some trifle without debasing your noble rescue?"

"Wisely said! We have already enjoyed a royal feast in excellent company and much invaluable information has been bestowed upon us. We consider ourselves rewarded beyond any possible merit."

"I cannot have Chun called an ingrate! At the very least permit me to stock your packs with choice preserves and viands to lighten your further travelling."

"A kindness we accept," burst in Bolan swiftly, frowning briefly at Orrolui. "To do less would insult the offer," he added emphatically.

They rose and arranged this matter to the satisfaction of all but Jebbin who was intensely disappointed that such an opportunity to acquire funds had been squandered. However, even he cheered somewhat when Chun, piling up delicacies for him to carry, winked at him and tossed a few golden ryals in with them.

As they prepared to leave, Jebbin noticed Orrolui in earnest conversation with Chun. The trader nodded vigorously, accepted a slip of paper from Orrolui and the two shook hands with the double grip of Shekkem. Jebbin frowned thoughtfully for a moment but shrugged and dismissed the matter.

Finally, they waved farewell to Chun and his men as the mules lugged the wagons uphill from the pool, a few despondently trudging bandits securely bound and roped to the hindmost wagon. As they quit the dell on the last stage of their journey together to the Golden Road, Orrolui capered comic imitations of their various endeavours on the field of battle. In his laughter at this uncharacteristic performance, Jebbin forgot his awkward questions.

The Staff of Sumos

They drew rein at the edge of a sharp slope and gazed down over a quilt of copses, leys and cultivated fields. A village had grown where the road crossed the largest stream and they were close enough to hear the pulse of its life; cries of vendors and children, rattling of carts and the ringing crash from the blacksmith's forge. The nearest building was the mill on the river; the groan and plash of its wheel underpinned the hubbub. Further along the valley they could discern two other little clusters of houses nestled in folds of the ground.

"Ha! Farralei at last, Jebbin. Once we have that staff, the greater treasure lies within our reach. Come on."

Orrolui clapped heels to his mount's sides and trotted down the escarpment but Jebbin turned from the view before him, just as Erridarch had described it to Hiraeth, and regarded the way they had come. The trail had been long since they had left Bolan and Hiraeth on the Golden Road, promising to meet at Lana Fair. Orrolui had seemed almost relieved when they had parted and he had stepped out for Farralei with increased vitality. Clapping Jebbin on the shoulder he had announced that now it was just two magicians together, they could get down to serious magical research. They had indeed delved deep into each other's spell systems. Orrolui had been particularly keen to expand his knowledge of western magic and to use it without his scimitar whenever possible.

There had been trials enough along that road and several occasions to practise new skills. After they had seen a party of Aelan tribesmen cantering westwards Orrolui had declared that they must acquire horses for safety and to speed them towards Farralei. Shortly afterwards they had stolen mounts from a group of cattle herders who had been insufficiently alert. As they galloped away from gesticulating figures, Orrolui waved back in glee, shouting that mighty magicians took what they willed from lesser mortals.

"This is more like it!" he had roared to Jebbin across the wind of their wild flight, "A bit of fun at last."

Together they had fought off a pair of woodland grimmigs, copper-skinned and ridge-backed, which had assailed them by stealth in an oak forest. The grimmigs were resistant to magic and the sorcerers had been forced to transform themselves with statemorph spells until they could trade blows with the ferocious creatures and withstand their razor claws. Finally, they had beaten them back but Jebbin had been almost Numbed by the pain and had fallen into a semiconscious stupor. Had the grimmigs returned later, they would have found an easier meal.

Days later they had stood back to back and hurled drops of clinging fire at a pack of wild dogs. A mighty illusion had routed more Aelans who had taken too close an interest in lone travellers. Jebbin knew that alone he would have fallen but he suspected that Orrolui too, for all his indomitable spirit, would have failed unaided. Yes, Orrolui had needed him for that grim journey of mental and physical endurance but what happened when he did not? Jebbin had grown steadily more apprehensive of his companion but his determination to solve the riddle was firmer than ever. Perhaps this staff would tell them everything. However, the tyrant in Ael rousing the tribes to war sounded apt for Echoheniel's riddles. The geographer said Ael could be the paramo of the riddle, something Jebbin had kept hidden from Orrolui. Lana was in Ael and Bolan and Hiraeth were in Lana. He missed Bolan's impregnable dependability and the warmth of Hiraeth's companionship and longed to rejoin them. He scratched his chin upon which the beard was now worthy of the name and followed the Gesgarian into the valley.

They elected to find accommodation and stabling for their horses before scouring the town for the source of the 'ghostly cries' but this proved more difficult than they had imagined. There was a large party in Farralei, travelled long leagues from Saleem on the Border River between Triva and Shekkem and they were occupying every nook of Farralei's only inn. It became evident that a celebration was planned for the whole town that very evening, paid for by Lord Rallor, who led the southerners. It was also plain that the innkeeper had no intention of upsetting these arrangements for the comfort of two itinerants of doubtful means and the magicians were forced to look elsewhere. Eventually they were able to take lodgings in a bunkhouse over the wrangler's stables. The wrangler often needed extra staff but having just disposed of his stock to an Aelan trader there was little work to do and space aplenty. Most of the animals still in his care were those from Rallor's party that had overflowed the stabling at the inn. The wrangler was glad of the extra income and by the time they found it, Orrolui and Jebbin were glad to have found anywhere off the street.

When their negotiations were complete, Orrolui took the opportunity to ask whether there was a graveyard in the village.

"Curious," said the wrangler. "That's the second time today. But why? You don't look like dying just yet."

"Glad to hear it," said Orrolui dryly, "but actually my grand-mother's family came from this region and I'd a mind to browse through headstones for any family names."

"What names?" the wrangler asked suspiciously.

"Well, if you're interested, I have a list of them all here some-where. Yes, here we are," Orrolui enthused, rummaging in his pack. "It's rather long, I'm afraid, but if you're a fellow genealo-gist..." He paused and looked up hopefully.

"Not really. It's by the Lady's chapel. First turning on the left just down Market Street a step and you'll find it on the right. Cash in advance for the room." The wrangler accepted coins and departed, muttering about peculiar coincidences.

The magicians dumped their packs and set off for the grave-yard in high spirits while the afternoon was still bright. Jebbin drifted through the headstones and slabs, ivy-covered and faded, and felt the gentle peace of the chapel's atmosphere steal through him like water seeping into parched soil. Here the dead made no demands on the living beyond the ties of earthly love and slid softly into oblivion with the stately passage of the years.

"This is no place of ghostly cries," he whispered to a sun-warmed statue as he leant across its attendant stonework. The statue gazed down with weather-greened eyes, a wistful smile bending immobile lips as it shared with the occupant of the tomb both the answer to the final question and the inability to communicate it. "We're looking in the wrong place, aren't we?" The statue remained silent, so Jebbin meandered inside to look for a crypt.

The chapel was simply built in yellow and dove-grey stone with pews and chairs carved from pale wood. A plain altar was constructed from three great slabs of shimmering marble, topped with two silver candelabra and a white wooden effigy of the Lady. Jebbin paused for a moment of contemplation and bowed his head in self-conscious humility, aware of the resentful attention of an elderly priestess. He turned to the back of the chapel where steps descended on both sides of the nave. His boots rasped on unpolished stone as he wandered down into the cool, damp air of the crypt. Here he could feel all was quietly ordered and peaceable, the mere thought of plundering seemed a desecration. By the dim light of a watch-lantern he could see a familiar figure at the far end of the crypt and walked towards him. Orrolui was standing with his arms folded, biting softly at his upper lip and glaring across the tenebrous vault. He remained motionless as Jebbin approached, then started into sudden life.

"I see nothing, hear nothing, feel nothing. We're chasing shadows."

"I feel a great deal, but agree the Staff of Sumos is far from here."

"Indeed. We must quiz more locals for news. There must be other graves or tombs; barrows, charnel houses, anything. Plague pits for all I care."

"Well, I could do with a shave and the best place for news is the barber's."

"Funny time to pamper yourself but I suppose you're right," Orrolui conceded. "The afternoon wears on and I want to get this done before the light goes. Quick as you can then and meet here as soon as possible. I'll walk round town and see if anything else is visible. Don't ask questions that might show our hand too plainly."

Jebbin held up his hands in protest at this tirade and marched away briskly. When he returned, Orrolui was waiting, drumming his fingers on the graveyard wall in irritation.

"Well?" the Gesgarian asked tersely.

"Interesting," replied Jebbin, scratching his smooth chin and rubbing fingers through his clean hair. "I had to wait because of the extra custom due to this group from Saleem and their shindig tonight. Apparently their leader is some paragon of virtue and a mighty warrior to boot. A wealthy lord of estates in the south who gallops round righting wrongs and supporting the oppressed while damsels swoon right and left. You'd think it would make him thoroughly loathed by everyone but I haven't heard one word against him."

"Someone to avoid for the present. What of our current issue?"

"Little enough but I have another idea. Hiraeth said those lines on Erridarch's map crossed to the north of the village. There was a dark spinney to the north we could see from the escarpment. Unless you've discovered something dramatic, we could investigate that?"

Orrolui sighed and nodded. "It's worth the walk. There's nothing else here for us."

At that moment they were disturbed by a burst of cheering and shouting from the northern end of Farralei. The magicians glanced at one another and shrugged. "We're going that way, might as well take a look," grunted Orrolui and led the way.

They rounded a corner to see a lean, broad-shouldered man riding towards them on a warhorse, glossy black in the afternoon sun. His fair, curly hair surrounded a strong face with lines in his cheeks and a deeply cleft chin. He smiled and waved as he led his retinue of knights through the villagers, boys prancing and mock-fighting before him, tossing their caps in the air.

"No prizes for guessing who that is," said Orrolui contemptuously. "The great Rallor and simpering sycophants. Quite a display for a free drink. We'll go out the other way."

Unnoticed, they left the village on a track that led northeastwards. Jebbin pointed out a gloomy copse on a low hummock to their left. Orrolui stared at it through narrowed eyes, behind which the fires of excitement were rekindled, but just nodded and set off across the quiet fields of Farralei towards the wood. The second field had been recently ploughed and its wet clay clung to their boots, reluctant to let them pass. Orrolui trudged on regardless, his gaze fixed on the wood ahead while Jebbin plodded in his wake. The ploughed field ended as the ground rose, thinning soils and heavy boulders rendering the land only fit for rough grazing for milking goats. The magicians scraped mud from their boots with relief and hastened towards the darkling trees, pines sprouting dense and forbidding in an unbroken rampart before them.

It had been a pleasant afternoon but now the westering sun shed little warmth and the breeze flicked their hair with chillier gusts. There were no croaking crows to wheel or black omens of foreboding but a subliminal tingle warned them that this was indeed the centre of that mighty cross on Erridarch's map.

"Do we circle round to find an entrance or hurry in while the light holds?" Orrolui wondered thoughtfully.

"Any entrance may be watched, even guarded. There may be no opening at all and we have little light left to waste. It's going to be almost pitch black under those trees as it is," said Jebbin.

"Courage," Orrolui smiled grimly, drawing his scimitar from its scabbard. "No playing without a focus in there," he nodded forwards. "Let's go."

They forced their way through the needled boughs and into the wood. Once inside, the lowest branches, long starved of light, had died and broken away and their progress, though uncomfortably hunched, was quicker than they had anticipated and silent on a thick bed of fallen needles. The dark was almost absolute beneath the canopy and though they were reduced to feeling their way more than looking for it, neither felt inclined to use a spell that would tire them and perhaps warn an enemy.

Jebbin started as he felt Orrolui grip his shoulder and he froze motionless. The clutch relaxed, then the Gesgarian's hand, just visible as a disembodied pale smear, appeared before Jebbin's face. With a tapping movement, the hand pointed a little to the right of their direction. Jebbin peered wide-eyed into the darkness, swaying gently from side to side in case an unseen trunk blocked his line of sight. He spotted an orange light that flickered and died, only to rise and dance once more before fading again.

"Smell .... smoke," Orrolui whispered in his ear and then moved on towards the light.

As they silently crept closer, Jebbin felt the familiar surge of adrenalin as his heart pounded, muscles feeling leaden with unused energy. They paused in the last trees before a small rocky clearing where the little flame still wavered. A dim light filtered down, sufficient for them to make out a black opening in a thick slab of solid granite.

Sensing no sign of life, Orrolui eased out of cover, scimitar poised, and darted to the side of the doorway. Jebbin joined him and knelt by the flame. He reached out gingerly and picked up the butt of a resinous torch. It burned brighter as he lifted it. He looked in consternation at Orrolui who was frowning fiercely at the little stub. He shook his head and shrugged. A creak in the pines to their left made them spin round, Jebbin tossing the telltale torch aside. The flame went out in a sputter of sparks and the butt glowed dully.

"It was nothing," Orrolui breathed quietly. "Down there, light gives us away instantly but I have no wish to die in the dark, seeing nothing. Agree?"

He waited while Jebbin considered a moment before nodding, then suggested that Jebbin controlled the light.

"Mind your eyes then," Jebbin replied and lifted *sear*. He

closed his eyes as the pain kindled his adrenalin. Then he held up his fist and brought it forward with three fingers straight, then two, then one. With a shout of power he launched a globe of light through the doorway. It flashed like lightning before fading to a lantern-like brilliance. Heads down, the magicians charged in and dived in opposite directions to stand with their backs to the wall, *sear* ready, spells hovering close to eruption. The chamber was empty. An open passage beckoned on their left, to the right, an unevenly shaped stone door stood ajar.

"Feel it?" demanded Orrolui sharply. Jebbin nodded, wrinkling his nose. The eldritch acridity bit at them both. "I've rarely sensed it so strongly. There's been an enormous magical discharge here," Orrolui continued.

Jebbin sent the light wafting down the corridor. For a while it led straight, a single opening leading off it on the right, then it dropped away sharply, the floor gleaming brightly. He began to inch in that direction but Orrolui stopped him.

"Look down," he barked.

A dark patch glinted in the light. Jebbin knelt to investigate and when he touched it, his fingers came away red. He wiped them hastily and backed away.

"There are holes in the wall just there. I don't like it. We'll try the other opening."

Jebbin drifted the light through the open door to brighten another small chamber and they edged in together. Thick dust was scuffed and trampled; a crude black-iron sword lay broken and half hidden. On a grey plinth, a marble casket lay open. It was empty. Quietly, Orrolui closed the casket and examined the runes graven upon its lid. At that moment there was a soft moan, so low it could only be felt as a vibration in their bones. Jebbin pointed into the dust where a feathery plume was raised as though by a gust of unfelt wind and then collapsed. Another again reared higher, curled and dipped.

"Let's get out of here," said Orrolui darkly, moving through the stone door.

"But the staff..." said Jebbin.

"Is gone!"

"We might at least search the other corridor," Jebbin suggested, following him into the outer chamber.

"You'll die if you do," said Orrolui carelessly.

"Well, you don't know..."

"Look," Orrolui spat in rage, "there was a trap by the entrance, the floor is waxed where it drops away. I dread to think what lies in that chamber to the right. Close this stone door."

Wordlessly, Jebbin put his back against it and heaved until it closed with a heavy thump.

"And now open it again."

Jebbin turned to the door and stared in amazement. With its irregular design, the door blended perfectly with the wall and no evidence of any opening device was visible.

"Now do you understand? The whole of the other corridor is a trap. And think further; a burning torch, undried blood, the casket empty. We are too late, as the foul Zaeboth prophesied, by just a few hours. Explore and die if you wish." Orrolui spoke stiffly, his whole face and frame rigid with tightly bottled emotions. He wheeled and stalked from the chamber.

They followed a faint trail away from the door and emerged from the wood at a point where the branches had been recently hacked down. Droppings and hoof prints told of waiting mounts.

"And now we know," Jebbin said quietly, "just why the great lord Rallor is in tiny Farralei and indeed why there's a celebration planned for tonight. Even why he was coming into the village as we left. It's a cruel blow."

"We must strike a crueller one yet."

"Meaning what?"

"So much power was expended in that tomb, either by a mage in Rallor's party or some arcane defence, and blood spilt too. They must be weakened and with their silly party to distract them, tonight is our only hope. We must steal the staff."

"Could we not borrow it?"

"What sort of fool are you?" exploded Orrolui, slashing the air just before Jebbin with his scimitar. "I'm tired of your naive bletherings. If you held an artefact, an artefact by Teltazzar, would you lend it to any vagrant who wandered in? You'd not keep it long! Any such request will only warn him of our interest and wreck our chances.

"Now listen. I need you tonight and you'd better not fail me. I must have this staff. I'll scout the building and plan our attack; stealth if possible, power if not. When the celebrations are at their height we'll meet at the wrangler's and agree tactics. I hope to have located the staff precisely before then. Then … we … fight. Accept?"

The two magi glared at each other only a hand-span apart, Orrolui's face suffused with blood and radiant with energy, Jebbin's cold and adamantine.

Jebbin said flatly, "If we must."

Orrolui turned on his heel and stamped back towards Farralei, embittered by such a narrow defeat in the race for the staff. He strode along the drier path taken by Rallor. As the glimmers of evening faded, the road was lighted more by the cold moon, flaring and dying behind drifting patterns of cloud, a light that lent his hurrying shape an eerie quality.

Shrouded in thought, he walked briskly into the outskirts of the little town and failed to notice a hooded figure leaning against the wall of the outermost house beneath an aged hemlock until a menacing voice interrupted his plottings.

"A Gesgarian abroad after dark. That must bode ill."

Orrolui jerked to a halt, his senses suddenly alert, questing outward. He turned with a fluid motion, his scimitar slithering forward in readiness, *sear* in his hand, and faced the stranger. His eyes combed the shadows for any further assailants but caught no hint of movement. Orrolui advanced cautiously on the stationary figure until scant steps separated them and waited, scimitar poised ominously.

"Speak," he commanded.

The stranger did not reply but after a pause he pushed himself away from the wall and faced the mage. As the clouds slid away from the face of the moon, he reached up and drew the hood back from his head. Beneath a bald cranium, the face was desperately gaunt, broad teeth glinting white in moonlight that refused to touch his eyes, leaving them as black wells of night beneath heavy brows. Orrolui gasped and his eyes widened as he faced the skull-like apparition.

"Ukanu!" he cried in delight, slamming his scimitar away and rushing forward to grip the newcomer by the shoulders. Grinning exultantly, Orrolui shook him in disbelief. "Teltazzar, I cannot credit this, tonight of all nights. How is it possible? Are you alone?"

"An islander waits at each corner of the village, looking for you. Marachin heads a band of us."

"Marachin of the Long Arm!" said Orrolui happily

"The same," assented the second Gesgarian. "We were west of Tu-Tanai when we received word from a trader, Chun. He had searched diligently to find us. I don't know how you managed that, few indeed are so generous to help Islanders for love."

"Saved his life, of course, how else?" Orrolui dismissed the subject with a wave.

"At all events, the summons was urgent and we came with all speed. What's afoot?"

Orrolui threw his head back and sighed deeply, blowing out through pursed lips. He looked back to Ukanu and regarded him steadily. "It's quite a story," he said softly. "We'd better save it for Marachin and the others. You're camped out of town?"

"Of course," shrugged the bald man, replacing his hood.

"I'll collect my things from the wrangler's and join you. There's no-one here of value to me now."

"Then I'll walk with you," replied the islander and the two tall men departed side by side.

*　*　*

Jebbin watched the light leach from the sky. A slow wave of pigeon silhouettes rolled towards the shore of another wood lost in the dusk. He sighed, thinking of other days and other sunsets, dropping warm and golden through the pear orchards where Sola lived or drinking in the evening sun while Hiraeth sang. Nothing had quite worked out as he had planned. He looked back to the copse that had been their goal for so long and was startled to see an owl regarding him steadily with yellow eyes from the top of the nearest tree. Surprised at the bird's fearless demeanour, Jebbin stared back. The owl slid from its perch and floated away on silent wings.

Jebbin plodded back towards Farralei, wondering what old Dordo might have counselled. He ambled through the darkened streets to the wrangler's buildings where he was surprised to find not only no Orrolui but no sign of his pack either. He sat wondering what the evening would bring, tapping a rhythm on a bran bin with his staff. His worries soon drove him from the empty dormitory to accost the wrangler who was filling hay nets below, but he was engaged upon his own tasks and proved taciturn, neither knowing nor caring where Orrolui's pack might be.

Jebbin wandered vaguely through Farralei and found himself on the bridge down by the mill, now silent, its wheel unresponsive to the playful slaps of the river as it pleaded for a game. Idly, Jebbin used his staff to flick pebbles into the swirling blackness under the piers and watched the moonlight catch the ripples as they were borne downstream. He jumped as a voice interrupted his reverie.

"You're with Lord Rallor's party, are you?"

"No. Just passing through at the same time. Why do you ask?"

"Strangers in Farralei aren't all that common."

Jebbin looked towards the speaker. She was slender with dark, tousled hair but the moonlight kept many secrets to itself. He became aware of a silence and spoke up hastily. "Oh, I'm sorry, my name's Jebbin. I'm a...well... a traveller."

He caught sight of the smile's gleam before she answered, "Yes, a travelling man you would be. I am Keline." She bobbed and continued, "I didn't mean to pry, only to ensure you knew you were invited to the party this evening."

"Both company and questions are pleasant, but can you speak for Rallor?"

"He's made it plain that all are welcome. In any case, my husband and I are the weavers here and we've enjoyed both business and conversation with Lord Rallor. I know your greeting would be cordial. Will you come?"

Jebbin hesitated. "I would like to, thank you. Would you ..." he paused uncertainly. "What can you tell me of Rallor?"

Keline eyed him quizzically for a moment. "Where are you going, traveller?"

"Lana Fair, I suppose," replied Jebbin, somewhat taken aback.

"Then you may answer your own questions, for you may have company on the road."

"Listen, I must know tonight," began Jebbin, clutching at her arm but she stepped back smartly.

"Sir Jebbin, enough!" she cried.

"Please Keline, I apologise. I have an urgent matter that weighs heavily upon me."

"I see you are troubled. Say on, then."

"Can I trust Rallor?"

She laughed lightly. "Can you trust me, a chance acquaintance upon a bridge? What have you heard of Rallor's character already?"

"That he's honest, honourable and unswerving in his pursuit of what he sees to be right," replied Jebbin slowly.

"Then what further description would you have from me? I cannot make your decisions."

Jebbin grimaced at her bantering, then spoke softly, "And yet you do. Mistress Keline, my grateful thanks. May I escort you to your door and hope for the pleasure of seeing you later this evening?"

He proffered his arm in the fashion of a true gallant. Keline regarded him archly but then laid her fingers on his arm and inclined her head gracefully. "Master Jebbin, you are kind." Together they strolled through the village, chatting as old friends until they reached the weaver's door.

Later, as Jebbin passed the well in the village square, he paused and leant over the low stone parapet. Gazing down into the inky water an arm's reach below, he could dimly make out his own reflection against the lightness of the sky. He thumbed a pellet of *sear* into his nose and inched his staff down until the tip touched the surface. Concentric circles danced outwards and the image of his head and shoulders bulged and shrivelled in time. As the water stilled once more, Orrolui's face was plainly visible as he sat in conversation with other dim figures. The pictured face tilted as though listening to a distant chime and began to look about. Hastily, Jebbin let the spell die and darkness collapsed back on to the well water before his own features peered up worriedly. Satisfied, Jebbin headed for the inn.

Rallor was sitting behind a table in the parlour when Jebbin was shown in to see him. He was settling some minor matter about the evening entertainments with the proprietor and Jebbin waited patiently until arrangements were finalised and his escort introduced him.

"My lord, this is Jebbin, a traveller who urgently requires to see you."

Rallor turned to face Jebbin with a blandly courteous smile but his eyes were intelligent and perceptive. "A pleasant interruption. Perhaps I might have the opportunity to speak with you at more leisure this evening but for now perhaps you could be brief. How may I help you, Lord Jebbin?"

Jebbin gazed back levelly. "Just Jebbin, if you please. Lord Rallor, later tonight may be too late. I beg to speak with you alone now."

Instantly, others in the room fell silent as their attention became bent upon one they had supposed a mere supplicant. Through the silence, Jebbin stared steadily into Rallor's eyes.

"Tell me," asked Rallor quietly, "are you a magician?"

"Yes." Jebbin became aware that a hand at his side was waiting for the staff and he passed it over without glancing round.

"It's just a stick, my lord," said his escort.

Rallor folded his arms and darted a look and a nod to the escort. "Thank you, Hol. Just Jebbin, I think you should go."

Mutely, Jebbin held out his hand for the staff and, when it was returned, conjured a globe of light. He heard a sword drawn fast and immediately held the staff out again. Hol took it from him and frowned at it dubiously, shaking his head.

"Intriguing. But you need to say more."

"I am engaged upon a quest and I need your help."

"Then why do you wish to see me alone?"

"Because I must divulge information that will endanger my life."

Rallor considered briefly, then drew his sword and laid it upon the table before him, holding it firmly in his right hand. He gestured to a chair set opposite him. "Please sit and place your hands upon the table."

Somewhat gingerly, Jebbin did as bidden and looked up at the brawny nobleman who leant towards him and asked, "Jebbin, do you mean me harm?"

"No."

Rallor sat back again. After glancing down at pommel of his sword, he pointed at the door with his left hand. The others began to file quietly from the room but Jebbin spoke up again. "Hol, will you alone wait one moment, please?"

When the door closed, Jebbin twisted round to see Hol standing stiffly beside it, sword ready in his hand. There was no sign of his staff. He turned back to face Rallor.

"Before we are alone, there is something you should know and which I beg neither of you to repeat, since knowledge of it has already caused me many troubles. Hol was right; the staff is but a stick. I am a mage but I need no staff. I still have my powers."

Rallor's expression did not seem to change, yet the merest suggestion of a smile hovered about his lips. "Await my call outside, Hol. Now," he said, feigning disinterest, "I really do have matters to attend to."

"I must demand on your honour that you reveal nothing of

what I tell you unless you feel honour-bound to do so. If you cannot grant me that, I will leave."

"Very well. Continue."

"You have today collected the Staff of Sumos from a marble casket in a tomb to the north of Farralei. I, too, have long sought that staff in the company of another. But we did not seek the staff for itself but to assist us in the unravelling of a larger matter." Jebbin paused, then squared his shoulders with an effort. "We hold a page from Echoheniel's Enchiridion."

"Lady's Light!" breathed Rallor, his eyes suddenly aflame. "And you guess the Staff of Sumos will reveal the hidden secrets of the riddle."

"Yes."

"You hold a mighty treasure."

"Yes."

"What is it, precisely, that you wish from me?"

"To use the Staff. But I want your word that you will not act upon the words of the riddle nor even seek to learn its contents."

"How then shall I tell you its meaning?"

"Lend me the staff that I may do my own unravelling."

Rallor snorted volcanically and tightened his grip on the sword. "Ho! How am I to be sure that there will be no feat of legerdemain, the staff disappear and you with it? You have your powers, you say."

"And you have my word."

Drumming his fingers, Rallor considered his options. He mused aloud. "What a tempting morsel you hold just out of my reach! Why do you think I would do this thing?"

Jebbin knew this was his only chance and chose his words carefully. "Echoheniel's verses tend to reappear when most vital and they have always aided what good there is in the world. You must give me your aid."

"Then by what right do you prevent me trying to solve it on my own account? The more that try, perhaps success becomes more likely."

"A just question. But would it be just to wrest scroll and rewards from us? You have your chance to assist, is that not enough? More, the verse has come to us, it smacks of arrogance to assume you can fulfil its requirements better than us, however likely it may seem."

"There's something you have not told me," rumbled Rallor after a pause.

"Yes. I told you I sought the staff in the company of another. That other is a Gesgarian."

"A Gesgarian," repeated Rallor colourlessly, yet a silky edge crept into his voice.

Jebbin watched Rallor carefully. "You are not one to believe slurs on every Gesgarian. Why is this so important?"

"You are stumbling into a larger matter that doesn't concern you. Suffice it to say that I was asked to fetch this staff by Pattacus, a sage from Shekkem. Pattacus is working to help the crown prince of Triva in a way that seems right to me. He told me where it was and something of its defences but he also said how a Gesgarian had stolen details of the staff from him. To find another Gesgarian so close on the trail, well, I don't trust coincidences - or your Gesgarian."

"He is a strong character, fiery and powerful and not given to niceties when baulked."

"So?" grated the southern lord.

"I'm here without his knowledge and at some personal risk. He would prefer a less open approach, I suspect."

"You seek to threaten me?"

"Hardly. Given that information, do you feel threatened by two of us? I'm seeking the best route for all concerned."

"You pose me quite a conundrum of your own."

Suddenly Jebbin grinned at the big man, "And if I need help, I'll know where to find it."

"Will you now?" queried Rallor, arching his eyebrows.

"Of course. Surely you will next be visiting Lana Fair?"

Rallor chuckled, then his face sobered. "Give me your oath."

"I swear on my life I intend no ill to you or others and I will neither purloin, damage nor alter the staff. By the Lady, lend me the staff for the good of all," pleaded Jebbin.

Rallor studied the pommel of his sword intently before banging it on the table in decision. "Hol!" he called and when the door flew open, held up his hand and shook his head. "It's all right. Get the staff, please."

When Hol, with a brief but clear hesitation, had retreated, Rallor continued, "There will be three conditions. One: I take you at your word. If you need help, you will come to me. Two: you will report to me regularly so I'll know if you have failed and I must take up the task. Three: if I am to accept the challenge if you fail, I must have a copy of the riddle."

Jebbin stared at him aghast. "Can you not retract that last clause?"

"No. I have named my conditions and made my decision. For the sake of what is good you say this riddle must be solved and the conditions are necessary. If I am to trust you with the staff, you must trust me when I say that I will not even read it unless you fail."

"Orrolui has forbidden any transcription of the verse," whispered Jebbin.

"Then you have it with you?"

"No. I have never even held it except when Orrolui has been by my side."

"How then will the Staff of Sumos be of value? You need a written version."

"I have memorized every word, every syllable, every spelling."

"Then if you have agreed to all my conditions, you will write out the riddle in full, learn its meaning with the staff and leave paper and staff with me. You're a magician: seal the paper with a spell so that it cannot be opened while you live. I would accept even that."

Jebbin's head sank into his hands. He was completely out on a limb and the consequences of failure now were dire, for he had utterly doomed Orrolui's stealthy approach. He had come hoping for a great gift and now found the price exceedingly high. Rallor was being just and honourable, only his intention was not to suit Jebbin but to ensure the riddle was solved. Jebbin's hands fell away and he gazed up at the southerner. "I can perform no such spell but there is no need. I will trust you and accept your terms."

For the first time, Rallor's heavy right hand came away from his pommel as he held it towards the mage.

Jebbin gripped it firmly. "Orrolui must never know," he stated. When Rallor nodded he went on, "How can you be sure that the scroll I give you is safe against theft, or indeed if anything should happen to you?"

"On that point you may rest assured. I have an adamantine chest that none can open but I. Your screed will be placed in a special compartment where any vigorous attempt to burgle the chest will destroy it."

Jebbin smiled as Hol returned bearing the staff wrapped in a cloth. "There's no reason for further delay then. May I trouble you for paper and ink?"

Jebbin had taken Rallor's seat with his back to the wall and painstakingly written out an exact copy of the page from

Echoheniel's book by the light from a copper sconce. Hol remained near his shoulder with sword drawn and several members of the group, including Rallor, waited patiently in other parts of the room. The innkeeper had twice knocked upon the door to say all was in readiness and on the second occasion he had been asked to proceed, they would all join him shortly. After that, a dim but ever swelling buzz in the background suggested he had lost little time in complying.

At last, Jebbin set aside his nib and inks. He blew upon the last of the writing and sat back in relief. "It is done," he pronounced needlessly.

An air of tension and unreleased energy developed as Rallor strode across the room, unwrapped a brown rod from its covering and wordlessly passed it to Jebbin. He took it and studied it. The rod was weighty beyond his expectations. Again he felt that haunting, tingling sharpness similar to that in the tomb, for the staff was redolent of ancient and potent theurgies. Although at a glance it seemed a simple, tapered wooden rod, carved into spirals, closer inspection suggested that it comprised a myriad separate slivers of wood, cunningly bonded so that no ends were visible. But even such marvellous construction and craftsmanship could not long hold Jebbin's attention. He swept his gaze round all the faces, lightly dusting expressions of wariness, wonder and hostility. Then he cleared his mind of distractions and lowered the rod to his text.

The shutters burst inwards with ear-popping force and a scimitar-wielding figure came diving through, rolling to his feet, running for the table. Jebbin barely had time to look up from his work before Hol's sword was pricking his neck and the staff had been plucked from his fingers. The eyes of the magicians met and Orrolui stumbled in shock.

"Betrayed!" he cried and for a moment it was as though they

two were alone in the room, Rallor and his interposing sword no more than a shimmer of air.

"Hold Orrolui, hold. It doesn't work, the staff does not aid us!"

"Liar - or some forgery," roared the Gesgarian while behind him, out in the night, dark figures slipped away unseen. Rallor rocked in consternation at Jebbin's words but his attention never wavered from Orrolui.

"No. The staff is the true Staff of Sumos - surely you can sense its aura - but recall its properties."

Oblivious of the weapons threatening them both, Orrolui narrowed his eyes and spluttered, "I've sought this staff over half the world! It renders written scripts legible, confers understanding, it translates..."

"No, precisely," interrupted Jebbin.

"The artefact confers the ability to understand unknown scripts and languages." snapped Orrolui, quoting exactly from Telmarion's Compendium.

"But Orrolui, we already know this script and this language. We may not be able to understand it but we can read it." Jebbin shook his head sadly. "All this," he waved an arm vaguely, encompassing both their attempts to gain the Staff of Sumos. "All of it, the journey to Farralei, solving the demon's riddle, even your rite with Zaeboth, all just chasing after rainbows. There is no easy solution to Echoheniel's verse."

Orrolui held his gaze, swallowing the bile of an even bitterer blow with a nod of comprehension. With slow, exaggerated calm, Orrolui slid his scimitar back into its scabbard and composed his features to studied blankness. He turned to Rallor, ignoring the heavy broadsword levelled at him.

"Your pardon, my lord, for the manner of my irruption. We have, as you have heard, been deceived. There is a vile creature called Zaeboth who laughs at the misery he causes and relishes the suffering. It is he who has led me, by the nose, to this debacle. I am sure I can count on Jebbin's aid to rid these planes of such a demon. Once again I crave your indulgence for my actions."

Evidently considering matters concluded with Rallor, he pushed past and addressed Jebbin. "Come now, we have perhaps both erred in our judgements here but at least the matter is settled and we know what we face. Let us leave these good people in peace with the relic they justly obtained before us and attend to our own business." Nonchalantly, he reached out to lift the copy of the verse from Echoheniel's Enchiridion but Rallor's fist landed upon it first.

"The writing stays here," the southerner commanded in a voice that should have brooked no argument.

"Just as the staff is yours, so that writing is mine," flashed Orrolui.

"I made a bargain with your colleague. I kept my word and I will not be cheated."

"But that is unreasonable! The staff was of no use to me, I see that now. You cannot rob me of my life's work with a hollow bargain made with one who did not possess what he offered."

"Orrolui, Rallor has promised not to study or even read the scroll unless he has reason to believe we have failed in the task."

Orrolui glared at Jebbin before sweeping a calculating stare round the room, measuring his strength against those glowering faces. After a lingering glance into the empty night he turned back to Rallor.

"Then we shall have to trust the noble lord to stick to another of these bargains he prizes so highly. With your permission, I will go. Come Jebbin, we must leave these folk to their celebration."

"Orrolui," Rallor spoke in a dangerous tone, holding his broadsword firmly, "do you intend any harm towards Jebbin?"

Orrolui turned again and raised his eyebrows. "What a curious question. You can be forgiven your rudeness after my own. I give you my word that I have no plans to injure him. And now I shall leave before I have to give an account of all my affairs to you." He stalked across the room and through the shutters, with none daring to block him. In his wake, Rallor frowned uncertainly at his sword hilt. Jebbin smiled and shrugged at Rallor and made to follow Orrolui but Rallor held up his hand.

"You have three weeks before I read that paper unless I hear from you."

"I'll leave word for you at Lana. I'm grateful for your assistance."

"You might not find me with the ease you imagine. Lana Fair is more than a village fete! Also, as you may have guessed, my visit with the staff is not the whole story and I may spend much time away from Lana."

"But protecting the staff gets you and your knights into Lana Fair and beyond?"

Rallor just looked at Jebbin. "You should be able to find a trader in Shekkemite jewellery and pearls from Torl by the name of Narbez. A message left with him should reach me. I hope we meet again."

"I'm sure we shall. Farewell until that meeting." Jebbin hurried out after Orrolui, collecting his staff on the way.

He saw the Gesgarian ahead of him on the street. He was talking in low tones, accompanied by vehement gesticulations, to a tall, dark-swathed individual. As Jebbin approached, the latter hurried away without glancing round. To his surprise, Jebbin found himself greeted cordially by Orrolui and he neglected to enquire about his strange interlocutor.

"So we got it all wrong, eh? I don't know about you but I don't feel like joining a great party tonight. On the other hand, a drink would go down well enough. I have a Gesgarian liqueur in my pocket. What about going back to the wrangler's and toasting our failures?"

"Well, yes, why not? I just can't get over the impotence of the staff. After everything."

"It seems that even your Lady Lessan puts lead on the wrong corner of the dice occasionally," chuckled Orrolui, clapping Jebbin on the shoulder and the two left the singing at the inn to fade behind them. Orrolui borrowed two grubby glasses from the horse dealer before they retired to the dormitory and perched on beds either side of a bran bin serving as a makeshift table. Orrolui kept Jebbin's glass full of a cloudy white liquid; sweet, herby and powerful, and the talk on the riddle of the seer. He seemed genial enough but keen to hear of all the details to which Rallor was committed. He questioned Jebbin very closely on whether he had learnt anything of the meaning of the verse in all the time since first reading it. Jebbin feared to reveal that he had long kept vital information secret and remained silent about Erridarch's suggestion that the castle of the riddle might be in Ael. At last Orrolui sat back in satisfaction. He regarded Jebbin thoughtfully, then reached forward and lifted Jebbin's hand. When he released it, it fell back nervelessly onto the bin. Jebbin stared at it in surprise but found himself unable to move.

"Wad...What's the meaning of this?" he demanded in horror, rolling his eyes up at Orrolui.

Orrolui rose without speaking and took the lamp to the window, raised it once and returned it to its place. He began to speak standing behind Jebbin, who was unable even to turn and look at him.

"You all think you're so clever. You think we are nothing but creatures from the Dark Isles to be reviled and defrauded when possible. You're a traitor; a stabber in the back, sneaking behind me and stealing all my treasure even though I'd shared it with you unstintingly. The great Rallor is nothing but a common cheat, robbing me with empty words. Why is it that you, who betray and thieve, consider yourselves so much better than Gesgarians? What have we done worse than any race? And the so-noble Rallor grandly demands if I intend you any ill. After you had given away that for which I have risked my life a hundred times? No, I am Gesgarian and for the honour that you should deign to be seen with me, I must endure all your injuries. Well, here's a surprise for you. I gave my word that I would not harm you and I spoke the truth or Rallor would surely have known it with that device upon his sword. I shall not harm you."

Just then the other Gesgarians filed into the room, their hoods raised, and advanced to stand round Jebbin's motionless form. Orrolui spoke to their leader.

"We have three weeks before Rallor will read the paper, Marachin. It is enough. And by the way it's concealed, we may be able to send some thief to try and recover it. He'll certainly fail and perhaps be killed but it should destroy the traitor's parchment in Rallor's chest." Orrolui reached down and raised Jebbin's head by his hair. "No, I will not harm you. I won't be here and if Rallor ever clutches that sword and demands how I last saw you, I can tell him you were sitting comfortably on a bed. Farewell, if briefly." He slammed Jebbin's head down and walked away without a backward glance.

Jebbin's face smashed onto the bran bin. There was an audible crack as his nose hit the iron hoop that served as a handle on the lid. Blood began to pool round his cheek.

Jebbin found his mind clear even though his body was all but useless. He wanted to scream after Orrolui that he hadn't meant to steal or give anything away, he only wanted to solve the riddle for them both, this wasn't fair. But he was surrounded by tall men with pitiless faces and racked his brain for a spell that might aid him more than futile supplications. Suddenly he re-called Dewlin's annotated spell lists and the last spell recorded. The page sprang into his mind with stunning clarity. Fired with the pain in his nose, he immediately attempted to deliver the words of power, heedless of Orrolui descending the stairs. His leaden tongue clanged a useless discord on coppery lips and a dribble of spittle mixed with the blood on the bin. Knowing the Gesgarians would only wait for Orrolui to leave the building be-fore killing him, he ground his broken nose into the handle, con-centrated desperately to control the exquisite pain and began the spell in a muffled voice while the Gesgarians watched him un-concernedly or talked in low tones over his head.

Orrolui must have felt the stirrings within the Web of Power that roiled out from the opening syllables for he suddenly roared up at his fellow islanders,"Stop him now - he casts a spell!"

But Marachin merely glanced down at Jebbin before calling back laconically, "He tries - but he has no staff."

Even as Orrolui cursed his natural secrecy and raced back to-wards the dormitory, Jebbin was grappling with the awesome strength of his chosen spell. He could feel it slipping from his control, its energies too massive for him to channel, the blinding pain from his broken nose beyond his ordering. His mind throbbed to the beat of Orrolui's pounding footsteps as the Gesgarian charged back up the open stairs and the syllables he uttered began to distort and writhe with a life of their own. Unconstrained power rippled in mighty surges, shivering agony throughout his body and he knew the spell was too great for him, his last gamble had failed. Still he laboured hopelessly to complete the straining words, his heart thudding rapid spasms of pain into his chest.

Through it all, he heard the gasp of someone choking on a

phenomenal quantity of *sear*. Just as he was expecting a Gesgarian spell to crash into him, a voice joined with his, steady and strong, shoring up his tottering edifice of sound, binding it with a will of adamant. Jebbin's own efforts ebbed and collapsed into feeble silence but the new speaker accepted the creaking burden even as the spell billowed out in chaos. Jebbin could feel the terrific stress as that dire magic was re-shaped by quivering but steely tones and wondered at his temerity in attempting anything so potent. Then the voice, cracking at the last, wrenched loose the final syllable with a mighty effort and cast adrift the spell of temporal stasis, catching Orrolui in the middle of his counter-spell.

Time juddered to a halt for those within the spell's radius and with it all else for without the seconds to measure its progress there could be no activity and the spell casters alone were shielded. The Gesgarians stood as waxen images, even Orrolui frozen into a mask of rage. But from the tip of his scimitar, cat's tails of blue fire lashed in corrosive patterns from his half-issued spell. Jebbin felt warm hands grip him under the arms and found himself being dragged backwards towards the stairs where he was briefly rested. He caught a glimpse of his rescuer, appearing as another Gesgarian though the stature seemed to be dwindling and the face was blurred and indistinct.

"I ... I know you," mumbled Jebbin as the new mage rushed back to collect his pack and staff, ignoring the immobile islanders but hastening to be away, for Orrolui's magic was ripping irregular chunks from the fabric of their spell.

Then, as the figure half carried him down the stairs, panting under his weight, events jumbled themselves into fragmented images as pain, exhaustion and the effects of Orrolui's potion took their toll. Later, Jebbin found himself with strange mental pictures of his rescuer's face as an owl, a salacious girl talking to a thief as they left Dadacombe, old Dordo who had joined him on the road and then returned to Bodd and Sola with half his gold and finally an owl again, all interspersed with isolated recollections of their flight, himself bound and bouncing across his horse.

Great Lana Fair

It was long before Jebbin opened his eyes. When he did, he looked into a face he knew so well. "Hello, mother," he said softly.

"Dear Jebbin." She patted his hand vaguely and seemed to look through him. Her face was careworn, the skin papery and pale

"I've had such a strange dream. You, Dordo, the owl..." he paused. "Only none of it was a dream, was it? You are Dewlin!"

"I am, or was. I thought I could guide you, keep you safe. I should've known better. Rest now, dear."

"I've never felt less like resting in my life! Mother, you have so much to teach me. Why did you never practise magic? Why did you never say anything to Marl or me?"

"Hush," whispered Dewlin wearily. "Magic was ever a dangerous art. I turned my back on the pain and the power for love of Tagg and with him I found the older magic in the slow turn of the years and the fruitfulness of the soil. The smell of rain on dry ground conjured a magic greater than any spell of mine. I promised I would never encourage any of you in sorcery for it is hard to turn pain into anything beautiful. We agreed when you left that I should try to protect you for a while. I have warded you all I am able. I must go back to him.

"I knew you would take up the art if fate willed it and I was content. Tagg never thought it could happen. You found the book but you did not come to me." She shook her head sadly. "In the end, it's not what you can do with magic, but what magic does to you. I was able to leave the pain and lose the power, mostly. Perhaps I should have burned the book. It's all too late now. Dear Jebbin, I must go back to Tagg." With that, she patted him again and tottered from the room while he called after her in perplexity. She did not answer but a stranger with grizzled hair above a leathery, pock-marked face entered; his thickset frame wrapped in homespun robes of brown and orange. Jebbin's clothes, washed and smelling of rosemary, were draped over his arm.

"What's the matter with her? What's happened?" demanded Jebbin.

The stranger placed the clothes on a chair, sat on the end of the bed and regarded Jebbin with narrowed eyes. Jebbin could sense the strength of his personality and held back the flood of questions burning within him. The man scratched the back of his head with a stubby hand before speaking slowly.

"I am Rilkas and I am well, thank you for asking, and we have healed your face as best we can but please don't mention it. As for the rest, you were the cause of all that has happened. I've seen what occurred and don't suppose you are wholly to blame. But it's hard. Dewlin Voryllion is lost to us."

"I don't understand what's wrong with my mother," Jebbin blurted when the pause became too long. "And who are you?"

"We are the Forshen. I see the name means nothing to you and that is as it should be. Lin aided our aims often in the past but now she is Numbed. Her power is gone, cauterised by the energy she expended to complete and control your spell. To take over a spell from another is difficult and complex. That was a great spell and hopelessly out of control. I would have thought it impossible. The challenge was far above even her capacity and only Dewlin's love for you lent her the strength to batter the web of power into order. But it was only lent and she cannot repay. I hope you will prove worthy of her sacrifice."

"This is terrible! Will she never cast a spell again?"

Rilkas shrugged as though the question were irrelevant. "From that Numbing? There will be no recovery from what you have done. And you think spell casting important? Do you understand nothing? She can't feel! She'll never feel again. An essential part of being human and you have denied it to her."

"I had no teacher to tell me how to feel pain. I see you don't need one to give it either."

"You are a mystery to me," said Rilkas harshly. "You were unable to see things that should have been obvious to anyone and yet you have discovered things hidden even from the great sorcerers of the past. We don't know what to do with you."

"Do with me?" echoed Jebbin in surprise.

"That's exactly what I mean. Sometimes you genuinely understand nothing," said Rilkas in exasperation, standing up to leave, while Jebbin looked at him in consternation.

"Rilkas!" Jebbin called after him. "Will you be able to take my mother home again?"

"Are you not her son? Is she not reduced because of you? Surely this is your duty and the very least of it," said Rilkas, glaring at Jebbin furiously.

"Yes. Yes and yes," he said quietly. "But if her loss is to have meaning then I must pursue another goal. It is vital that I reach Lana Fair as soon as possible."

"More important than your own mother, crippled when saving your skin?"

"If you do not accept this burden, I will not neglect her. But you will have failed us both."

"What could you know of that could possibly take precedence?" Rilkas's glare became an intense scrutiny. "Shadows and hints," he muttered, turning away. "This calls for heads wiser than mine. Please stay here."

Treading silently on the stone floor, Rilkas strode out, leaving Jebbin's face crumpled in a deep frown and his mind in turmoil. After a rare period of honest introspection, his mouth hardened in determination. Too long had he dreamed of power falling in his lap, hanging on the words of a cunning old woman preying on a boy. He had reckoned nothing of the value of his gift nor realised the enormity of what Orrolui had committed. He had played like a child under his mother's protection. Now that protection was gone. The words of the seer burned in his mind and he must solve them alone.

He dressed resolutely, sat on the chair and rested his hands lightly on his knees. He emptied his mind as though preparing for a spell and waited. After a while he felt the gentle, insistent pressure of a skrying. Like a distant music swelling in volume, the pressure grew. Jebbin gave back no resistance but let it waft round and over him until it lapped away into silence and he emerged like a rock from soft surf. Long he waited, immobile and receptive, until he could sense the distant emotions: anger, disappointment and scorn losing ground against tolerance, sympathy and above all, hope. He knew the outcome long before his mother came to see him once more.

"Rilkas is heading a party coming with me back to Dorning. I don't know why but he says he has some business."

Jebbin stood and wrapped his arms round his mother and held her close. He had no words to thank her and none were needed save for the silent kind that passed in that embrace. At last she squeezed him gently and moved away as Rilkas appeared in the doorway.

"Forshen travel light, Master Jebbin. The others will be waiting by now."

"Mother, did you go back to Sola as Dordo? I thought you had. Tell Sola again that I will see her when this is all over. I'll try and be worthy of you."

"Be worthy of yourself," she smiled at him wanly and shuffled out as though her age had doubled.

"You must leave too," said Rilkas. "Since there are some that consider your secret matters of importance, you have a guide. And since there were others of us with different opinions, your guide is Nith. Farewell." With a playful cuff, Rilkas sent a red-haired lad scuttling into the room and departed after Dewlin.

Nith waved a fist in mock revolt after Rilkas, then straightened up and grinned hugely at Jebbin, his blue eyes sparkling with amusement.

"Yeuch! What happened to your nose? Oh, I wasn't supposed to mention that."

"Is it bad? It's Numbed, I can't feel a thing."

"No, it's fine. The blackened pumpkin look is probably really big at court these days. Nith, guide extraordinaire, at your service!"

"What's so extraordinary?" asked Jebbin, shaking hands Marigor-fashion.

"Well, I don't know the way which must be fairly odd for a guide. Odd guide doesn't have much of a ring to it. What about unusual guide as a happy medium?"

"Unusual it is, then," chuckled Jebbin. "Tell me, did Rilkas select you personally?"

"No idea. I was summoned from a deliriously happy time beheading turnips by the ungenerous sobriquet of 'incorrigible lout' and offered more congenial employment. I don't think I fit in with this lot - Lana Fair sounds much more to my taste and I'm in your debt for the opportunity to go."

"Let's hope we get there before it finishes then. How do we go?"

"All arranged. Riding animals with, I shrewdly suspect, the barest minimum of provender, doubtless ready for our instant departure, if you're fit?"

"Certainly," declared Jebbin, collecting his staff from a corner and striding out after his guide, "How do we get to Lana?"

"All roads lead to Lana when the fair is on - I hope. If I escort you as far as the nearest trail westwards - which I think I can find," he paused to wink jovially at Jebbin, "then we can join the merry throng pressing towards Lana Fair where I have secret business to conduct for the order. Oops, well, that's off my chest already! Still, if it were that secret, I doubt I'd have been given much of a look in."

Nith collected two aged and portly nags and they rode away. Jebbin looked back at the house they left. It blended so well with its surroundings it might have grown there as part of the little garden, an oasis of matched colours yielding an atmosphere of tranquillity.

"What can you tell me of these Forshen?" Jebbin asked curiously.

Nith raised his eyes skyward and folded his hands piously before answering, "Hail to the Searchers. Their wisdom is deep, their lore is old and their goodness springs from the roots of both."

"Pardon?" exclaimed Jebbin in surprise.

"Oh, don't ask me. That's what I was told when I came. They're just another group with their own plots and schemes. They don't do anyone any harm, except for making you feel like a lost child at a cleric's convention whenever possible. Come on, let's see which of these carthorses goes least slowly. Race to that tree!" With that, Nith booted his mount into a lumbering stumble, whooping as though he were riding a war destrier and the matter was left behind as Jebbin lurched into an elephantine pursuit and galumphed after his guide.

When they passed a winding track from the north, a plodding convoy joined their road. Three oxen each drew a small wagon. A motley assortment of folk lolled on the wagons or ambled beside them, coarsely dressed and mud be-spattered.

Nith hailed them. "Are you bound for Lana Fair and if so, would you object to company on the road?"

Answer was returned in a grim voice by a heavy, dour-faced woman, "If you've a strong arm, we'll be pleased to have you with us when the Aelans are about. Others have been more choosy."

Even as she spoke, Nith's nose wrinkled as the smell from the wagons struck him. "Fish?"

"Fish," said the woman. "Go or stay as you please. We've no victuals to spare for you either way - unless you care to buy fish."

Nith bowed gallantly. "We'd be glad to stay. While I have no pretensions to a military nature, my friend Jebbin here is a powerful sorcerer and the fires of his staff would quell an Aelan army!"

"Doubtless," said the woman indifferently while Jebbin winced, "Though he looks as though he lost a fight with a doorpost. Tag along then. I am Clupea. These two," she indicated a pair of bristle-chinned and spike-headed fishermen, "are Hyas and Corystes, my twin sons. Alaria and Taonia are my daughters. Also with us, or partly with us in Mugil's case, are Mugil and Byssus."

As she spoke, a stolid figure glared at them suspiciously from beside the first ox and a vacuous face smiled dreamily from one of the wagons before returning to a piece of wood being aimlessly whittled.

Nith and Jebbin mingled with the others and soon found they became inured to the odours from the cargo. Nith investigated the contents of the wagons in Alaria's company. There he found fish in all forms; smoked, salted, dried in strips and blocks, even live in barrels. Also there were packs of harfisk livers, soft bladders and even tiny phials of the powdered scales of rare blue natheriks, allegedly a mighty aphrodisiac. Alaria's large eyes loomed at him over a bottle and he admitted there might be something in its powers.

Jebbin talked to Clupea about the fair. She was dubious of the reactions of her children and fellows in the lures and traps that would abound in Lana. Taonia interrupted their talk to ask Jebbin questions about himself and to preen before him. Clupea sent her away crossly but she returned again with a drink for Jebbin. He took it gladly but tasted something vaguely fishy behind its sharpness and disliked the flavour. Taonia departed giggling and flouncing her skirts. Clupea stared after her despondently and became even more morose and taciturn. Jebbin bought some smoked fish for his supper with Nith, mostly to relieve her mood.

After they had pitched camp beside a small copse that helped break a cold wind from the west, Taonia brought him the fish. As he divided it between Nith and himself, Taonia nodded salaciously to the trees and raised her eyebrows expectantly.

"I thought you and me could go for a walk," she said when Jebbin failed to respond.

"I've had about enough exercise for one day, thanks."

"It don't have to be a long walk," continued Taonia, hitching her skirt even higher on her thick brown legs and sounding even more obviously lascivious.

"We were about to have our supper," protested Jebbin, comparing her large and grimy frame with Sola's lithe beauty. "Would you like to join us?"

"Not very bright for a magician, are you?" snapped Taonia. "Aren't you feeling a bit passionate after your little drinky?"

"I'm really very tired," Jebbin began but at that moment Clupea called sharply for Taonia. The girl looked down at Jebbin contemptuously.

"I don't care for being slighted, however grand you think yourself." Her parting shot delivered, she stamped away to the wagons and left Nith to snigger at Jebbin's discomfiture.

"You just don't know how to treat a lady. You could have been whisked away in transports of delight before the moon moved! Take Alaria now; eating out of my hand, she is."

"Have some fish," said Jebbin wearily, "and eat out of your own hand."

They noticed that Clupea ate with only her sons near her, chomping bread and fish in sullen silence and grinding each mouthful heavily. The others sat in a huddled group, talking in hushed tones while they passed a bottle. Occasional laughs splattered across the quiet and were stilled. Later in the evening, Jebbin mentioned a feeling of disquiet to Nith.

"Nonsense," replied his guide sturdily, tossing more wood on the fire and settling deeper into a hillock of blankets. "Just Alaria and Taonia comparing notes, doubtless with unfavourable remarks aimed at your good self. These are solid fisherfolk, the salt of the earth!"

He had cause to review this opinion when he was roughly awoken by someone pulling his pack from beneath his head in the dead of night. He recognised Mugil in the fire's glow.

"Hey, what're you doing? Get away from that!"

Mugil smiled at him gently and placed the pack next to Jebbin's by the fire. As Nith tried to rise, Byssus' meaty fist landed on his shoulder and a heavy cudgel tapped him on the head.

"Don't move. Whatever you lose, it's not worth dying for." Byssus' voice was as leaden as the weight of his club.

Nith rubbed his eyes and looked across the fire at Jebbin, who shrugged at him glumly. Alaria built up the fire. Taonia stood before Jebbin, holding his staff and running her hands up and down it tauntingly.

"Not much good without a pole, are you magician?" she said and spat on his staff. She waved it over the flames and grinned maliciously.

In the firelight, Mugil's quick fingers filtered through Jebbin's pack and extracted the remnants of Chun's ryals while Byssus stood with his cudgel against Jebbin's ear. Mugil turned his attention to Nith's pack and whistled softly as he lifted out a leather pad from a soft cloth. The pad was studded with small gems in a complex pattern. Mugil dangled it on its short leather thongs and admired its glints in the firelight.

"No, drop that!" yelled Nith, leaping up. He ducked under Byssus' clumsy swipe and rushed towards Mugil. The normally lethargic fisherman whipped a thin filleting knife from his belt and stabbed towards Nith's unprotected belly.

Jebbin bit down on the ball of *sear* ready in his mouth. He smacked the edge of his hand onto the earth and sent an invisible Argen wall crackling between them. Mugil's knife drove into it and fell from his jarred fingers. Nith jolted to a halt and slid gracelessly to the ground. Byssus spun round from chasing Nith. Guilt, fear and surprise wrestled over his face and left it a contorted mess. Jebbin stretched out his arms, the left hand pointing to Byssus, the right to Mugil, the first two fingers spread and spat words of power as sparks over the fire. Writhing pain lashed into them and both doubled up. Taonia gave a horrified glance at the staff and dropped it as though it had bitten her. As Jebbin's blazing eyes pierced them, both girls fled shrieking for the wagons, Byssus and Mugil crawling after them, gasping and groaning, while Jebbin stalked behind them.

He stopped when he saw Clupea standing in the shadows and raised his arm again. The shape of Corystes loomed towards them and Hyas could be seen hurrying after the girls.

"I knew nothing of this," Clupea stated flatly.

"You did little to help us."

"The first I heard was Nith calling out. We'd have been too late to help had you not... I saw ..." she faltered, her voice hoarse with disbelief. "I'm sorry," she added simply.

"Byssus and Mugil will regret tonight's labours with the aid of many more," interrupted Corystes darkly.

"Do you vouch for them?" Jebbin asked, regarding the youthful features beside Clupea.

Corystes nodded decisively and returned his gaze steadfastly. "Hyas and I will take responsibility - if you give us the chance."

"Will you get our horses together then? We'll make an early start," ordered Jebbin gruffly, electing to trust Corystes immediately, and turned his back on them both.

Almost in silence, he and Nith had gathered their things back into their packs, mounted and ridden into the darkness. Clupea nodded heavily as they rode past. Corystes, standing tall at her side, waved briefly.

Nith was subdued and thanked Jebbin for his intervention hesitantly. "I'm sorry too."

"What?"

"I was a bit impetuous. We could've got them back later, couldn't we? The money and the disc?"

Jebbin shrugged. "Probably. The disc is your secret business for the Forshen?"

"Yes. I have to deliver it in Lana. But because I went charging at Mugil, you had to use a spell to save me and now the story will be spread all round the fair. The mage without a staff. It was what you most wanted to avoid, wasn't it?"

"Doesn't matter now. Couldn't be helped."

They rode through the slowly lightening morning in silence. Eventually the sun blew on the chilly fingers of the trees and launched their shadows towards Lana as it drifted clear of the horizon. They moved less stiffly in their swaddling cloaks and began to look for other company.

"Nith," said Jebbin suddenly, "for one that pretends scant regard for the aims of the Forshen, you risked your life very readily when Mugil touched the disc."

Nith gazed at him steadily with a half smile. "Well, no-one likes to fail in a trust, do they?" he replied at length and changed the subject.

* * *

Jebbin peered through the rain to see Lana Fair camped before him. He had heard tales of the many-coloured splendour and riotous blazing of the tents and pennants of the fair; Aelans called it a burnished jewel lighting the city walls of Lana. But the drumming rain leached away the brightness and dimmed his sight with grey. It pummelled the night's covering of snow into dismal slush and, when he turned to scowl mordantly at Nith, slipped wriggling eels of cold down his spine.

The two of them had been riding at the head of the column but there was little need for scouting now and they reined to one side to allow Joss and his carts of coir and copra from Shekkem to squelch by in the icy mud of the road. Joss sat huddled like a heap of mildewed sacking at the reins of the first cart, immobility his best defence against the worms of water. He raised his eyebrows at them and was gone.

Next in the column rolled the perpetually gloomy Olcomd with ginger, pomegranates and lapis lazuli, then Ygyrd riding on his tall wagon; huge, gnarled hands tirelessly gripping the soaked thongs. A leather hat jammed low shed water in cascades when he turned to grin at the riders. His eyes were heavy-lidded and inscrutable. A stiff white beard clung to his slabby flat face like moss. Jebbin urged the Forshen's horse into the road behind the fur trader's wagon and hitched its reins to the back. As Nith followed suit, he scrabbled up beside Ygyrd, who made room for them both.

"Rain not good," boomed Ygyrd in a subterranean voice. "Whatever happened to the famed Aelan winter?"

Jebbin laughed. Ygyrd's views on the weather were infamous: when the air grew chillier as they climbed the foothills of the Aelan mountains, he had smacked his hands together in glee; when the sun slid behind a monochrome blanket and the first snows tumbled down, he had roared with delight and mentally raised the price of his furs; when the wind lashed them all with frozen spite he had beamed from behind a massive cloak and cheerfully derided his shivering companions. While the other traders had moaned that the fair would be at its height in the middle of the winter; Ygyrd had declared the timing perfect and said it might even make his journey worth the hazard.

He had taken the two youths under his wing and told them tales of his long trek from Gelavien over the evening campfires. He had rafted three hundred leagues down the Oropin to Habban, taken a barge on the Ailya past Rareton, buzzing with the news of a religious uprising blocking the Golden Road near Rulion, right down to the great Guild-run city of Tarass. That city hummed with rumours of Lana Fair recurring. Ygyrd had promptly elected to risk his luck on the Great Fair rather than trade out to the grim fortress-city of Jerondst as he had planned.

Deciding to avoid the Golden Road with the uncertainty at Rulion and sure taxes in Algolia, he took ship. A daring captain had taken advantage of a favourable wind to brave the Tuin Gap, most northerly break in the mountainous line of islands that stretched southward into the ocean from the Sultanate of O-Ram. It was the shortest trip but the most at risk from pirates. Just after they thought they were safely through the strait, a lone pirate sloop had closed with them. Ygyrd had waved the memory aside for another evening but gleams behind the slits of his eyes spoke of a savage battle. A skeleton crew had struggled into Saleem on the Border River and he had made the long trek north.

"And now," he had finished, "the weather turns clear and bright, the sun will rise tomorrow and people will be giving me their old furs thinking I collect rags!" Then he had lent them furs against the bitter chill of the night and gone to bed chortling.

Jebbin thrust his staff against the footboard and leant forward keenly, buoyed by the prospect of seeing Hiraeth and Bolan again. He was as yet undismayed by the sheer size of the fair, unaware that he could only see the outlying tents and that Lana itself was leagues away.

As they passed between the first awnings they were idly inspected by a small military detachment huddling under cover, apparently too warm and comfortable to bother to ask questions. Then they were subjected to a rigorous scrutiny by another group trying hard to look disinterested as they loitered round the public information notice boards. They were clearly resentful that the proper demands had not been made: goods should have been declared and information gleaned by thieves and spies.

Jebbin elbowed past Nith and jumped down to study the boards while Ygyrd began negotiations with an Aelan flunkey for a vacant pitch in the main part of the fair. The main board held lists of the principal events funded by the authorities. Jebbin conned it over until he found wrestling mentioned and was relieved to discover that the opening bouts were not scheduled for another two days yet. He moved to the personal boards that held messages of greeting and rendezvous and was surprised to find Nith coming away with a satisfied mien. Then Ygyrd was bellowing that he was in a hurry to claim his pitch and Jebbin only gave the personal boards a cursory scan before jostling back to the wagon. Behind him, a note hastily tacked by a single pin fluttered vainly as though trying to catch his attention.

Back on the wagon with Ygyrd, they rode through the ragged, outermost areas and into the well-ordered lines of marquees and booths that represented the real fair rather than the hangers-on near the boards. They passed two lines of livestock enclosures; dairy cattle, yaks and fat-tailed sheep. Covered over with canvas and bedded on straw, the animals chewed the cud and ignored the passers-by in the rain. Only when someone came too close did they start into alertness and blow plumes of curiosity before backing further under cover.

Before they reached their appointed area, the day was fading and they stopped one of the ubiquitous vendor's carts to buy sticks laden with sizzling, spicy meats and waxed paper cones of vegetables. The seller himself was barely visible behind a cloud of steam and smoke from the braziers beneath his handcart. Though soaked to the skin he still had the heart to crack jokes and grimace a gap-toothed grin at Jebbin.

The rain faded to a light snow and finally stopped altogether. The cloud cover ripped like wet paper on the teeth of the mountains and was swept away by the wind. The temperature dropped steadily and the wheels of the wagon were breaking through a crust of ice when Ygyrd grunted in satisfaction, pointing down an alley thronged with people haggling and arguing over tapestries and woollen goods.

"Ha! The street of weavers and dyers. We're on the next street. Yes, this is it. What number do you have there? Look sharp!"

"One," said Nith keenly. "Numbers must start on the main road towards Lana gates. What number are we?"

"Two hundred and thirty-four," intoned Ygyrd funereally. "The fair is larger even than hearsay builds it." He clicked his tongue to his weary beasts and pulled them to the right. "If our marquee is occupied," he said darkly, "we will empty it."

Fortunately, they found it vacant but for a young couple who skittered away without need for eviction. Ygyrd skilfully wedged his wagon into the small gap between adjacent marquees and the three of them set to unloading and arranging the interior to Ygyrd's satisfaction; an arduous task which consumed the last of the day. When all was ordered, Ygyrd offered to buy supper.

"You aren't going to leave all this unguarded, are you?" queried Nith in surprise.

"What should I do? Starve to death sitting on all my furs, gnawing them into holes?"

"Well, it's a bit of a risk. I don't want to sound alarmist but some of those who eyed your furs didn't seem overburdened with scruples."

"Lady preserve me! The thieves of Lana Fair would fleece this place to the canvas in an hour, given the chance. However, in case you have the desire to wander round any marquee at night, I warn you that the methods we poor traders use to thwart robbers are many. Ignoring the vendors that pay off the Guild, a few leave traps amidst their wares, though thieves may prove equal to these. Some pay warders, whose reputations depend upon their success; others rely on savage beasts that roam unchained. Of greater subtlety are those who leave poisons strategically placed so they alone can render their wares safe. Still more combine fear and venom and leave snakes gliding softly through their chattels.

Me, I hate snakes. But I find these little fellows highly effective," Ygyrd rumbled in his deepest voice, opening a wooden crate that Jebbin had been sitting on and idly kicking. Inside were several glass boxes and in each box squatted a spider a thumb length across. They were glistening smooth and sturdy legged, black as a headsman's hood with a single band of leprous orange.

"They stay where you put them and, providing you come from behind, they are not too difficult to recapture. Come from the front or the side and they jump - I've not known one miss. A single bite is usually enough. They aren't infallible, of course. There are those who understand spiders and might recapture my pets for themselves. Protective gear is possible, but ungainly and likely to attract questions from the Fair Wardens who dislike robbery and dispense summary justice upon suspicion." As he spoke Ygyrd drifted round the marquee, shaking spiders into concealed points where they nestled into the furs, crouched, in-visible and patient.

"Of course, there are two tricks to this game. The important one is to leave an unopened box near the entrance. Once thieves see the defence, they rarely come further."

"But why give the game away? Why put them on their guard?" demanded Jebbin, who was developing a serious dislike of thieves.

"Because my aim is to deter, Master Jebbin, not kill," said the trader. "How would you like to risk your luck in here now, on guard or not?"

"But you said some could deal with your spiders. The Guild could hire such a one?"

"True," admitted Ygyrd with a shrug. "But the risks are great even for the skilled and the fee large. One would have to irritate the Guild enormously before they would bother and I do not in-tend to give them such cause."

"I must leave you then. I've already run foul of the Thieves' Guild and their irritation was extreme."

"Thanks for the warning. Yet you may stay. I have no liking for the Guild."

"And the second trick?" prompted Nith after Ygyrd had lapsed into silence.

"To remember exactly where you placed the little devils!" Ygyrd turned to face his two helpers, who were standing as far as possible from any furs with their lurking perils and regarding Ygyrd's distribution with wide eyes. "Now let's find that food!"

"Must we walk to a street of inns?"

"No. There are special areas for hardtack provisions - salted beef, biltong and travel biscuits - and wine and spirit merchants have their own row but there'll be inns aplenty on every street. We'll not have far to go."

Outside, the evening sun slanted across the fair, leaving tents and awnings in shade but lighting the flags and pennants in a wash of gold as though to help them descry their destination. All pennants marked their street by symbols but the inns were particularly gaily bedecked. The nearest sported a black bottle and glass on a yellow background, the flag wriggling and snapping before the rising wind. Noise and warmth bustled out to meet them, bearing the smells of cooking and damp people. Lanterns blazing, the inn was three-quarters full already with traders keen to squander the fruits of a day's haggling for a convivial evening with those they had argued with so fiercely an hour before.

Over night the wind died and collapsed to the ground as heavy snow. Morning found traders all over the fair pushing mounds of snow from bellies in the canvas to land with solid thumps in sculptures of white. They shovelled and brushed until safe paths enticed early buyers towards open flaps and the goods within.

After a breakfast of herb sausages, Jebbin had no set tasks and donned his pack to explore the fair. He collected his staff after a moment's hesitation, convincing himself it was to aid his balance on the ice. Nith refused an invitation to join him, patting his own pack meaningfully, evidently intending to discharge his own duties without company.

Rubbing his hands to keep out the cold, staff thrust under one arm, Jebbin strode out briskly. He was acutely conscious that his wallet was light and wished for a few of Ygyrd's furs to sell. In this weather, Ygyrd's might be the busiest street of the fair. Except, he mused, the street of the weaponsmiths, if the rumours about the rousing of the Aelan tribes were true. He listened carefully to these tales, but there was no mention of any war leader called Garwaf, the name from the riddle, and he grew disenchanted.

He soon reached a ride running across all the streets and turned towards the city of Lana, first crossing the street of scrivenors. He remembered he was supposed to contact Narbez to give Rallor a message but he could not recall what Narbez traded and hoped for something to jog his memory. To chance upon the man himself would be too improbable.

As he paced onward, the number of people grew from isolated spectators to a trickle of idle wanderers to a throng that sometimes milled so thickly he could only elbow his way along with difficulty, past faces from every country, especially the dark-haired, flat-faced natives of Ael with their narrow eyes. He ticked off the streets of booksellers and masons and the street of curios, which he marked down for further investigation, and eventually reached the first street, nearest to Lana. It was the street of the weapon-smiths. Jebbin nodded to himself as he looked into the nearest marquee. A sign proclaimed 'Wensla, specialist in knives'. Jebbin studied ranks of knives and daggers clipped to a felted board in amazement at the range; chunky thick-bladed knives that might gralloch an elephant right down to the finest stiletto for a lady's hand. A thin man with a bent back and grey hair hunched over a vice, delicately chamfering the handle of a throwing knife. Jebbin was captivated by a gently curved dagger with a matt black grip and grey blade that reflected no gleam of light. An assassin's tool. Other blades were beautifully engraved with animals, motifs and runes or spotted with gems.

Without warning, Wensla spun round and sent his knife whirling through the air. Jebbin leapt back with a cry but the knife sped by to strike in the centre of a tent pole. The blade never quivered and the single eye of its haft glared at Jebbin contemptuously.

"Sorry to startle you," said Wensla. "It still ain't perfect and nothing less will do here." He plucked the knife from the pole and returned it to his vice. Jebbin deigned no reply and forced himself to a further nervous study of the daggers on display before marching out, reflecting that some merchants had the oddest means of attracting custom.

Between the street of the weapon-smiths and the city walls was a large area of folded rocks that formed a natural amphitheatre. Carved and improved with stands and awnings, many of the contests were held in its stone bowl. Jebbin bought a token for the first day of the wrestling on the morrow without knowing whether Bolan would be appearing, or indeed whether he had arrived at all. The clash of metal and sounds of cheering forced him to shout at the Aelan token seller, who seemed unhelpfully deaf and stupidly gave him insufficient change.

Jebbin lunched on the street of the masons. He sat in the pale sun munching bread and pickles washed down with a tangy beer and watched the relatively few customers discussing their needs with the masons and carvers. Of the two establishments opposite him, one dealt in large scale works and displayed diagrams of barbicans, bartizans and clerestories with examples of carved corbels and a section of ashlar - stone cut and worked until it filled together smoothly enough for a castle wall safe against climbers. The other showed little statues and advertised other figures and lilins within. Jebbin was reminded of the smiling bust on the grave in Farralei and lost himself in recollections until his meal was over.

Stamping warmth back into his feet, he moved off again, recrossing the street of the furriers and heading on towards the outer fringes through streets of spice merchants, provisioners, coopers, vintners and alesmen and on. He rested in an area designated for horse trading and found himself by an office for recruitment into the Belmenian army: an imposing marquee situated next to an inn offered free drinks to interested parties. While Jebbin watched, an insensible man was furtively thrown into a covered wagon by dark clad men with truncheons. Belmenian recruiters were not your friends even when they were buying the drinks. Especially when they were buying the drinks.

He trudged on past the street of agencies where sages and philosophers held court, religions attracted converts and spies awaited assignations. He passed the streets of potters, carpenters, wheelwrights, tailors and barbers and finally exited at the last street before the squalid ranks of hangers-on lurking at the extremities, the street of cobblers. He wondered why the cobblers should be last, then groaned at the wit of the organizer. He was tired and it was then too late to plod all the way back again. Several entrepreneurs had anticipated this eventuality and hired out little carts drawn on skis. Settling into one of these, something niggled at the back of his mind. He had the strongest feeling he had missed something vital. He did not enjoy the journey.

A night's sleep failed to elucidate the problem but he thrust it to the back of his mind with a conscious effort. Nith had not returned and Ygyrd was busy so Jebbin set out alone for the great amphitheatre to watch the early wrestling bouts and hope for an appearance from Bolan. He elected to leave his staff behind to make himself less conspicuous.

He reached his allotted place while the fine sand of the arena was still being swept by a thorn bush towed by a donkey. The stands were filling rapidly and Jebbin noticed that all the experienced visitors brought cushions and blankets. The bleak hardness of the stone bench had already made itself felt and he squirmed uncomfortably at the thought of a long day ahead. To his surprise, a pillow hit him on the head and he heard a chuckle from an overloaded merchant who was plopping himself down on a liberal supply of cushions.

"If you are wriggling like that already, you'd better borrow one of these or you'll drive us to distraction."

Jebbin looked round to see a party of three richly dressed men wrapping themselves in well. While his companions settled down, fighting a place for a large hamper carried by a lackey, the merchant who had thrown the pillow introduced himself as Wirral. He seemed delighted to be next to a tyro and cheerfully plunged into explanations of the few rules. He pointed out the silk-covered enclosure where the highest nobility reclined. Nammerlan, crown prince of Triva, and his family would be there today. A great supporter of wrestling, Nammerlan had provided the winner's purse of five thousand ryals and the Aelans had granted him the honour of presenting it himself. Jebbin was content to let Wirral prattle as the contests began and accepted a drink gratefully, hot tea spiced with citrus juice and heavily laced with alcohol. The tea, poured from a battered silver urn warmed by a lamp, fought back the cold seeping up from the stone and Jebbin wrapped his hands round a generous refill thankfully.

He found himself becoming involved with the wrestling and turned partisan when Kelebegi, King Orthogon's champion from Marigor, stepped into the arena to fight an Aelan supported by Wirral. The trader immediately offered a wager and Jebbin risked a ryal on his countryman. The two cheered and booed lustily at opposite moments during the fight. The Aelan seemed the stronger of the combatants but the experience and guile of Kelebegi won him the victory. Wirral paid up, moaning good-humouredly that he would be ruined before the day was out.

The next bout was a vicious affair between an ex-army Belmenian and Gartok, the colossus from Grimcairn in Torl. The Belmenian was fast and tough but the might of Gartok broke him and he was left bleeding on the sand, ribs crushed and splinters of bone protruding from his shin. Gartok, who had continued belabouring his opponent after victory was awarded, strode away with a final kick at his prostrate rival, ignoring the mutterings and reserved plaudits from most of the crowd who disliked such treatment of a brave competitor. As he left, several grey robed figures converged upon the motionless Belmenian.

"Who are they?" Jebbin enquired as the newcomers circumspectly approached the fallen warrior.

Wirral answered with disquiet in his tone, "The medical practice."

"Why are they so unpopular with the crowd? He sorely needs a doctor."

"Twice the pity he'll not be treated by one. These scurrilous creatures are aspirants to the Physicians Guild," Wirral explained as the still form was rolled onto a stretcher. "There are many accidents and injuries in these contests. Some victims are unable to pay the extortionate fees of the surgeons and healers. Therefore apprentices are on hand to tend the wounded for no fee, any debt considered discharged by the practice they afford the students, who must demonstrate competence before they are admitted to the Guild. These apprentices are universally feared for their horrendous errors but frequently the sufferer has little choice. Agreement for treatment may be tacit so if a patient is unable to communicate coherently in their language or even to speak at all," he jerked his head towards the Belmenian, "it is assumed consent would be given and the students launch into their endeavours."

Wirral shook his head grimly. "Often enough, friends or religious groups bring reputable aid only to find the medical practice has beaten them to it. It seems a ghoulish business but I suppose there is truth in the slogan of the apprentices that medical practice makes perfect physicians."

The next contestant was introduced as Brethanqui from the Sultanate of O-Ram. A giant of a man, hair pomaded, stepped forward and bowed. He was dressed in no more than a rich purple loincloth with gold trimmings and copious body oil. Body gleaming, he postured to the crowd, roars of approval sounded for his mighty musculature and applause clattered raggedly round as Brethanqui slashed a scissoring kick through the air. He faced the silken enclosure and flexed his muscles once more.

Almost unnoticed in the din, his announcement unheard, another figure plodded onto the sand. Jebbin's exhilaration collapsed like a burst bladder as he recognised Bolan. Brethanqui would have over-topped Orrolui by a head; he dwarfed Bolan.

Beside Jebbin, Wirral noticed Bolan's arrival and groaned. "Errela! Why has this happened now? Jebbin, my friend, in every games the draw throws up some appalling mismatches. They should call this a no contest."

Jebbin nodded his head, watching dismally as Brethanqui's

massive form moved lightly round Bolan with dancing steps, feinting and weaving. Bolan turned slowly to keep facing the giant and waited patiently when Brethanqui broke away to play the crowd again, preening before the enclosure.

"I tell you, I'll lose another wager here," went on Wirral morosely. "I'd have liked to have seen more of Brethanqui."

"Brethanqui? You think Bolan can win against him?"

Wirral shrugged. "Maybe the big lad will get lucky. Otherwise..." he shook his head.

"I hope Bolan makes it. He's a friend of mine."

"Really? Many know him but he has few friends, I hear. A frustrated man - and Brethanqui's capering to the enclosure won't endear him to Bolan."

Jebbin sat back, startled by the truth of Wirral's words. He knew Bolan, but how little he knew of Bolan.

Wirral was still talking. "Did you meet him on the road, then?"

"No, in jail actually," replied Jebbin absently and immediately cursed himself for his foolishness.

Wirral chuckled. "Yes, I heard about that. Amazing thing."

They were interrupted as Wirral's neighbour leaned across him and darted questions at Jebbin. "You were there? Was it true?"

Wirral smoothly covered Jebbin's confusion and his colleague's rudeness. "Ah, may I introduce you? Master Jebbin, this is one of my partners, Biwa. He's an unconscionable meddler, I warn you!"

"Was it true?" demanded Biwa, "Did someone use a spell on Bolan?"

"Oh that. It can only have been trickery, surely."

"But it did happen then? A spell with no staff?" pressed Biwa.

"I was in a different cell."

"But you said you met him there!"

"Yes, that's right," said Jebbin blandly, regaining his equanimity. "But it was overcrowded and I was moved before the incident."

Biwa gazed fixedly at Jebbin another moment, then relaxed and drew his blankets up, murmuring, "Yes, it was said to be crowded. Well."

Jebbin looked back to the fight. While Wirral shook his head over the error, Brethanqui was taunting Bolan, trying to force an ill-considered attack.

"Come on, toad. It's no good being afraid of me. The only way out of this stadium for you is on the stretcher of the practice - unless you care to submit now!"

Bolan was unmoved. Beside Brethanqui's fluid grace, his slow pivoting seemed as clumsy as an ox.

"Toad man," sneered Brethanqui. "You don't know how to treat a woman; don't you know how to deal with a man either? No wonder she won't look at you! Maybe if she kisses you, you'll turn into a prince!" He laughed warily but Bolan's steady gaze never faltered. Brethanqui whirled again, shadow boxing, then stamped to a halt with rage in his eyes.

"You can't stare me out like a stoat with a rabbit!"

"Don't be a rabbit, then," said Bolan.

Brethanqui attacked with breathtaking speed, lashing a chop at Bolan's neck and darting back. Bolan merely lifted slightly on the balls of his feet and took the blow on his chest. The smack resounded in the cold air but Bolan's stance never wavered. In a rage, Brethanqui showered chops and punches at Bolan, then leapt at him. Bolan methodically blocked the strikes and swayed out of the way as Brethanqui sailed over him. Then Bolan balled his right fist and drew his arm back slowly as though winding back an arbalest. As Bolan moved forward, Brethanqui met him, committed to the block and counter. Instead of the expected punch, Bolan blasted his right leg out to impact crushingly on the inside of Brethanqui's knee. As the huge man staggered, Bolan's left fist cracked him on the side of the jaw and Brethanqui went flat.

"Submit?" enquired Bolan.

Brethanqui shuddered and groped his way to his hands and knees.

"Yield?" Bolan asked again, sounding disinterested.

Brethanqui shook his head desperately, trying to force his gigantic muscles to obey him. He clawed downward for a handful of the sand. Bolan had seen that done in a hundred fights and kicked the hand open. Reaching out, he sank one hand into Brethanqui's throat and, with power that drew a gasp from all round the amphitheatre, raised the giant like a puppet. He grabbed the loincloth and lifted Brethanqui clear above his head before bringing him smashing down. Bolan dropped to one knee as he did so. Brethanqui landed belly first on Bolan's raised knee and his face thudded into the sand. He rolled limply to the ground and lay still. Bolan moved over and checked that he was still breathing. Sending back the medical practice with a glance, he waved forward two other warriors to help with the fallen before raising his arms to acknowledge the cheering spectators. He bowed low towards the enclosure, paused for an instant with his eyes burning towards it, then trudged away.

"Bolan does it every time. Moves like a carthorse until they think he is one - then kicks them like a carthorse!" Wirral was crying hoarsely. "Hoisted him like a sack of flour! Well, he asked for it - and got it!"

"Wirral, what's that all about? What you said about a woman and the enclosure?"

Wirral looked at him quizzically. "You do know why Bolan was in jail, don't you?"

"No, he never said. And I never asked." Jebbin was aware of, and ignored, a sidelong look from Biwa.

"I don't suppose you had time for idle chitchat in prison, even if Bolan would have spoken of it. Still," Wirral leant forward; his eyes alight with the promise of gossip, "Bolan is a man in love. The object of his affections is in that enclosure beside Nammerlan, which is why Brethanqui, who considers himself utterly admirable, especially in the eyes of women, was unwise to prance before it. The love is doubtless unrequited for Bolan will be the first to admit that he's not a handsome man and she is Rhesa; Rhesa the lovely, Rhesa the daughter of Nammerlan, Crown Prince of Triva! Yet she inspires her devotee. She awarded the victor's wreath in Mellu and Bolan won it. Defeated even Hophni! Now there was a rare bout. At the start...."

"Yes, but why was Bolan jailed by Tremenion?"

"That was after his victory at Mellu. Bolan was passing through, er, yes Talnavor, thank you Biwa, and the local bullyboy picked a fight with him. That often happens, for if a thug can thrash some noted champion the way may be open to training and the gladiatorial circuit. Bolan is proof against insults; he's heard them all and better before. However, this fool persisted, vilifying Rhesa and even defiling a picture of her. Bolan hit him. Only once, I believe, but he died of that blow. All testified that Bolan had been sorely provoked and even struck but Lord Tremenion deemed that a trained warrior should have been able to control the strength of his arm and since a man was dead he was obligated to detain Bolan so that justice was seen to be done."

"You are incredibly well informed."

"As a confidant of Biwa, I am indeed well informed," admitted Wirral cheerfully.

"And what of Rhesa?"

"I know of nothing to her detriment," Wirral sounded regretful, "but I doubt Bolan has a future of connubial bliss with a Prince's daughter."

"What of the king?" Jebbin asked absently, his mind filled with matters more important than the books at home.

"The king is Inchiron of Algolia but the real power in Algolia resides in Lord Reinbeck's Comminators and Inspectors. Nammerlan of Triva may be theoretically subservient to Algolia but he maintains his own troops where Inchiron has only a few retainers. I could tell you much about Algolia's endless paperwork and Reinbeck's plottings but I suspect you've lost interest."

Jebbin was sitting staring at another bout with vacant eyes, his mouth open in a slight grin. His fists were clenched and excitement welled out of him in palpable waves. "Lilins!" he breathed. "By the Lady, the mason's lilins are in the riddle!" He jerked round when Wirral stopped talking and apologised for his inattention. "I'm sorry but I have just realised how to solve a puzzle. Ha!" he cried, smacking his fist against his thigh. "Pick your favourite of those two slugging it out down there and I've got two ryals on the other one!"

"You must be pleased," commented Wirral drily, "but before you change your mind, my money's on the fellow in blue."

Jebbin hugged his thought to his chest and bellowed encouragement at the fighters to relieve his tension. Eventually, the wrestler in blue fell to his knees and submitted. Wirral had to pay up again and complained with mock bitterness about beginner's luck for the bout had gone against all the rankings. Jebbin chuckled unsympathetically and pocketed the coins.

"Wirral, I must see Bolan. Would that be possible?"

"Surely. There'll be apartments set aside for all the wrestlers who get through the first round. Ask directions at Lana gate, but if Bolan doesn't wish to see you, there'll be no gaining admittance."

"Thanks Wirral, thank you for everything. I must go."

"Hoi, you can't go now, three of my ryals jingling in your pocket!"

"There'll be another time for wagering. May I offer them back to you in recompense for the drink and advice?"

"Don't you dare insult me so," laughed the merchant. "Master Jebbin, you will never be a rich man. Fare you well."

Jebbin hastened away, aware that Biwa watched him go with speculations dancing in his eyes. Jebbin wormed his way from the cramped amphitheatre with difficulty he scarcely noticed, being borne on the wings of elation. Outside, he bought an expensive pie stuffed with quail breasts and munched it happily on the way to Lana Gate.

It took him so long to persuade the guards to admit him and give directions to the barracks that he might as well have been in Algolia. He hurried through ice-crisp streets, past thick-walled houses, the faint acridity of smoke tickling his frosted nostrils. More, and he fancied larger, guards barred the entrance to the wrestlers' quarters and it took more explaining and waiting, stamping in the cold, before he was permitted to enter. Bolan was already in his room. He greeted Jebbin heavily and sat down beside a glass of viscous, brown fluid which he regarded unfavourably.

"Well, mission accomplished and puzzle solved, lad? Still got that Gesgarian with you?"

"Mission a total failure and I parted from Orrolui after he nearly killed me."

Bolan harrumphed without surprise. He stirred the glass

round and round gloomily then dragged himself up with an explosive sigh.

"Won't do at all. Hardly a welcome for a friend. Hey, a bottle and glass, if you'd be so kind!" he bawled at a passing lackey after opening his door. "Now, you have some telling to do."

"That can wait. I watched you fight today."

"Oh," said Bolan and collapsed back into his chair.

"Can I help with whatever's wrong?" asked Jebbin quietly.

"No, laddie, thanks. Don't like the opening rounds, that's all. Silly oaf today; no idea."

The lackey knocked on the door, brought in a bottle of wine accompanied by a single glass and scuttled off again.

"Won't you have a drink?"

"No. Have this," replied Bolan, indicating the repellent contents of the vessel before him with disgust. "Raw liver and eggs and Balgrim knows what else. Anyway, did you find Hiraeth? Know where he is."

"Is it Rhesa?" Jebbin asked softly.

"Ah. Know about that, then."

"Bolan, she's the daughter of the crown prince."

Bolan faced him squarely and spoke with his old irrefragable dignity. "Don't speak of the impossibility of queens marrying paupers or offer wise words to forget her. You think I have not tried? Like a loon, have stared in the glass and called her face to appear and talk to me but it does not. In desperation I've fought her to quit my heart but she will not. No part of any day passes without her in my mind. Every face I see, every lock of hair, catches at me with an echo of her."

He turned away with a deep sigh, then downed the drink in three gulps, banging the glass back on the table, and spoke to the wall. "She signalled to me today. My love is not blind, for she is lovely beyond measure. But sadly her love is not blind either and as Brethanqui remarked so loudly today, I'm more like a toad than a man. Yet she tried to convey something. No foolish token of love but a sign of some need. Don't know what. Brethanqui displayed before her, yet she signalled to me. Furtively, from behind her father. But for what?"

Jebbin rested his hand on the wrestler's massive shoulder and swallowed his own excitement over the riddle. "We'll know soon enough, I feel it in my bones. And whatever it is, if I may help in any way, I will. May I stay?"

"No good at this sort of thing. Be glad to have your back to mine." Bolan had his chin stuck out and his head hunched. He looked as though he were about to tackle the Belmenian cavalry single-handed and Jebbin had the feeling he would prefer to do so.

In the event, it was the evening before they heard anything. For most of the time they sat in silence; Bolan nervously knitting macramé patterns in the muscles of his back, Jebbin quietly pondering his solution to the riddle, how best to go about it and what Hiraeth would say. The knock on the door startled them both.

"Yes," called Bolan, tensing sharply.

A guard opened the door and addressed Bolan without seeing Jebbin, "Two others asking to see you, sir. Odd sorts. One said to tell you he was disturbed. His name is Heras."

"Don't recall anyone with that name," rumbled Bolan but Jebbin interrupted him.

"We will see them. Please show them in."

The guard looked round at him in surprise, then, rather doubtfully, back to Bolan for confirmation. When the wrestler nodded, the guard backed out and closed the door. Bolan looked a question at Jebbin.

"He said he was disturbed. If you disturb the letters of Heras, you could get Rhesa."

"Balgrim's beard," muttered Bolan uncomfortably, wiping his hands on his thighs. "What does she think I am?"

When the next knocking sounded, Bolan was standing before the door with his arms held stiffly at his sides. Jebbin was still sitting quietly in his corner.

"Yes," Bolan uttered, as though accepting death.

Two people stepped smartly into the room and closed the door behind them with evident relief. The first was a man with cropped, greying hair and a receding chin; his robes seemed ill fitting. Bolan sensed the fear inside him and unconsciously moved into the wrestler's crouch. Then the second figure drew the hood from her face and Bolan rocked back onto his heels, the colour draining from his face. Rhesa smiled at him nervously and then spotted Jebbin. She clutched at something under her robes but spoke steadily in a low, rich voice.

"Who are you?"

Before Jebbin could reply, Bolan spoke for him, "Someone to trust absolutely."

"Then we are both well served. This is a retainer of my father's but he has always aided me unstintingly."

Jebbin looked at her wonderingly while she was speaking. Her brown hair was thick and wavy, lustrous with red glimmers. Wide-spaced eyes were clear and large and warm. With her perfect skin and teeth it was a face of renown. But her chin was strong and she held herself proudly: she was more than her face would tell.

"Bolan, please do not think badly of me. I have heard of the way... that you...."

"That I love you, my lady. It is so." His tone reverberated with strength and steadfastness.

"This is very hard for me, Bolan. I do not know you well. I cannot say I love you. I do admire you. Please don't drop your eyes. What I say is true but I do not wish there to be any misunderstanding between us. Neither do I want to trade on your love for me. You must know that I have been promised to another."

"Yes?" prompted Bolan quietly, his voice empty and hollow.

"This other is Matico, the son of the chief of the Snow Leopards, one of the foremost tribes of Ael. It seems to us of Triva that the tribes of Ael are being raised and driven towards war and conquest. We guess that at the centre of this lies Lykos, a ruler dwelling in a great fortress high on the upland plain. He has imprisoned Matico and holds him to ensure the co-operation of the Snow Leopards. Matico, who is fiery and reckless, openly urged rejection of Lykos' overtures and his father sought external alliances. To marry into the royal house of Triva seemed expedient to them and my father sought a great trading coup. But now Matico is held under threat of death and my own future looks bleak.

"If the marriage goes ahead, Triva will also be bound to Lykos, for I will be forced to join Matico in captivity. If we back out of the marriage contract we lose great face and abandon poor Matico to be executed by Lykos, thus earning us the enmity of the Leopards. Yet the status quo leaves us both enthralled and Lykos might even marry me to another to further his own designs once I am in his power."

She paused, pink spots of colour blossoming on her cheeks. "Ah, Bolan, I can make no claim but we are in such peril. The house of Nammerlan has troops but we cannot storm through all Ael: the Snow Leopards cannot aid us and risk the life of their chief's only son.

"There are even those who suggest we hire an agent to murder Matico in his cell and buy us release from this contract but that price is too high and no good can come of such an action. We have perhaps a month, little longer, before we must decide. This situation cannot continue, so either I must marry and Triva will fall under the yoke of this grasping tyrant, or my father must break his word, humiliating Triva and destroying the alliance.

"There is no honourable way except marriage for Triva and no chance of happiness for one poor pawn in this game." Rhesa fell to her knees and lifted her face to Bolan, her great eyes filled with unshed tears and desperate hope.

"Bolan, I beg of you, can you help me?"

"Rise, my lady, please," cried Bolan, pulling her upright and allowing her to sink into a chair. He turned to Jebbin with granite determination etched on every line of his frame. "What say you of this business?"

"This fits with other things I've heard. Ael is being raised, but are you sure this leader is Lykos? Have you heard of Garwaf?"

"It is Lykos. The other name means nothing to me."

"You murder an infant hope. Nevertheless, we know who rouses Ael but not their target: the leas of Marigor, riches of Shekkem, trade routes of Triva or the free lands on the margins of the declining Belmenian Empire could all be attractive. Of Matico, the Snow Leopards will dare nothing that might endanger his life and Triva cannot be associated with any underhand action, where it risks the blame as well as disgrace and loss of the alliance. Hence the secrecy tonight."

Here Rhesa nodded assent, biting her lip, and added, "Even my father does not know I'm here. I know in my heart he must decide, however reluctantly, to honour his word and submit to the wedding in Lykos' louring castle. I do not wish it," she finished in a tiny voice.

"However," continued Jebbin, "if Matico could be released without any hint to implicate Triva in the event of failure, then the Leopards would be freed with him and the chief and the crown prince would be masters of their own fates. Some campaign might then be mounted to stop Lykos from this incitement to war."

Rhesa's gaze never wavered from Bolan's face, her eyes radiant with hope and supplication.

"Then it shall be done, if it lies within my power," Bolan stated solemnly. His eyes lost in Rhesa's, he continued, "My lady, do not consider you are compromised by coming to me in this way. Neither are you beholden. I hear you; you are promised to another. But when you look to Bolan for a friend, you do not look in vain. I have spoken."

Rhesa flung her arms about him, then stood back, her poise regal but her cheeks glistening with the overspill of emotion. "By the great god Rashen-Akru, you are a greater man than I could have dreamed. There is not enough in Triva to thank you. Grant me one last boon, I pray you." She drew the only ring she wore from her right hand and held it out to him. "Keep this with you. It is but a little thing with no power, save that of my love."

At that last, both her voice and hand shook as she held out the ring. As Bolan's thick, scarred fingers gently held its other side, the ring gleamed in a strangely bright reflection of the lamplight.

"Do not risk yourself too much. I don't think I could bear.... May the Lady keep you," she whispered and fled from the room with her retainer close behind her.

Bolan stood stock still holding her ring as though he had been struck blind.

Solution

Jebbin sat with Hiraeth at the inn on the street of the masons where he had lunched on his first excursion into the fair a week previously. The snow was deeper and the cold more intense but the sun shone, igniting fires of ice all about them and creating glaciers of light on each sloping roof. Jebbin's empty mug and plate were limned with brightness. Steam that had once plumed like smoke still lazily curled from a half-eaten dish of savoury pancakes topped with a fiery sauce in front of Hiraeth. The bard shook his head, swapped the paper he had been studying for his spoon and attacked the pancakes with renewed hunger. Jebbin swept up the line he had written from Echoheniel's verse and then carelessly tossed it back onto the table to disguise its value from any observer.

"The rest of the verse is all like that? And you've solved it here?" demanded Hiraeth, his voice indistinct behind a mouthful of pancake. "Bolan told me you said the answer could only be found at Lana Fair. I should've thought the street of agencies more likely to supply your needs than this place."

"Some of the sages there might have knowledge to unwrap it but any such would surely know of Echoheniel and my problems would increase rather than the reverse if they began meddling.

Any yet there is nowhere but Lana Fair where all the people I need could be assembled. Look around you."

"I have peered – 'scuse me -" Hiraeth scooped sauce from his chin with the spoon, "round and round at your strange insistence until my eyes are near bursting and all I've seen are flint-handed masons and an innkeeper who might very well be encouraged to fetch us a drop more ale."

Jebbin laughed and dealt with the order.

"In any case, Bolan has told me of his recent affairs and that you are going up country with him in a week. What then all your solvings?"

Jebbin was not surprised that Hiraeth knew this. Everyone talked to the bard. "I am. And I must have done all I can by then."

"I suppose you'll explain eventually. And as for your solution, I give up."

"Very well. Read that little sign over the street," Jebbin waved his replenished mug towards the tent of the statues.

Hiraeth read it through, shrugged, then jerked violently. "Lilins!" he cried in an explosive whisper, snatching up the paper again. "Yes, "excind fallal lilin". So he must know what a lilin is."

"He did. And so do I now - if not a fallal one."

"Brilliant!"

"Hardly. It was happenstance that I sat here and then I nearly missed it. You cannot tell the meaning from the context but sometimes you can tell what the subject is. For example, the first line says a castle is on something. It might have been a mountain, lakeside or volcano but it had to be a description of where the castle was and a geographer might know the term used. We were a bit lucky with Erridarch, but still.

"And since then, I've had more luck. The riddle mentions a portal, so I've been trying to find what a proceleusmatic one might be. That remains unanswered but the carpenter was able to tell me straight off that a soffit is part of a lacunar."

"How helpful," murmured Hiraeth.

"It's the underside of an architrave."

"Who was this, Echoheniel's grandfather?"

"Might as well have been but he did explain it to me. He also said a kerf is the mark made by a saw cut. After that I didn't dare question him further but on the same street I found a woman who had actually made an aumbry, a little cupboard."

"And these are all things in the riddle, I suppose. Can I give you a word of warning? While you're wandering round the fair making yourself the subject of endless speculations, avoid almshouses."

"Why?"

"They're all run by the Thieves' Guild. You should try harder to be inconspicuous."

"I'd forgotten the thieves and hoped they might have forgotten me."

"I know they have not. Everywhere there are rumours of a mage without a staff and thieves offer gold for something more tangible."

They sat in silence awhile, Jebbin regretting errors and events along the way. Suddenly Hiraeth reverted to an earlier topic.

"Are you sure you're in the right place? Is this plain western enough? It's the easternmost of the ones Erridarch mentioned."

"My guess is that it is here. We know there's an element of disorder in these verses; words misplaced or having their most abstruse meanings. I think I'll find what I seek at the western end of the upland plain of Ael.

"But more; it's been said that these verses come to light at opportune moments. I sense these strands will all lead to the same place. Surely Lykos must be the angekkok or sorcerer of the riddle. If there is any use in solving the riddle now, surely it must be stopping Lykos from his schemes of raising the tribes of Ael for conquest. Lykos rules a forbidding castle high on the plain - maybe Bolan and I seek the same place and perhaps the Garwaf name Echoheniel mentions is one used long ago."

"Are you trying to convince yourself? There is revolt in O-Ram and who knows what happens on the far plains beyond Jerondst. I wish you luck."

"Can you help with my search?"

Hiraeth made a rueful face. "Sorry, but I'm going to be busy until you leave. There are the major festivals of song coming up, prizes and renown for bards. I'll get you a token, if you like." After a pause, the bard cocked a quizzical eye at Jebbin and said, "Bolan's told me what he's doing and why. Ah, Bolan and Rhesa. He'd do anything for her. You know, he once told me that he'd seen her in a gown of ivory and charcoal and he'd never seen such glowing colours? I'm amazed he isn't hurrying off already - except that you advised him to wait. Is that just for your convenience?"

"Partly perhaps, but if Bolan decamped in the middle of the wrestling, there would be talk. Many know of his association with Rhesa; her dilemma is not secret and the truth might be guessed. Furthermore, if it were the same castle, I think the riddle may provide a route inside. If only it is. My heart is sure it's one and the same but the fear I'm searching the wrong paramo gnaws at me. Why's no one heard of Garwaf, if he's the chieftan of this fortress?

"Garwaf? I've heard the name, some old story," said the bard slowly. "Something about a wolf."

"Ha. We know we look for a castle, not some wolf-den in the mountains."

"That's it! Garwaf and Lykos - they both mean Wolf! Do you remember the Song of the Wolf? Lykos getting Asharne of the

Condor tribe to start rousing all Ael? You're putting your head into the wolf's lair."

"Really? By the Lady, it is true then. It must be! Still, if, if, if it's the same, we'll both be served by the company of the other."

"All right," chuckled Hiraeth, "but the wrestling won't have finished in a week, will it?"

"Not entirely but this championship sponsored by Nammer-lan will have ended. The next will be fought for a belt said to be the image of that worn by Baelar of Carnen. If all goes well, we may even be back in time for that."

"Well, I must hurry off, I have a trio to arrange for the festival," cried Hiraeth, jumping up after squinting at the sun. "Try to listen to it. I'll send the token to Ygyrd's. Fare you well, Master Jebbin!" he called over his shoulder as he hastened away.

Jebbin sat for a while, ruminatively tucking the line of verse back into his new shirt, bought with Wirral's coins. A ragged urchin sitting just off the snow under an edge of the awning stared intently at him with a frown on his face after Hiraeth's valediction. Suddenly, the lad's face cleared with an avaricious if gap-toothed smile. He scrabbled to his feet and pattered off with bare feet on the packed snow.

Jebbin strode along the street of the curios, delighted with his afternoon's work. It was that dead time of early evening after most of the traders had closed their flaps to tidy their wares and sort the day's takings but before the light and bustle of the inns took over the night of Lana fair. The lucent glimmer that only comes with snow in the mountains lent a soft halo to the tent streets. But the light was deceptive, details were blurred and motionless figures could not be seen.

Jebbin had lost his morning drifting through more books than he thought existed: rambling vanities of forgotten lords; the distillation of wisdom from ancient sages, written in crabbed writing on cracked vellum; bestiaries and natural histories, glow-ingly illustrated; legends from other lands; details of campaigns and battles, armies and conquests; the lucubrations of philoso-phers, lovingly bound in leather and gold and never read; iron-bound grimoires clutching spells and lore behind heavy locks, the keys long mislaid or destroyed, challenging anyone to risk their curses for hidden magic; poems and plays well-thumbed or pristine. Jebbin wafted through the atmosphere of preserv-ative oils, dust and mould until the trader ushered him out at lunchtime. Lost passages swam before his eyes as he ate a cone of diced chicken in a honey and lemon glaze and a triangular loaf, his eyes vacant.

On the street of curios he had found a trader advertising his speciality in bibelots and gewgaws. Astonished, Jebbin had en-tered an emporium of bric-a-brac. Phials of fluids without labels, pictures of unnamed scenes and untitled portraits, old tools, carvings, idols and keepsakes. When he expressed interest, the trader pointed out what he hoped were salient items such as a contraption of wooden flaps and silver wire, use unknown, and a strange box, weighted with vertical plates of lead. He proudly demonstrated a pair of crude effigies, aggressively sexed, saying they were xoana from Tachenland where the little tribesmen be-lieved they had fallen from the skies. Jebbin had grinned euphor-ically, his insides constricted with delight, for a cargo of bibelots should gain access to the castle. He promised the trader he would purchase a whole consignment, stepped out onto the darkling street and almost trotted for home. Rubbing his hands in excite-ment, he paid no heed to the scruffy child who sped away in front of him.

Despite his preoccupation, when the street was virtually de-serted and a woman with wild, knotted hair changed course to intersect with his own path, he was immediately alert. When Jebbin stopped, the woman also halted. She threw back her cloak to reveal a short staff, carved and potent. Her left arm was covered with open sores which she picked at with long nails. Jebbin glanced behind him. Three men with daggers and coshes were spaced across the road, their faces wary and expectant. A fourth was slipping coins to the urchin.

The tendrils of a skrying spell wreathed about Jebbin but he sucked *sear* from a fingernail and flung them back with a mind shout. The woman gripped her staff more firmly.

"Yes," she said, "it's him."

Jebbin heard movement and looked behind him again but the men were backing away cautiously. He understood then that the Guild had both found him and hired suitable aid against him. They were learning fast, he thought grimly, and he had no option but to teach them more.

"I'm Hamaga. I like jellyfish. But it's going to kill you," the woman said, her eyes rolling.

"The last few magi mustn't fight at the behest of thieves," said Jebbin.

A voice from behind Jebbin cut across him. "Get on with it, woman. Let's see which of you can hurt yourself the most."

Hamaga shrugged. "I've had a better offer than that. I invoke the Mage's Duel." With a horrible laugh, she shook long strands of white over the sores on her arm and started shivering. Her breath hissed over her teeth as she began to chant the spell.

Fumbling a full four minims of *sear* into his nose, Jebbin felt someone had hammered a tent peg into his nostril. His whole head blazed with blinding light. Even as he forced his watering eyes open, Hamaga whirled her staff and spurted its power at Jebbin. He ground out the spell of the Mage's Duel and hurled his pain back at her. Energies collided and his green fog fought a seething cloud of grey, annhiliating each other. When the green was all consumed, the remaining grey surged into him, grinding a dull ache through his frame, a sickness that would blot the bright blade of *sear*. He fell to his knees and gasped for air. Hamaga gave a humourless grunt of laughter and signalled success to the thieves. She readied her staff once more.

At that moment, the flap to one of the tents was wrenched aside and a crumple-faced trader peered crossly out at the scene. One of the thieves stepped across to him with an enquiring look. A twist of his wrist flicked a dagger into his hand. Without a word, the trader moved backwards and quietly hooked up the tent flap again.

Jebbin felt blurred and empty. His last ball of *sear* had been insufficient and he dared not try even that much again. Taking half as much, the pain still roared across his face like steam but it lacked focus for energy. He was dangerously close to being Numbed. Another touch of Hamaga's grey cloud would finish him. He could control just enough pain to launch the Gesgarian disruption spell at Hamaga's staff. The woman wrestled fiercely to counter his spell, power leaping in shuddering arcs round her staff. Jebbin regained his feet and took stilted steps towards her, concentration on his spell lining his forehead as he searched for the harmonic frequency. Hamaga was a stronger mage but this spell was foreign to her and Jebbin's theurgy wormed deeper beneath her defences until her staff pulsed and bulged wildly in her hands. The wood blistered, then shivered into splinters. Hamaga fell back with a cry, her powers reft from her. Jebbin sprinted away from the surprised thieves. Mouthing curses at the woman, they sped after him.

Jebbin fled with no spells left to battle four men close behind him. Although at least one was gaining on him, he dared not look round but darted for a marquee flap which showed a chink of light. Skidding and flailing his arms, he charged through the canvas and found himself surrounded by rocks. There were great round stones from Torl that sound like a bell when struck, glittering geodes and rocks showing imprints of the gods. Of more importance to Jebbin was a leathery-skinned man with sandy hair who shouted in alarm and reached for a ready-cocked crossbow. Jebbin dived flat behind a table of amethysts and scrabbled onward. The first of the thieves ripped the flap aside and glared about him, knife in hand. The crossbow bolt took him in the stomach and pinned him to a wooden upright of the marquee. The thief's knife was already in the air and the trader ducked as the blade sliced his cheek. The other thieves arrived, the first trying to wrench out the bolt. The leader waved the others on impatiently as Jebbin wriggled through a hole he had hacked in the back of the marquee.

"Go! Go! If he gets out of sight in a tent, kill everyone in it. He may be able to change his face. Get help if you can. Move!"

On Jebbin ran, unaware how many were left to pursue him. On the street, the few folk abroad pointedly ignored both him and the panting figures behind him. Jebbin was sure that once again they were reducing his lead and abandoned his hope of reaching the strength of Ygyrd and his defences. In desperation, he flung himself beneath a wagon and rolled into a different street, squeezed between two more marquees and so struggled from street to street, pulling anything loose into the path of his pursuers. The thieves tripped and swore but they were lean and agile and still drew on.

Finding a tent still open, Jebbin pelted through it. Towering pillars of confectionary rose about him; coloured sculptures of icing; sailing ships of sugar strands, each net and sail carefully constructed; perfect blooms and sprays of flowers, each tiny petal edible. Gasping, Jebbin scuttled under a trestle, scrabbled beneath a loose awning and so out into the street once more. As he went, his foot knocked the leg off a small table supporting a fairy castle of gleaming sugar. Slowly, the edifice toppled over and smashed down on the thieves.

Jebbin rolled out near five ruffians standing idly in a group and loped away. He could hear furious squawkings from the tent and cries of pain. Resting his hands on his knees and panting through a grimace, he spared a moment to glance behind and saw one of his pursuers with his head and shoulders protruding from the bottom of the marquee. He was thrashing madly but evidently somebody had hold of his feet and he could not break free. Jebbin allowed himself a smile but just as the thief was dragged backwards, he waved and called to the ruffians. Even as the canvas wiped him off the street, the other thieves faced Jebbin and started after him.

Horrified, Jebbin turned and goaded his quivering legs into flight once more but he could not hope to outrun the fresh thieves and they gained on him rapidly. Putting on a final spurt, he slashed his way into a new tent. He dived through a rack of flowering plants into a warm area. All about him, flowers wagged heavy heads in disapproval of the cold airs he had let in. He ran down an avenue of bright-leaved plants, past regularly spaced, glowing oil lamps. Above them, porous stones soaked in aromatic compounds steamed heady gases. Beside one of them, a small transparent box held a little scorpion. Ranged on the far walls were crates of bulbs, corms and rhizomes. Jebbin realised that the flowers themselves were merely demonstration stock advertising the real wares.

Then the thieves were outside the tent, one grunting as he crawled through the hole. Jebbin wiped sweat from his eyes and thumbed *sear*. The pain was hangover sour, flaring and stabbing in a queasy maelstrom. Almost vomiting, Jebbin fought for control. He stepped onto a patch of sweet, moist earth and cast the spell that had come upon him unawares on the hill above Felice. He felt his ragged gasping drift away into steady transpiration, his up-raised fingers drinking in the subtle glow of the lamps. The fumes that had been making his head spin swirled about him and supported him. The thieves were nothing: animals that came and went in a blink of time. He was barely aware of the sudden outcry as a searching hand brushed against a black body with a needle tail.

It was only a vegetative instant later that he forced the spell to waver knowing that the longer he spent in that form the more footling and evanescent would seem all his hurryings and strivings. He blinked slowly and descended creakily from the patch of soil. The lamps still burned but the oily stones were gone. He frowned owlishly at the nearest lamp for a moment, then straightened, becoming aware that there were several people in the marquee. His momentary panic dissolved when he recognised the folk as buyers congregated round the bulbs. He had no idea of the time but guessed that day was bright outside. The lamps would be the only light the plants received, since the frigid air of Lana was deadly for them. The cut Jebbin had made on entering was carefully patched and stitched.

Hurrying towards the exit, Jebbin found a small man blocking his path, almost shaking with fear but looking nonetheless determined.

"Yes?" Jebbin enquired in a sibilant voice, his brows crumpled.

"Er, my lord, you …. there should be a reckoning," the little trader stuttered, then stood still, gulping like a fish.

Jebbin looked at him crossly. "I have none of your plants."

"No, your eminence, but you did give me another for a while. I am not a man given to talk but…." he trailed off, his face turning grey.

Jebbin frowned darkly at him in perplexity but then laughed

shortly. "Of course, yes, you are perspicacious. You must forgive my presumption amongst your excellent foliage. What fee would you regard as suitable for a night's quiet lodging?" he asked, stressing the word quiet.

"Perhaps your lordship could spare a noble?" asked the trader, blushing in hot relief.

"You must be Trivan; nobles aren't legal currency elsewhere. Here angels are their equivalent and too little for your worth." Jebbin proffered a fistful of change and left while the little fellow simpered, clutching the coins in victory and perhaps rehearsing the tale for his grandchildren of how he had bested the magician of Lana in a duel of words.

When Jebbin next saw Bolan, the wrestler was in ebullient mood and had company. Jebbin was introduced to a man of slightly over his own height, with wiry hair, dappled with grey, and a broken nose set in a broad face. His chest was deep and his hand as hard as stone when Jebbin shook it but his face was suffused with mirth, eyes twinkling behind crinkled slits. Bolan introduced Hophni as the greatest wrestler of his time. Before Jebbin had entered he had heard the two of them giggling like schoolboys; it hardly fitted with his image of a champion. However, it seemed Hophni was not the only one not to live up to expectations.

"Ho now, Bolan, this little beanpole is really your master magician? I must mind my words or be hurled hence in a whirl of wizardry!" Hophni laughed with the calm assurance of one whose indomitability was proof against any assault he could imagine.

"I'll try and hold myself in check," said Jebbin dryly, piqued by Hophni's air of superiority, more so because he did feel inferior before the man's presence. Nevertheless, he found himself so naturally included in their bonhomie that his irritation rapidly faded and after an exchange of ribaldry he asked what they were planning, thus closeted together.

"We plot against this Gartok. He hasn't played by the unwritten rules," said Hophni, wagging a cautionary finger.

"I saw him fight a Belmenian. Not pretty."

"That's right. We have to put him out. Not fair on some of these boys," Hophni added with calm self-confidence.

"We're both in the last eight," Bolan said, "so's Gartok. Obviously don't know how the draw's going to come out and who'll face him but Hophni's been making a few suggestions on the best way of sorting him out."

Bolan and Hophni looked at each other and burst out laughing afresh. "And then," added Bolan, "after the final, Hophni's said he'll join us on our journey."

Jebbin's smile died an unnatural death as he turned a worried visage to Hophni. At the sight, the wrestlers collapsed in a round of guffaws.

"Enough, lad! By Balgrim, give you my oath that you have no cause to fear aught from mouth or hand of Hophni. This is cause for celebration!"

"Fine, then, for us, but why would you come?"

Hophni paused while he sat down, folded his arms so his massive forearms looked like a couple of badgers strapped across his chest and regarded Jebbin from half-closed eyes. "And what should I do after this contest? Loaf around here, suffering the visitations of every weaponsmith, hardly enjoying a mouthful of food lest the assassins have spiked it with a debilitating potion so some lord can win a bet against me? Listen to the bellicose ravings of the rabble-raisers in Ael? No. Bolan suggested I could have a little entertainment in your company. Would you deny me?"

Jebbin grinned and shrugged. "There are those I might wish to deny. There is something about you which makes me glad you're not one of them."

"Well spoken - in a wizardly sort of way," cried Hophni, smacking the tabletop with the flat of his hand. "And now that's settled, we can concentrate on crushing the beastly Gartok. There's a different matter I don't understand, Bolan," Hophni continued in a quieter tone. "You've heard of Ommak?"

Bolan shifted uneasily and nodded.

"Why isn't he here?"

Hophni's question fell into a well of troubled silence until Jebbin piped up, "Ommak? Who's he?"

"Gartok comes from Torl. Ommak is another monster from the same place: said to be twice the size and half as polite," Hophni said, scratching an ear reflectively. "The sort of story one normally laughs off but I've heard this one too often. Someone in Torl is practising arts best left to rot. But I'd also heard Ommak would be here."

"May yet come; best be glad he has not," Bolan put in gruffly.

Hophni sighed and turned to Jebbin. "Bolan said you pursue some darkling business of your own."

"What?" burst out Jebbin. "So much for secrecy!"

"Hold hard, lad," Bolan interjected in a warning voice. "Have vouched for Hophni."

Jebbin passed his hand over his eyes, making a deliberate effort to unclench his jaw muscles. "Yes, it's true. I search for the answer to a hidden riddle."

"And you seek your answers amid the timber merchants and hucksters, Bolan said. Have you thought of approaching the savants on Agencies? They might know something."

"A good deal too much! At the moment there are still a few in ignorance of my activities and I hope to keep it that way."

"Yes, well, you know your own affairs, I'm sure. I merely

wanted to know if this other matter will interfere with Bolan's mission?"

"It'll do no harm and if I'm right then I know how to get you into the castle. That's what I wanted to talk to Bolan about."

"Oh ho, a way in! Say on indeed."

Jebbin hesitated with a sidelong glance at Hophni. The wrestler steepled his fingers and gazed down through them at his feet, waiting patiently.

"Well." Jebbin cleared his throat and plunged into his story. "I'm almost certain that the riddle also leads me towards Lykos' castle, the Rokepike. If I'm wrong then the riddle will cease to have value to me except as a curiosity. If I'm right then the riddle tells me that the gerent - who must be Lykos himself -has an engoument for bibelots."

Jebbin felt a flicker of vengeful amusement watching Hophni trying not to look blank. "So we know that Lykos is a passionate collector of relics and ornamental knick-knacks. I've found a trader specialising in such oddities. I suggest we travel into the depths of Ael as merchants taking a consignment of these commodities to Lykos. That gives us a legitimate excuse to go up-country and, with luck, right into the fortress. Once inside, the riddle may provide further clues or it may only give directions for my quest, I don't know yet. At least we should be on the inside and that will give you a chance. What do you think?"

Bolan looked across at Hophni. "Told you. Sounds good. Is there some problem?"

"Beyond the fact that he may not be a collector, we know nothing of trading and may look like complete idiots," put in Hophni.

"Yes. Apart from the risk of attack from tribesmen because we are carrying goods and the usual perils of travel, there is a major drawback. We need to buy everything: wagon, horses or mules, provisions, the cargo itself, weapons, tack and tackle - the lot. And I have virtually no money."

"No problem," yawned Hophni. "How much do you want?"

"I don't know. Hundreds, perhaps thousands of ryals!"

"Right. When do you need it?"

Jebbin stared at Hophni in astonishment and found no reply.

"Money's nothing to us," Bolan said. "Have money in treasuries and strongboxes from here to Kathos. Forgotten where half of it is. Hophni has more. The money...." he shrugged eloquently, "it's the contest, the moves."

Hophni cut in. "There's a purse of five thousand ryals to the winner of this contest. How do you spend that sort of money? Some lose it to conmen, others give it to religious institutions, some just stuff it away. One thing is sure, those that spend it on high living don't win many more bouts."

"So why do you go through all the hurt then?"

"A magician asks why we put up with pain? That's rich! It's who we are, same as you. Occasionally the money comes in useful for helping out friends or buying favours. That's all. So, we'll provide the funds, you see to the necessary arrangements."

The subject dismissed, conversation turned to other matters. Jebbin stayed and lunched with them but then hurried away to consider their purchases, having agreed they should depart as soon as practicable after the final bout, assuming that one or other of them would be there.

That night, Jebbin dreamed. He floated through ancient woodland of gnarled trees covered with leafless strands of old-man's-beard. His presence sailed into a glade where the yellow light of the moon washed over a ruined tower, squat and crumpled. He passed through dead stone and sank into the depths beneath the tower. At first, he hung suspended in a sea of black but then a slow circle of light was drawn in the dark: a perfect figure of unwinking flame. A second circle was drawn outside the first and by their light he could see several forms seated cross-legged round the circles. In turn, each of the robed characters reached forward with an edged weapon and inscribed a glowing rune in the gap between the two rings. Jebbin found himself drifting widdershins round the circle. He saw faces he knew; black hair and blacker eyes; a bald head and broad teeth clenched in effort. None were aware of him but concentrated on their task.

When each had inscribed their rune, fire burst up beneath a black cauldron. Sulphur, laurel leaves, salt and camphor were thrown upon the flames from the four quarters. When the smoke cleared, a chant rose from the circle. Galbanum and mandrake were cast into the cauldron, already bubbling. From the eight points of the compass, a Gesgarian spoke and threw another item on the flames; liquor of black poppies, henbane, hemlock, coriander, myrrh, hellebore root, fennel and sandalwood. Fumes belched and coalesced above the seething cauldron. The chant grew more urgent, strident, as a creature grew above the fire. A heavy porcine head with savage tusks leered round, suddenly lunging one way. Blackness spilled from the cauldron and threatened to swamp the narrow fire of the circles. The seated figures lurched and poured their pain as power into the rings. Light flared and dominated.

The demon thrashed and roared, flinging handfuls of midnight at its concentric manacles. They wavered but they held, though the very flames beneath the cauldron turned black and deadly. The demon's initial strivings proved fruitless but cunning might yet serve its turn. It lowered its wicked head and revolved slowly. Then came a voice from amidst the summoners.

"I, Marachin of the Long Arm, command you to answer my questions!"

The demon raised massive arms and brought them smashing

down, splattering blackness towards Marachin. An answering blaze of light met the darkness and the concussion knocked Jebbin flying into wakefulness.

He started up, pale and hag-ridden. In the dimness of the tent he could just make out Ygyrd watching him impassively.

"All right now?" rumbled the fur trader in a voice that supported Jebbin like a rock foundation.

"Yes. Thanks. Things just aren't as easy as I had hoped."

"They never are," said Ygyrd.

After a quiet breakfast, Jebbin helped Ygyrd sort his dwindling stocks. The trader was chuckling over his profits and wondering what manner of goods he should be buying to trade back towards Gelavien.

"What I buy depends on which way I go and I'm in no hurry for a swift return. I hear nothing from Rulion except that it goes from chaos to disaster so maybe I'll leave the Golden Road at Numery, perhaps cut across northern O-Ram overland. But then there'll be Algolian taxes to pay, so I could sail down the Border river and thence to Armeen. Or then again take ship back through the Gaps to Tarass. And I still have a mind to trade out to Jerondst. Always wanted to see the place."

"I've no knowledge to offer. My road's shorter but even more doubtful," shrugged Jebbin while Ygyrd scratched his beard with crooked fingers, mulling over the map in his mind.

"I must decide soon. I'm getting cash-rich and depleted of goods. There'll be plenty of other fur dealers glad of this pitch. Another couple of days, then I must go a-buying and move on. What of you? Fancy a ride?"

"I wish I could, thanks, but I still have my other matters to conclude. A moment, though. I have to take a wagon of goods in through Ael. We don't have the least idea about the ways of merchants and we'll probably stick out like millers at a dance. You wouldn't consider a commission with us, would you? To have you with us would be a boon beyond measure! We're going in a couple of days. We'll buy everything you need and you can have the profits. What about it?"

"No traders on a trading mission? You're up to something a good deal more dangerous than travelling through Rulion. I'm a trader, not an army. I'll think about it."

"It's not the money to us. We could pay you in advance and you buy everything we need. Then..."

Ygyrd cut him off with a curt wave. "Money is not worth dying for. I said I'd think about it. I'll let you know tonight." And with that, Jebbin had to be content.

Jebbin was busy during those last few days. He even missed the remaining bouts of the wrestling. By a poor chance, Bolan was drawn against Hophni in the next bout. After a long and entertaining fight that drew the crowd into wild cheering, Hophni managed to pin Bolan for a count of five to win. Bolan was irritated with himself but the loss was no disgrace and he was the first to congratulate Hophni.

In the semi-final, Hophni was delighted to be drawn against Gartok. He was at his finest. Every attack the man from Torl attempted was neatly switched, its power turned back against him. Gartok's roars of rage turned to cries of pain and finally terror as the implacable Hophni took terrible revenge for all the promising wrestlers whose careers and bodies he had destroyed in his unchecked savagery. Hophni eventually tied Gartok into a cruel knot. Both his shoulders were dislocated and such was the agony of his position that he had to offer a humiliating submission. Hophni accepted curtly and left the medical practice to disentangle Gartok's wracked arms. They were unknowledgeable about such things but, judging by Gartok's screams, they were gaining much valuable experience. It was deemed unlikely that Gartok would wrestle again.

In the final itself, Hophni was up against one of his old rivals, Mason; a bull of a man from Azria who had learnt his trade in a hard school. Mason intended to win and was too well aware of Hophni's abilities to allow the few rules to discommode him. When they moved into the first trial hold, Mason raked his fingernails into Hophni's eyes, gouging blood. As Hophni jerked backwards, Mason kneed him in the groin and swung a mighty roundhouse punch to the side of Hophni's head. Heedless of the jeering of the crowd, disregarding even Nammerlan, standing at the edge of his box and shouting inaudibly, his face congested with rage, Mason pressed his advantage with lightning speed, dropping on the prone master with his full weight and trying to gain a rapid win by pinning him.

The meticulous, black-clad marshals were just raising the fourth flag in their count of five, unhurried by however much Azrian gold, when Mason was suddenly flung away in an explosion of power. Hophni rolled to his feet, wiping blood from his eyes. The Azrian must have known that his gambit had failed but he did not lack courage and immediately attacked. But when he charged in, he found himself hurled away by a perfectly executed arm roll. Again and again he closed for combat, racing or cautious, only to be thrown anew until he barely knew which way was up. Waiting for the perfect opening, Hophni stalked Mason as he reeled about the arena. Suddenly Hophni pounced in an acrobatic move and Mason was pinned. The victor's wreath was Hophni's.

Although this was Jebbin's final day, and that only granted him when Bolan and Hophni had both been summoned to a final ceremony with Nammerlan, he determined not to miss the bardic contest; or at least not Hiraeth's contribution. He had made little progress on the riddle recently. The words "don yataghan" appeared and he had assumed that the yataghan must be some sort of clothing or armour which had to be worn but all in vain were his researches amid the clothiers, outfitters and armourers, although one of the latter thought she had heard the word. She had, not unreasonably, asked Jebbin in what context he had come across it and he had brushed the matter aside with assumed nonchalance. He hoped that what he knew would prove sufficient in the fortress.

He set out early under a leaden sky, dead and unresponsive to the scourging wind. Ygyrd's cloak pressed against his back and legs and flapped before him. He pulled it tighter about him and struck out for the arena. There were far more people about than he would have predicted and many of these were heading towards Lana, clutching rainbows of cushions and blankets. He supposed that even without tokens, many would sit outside the arena and still hear the singing within. His long strides reduced through shufflings and elbowings in narrower places to a near standstill.

A lad had been taking a cow and calf through the streets but had been caught out by the early crowds. A broad youth with curly hair and enormous hands that told of greater strength to come, he had but a felt shirt, red as a holly berry, and his exertions to keep him warm. The calf was gripped about his shoulders where it struggled occasionally and bawled to its mother. The cow, a huge, tan-sided beast, had followed docilely enough to begin with but was becoming unnerved by the pressing throng. She baulked and snorted with her head down.

Lifting her tail, she mucked copiously at the entrance to one marquee and backed into the side of it, tearing a rope from its moorings. The tenant, a solid individual with a face always round and currently red, sold olive oil in little jugs, specially primed with aromatic scents for burning in lamps. He was none too pleased with the new odour and came charging out waving a broom with which he proceeded to belabour the cow. The beast lashed out and sent him sprawling in the worst of the mess she had created. The crowd laughed as one, gawping delightedly at this unscheduled entertainment as the trader scrabbled back to his feet with a screech of rage. He swiped at the cow once more, connected with a solid clout and watched the head sail off his broom.

Jebbin laughed with the rest but, glancing ahead, he made direct eye contact with a thin, bearded man who was struggling precisely towards him. There was a glint of a drawn dagger. To his left, another character forged towards Jebbin through the crush.

Dropping into a crouch, Jebbin thrashed madly to rip off his cloak. He reversed it and pulled it back about his shoulders. He dug frantically in the pockets for *sear*, spilling grains on the snow. Jostled and bumped by the crowd, concentration was difficult to achieve but he managed to cast the spell to change his appearance, moulding his features to resemble the chunky, straggle-haired trader. By the time he was able to straighten, the bearded man was very close and Jebbin could hear him bellowing over the general din.

"He's gone! Where's that bloody Looker?"

"She was talking to that red-headed lad," came a strained voice. "I think she went off with him."

"With Nith? Now? By the left hand of Larkeno, we'd have had him." The bearded man's voice was drowned in a fresh roar of laughter from the crowd while Jebbin edged further away, wondering just what his erstwhile companion was up to now.

Gradually, Jebbin sidled further apart from the men he guessed were from the Militant Arm, anxious not to look furtive, then hurried on for Lana, keeping his unusual outward appearance despite the risk of being seen by a Looker.

By the time he reached the entrance to the great arena, he was feeling the strain of maintaining his false visage but the sight of a couple of sharp-nosed loiterers strengthened his resolve and he passed by safely. His token was treated to a close scrutiny by a sceptical guard who eventually admitted that it did appear genuine and, with grudging respect, pointed out a reserved area on the inner perimeter.

Jebbin collapsed into his seat with a sigh and allowed his own features to surface through the evanescent bubble of the oil trader's face. He took stock of his surroundings, blinking and rubbing his face with cold hands. There was no friendly Wirral to hand, overburdened with cushions and hot drinks, and this seat was no softer or warmer than the last. However, he was closer to the centre and could buy something from the vendors struggling through the packed rows.

While the huge stadium was filling, lesser jongleurs strolled about the edge, playing and singing to sections of the crowd. Once the main event began and quiet fell, the acoustics of the arena would ensure that even the furthest could hear clearly but at this stage the tumult was so loud that the different players scarcely interfered with each other. The jongleur before Jebbin had a nautical bent, his songs all sea-shanties telling of tragic wrecks off foreign coasts and the consumption of improbable quantities of rum. Jebbin was unsure how the two were related unless the second led directly to the first and was glad when the man moved on.

An imperious clarion call stilled the babble. Sentences were snapped in half and conversations assassinated as all eyes turned to the entrance. The jongleurs were gone and the silence waited. The voice of a herald called out, clear as a trumpet.

"The Bardic Fair is opened. The Lay of the Troubadour is performed by Brya as the Lady, Evenor as the Lord and Hiraeth as the Troubadour. Listen, then, and see."

With that, three bards marched into the arena to the steady beat of a martial drum tapped by Evenor, a barrel-chested man wearing a fine chain hauberk and a silver helmet. A great sword glittered and swung at his side. Brya was richly attired in flowing silks of pale blue and white. A tall headdress set with sparkling shards of glass caught the light like a breaking wave. Demure and graceful, she bobbed by the side of the lord, her flute cradled before her. Hiraeth, carrying a harp, was dressed in the many-coloured motley of a court fool.

In the middle of the arena, the three halted as the last drum-beat reverberated away into the tense hush. Each bowed once to a different section of the crowd, then acted, played and sang in the Lay of the Troubadour.

Trou.	I carried the news of Karramon's curse
	I told the tales I heard in verse,
	Sang of the slaughter the pagans wrought
	And upon us all this grief I brought.
Lord	The honey'd fire and dream of this fight
	Pulsed through my veins with fierce delight.
	I donned my helm of silver bright,
	My mail, my shield, my spear of light.
	To dare the darkness, fight the foe,
	Forth to greatness and glory go!
Lady	My lord, don't leave me.
	Here are hearth and heart and home.
	Here are children's mouths to feed.
	Plough and tine are the tools we need,
	Cast forth these weapons of death's misrule,

Stay with your love and be not cruel.

Trou.   I sit silently seeking in secret thoughts
Repose and respite from the world's whirling round
And pondering, pensively, passes my life
For nothing, and never do I notice it's gone.

Lord   And shall the heathens win the day?
Shall all men say I idly lay
Whilst light was dimmed and honour shamed?
I'll fight this fight and be not blamed.
My sword shall cleave my fiercest foe
Though he be armed from top to toe
And from the furthest land or sea
Tales of my prowess shall come to thee!

Lady   What use are stories three months cold
Till you return wounded or old?
Do we wait for the tale that tells of your fall?
When you hazard your life, you hazard us all!

Trou.   Softly, sadly, sweep the strings
And sing of old forgotten things.
For thus and so it has ever been
For men are fools and women grieve.

Lady   Sorely I missed my beloved lord,
He fought so distant, far abroad.
I sought comfort in the troubadour
Till he became my paramour.

Lord   I braved the blast of fire and smoke,
Five years I slew in the warrior host.
Backward the hordes were hurled and harried.
Homeward on rugged roads I've galloped
Only to find my lady true
Soft in the arms of my friend, the fool.

Lady   My lord was burned by the bane of betrayal,

The bard he savaged, his body flailed.
All of the servants he put to rout,
My hair cut off and cast me out.
Friendless, penniless, to the world I wept,
By old love spurned, from family kept.

Lord   Then I found I'd fought in vain
In madcap pursuit on the eastern plain.
In folly I groped for glory and fame
But pride became arrogance, respect is now blame.
I lost my friend, my honour, my wife,
But it was I alone that took my life.

Trou.   I carried the news of Karramon's curse.
I told the tales I heard in verse,
Sang of the slaughter the pagans wrought
And upon us all this doom I brought.

As the final soft chords wavered and drifted through the air, the spell faded. Jebbin gaped at the scene of devastation before him. The lady lay crumpled in a swoon where the lord had thrown her. Hiraeth sat in a heap over his harp as though his bones were broken and each note was an agony to play. The lord was stretched full length beside his shattered drum, burst in a final blow when he had fallen upon his sword. The three had held thousands in utter silence and still gripped them in their final pose.

Slowly they stirred and rose to their feet. About them a rumble of noise rolled and swelled in crescendo until the stadium was engulfed in a tidal wave of cheering and applause. Jebbin stamped and whistled with the rest until the trio had retired and the high notes of the clarion demanded quiet once more.

The next song was a solo by a bard with a lute. In a haunting melody with a simple refrain he sang of the grim, bulwark city of

Jerondst in the west and its endless labours against the creeping wilderness. The crowd picked up the chorus and, urged into song by the bard, the mountains echoed and volleyed with the roar of ten thousand voices in slow melody.

But Jebbin's mind had wandered back to the riddle. They were ready to leave first thing in the morning and he had only a few hours left to glean any last grain of information. Ygyrd had agreed to join them and had taken charge of all their procurements, re-selling half Jebbin's purchases and buying anew. He had bought the consignment of bibelots yesterday and had left them with the new wagon under the care of hired guards. Today he should be buying the last of their provisions and getting everything stowed on board.

Jebbin cracked his fingers impatiently. Though the excitement of the choruses made the hair on his neck stand up, this singer failed to exert the utter compulsion of Hiraeth's trio and Jebbin chafed to be away. The moment the song was over, he hastened to the exit, treading on toes everywhere and apologising constantly. Pausing only to check that the watchers had abandoned their post and to accept a surprise offer of the enormous sum of twelve ryals for his token, he headed back to the fair.

A hailstorm began before he reached the first street. Chunks of ice bounced and rattled about him on the packed snow and frost-crisped canvas. Crowds melted off the street like heated butter and he too scurried into the nearest tent.

He was on the street of the weaponsmiths, in a marquee similar to that of Wensla, the knife seller who had thrown one of his specimens past Jebbin's ear. This trader specialised in exotic swords. Jebbin looked for him and spied a bundle hunched over a brazier of glowing coals. When he investigated, a long nose, red and dripping, became visible behind the shaggy furs, then a sad, lined face with yellow-rimmed, watery eyes.

The face offered Jebbin a weak smile which wilted as he looked out at the pelting hail. "Be a good fellow and hook up that flap, will you?"

Jebbin shut out the flailing white, wondering what had happened at the arena.

"I am Pok. Before I leave the meagre comfort of this glowworm, tell me whether you have just come in out of the storm or would you actually like to buy something?"

Jebbin's eyebrows shot up in surprise as he considered this revolutionary concept. "Yes," he said.

"Funny. I knew it would be one or the other. I must be getting better," said Pok expressionlessly.

"Sorry. Yes, I would like to buy something. Something I can conceal but also, well, workmanlike."

"Take a look round and see if anything takes your fancy and then we'll get you fitted up properly." Pok shuffled to his feet, took a swig from a flask plucked from the recesses of his furs and arranged a kettle on the brazier.

Meanwhile, Jebbin scouted round the racks of gleaming metalwork, all carefully labelled and marked with weights and details of manufacture; passing massive, two-handed, armour-crushing affairs with scarcely a glance on his way to shorter, more wieldy weapons. He dismissed the scimitars and positively jumped back from a cheap misericorde whose iron handle bit at him with cold. Jebbin fingered a gladius thoughtfully, then took down a gently double-curved blade without a guard and gave it a few trial swishes. Shaking his head, he carefully returned it to its pegs and stopped stock still gazing at the label a span from his nose. Above the glyphs denoting its details was its name in large letters: yataghan.

Pok's voice startled him. "Cup of tea?"

"Thanks. With a dash from that flask of yours, if you could spare it."

Pok obligingly tipped the bottle over both mugs of tea and then, after a second's thought, took another hefty draw from it himself before tucking it away.

The two set about arming Jebbin to their mutual satisfaction, Pok telling Jebbin about his hometown of Osta-Kerina in Shekkem. "I want to be back where the green seas beat on the sun-yellow rocks, where there's salt and peeling paint and hot sand between my toes, where the lizards flicker over baking stones and snow is a myth." Pok had not taken to the bitterness of Ael nor was he averse to an early return to Osta-Kerina. However, he knew his trade and equipped Jebbin with a tough poinard set in a leather scabbard that he could wear beneath his outer clothes. It would be slow to draw but very inconspicuous, Pok pointed out. Jebbin was pleased with the purchase and his discovery and didn't haggle over a price that already reflected Pok's eagerness to leave Lana's winter behind him.

The hail had long stopped when he emerged, leaving Pok to cringe over his brazier and cuddle his flask. Jebbin kicked through a little drift of ice pebbles, sending a glittering shower clicking and ricocheting across the street.

At the same moment, Ygyrd booted a smouldering heap of furs. Choking smoke and a spiral of black ashes whirled about him from partially doused cloaks, flecking his face and clothes with soft darkness. The marquee was gone, his stocks, tables and stores charred and ruined. Ygyrd glared venomously at his neighbours, busily re-erecting their own tents, stained with smears and splotches of soot but essentially unharmed. He marched over to one of them, a man he had helped earlier with a small loan.

"And you, of course, saw absolutely nothing?"

"No," returned the trader, concentrating particularly hard on tying a knot. "As soon as we realised your place was ablaze, we had to drop our marquee to set up a firebreak."

"Leaving my stock to burn," said Ygyrd bitterly.

"No sense in letting the whole street go up."

"You didn't hear anything at all?"

"Look, I'm sorry, Ygyrd. But you know how it is."

"Yah. I know how it is."

The trader shrugged in resignation. "Oh, come inside a minute," he said, glancing round furtively. He led Ygyrd into his marquee and pulled the flap closed. When he turned back, Ygyrd was regarding a small pile of sheepskins. The glossy black, tightly-curled fleeces were unmistakeably from Gelavien.

"Those are mine," Ygyrd stated.

"You have no stock. You're alive and you'd almost sold out anyway. Quit while you're ahead. If you don't clear out, you'll only get the account for sousing the fire."

Ygyrd pointed his finger to the fleeces and paused, staring at the trader. "For those, what do you know?"

"Look, for Nakki's sake," the furrier licked his lips, then burst out, "What did you do to them?"

"Who?"

"Come on! You know this is Guild work. Maybe you're some big wheel but I can't afford to cross them. I shouldn't be talking to you."

"But you are."

"We're all vulnerable, right?" fretted the trader, "And maybe I owe you," his glance sidled over the black fleeces. "I heard something about harbouring someone but that's all I know. They even gave us a warning. That's why I had time to... Look, I'm sorry, all right? In the confusion we were able to beat your pet out of those. If it's any consolation, one of the fire-raisers was less fortunate."

"Not much," said Ygyrd and turned to leave.

Outside, the air was full of the stink of singed wool, scorched fur and climbing columns of weightless black from the goods that had escaped a drenching. Ygyrd glared at the wreckage briefly, raised his eyebrows in a fatalistic shrug and shambled away up the street.

He spotted Jebbin standing gazing at the black hole of his pitch and altered course to walk past him. Quietly, Jebbin fell in by his side.

"By the lady, Ygyrd, I'm sorry. I have repaid kindness with ruin!" Jebbin whispered, his mouth and nose full of the acrid taste of Ygyrd's loss.

"Saves wasting time selling the remainder," commented Ygyrd stonily. "If I hadn't agreed to come with you, I might have thought you set the place on fire."

"Don't! The noose round my neck may strangle us all. The lady knows why they pursue me so. I must duck out of sight until we go."

"Can't you change your face?"

"Yes, but they employed a Looker earlier. They'll have more now and to them I'd stand out like a beacon. No, the net is pulled tight and if I don't dodge it now, I never shall. I'll evade your hired guards somehow and conceal myself on the wagon. Just leave as though I'm not there. If indeed I am not, good luck. Hope to see you tomorrow."

"I'll be there tonight. I have but to buy herbs; vervain, fever-few, and the like. That done, I am rootless." Ygyrd looked back to the dissipating whorl of black. "D'you know what those spiders were worth?"

"Avoiding."

There was a long pause, then Ygyrd softly snorted. "Yah. Avoiding."

Jebbin squeezed Ygyrd's arm briefly, then drifted away from him in a dense group of people. He wondered whether illusions or a spell to induce queasiness in the guards would enable him to board the wagon. After that, it would be a matter to staying very still and hidden until Lana Fair was left behind.

The High Hithrogael

Buried under boxes and blankets, half-stifled by the reek of lanolin, Jebbin lost all sense of time and was convinced that perils had overcome his friends. He rolled a ball of *sear* between his fingers, trying to persuade himself that they would be safe without his presence drawing attention to them but always the sour thought surfaced: yes, just as safe as Ygyrd's marquee had been.

Every so often he heard the rumble of voices, muffled to indistinctness by his itchy coverings. Sometimes the wagon lurched as it was boarded and Jebbin waited with thumping heart for searching fingers and cries of discovery. At last the wagon jolted into movement. Jebbin lay utterly still, eyes wide in the blackness of his retreat, while adrenalin burned through him, screaming for action. The harsh blare of a mule startled him into an involuntary twitch that brought the sweat prickling onto his skin, *sear* at his lips.

Then the wagon was outside the protected tent. The garbled pandemonium of the fair leaked down to Jebbin as the wagon jerked and jarred its way through the concourse, shouts and curses rising over the growling clamour of the traders. Jebbin thought he recognised Ygyrd's stentorian tones from the driving seat but could not be sure and huddled deeper down, fearful of the inspection to come at the entrance.

Only when the fair had long dwindled to silence and he could hear nothing more than the creak from the wheels and occasional murmur of conversation did Jebbin consider emerging. As he crawled from his cocoon, he stopped again. Music nibbled at his ears. He eased further forward, craning his neck and blinking in the light. There was no doubt. A harpist was sitting next to the driver, gently strumming a tune. At that moment, the musician turned and spotted Jebbin. He winked and motioned with his head that it was safe to sally out.

"Hiraeth!" Jebbin cried, scrabbling and clawing his way forward, staff abandoned. "By the lady, what are you doing here? It's good to see you. Did you win the contest? You were fantastic!"

"Ha," grumbled Ygyrd's rolling bass. "Stowaways should have the decency to creep out quietly, not burst forth like new-wakened bears."

Jebbin leapt forward, clouted Ygyrd on the shoulder and wedged himself between them, grinning with elation.

"Ah, the bardic contest," sighed Hiraeth. "What a fiasco!"

"You jest, of course. Your trio was superb."

"Thank you. A view not shared by the adjudicators. Not winning was one thing but actually we were all reprimanded."

"No! What for?"

"Bringing the purpose of the bard into disrepute."

"What does that mean? You're all disreputable!"

"The purpose of the bard is the bringing of news. In our song, the bringing of news was the catalyst for disaster and this was not approved. Furthermore, the bard is supposed to work solo and not in a circus, as they called it. As if that were not sufficient, we relied too heavily upon instruments and acting and not upon simple song, the hallmark of the skaldic tradition. The voice should be paramount.

"To underline the point, the winner was a song from Rulion. It was a brilliant and worthy winner, telling of a chapel to the Lady Lessan. The priests and supplicants were at their evening vespers when the chapel was surrounded by masters and initiates of this vile black religion that has cankered the Golden Road. A harsh, repetitive chant swelled and beat against the chapel walls. The abbot and devotees of the Lady fought back with hymns of piercing purity but they were whelmed in a crushing pulse of base music. Though a tiny ribbon of argent light coursed skyward, their final paean was snuffed and the chapel fell in desolation, grinding the worshippers in a deadly sacrifice."

"The Lady preserve them," breathed Jebbin automatically. "Is evil everywhere?"

"Only where we permit it," said Ygyrd.

"Ygyrd, why did the thieves burn down your pitch?"

"Does it matter? Maybe they were trying to flush you out, perhaps it was just spite. More likely one of the thievish hierarchy was just doing something demonstrable to impress a Master." The northerner closed the matter with a fierce clack of the reins, which the mules ignored.

Jebbin ducked back inside the wagon to collect a cloak. Away from the fair where the tents broke the airflow, the wind was cold and too lazy to blow round him. He looked ahead to the rising peaks of Ael and shivered. Old stone teeth that chewed once an age, he thought, but they chewed small.

"Not cold already, shrimp?"

"Bolan! What makes you so impervious?" laughed Jebbin, eyeing the wrestler whose torso was only covered by a sheepskin jerkin, his mighty arms left bare.

"Might dig out a shirt up there. This is invigorating. Even our questing bard isn't muffled to the eyebrows yet!"

"Maybe not, but having visited Lana Fair, I'm wearing the finest silk undergarments, moleskin shirt and trousers, fine and thick woollen sweaters and socks aplenty!"

"Which brings me back to my original question: what are you doing here? What's all this questing business?"

"I've learned from my distinguished masters. The purpose of the bard is to bring news, they say, and I agree. I intend to be where the news is generated and thus steal a march upon my colleagues at the next bardic festival. You are a true magician; perhaps not like fabled Alledax, who used the pain of passing a kidney stone to cast a spell of such potency that it precipitated the collapse of Siuda Reyes itself, or even Perumor the Lame, who suffered such agony from his gouty feet that he continually vented pale spires of crimson flame. But a magician nonetheless and I shall be witness to your deeds. It will be my songs that are learnt and repeated across the land. I shall record your valiant struggles, heroic victories and tragic demise!"

"Avaunt, ye auguries," muttered Ygyrd.

"Couldn't you stop at the victory?" Jebbin smiled, rather too broadly.

"I'd prefer to do so. Doesn't make such a good song, though." Hiraeth's voice was bright but his tones rang hollow and the jest was abandoned, hanging heavily in the brittle air.

A short while later, Hophni came back down the trail ahead of them. He waved a greeting to Jebbin. "Way station ahead," he reported in a theatrical whisper. "Definitely occupied. This could be our first test." He rubbed leathery hands together enthusiastically. "The first skirmish, eh?" he grinned, shadow boxing at Bolan.

"Doubt it," said Ygyrd flatly.

The wagon groaned up the slope towards the hut. Most of the snow had blown off the roadway and rocks showed through the packed white. The mules lugged the vehicle up the hill without slipping but Ygyrd had already hung the iron drag-shoes behind the wheels in case of accident.

Bolan and Hophni both seemed poised, even keen, for battle. Bolan's eyes flickered round the trail checking for ambush points while Hophni rolled his shoulders and gave a few trial clenchings to his fists, still looking like a schoolboy enjoying a war-game. Ygyrd was as unruffled as usual and Jebbin took his cue from the trader, relaxing his grip on his staff. Unless the thieves were on his trail, they should be safe. Unless the Aelans would despoil the poorly guarded wagon. Unless something gave away the true nature of their mission. Unless... His fingers whitened back round the staff but he remained still.

The black stone station, paled by driven snow, loomed over the trail. Heat haze wriggled from a stumpy chimney and made the mountains behind shiver. A short distance back from the station, other buildings huddled haphazardly in the lee of a cliff.

They drew up outside the way station which smelt like an old urinal. The mules steamed and blew, looking vaguely for anything edible. A guard in a fur hat and armour of overlapping plates with spiky epaulettes favoured them with a bored expression. He stopped chewing and spat into the icy rocks at the edge of the road.

"The usual," he grunted.

Four members of the party gave a long look at the massive, ready-cocked crossbow that would stop a chilarth beside him and a longer one at the lone trader.

"Yah," nodded Ygyrd, stretching slowly. He climbed down from the wagon, moving stiffly. "New guards," he said to the armoured man, jerking his head at the others. "Doubt they'll make a career of it," he added sombrely.

Ygyrd clomped up a few steps and into the station, giving the others a brief vision of a fire-lit office, an occupied chair and a ledger-strewn table. With a final dismissive glance at those left in the cold, the guard hastened in behind him and the door closed with a solid thud. Jebbin and Hiraeth watched the door nervously: Hophni and Bolan were eyeing the crossbow.

"Just declaring the goods carried, I suppose," said Jebbin, trying to sound confident.

Hiraeth shook his head uncertainly. "Possibly but normally that is jealously guarded information. Merchants privy to details of impending cargoes could profiteer by trading in the cargo goods before they arrived, selling ahead of delivery and buying to meet commitments when the shipment is in and prices are down. Perhaps at national boundaries for taxation and at Lana fair, for example, so the right pitches can be allocated but it's always given reluctantly. I see no reason why it should be declared here."

Jebbin shrugged and sat back, listening to Bolan and Hophni. They were planning a speculative raid on the station to rescue Ygyrd, guessing at the number of guards, their putative abilities and discussing how to prevent word reaching the buildings behind. At that moment, a door opened on the far side of the station and someone plodded away towards the rest of the houses. The wrestlers nodded approval for this change in the odds.

"How about playing your harp or something? Otherwise we could be in trouble."

"I can play an or something, if my fingers aren't too cold. What are they planning?" asked Hiraeth, rummaging behind his seat.

"Our worthy pugilists are pondering an assault on the station.

At the moment, they are using words like 'hypothetical', soon it will be 'immediate action' and I want to stop them before they get to 'sustainable losses' which would, I fear, be me."

Hiraeth chuckled and began to play. When the wrestlers looked up in surprise, Jebbin spoke in his most reassuring tones, "Ygyrd knew what he was doing. I sense no peril here - unless we bring it upon ourselves. We must wait awhile."

The two big men seemed to trust the words of the mage and settled down uneasily to listen to Hiraeth's harp. The full richness of his notes seemed to coalesce warmth from the chilly air and banish the cold from Jebbin's feet.

"I thought you were going to play the or something, not the harp?"

"But this isn't a true harp. It's a sambuca from Shekkem. Just listen to it," Hiraeth said wistfully. "It's old and so mellow, much warmer than a real harp. It calls to the sun of its native land. Ah, Lana fair, what a paradise you are. Long have I sought one of these, even in Shekkem, but only at the great fair was I given one."

"You were given it?"

"Of course. By the time I'd spent an afternoon playing his instruments, he'd sold most of them. He also gave me a long-necked lute which Ygyrd wouldn't let me bring saying that it would probably get broken and there wasn't room for it anyway. One reason to stop me bringing it and one genuine reason, I suspect."

"Balgrim's beard!" muttered Bolan darkly with an accusing look at Jebbin. Startled, Jebbin looked up to see three people heading towards the station. Bolan and Hophni hastily fell to re-analysing their schemes.

"Right," declared Hophni briskly as he straightened up, his scabbed eyelids giving him a piratical air. "Before this place is further reinforced, Bolan and I will force the door and get to grips with them. Jebbin, follow as quick as you can and give us some arcane support. Hiraeth, take the crossbow and stop anyone leaving to spread word. Let's go."

Just then, the door swung open and Ygyrd strode out, stuffing papers into his furs. He paused, giving his stilled guards a disparaging stare, and trudged down to the wagon, shaking his head. Two Aelans followed him. Although they looked young, their flat faces were already creased and their eyes were almost hidden behind heavy lids. They were dressed in dark clothes, thickly padded, and carried large packs. In addition, one carried a box of fresh provisions which was stowed in the wagon.

"Hophni, Bolan, Hiraeth and Jebbin," said Ygyrd, pointing out each of his fellows. "These are Tywy and Arwain, who are to be our guides through the mountains. As, of course, you will have assumed," he added witheringly.

"Of course, of course," said Bolan in a burst of geniality. "Be welcome in our company, gentlemen."

"Ladies," corrected Ygyrd expressionlessly.

Bolan made a few harrumphing noises, then scuttled off to attend to the entirely unnecessary tightening of a few ropes. Hophni, his whole frame shaking, seemed to have developed a fascinated interest in the local geology.

Hiraeth grinned and introduced himself with a courteous grace, accompanied by a musical flourish. The Aelans took little notice of anyone and busied themselves strapping their packs to the outside of the wagon. One mumbled something with a tiny nod towards the bard. This, at least, the other found humorous and Hiraeth settled back with a shrug.

With no further delay, the two girls set off up the trail with a rapid gait which never altered, however steep or rocky the road.

Their wiry limbs were apparently impervious to weariness and even Hophni was glad to take his turn sitting on the wagon.

After one day of such treatment, Ygyrd asked them to slacken their pace somewhat. When Arwain questioned the reason for this in feigned astonishment, Ygyrd said his mules would not long brook such travel, the yaks they must soon acquire would be slower yet and neither he, nor anyone else in his party, was accustomed to the thinner air of the heights. If his guards were to be of any use whatsoever, they must progress steadily, not assault the mountains in a headlong rush.

"Naturally, as the expedition leader, you must set whatever speed you consider appropriate," said Arwain sweetly. "However, our remuneration was calculated on the basis of our usual rate of travel and if you intend to halve this then our wages should be doubled."

Ygyrd received this prepared speech from the smiling girl with a nod of comprehension. "Yah. Very well, we may enter negotiations but I'd assessed the payment on the basis of a job to be performed and I'll only pay upon reaching our destination or the next relevant station."

"How will you know a relevant station from an irrelevant one?" asked Tywy archly.

Ygyrd pondered their situation if abandoned without a guide in the fastnesses of Ael. He realised this was a standard practice by the guides and he had been trapped into agreeing a fair price in the first place, like many before him he suspected. Now it would be down to haggling afresh.

"Of course, it's fair to remind you that we cannot guarantee that the wagon isn't attacked by raiders," Tywy added.

The implication was not lost on Ygyrd: should they so wish, the two girls certainly could guarantee that the wagon was despoiled. Doubtless others had called the girls' bluff and allowed them to proceed at their rapid pace in the hope that they would be unable to maintain it. That would have left them doubly vulnerable to marauders.

"A modest increase might be possible to recompense you for the burden of our sluggishness but much of a raise would jeopardise the profitability of this mission and I will turn for Lana now, when you would get nothing."

"I suppose it is possible that you could retreat safely without our benison" conceded Arwain. "Come then, let us settle what bonuses and emoluments should properly be deemed equitable between our worth and your ability to pay."

While Bolan and Hophni scouted the area, Jebbin attended to the mules and Hiraeth busied himself with the supper, Ygyrd invited the girls to discuss terms, a skill in which they proved well practised. Another reason why so few traders ventured into Ael made itself apparent. Ygyrd looked up at the warriors skipping about the nearby crags with gentle dismay: the Aelan girls would have fleeced them in days.

Having established their new rates of pay the two girls proved companionable and willing enough to do their share of routine work, even of night watches. Although Ygyrd and Hophni were suspicious of this, if the caravan were attacked except at their behest, they would be as much at risk as everyone else.

As the path wound ever more steeply up into the mountains, their rate of climb diminished steadily but there were no more cavils over money from the Aelans. Already Ygyrd found himself breathless; he knew the younger men would begin to suffer soon. From a physical viewpoint, it would have been much better to have taken an extra fortnight over the ascent. However, even without their other pressing affairs, a genuine trading mission would have found this prohibitively expensive and too demanding on limited supplies.

They took the Aelans' advice to trade their mules for yaks at a great corral where scores of both chewed hay, the mules huddled together, the yaks standing alone for they were nearly immune to the cold beneath their piled coats of coarse hair. Ygyrd complained that the yaks' unresponsiveness made even the mules seem biddable and their great strength only made control even more difficult.

They began to hear eerie noises, quietly reverberating round the cols: soft clonkings and low hootings like titanic flutes blown by the breath of the mountains. The girls listened attentively to these but to all questions on the matter they replied that the company should soon see for themselves.

At length they came upon the first wind sculpture. At a junction in the trail, huge boulders were carved and hollowed into sounding stones, the mouths protected by stone hats that stopped them filling with stone-fall or gravel flying on the wind. The bas-relief figures that pranced and postured on the stone gourds were worn, in some places completely effaced, where winter storms had ground them away. A stone gantry reared out from the rock wall, ending in a carving of a bestial face, teeth bared in a savage snarl. A cord of plaited yak-hide was knotted in the creature's teeth and from this a heavy polished stone hung in the centre of the ring of hollowed boulders. As the wind blew, moaning notes sounded from each of the mouths in the boulders and the clapper moved to tap against a stony gong, depending upon the direction of the wind. Marks upon the gourds showed that they had received some terrible batterings in bygone storms. Jebbin shivered, imagining that clapper swinging madly, rebounding and tonking into sounding stones, all screaming their monotones into a tearing gale.

Arwain told them that each wind sculpture sounded a different chord, so it was impossible for a trained native to become lost in the mountains, providing there was enough breeze to sound the stones and less than a full storm blowing. While the stones' lowing whisper swelled to an outrageous bellow in a gale, the storms in Ael roared with the voices of thunder gods and were contemptuous of competition.

In good conditions the best stone readers of Ael could detect the location of travellers in the mountains, just by the minute shifts they caused in the air currents. "The great Varga could even count the men and their beasts separately, and tell their rate of travel within five minutes. When he wasn't drunk, of course," Arwain added, ruining the impression.

There were occasional shelters, most of which were freely stocked with fodder for draught animals - all the disparate tribes of Ael feared only the weather as a common enemy. The girls were well acquainted with these and always called a halt to the day's travel at the most convenient site. Furthermore, Arwain, particularly, demonstrated an excellent understanding of the weather, aided by the changing notes of the wind sculptures. When she recommended taking shelter, they hurried to do so.

The girls erected their own tent every night in the shelters. It was tensioned by hoops that were bent into a light frame and required no pegs in the ground. Ygyrd assumed that it must be well insulated for the cold was intense and though the Aelans' packs were too small to contain thick furs, they neither complained of the chill nor accepted offers of further coverings.

Bolan had been the last to be enveloped by one of Ygyrd's heavy cloaks but he too was soon grateful of its protection. When the first snowstorm came, hoods went up everywhere and when the air cleared, the hoods remained in place.

The Aelans had rapidly unbent far enough to share their meals in a group with the others. They had listened in riveted silence to Hiraeth's superb playing and had joined in the singing with great enthusiasm. They had sung some of their Aelan songs and been astonished when Hiraeth immediately joined in with an accompaniment.

They were especially delighted when Hiraeth sang The Song of the Wolf but they told him there was now more to it and taught him fresh words. Hiraeth repeated the words softly through to the end.

"...Then the Goat man ran and the Condor man ran
and the Bear men, they ran too
and they told of a man who would brook no ban
to his word and his will to rule."

Then the bard stroked his harp and spoke again; "Listen, then, and see...

Controlling his truculence, Buoch faced the line of impassive faces: Castellan Kistmaen in his oversized Bear helmet, Asharne wearing the spike of the Condors, Lykos bareheaded and another Buoch did not recognise, but Goat tribe from his dress. It troubled Buoch that anyone from the Goats should be here, for if they sided with the Rokepike and his Ravens against, then allegiances would shift unpredictably. Buoch had listened carefully to the blandishments from Lykos, perhaps the very ones that had swayed the Goats - but had the Goats joined with Lykos? Was he perhaps watching Buoch to see if the Ravens would hold to ancient allegiances? Buoch made his decision.

"I defy you all! You've abducted me here by force and offer me putrid words for a future of Aelan blood spilt at the behest of a flat-lander! The Ravens stand against the foreign usurper and his Condor allies, against whom we have sworn vendetta. All the North Cols are thus closed to you."

"Then you shall not leave here and if the Ravens deny me passage, your life will answer for it!"

"Take my life if you can. Never will I deliver the Ravens to you."

At a signal from the enraged master of the Rokepike, Buoch was seized. "Hold him still," commanded Lykos, advancing upon the man who baulked him. He reached out and plucked first one, then both of Buoch's eyes from his head. Ignoring Buoch's agonised howls, he tossed the twitching orbs upon a table. "Deliver these to the chief of the Ravens with the message that his son lacked the vision to grasp my dream. The father will have one chance more."

Defiantly, Buoch staggered up from the floor, drew bloodied hands down and thrust his grisly face towards where he guessed Lykos stood.

"My Life's Curse!" he cried. "May your eyes too be wrenched from your head within the year!"

Lykos spun round, his face made hideous with rage, his eyes glaring yellow from a skin turned suddenly grey. The nightwood staff stretched out and streaks of violet force threw Buoch into the wall, then ground against him with such power it seemed that the stones themselves must part. The Aelan should have been unable to speak but even as his ribs buckled, Buoch's last words sounded clear in the room like a tocsin.

"As I can see nobody, so all your plans shall be destroyed by a nobody!"

Then Buoch's skull split with a ghastly, moist crack and the force subsided. Leaving grey-pink stains on the wall, Buoch lolled lifelessly, looking as though he had been crushed beneath a rock-fall.

"Enough of such superstitions. Nonetheless, he was right in that I must have access to the cols through the Ravens. Does the chief have other sons?" Lykos spoke lightly in a leaden silence.

"No, my lord," croaked Kistmaen in a husky voice, "but he has a grandson, Buoch's boy, on whom he dotes with obsessional fondness."

"Excellent. Fetch him hither and the Ravens are ours."

"The matter will be difficult to arrange now. The grandson will be guarded."

"You have forgotten, Kistmaen, that I have formidable experience of acquiring whatever I want by stealth. We will have the boy."

Kistmaen shuddered as Lykos left, looking back at the dripping stones where Buoch had died. He brusquely ordered some guards to remove the corpse; others to conduct the Goat man back to his pampered durance. News of what had transpired would doubtless quell any doubts as to Lykos' ruthless determination to achieve his aims.

"How much pain did that spell cost," said Jebbin after a long silence.

"This is where we're going?" said Ygyrd. When no one answered, he snorted softly. "Good song, but I should have gone to Jerondst."

"Buoch's curse was foolish. Destroyed by a nobody? Only the most powerful could trouble such a leader," said Tywy.

"But it was a Life's Curse; and Lykos did not ward it," shrugged Arwain, applauding Hiraeth with the rest. His ability to turn their simple words into a vision was a revelation to them but his gentle attempts to initiate a closer friendship were equally gently rebuffed. They retired alone to their tent every night and the men were left to guess at their figures beneath their padded clothes.

Halfway through a cold morning march, Arwain stopped suddenly, her head canted on one side as she listened. A steady wind was blowing towards them down the valley, gelid from the upper heights. Hophni was driving the wagon while Ygyrd rested in the back with Hiraeth. Jebbin was walking in the rear and using the wagon as a windbreak. He checked that nothing approached from behind, then stayed where he was. Bolan and Tywy hurried to Arwain's side, stepping quietly.

"You hear?" whispered Arwain, her mouth open. "Argrenlah three is muffled."

"Argrenlah speaks as she should in this wind. I hear no more," said Tywy, frowning and pouting her lip.

Arwain said nothing but shook her head slightly. When Bolan

asked what this meant, she answered, "Probably nothing. At least I'm not sure yet."

A quarter of a league further, Arwain stopped once more. "There! Now do you hear?"

Tywy listened with her head bent forward, eyes closed and strained to pick up this slight change in timbre. She shook her head in frustration.

"Arwain, what if the stones were muffled, what then?" said Bolan again

"Argrenlah three was muffled, I'm sure of it. It means that some things were grouped about the stones for as long as it has taken us to walk from that spur. Either a herder paused at the stones with his stock or ... or a group of tribesmen is on the move."

"That means raiding?" guessed Bolan, studying Arwain's expression. "If they're coming this way and not heading deeper into the mountains, will they see us?"

"They can only run straight into us," said Arwain bitterly.

"Arwi, from Argrenlah, they could be Condors," Tywy said.

"I know that!" said Arwain through clenched teeth.

"Can we not avoid them?" asked Bolan.

"We must! We must flee back the way we came, at least for a while."

"They are too close and mounted," Arwain reminded Tywy.

"Then we must abandon the wagon immediately."

"None of that," said Bolan. "Is there no other course?"

"Yes. One fat old man can die for nothing," shouted Tywy, unkind in her fear.

"Wait," said Arwain softly, a strange light gleaming in her eyes, "there is the High Hithrogael." Tywy glared at her for a moment, then the two moved apart and fell to bickering in passionate whispers.

"If only we knew what that's all about," complained Hophni.

"Arwain wishes to try a strange route, dangerous but new to her. Tywy is keen to avoid both the tribesmen and this new road. She tells Arwain they owe no allegiance to foreigners and we should all flee for safety. So much is plain," murmured Hiraeth who had clambered from the wagon when they stopped.

"Is it? Well forgive me but I have neither the spells of a mage nor the ears of a demon," huffed Hophni.

"Nor I but people don't change and much is clear to the observant eye. The question is, who will win the argument?"

"I'm not sure who I'm backing," rumbled Ygyrd, just his head poking from the wagon.

Bolan, standing nearest to the furious dispute, shrugged towards them in helpless perplexity. But then Tywy flung up her arms in a graceless surrender and wheeled to face them.

"Well, get a move on," she shouted impatiently, waving them forward vigorously. "Arwain has decided we should all be allowed to die in the peaks. But hurry or the Condors will reach the turning before we do and it'll all be for nothing." She turned her back on the wagon and stamped up the trail.

Hophni relinquished the reins to Ygyrd, saying that Ygyrd was the better driver and if there was to be either fighting or pushing, then it had better be him on the ground. Ygyrd accepted this with a nod and set about convincing the yaks that they really could manage a faster walk than their current amble. Hophni and Bolan discussed tactics should they encounter this other force while Hiraeth joined the Aelans.

"What is it about this high road? Who are these Condors? Are you sure they're coming this way? What happens if they do find us?" he asked, pausing for answers but getting none until Tywy turned on him,

"Pray they do not. If you've nothing better to do, why not help the yaks pull the wagon?"

Baffled, Hiraeth retired to tell Jebbin the details he had missed. Fortunately, they were travelling over one of the best stages they had encountered. It was level, mostly clear of snow and had a good rock footing unlike the broken, sapping shale they had faced earlier, giving back one step for every two they had struggled forward.

The yaks tugged and slithered onward at Ygyrd's steady urging, the wagon bumping and jolting, by turns clattering over rock and crunching over ice-hardened snow. The two wrestlers hurried along at the back corners of the wagon, lifting and shoving every time that the wheels stuck on ledges or rocks in order to spare the yaks as much as possible. Hiraeth and Jebbin walked behind, leaving the scouting to the tireless girls.

They were puffing and giddy by the time Arwain waved them to their right, off the main track. Sparing only a brief glance up the valley, Ygyrd turned the yaks and forged into the new path. Here the scouring winds had been baulked and eddies had piled weirdly carved drifts across the road, making an uneven and awkward task for the yaks. The poor creatures' feet were almost supported by the icy crust but at each step they broke through and had to drag themselves out and onto the drift once more. The wheels ploughed a rut in the yaks' wake and then juddered to a halt. The wrestlers bent to their task, Ygyrd clicked the reins and the wagon lurched on again.

As Tywy and Arwain left the junction to resume their place at the front, Hiraeth pulled at Tywy's sleeve, "Look at these tracks! How can we stop them following us?"

"Unless they actually see us, nobody," Tywy told him with a pitying look, "but nobody will follow us on the High Hithrogael."

She pushed past him after the wagon, frothing complaints to Arwain.

Hiraeth beckoned Jebbin over. "I have a funny presentiment I'm not going to enjoy this jaunt on the High Hithrogael. Since Arwain was unsure whether or not there is anyone coming down the trail from Argrenlah, what about staying here for a while and keeping an eye up the valley? I don't think we add much muscle power shoving that crate through those drifts. I'm not even sure whether the front team or the back team is the stronger! If nothing comes, perhaps we won't need to risk the High Hithrogael at all."

"Sound planning," agreed Jebbin. "We can see far up the valley and we can vanish round a turn in this new trail before they could catch a glimpse of us."

"Arwain seemed in a dreadful hurry," continued Hiraeth, settling himself comfortably and closing his eyes, "so if nothing's appeared at the top of the valley in forty winks, we can assume there is no-one or they've gone another way. We can easily catch up with the wagon. Frankly, after all that chivvying to get us to this fork, I need a rest. I can hardly breathe and..."

Jebbin snatched a handful of Hiraeth's clothing and hauled him backwards with desperate strength. "Great Lady save us! Run, Hiraeth, run!" he hissed.

Barely a stone's throw up the valley, the first pair of a column of riders rounded a shoulder of rock and advanced towards the turning. Their horses and clothes were shaggy, their moustaches long; swords and bows within easy reach. They sat astride their blocky mounts with indolent ease born of long practice. Beside each rider, a helmet topped with a spike bounced against a leather pad.

This much Jebbin took in with a horrified glance before dragging Hiraeth away in floundering flight. Ahead of them they could see the wagon at a turn. The yaks were round the corner and invisible but the wagon was stationary. The snow had built up thickly where the trail altered direction and the wagon had bellied out on a ridge and stuck. Beside him, Hiraeth lost his footing and plunged headlong into a drift, showering snow upwards in great sprays. Jebbin dived flat beside him as he tried to scrabble up.

"Stay down," he gasped. "We'll never make it round the corner. Be still." Jebbin wrenched off a glove and scraped in a pocket for *sear*. The pain seemed almost comforting, like a weapon in the hand. He clasped his hands to his head and remained motionless. About him, a shimmering illusion of undulating white floated outwards and back to the Argrenlah trail. Hiraeth looked in despair at the black pits of footprints and ruts that showed clearly through the sparkling mist that wavered and cleared before his eyes. But there was no time for further efforts: the riders appeared. To Hiraeth's amazement, the leaders looked neither right nor left but continued steadily on their way. Others in the long column glanced up the Hithrogael road but saw nothing upon it to interest them and passed on.

Long after the last rider had passed, Jebbin struggled back to his feet. The wagon had now disappeared but neither of them knew whether this had happened before or after the riders were in view. With frequent backward glances, they hurried in the wagon's tracks.

"In the name of the great god Rashen-Akru, how did we get away with that? Our tracks were as plain as your nose - which is to say, very plain indeed."

"The tracks were plain to you, but you knew they were there. I doubted they'd seen us; only our heads were visible for an instant and they weren't alert. Why should they be, up here? When they looked up the Hithrogael, they saw what they expected to

see and no more. After all, as we have been told, nobody comes
up here. So the illusion held. Had we been spotted to begin with,
it would not have been sufficient. And my nose is fine; the Forshen said so, thank you very much."

When they rejoined the others, they discovered that their absence had not been noticed. Hiraeth quickly told them all they
had seen, congratulating Arwain on her perfect interpretation of
the wind sculpture's singing.

"They wore helms with blades upon them?"

"They had such helms with them, certainly."

"Condors," Tywy spat. "The worst!"

"And Lykos' henchmen too," said Jebbin.

"Be that as it may, surely they have now passed and we can return to the other road, head westward on our old route and leave
the High Hithrogael to its slumbering unchallenged."

At this even Tywy shook her head. "No, we are now committed, with however much reluctance, to the Hithrogael. That was
but one band of Condors. There will be many such and I have no
wish to be sandwiched between two of them. We can neither retreat nor advance upon the old road. High Hithrogael is our only
option, now we are here." She looked venomously at the uncaring
white peaks.

Their climb up the Hithrogael was steep and icy. They wound
up lichened cliffs in a series of switchbacks, forever with the cliff
face on one hand and a sheer drop on the other, snaked through
boulder fields and picked their way across rumpled sheets of unsullied snow. There were few shelters, little fodder and no wood
for fires. Arwain rationed all of them severely, admitting that
there would probably be nothing stocked in the few stations that
were said to be on the route. It was supposed to be the duty of
the local chief to ensure that the shelters were provisioned but

Arwain could not imagine who would take responsibility for the High Hithrogael and she would not rely upon them.

On this road they were utterly alone and entered a new world. Here was only rock and ice and a sky so close that it seemed barely supported by the mountain spires. Wave after wave of grey and white peaks loomed over them, threatening to engulf them forever. Each move they made was slower than before and took more effort but they made the best speed possible while conditions were good. They toiled past the vertiginous outlines of sheer pillars, shattered and split. Crumbling and rotten rocks teetered in the constant wind, toppled and smashed down towards the party. The path was scarred and splintered by stonefall from the heights.

They crossed a barren valley full of giant, broken stones and found an open tarn, strangely ice-free and deep as night. The cold waters had an acrid tang that made the travellers pause but the yaks showed no inhibitions and slurped noisily. Arwain assured them that it was safe to drink. She also said that visions were seen in its glassy surface when the waters were smooth. Hiraeth viewed the rippled waters and regretfully suggested that any visions would be confined to their dreams, unaided by mountain lakes.

A shelter here was stocked, the first such they had found. Rare fire blossomed and while the yaks munched on dusty hay the party huddled greedily round the flaring fingers of light until their faces glowed, though the cold still slunk round in the darkness and gnawed their backs. They sang songs and laughed until the realisation that they were a minuscule pocket of life dwarfed by the cold vastness of the mountains weighed upon them, quelled them and sent them to bed almost in silence.

The following day they took what they could from the shelter without denuding it and hurried on, still climbing. Plagued with headaches and nausea, they were forcing themselves to eat their midday meal when Arwain warned them a storm was coming. There was another shelter not far ahead and they would do well to stop there early and wait out its violence. Hiraeth took a last look back at the tarn below them but its wavelet-crinkled surface showed nothing more than glints of fractured mountains. He shrugged sadly and plodded after the others towards the next point of safety.

When they reached it, they found three walls collapsed and the roof canted at a crazy angle. While the others stood panting like dying fish, Arwain and Tywy discussed whether they could survive if they crept into the recesses of the shelter, accepting the loss of the wagon and leaving the yaks exposed. However, they decided to press on to the next shelter, Arwain promising that they could reach it before nightfall even at their current pace. Wordlessly, Ygyrd clouted the yaks into movement. The others plodded wearily behind the wagon, looking like refugees from a rout.

By mid-afternoon the wind had freshened to a gale, although the sky was cloudless blue and bitter cold. All of them could now hear the change in the wind sculptures. Somewhere ahead, vessels vented a tortured screaming while the clapper careered about in mad carillon. Tywy blanched, first urging the company forward in an unsustainable rush, then hanging back as though she wished to turn and flee hopelessly for the shelter by the tarn. Arwain's whole frame was clenched in determination as though she would drag the entire group forward by main force of will.

For the lowlanders, the journey became agony, then a nightmare. The freezing wind lanced through furs with icy knives and wrenched away each hard-won breath. No step was taken without a mighty conscious effort - and still the wind strengthened until it threatened to hurl them bodily from the trail. On and on they laboured, thoughts of safety pummelled from them, only the hideous rhythm of breathe and step left to them. Spicules of ice and rock lashed and tore at any scraps of exposed skin. They barely noticed as the sky darkened, huge siege engines of cloud boiling and seething up from the violent commotion where the sky snagged on the mountains' jagged edges. Arwain bawled at them but her words were lost and even her urgency dulled by the torpor of their condition. Breathe, breathe, step. The light suffocated under the cloud and failed as the first flakes came towards them, not falling, but flying horizontally like crossbow bolts. They could see nothing, no slope, no drop, no rock, no cliff. Only the shambling, stumbling figure immediately before them. All else was lost. Breathe, breathe, step. Fresh snow dragged at their feet until each tottering step advanced them but a hand's width. Pant for air, step, pant, step again. Vision failed. Only will remained to tell them stop is death. Pant, step, pant, pant, step.

Arwain had to push each of them into the shelter or they would have limped on into the blast until their dwindling strength failed and they died where they fell. Only the yaks had the sense to turn into the doors and life. When Arwain finally dragged the shelter door closed, the noise inside was deafening but it seemed like pure calm after the colossal roar outside. Arwain ran about the shelter checking on the travellers who lay where they had dropped. She almost cried with relief when she found firewood stacked by a hearth. Without it, she would have wrenched timbers from the wagon for vital fuel. Forcing Tywy to attend to the immediate lighting of a fire, she turned to the wrestlers, sitting stupidly together, gazing at nothing. Shivering, with pathetically slow movements, Bolan was trying to chafe his hands to get some feeling back into them.

"No, don't rub them. Just warm gently. Not at the fire, you'll burn them," she panted. Turning to Hiraeth, she looked at his dead white fingers. Unhesitatingly, she opened her clothes and placed his hands under her armpits and held him while he groaned with the pain.

Tywy was roused enough to check Jebbin, who was lying unheeding on his side. She shook him fiercely but his strength was spent and he only responded, "Let me sleep."

As the two wrestlers crawled towards the fire, she pulled Jebbin to lie between them and threw dry cloaks over them. She looked round the cramped shelter; the fire slowly pushing heat outwards; the yaks standing with their heads down and eyes halfclosed, still too cold to steam and too tired to eat; the damp huddle by the fire; Ygyrd, unable to straighten but still trying dismally to unhitch the wagon from the beasts. She caught Arwain's eye where she stood still clutching Hiraeth and nodded grimly. They would live, at least tonight.

Driven by her responsibility, Arwain had dragged off all their frozen boots, made a strong, hot broth for everyone and ensured that they drank it before she allowed herself to join the general slump of exhaustion. There was no light save that of the fire and nobody spoke. They were too drained to shout over the storm even had there been anything to say. They slept without watch, only Arwain stirring occasionally to put fresh wood in the grate.

It was very late before they stirred in the morning, lying luxuriating in the comfortable warmth, free from travail and shivering at last, enjoying even the warm air smells from too many closely confined bodies. Eventually the two Aelans rose and checked the hands and feet of the entire company. Owing to the excellence of Ygyrd's mittens they had suffered little longterm damage, but Hiraeth's hands were still pale, swollen and slightly blistered. None could face the thought of having to pull on boots and Hophni voiced the fear that he might not be able to do so. A day of rest and general drying-out was tacitly agreed upon, despite their diminishing supplies.

Arwain spent the day encouraging the rest of them, telling them they had nearly reached the highest point of the Hithrogael and then it was a gentle descent to the plateau, which descent, combined with their developing acclimatization, would soon have them feeling fit again. And then they would have traversed the High Hithrogael, a deed for the bard to extol!

"After all," said Tywy, "it's not as though we must climb the peaks themselves. Before a boy may take his place among the men of the Ptarmigan, he must stand alone upon the summit of Eryrfyn and afterwards describe what he finds carved there."

"A rapidly waning tribe, I imagine," muttered Hophni, drying his feet with delicate dabs after laving them in salt water.

The storm died away completely during the day and they even opened the doors to allow in a brief waft of pale sunlight, retaining an illusion of warmth. All was still and quiet except for the occasional cracking booms that told of avalanches sliding down under the weight of fresh snow, loosened by the sun. They saw one on the opposite slope: a ribbon of dark tearing itself from the white, moving unbelievable slowly, and widening until it was lost in its own mist and spume. Only then did its echoing din roll round to shake the shelter and awe the watchers. Tywy eyed the slopes above the shelter critically and pronounced it well situated. Perhaps, most oddly, the broken shelter they had passed had been less well sited.

The following day Arwain rousted them out early after a night of savage frost, saying, "We have quite a short trek again before the next station. It'll be easy if the paths are clear. Should steep drifts block our way, we may have great trouble. If there's been an avalanche..."

There was much good-natured groaning and grumbling as

they dressed themselves anew, accepting the dark veils Arwain insisted they wore to ward off snow-blindness and harnessed the smelly yaks back to the wagon, having rolled it out backwards by hand. However, they all felt they had survived the worst that the Hithrogael could throw at them and now all was plain sailing.

Last night's aching frost had stabilised the drifts and they found that where these crossed the trail, the Aelans were able to find a way for the yaks to pull the wagon on top of them and the icy crust bore the combined weight without collapsing. All were good-humoured and elated with their rapid progress except Arwain, who seemed to miss the lowing notes of the wind sculptures in the stillness after the storm. By the afternoon they had little more than two leagues to travel before the next shelter and their high spirits increased when Tywy revealed that they had reached the zenith of the trail. A light breeze had revived the wind sculptures to once more send soft hooting chords rolling over the slopes but, if anything, Arwain seemed even more worried and introspective, though the ever-sympathetic Hiraeth was the only one to notice.

Within the hour, they could see their night's lodging ahead, incredibly clear in the crystal air. The trail headed straight towards it down a gentle incline. The mountain slope itself swept down from their right and plunged vertically downwards on the left edge of the trail. Between them and the shelter, an icewall from a meltwater trickle had mounded over the trail and fell in a titanic icicle over the cliff. There would be no grip on its hyaline surface: neither yaks nor wagon could cross without slipping and crashing over the cliff. The party moved to the very edge of the ice and stared at it in disbelief. Bolan booted its gleaming surface to chip out a foothold, but his foot glissaded over the shimmering mass and left no mark.

"Well, that's it as a trading mission," said Hiraeth dispiritedly.

"No; must be a way," said Bolan, determinedly hacking glassy flakes with a hatchet. He turned to look at Jebbin who neatly handed on the whole issue.

"What do our mountain guides suggest?"

"This is my business," declared Tywy, giving him a warm smile and ignoring her dejected colleague. She selected two skeletal boot soles from the outside of her pack and attached them to the soles of her ordinary boots. Sharp pins descending from them gave her some sort of grip even upon the ice. "I can climb even this. From a vantage on high I can attach a rope and belay you over the ice. We can sling the gear, trade goods and supplies over in sacks on the rope and carry what we can from the other side."

"The wagon and the yaks?"

"Will have to stay here."

"But with a couple of ropes on each yak and a bit of muscle power, surely we could manage it?" asked Hophni.

"I don't think you know what it is like, or the weight of a yak," chuckled Tywy, "but it would present an interesting problem if we had fifty people here."

"Might as well let them try it, Ty. For flat-landers, they've done more than I thought possible already."

Tywy shrugged. "It'll depend on what points we can find to belay from." She attached a rope to her waist and tossed the other end to Hophni. "You'd better hang on to that, muscle power. Better still, get Arwain to knot it properly about you. If I slip, haul it in as I come down and stop me going over that edge." With that, she turned, dropped a second rope over her shoulder and began to inch her way up the ice.

With spikes clasped in each fist, she steadily chiselled her slow path up the ice face. The others watched almost in silence; Hophni gradually paying out loops of rope with grim concentration. Tywy paused unmoving for a while, then traversed to her left before working still higher.

"What's she doing?" Jebbin asked nobody in particular. "There's an obvious outcrop through the ice just over her old position, surely?" No one commented and he too fell quiet.

At last, Tywy found herself a safe position and spent a few moments roping herself in before calling down to Arwain to make ready. Next, she threw down an end of her spare rope. Arwain tied herself to this and, with another rope trailing behind her to Bolan, she slithered her way over the icewall. She slipped several times but on each occasion Tywy's rope saved her from sliding downwards and she was able to press on. Once she was over, Hiraeth was able to cross, Tywy stopping him falling, Arwain pulling him over and then they began moving the supplies, a bundle at a time lashed securely and dragged over.

When this was accomplished, Tywy called to Hophni in a mocking voice," If you want to try moving wagons or the like, you had better climb up this rope to your own little eyrie." She indicated the outcrop of solid rock that Jebbin had spotted earlier.

Hophni barely hesitated before grasping the rope and swarming up it, ignoring the slippery ice altogether. When he reached a suitable height, he was able to swing himself like a pendulum across the icewall until he could reach the outcrop. From there, he lowered a new line which Bolan attached to the wagon alongside Tywy's rope. Bolan then tied Arwain's rope to the front of the wagon and helped Ygyrd and Jebbin to push it on to the ice. Much to all their surprise, it trundled easily across and in no time was back on the relatively safe rocky path.

After a quick cheer, Hiraeth started to reload the wagon while Bolan began tying the ropes to the first of the yaks. When all was secure, Tywy and Hophni braced themselves above and

Hiraeth and Arwain hauled on their rope while Ygyrd and Bolan coaxed the first beast forward, baulking and snorting. Three paces onto the ice, the yak's feet slid from beneath it and, thrashing madly, it crashed to the ice. With a crack like a whip, Tywy's rope snapped and came lashing down the mountain like a striking snake. Hophni's rope was looped round the top of the outcrop but with the mighty jerk this rotten finger of rock broke away and skittered downwards. Hophni was plucked from his scant footing and rocketed helplessly down the ice, flailing wildly for nonexistent handholds. The yak slid back to land on the path two strides from Ygyrd but Hophni, unable to turn his course, accelerated straight down the icefall. There was an awful quiet as first the rotten pillar of rock and then Hophni sailed off the ice and into space.

"Hophni!" bellowed Bolan, clawing futilely at air as the great wrestler dropped from sight.

Then a sharp snapping noise was followed by a steady thrumming. A rope still connected Hophni to Tywy and with her climber's training she had also made this fast. It was Hophni's fault that there was so much slack and now he was suspended like a spider over a huge drop. There was no reply for a time when they called to him but he had been winded in the fall with the rope about his waist and at last they were rewarded with a wheezy response. His weight was too much for Tywy to shift but, hand over hand, the stalwart fighter winched himself back up the rope, over the rim and into sight. Then he studiously ignored all those calling to him and continued towards Tywy. Laboriously, he swung himself once more until he regained his even more precarious ledge. After thanking Tywy briefly and shortening his rope, he called down for a new rope for Tywy, then urged them to try once more, this time, he suggested, hog-tying the yaks and dragging them over by main strength.

"It's a yak," called back Arwain in amazement, "not some sheep to be trussed!"

"You have Bolan there," replied Hophni laconically. "What further need is there of strength?"

So indeed it proved, although Bolan found it necessary to first tie the yak's front and back feet to a beam of wood, then use his incredible power to boost the beast onto the ice. Then he had to cross the ice himself to heave it over, since it would not budge with the best efforts of Hiraeth and Arwain. The whole process had to be repeated for the second yak. Ygyrd crossed last on the lower rope and went to attend to the injured dignity of the ponderous yaks. Hophni swung himself over on Tywy's rope and held it for her while she simply finished her traverse across the ice.

"I knew it would be easy," said Hophni as they rolled down towards the shelter, "but I'll never feel the same about mountain air now I've had so much of it about me."

In the morning, Hiraeth walked with Arwain. She was more withdrawn than ever and sought to shrink away from the bard but he would not permit this.

"Arwain, you have led us faultlessly from the very borders of the mountains. Why do you suddenly fear your precious skills have deserted you?"

"How could you know such a thing?" she barked defensively.

"You read mountains, bards read people. What troubles you so?"

"I should know mountains," she cried. "I've learned every route from Lana to the Aingal." She glared at him, daring him to contradict her.

"And you know the High Hithrogael," prompted Hiraeth.

"Yes. And there is no icefall across it."

Hiraeth shrugged. "I don't think you are saying we're lost."

"You don't understand, there is no icefall," she groaned.

"Your maps may have been a little dated?"

"You're saying my knowledge is antiquated and useless?"

"Not at all. The melt water might be taking a different route. Erosion, perhaps an avalanche?"

"Then all is futility."

Hiraeth walked on alongside her for a time before softly adding, "So what is it really? What is it you have not mentioned? Something you hoped Tywy would notice?"

Arwain shrugged in surprised resignation. "Yes, exactly that. But she has said nothing. There is a silent voice."

"You mean you should be able to hear another wind sculpture?" hazarded Hiraeth.

"For a long time now," she sighed. "If I'm right, there should have been Nethangard four and no ice. There is ice and Tywy is silent, so should we hear this outlying voice of the Nethangard?"

"Keep confidence, Arwain," smiled Hiraeth, taking her arm. "Time will tell. Do we pass the site of Nethangard four? How far is it?"

"Not far. We should even see where I thought it should be when we round that." She nodded towards a bend in the trail.

Hiraeth immediately summoned the two wrestlers and explained that there might be something unexpected ahead. He grinned as he saw them both shrug off their lethargic plodding for something like their old alertness. But there was no preparing for the Nethangard.

Arwain stared at the ruins of the wind sculpture with her mouth sagging open in horror. "No," she wailed, "no, no!" She ran along the narrow trail towards the shattered remnants of the stone gourds, heedless of the treacherous ice and the precipice on her left.

"Arwi, stop!" screamed Tywy, her voice high with terror. "Can't you see? Stop!" She pelted desperately after the other girl, who ignored her completely in her outrage over the wreckage. The wrestlers, Hiraeth and Jebbin hurried after the Aelan girls, leaving Ygyrd to control the yaks as best he could. They were stamping and snorting with unease.

Arwain reached the debris of the sculpture and fell to her knees amid the fragments. She clutched a curved shard of rock, the broken half of a dancer's face, and touched it to her forehead, rocking gently back and forth.

Tywy caught up with her and shook her by the shoulders. "By Rashen-Akru, will you LOOK. We must go or die! Arwain, this grief is madness. No human raider smashed this sculpture. Look - or must we all perish?"

At last, Arwain raised her tear-tracked face from the violated carvings and viewed the cliff about them in sudden silence. It was honeycombed with round holes, blue-white tunnels leading into ice and rock. "By the levin," she whispered, "oh no."

Before she could scramble to her feet, a clicking, scraping noise grew rapidly in volume. A black creature exploded from the nearest pit, many chitinous legs biting into the ice for grip. In an instant it was striking down at the paralysed Arwain with double pincers. But the pincers closed upon the cold iron of Bolan's wrist guards, still worn over his furs. The wrestler hurled himself sideways to avoid the girls, pulling the creature off balance, and smashed his booted feet into its monstrous face. Using its own grip upon him, he gave a mighty heave with his legs and lifted it over his prostrate form to land on its back in front of Hophni. The beast released Bolan and scrabbled to right itself but Hophni had seized it by its weighted tail, avoiding the poisonous spike. With a roar, he pivoted round and slid it over the edge of the trail to dash itself to pieces on the scree far below.

Already two more ice demons had burst from their holes, one thundering towards the group from the trail ahead, another clat-

272 - ACM PRIOR

tering down from high above them. Over the noise of their approach rose the singing thrum of a whirling stone. Bolan was spinning the stone clapper round his head on its length of hide rope. Faster and faster he swung it until it blurred into a circle and howled its cry for vengeance. The ice demon was almost upon them before Bolan released the stone. It crashed into the beast like a pile driver, snapping forelimbs and crushing the head back into the torso. The remaining legs shuddered spasmodically but, astonishingly still alive, it began dragging itself back towards the nearest hole, trailing ichor behind it. Bolan snatched up his makeshift weapon and, taking care to avoid the randomly lashing tail, pulped the vile creature with thunderous blows.

Meanwhile, Jebbin planted himself firmly on the trail, clearing his mind. He looked for a moment at the small pile of *sear* in his hand, then dragged it all into his nose. Pain erupted through him as though he had dipped his face in molten lead. He thrust his fist forward and fired the blast spell at the careering ice demon. Snow belched upward but the beast charged through it. Again Jebbin launched his spell, keeping the harmonic low but still the ice demon careered downwards. Then the exhilaration of white pain took Jebbin and he let the power flood through him, losing control in an orgy of violence. He hurled a shuddering rain of droplets from the web of power upward in spell after shrieking spell, detonating in halos of shattered ice and rock. His staring eyes watered with pain and power until he could see no more of the on-rushing beast than an expanding blot of blackness. He was caught in his own snaring magic, feeling the mad, screaming laughter welling up in him and he could only remain where he was, still catapulting weakening bolts of power towards the demon. Then suddenly Hophni leapt upon him and bore him out of the path of the beast. It should have been upon them both but too many of its ferociously scrabbling legs were splintered and useless. It struggled to snap at them with broken pincers, twisted, rolled across the trail and plunged downward.

In the quiet that followed, Tywy looked at Bolan in wonder and amazement. "What are you?" she asked, bowing in respect.

"Fat old man who didn't want to die," replied Bolan. "Must hurry from this place. May be more of those nasties. What were they, anyway?"

"Ice demons; we call them Grwnwyr. They are a deadly and implacable foe. They were driven back at enormous cost from the travelled districts of Ael and were thought to have been exterminated, although a few unreliable trappers still mentioned dark tunnels in the Duvvenpeaks. Perhaps they worked across to the Hithrogael? Few indeed survive the assault of even a single Grwnwyr." She lapsed into silence with a shrug of disbelief.

"We now all understand your missing voice, Arwain," said Hiraeth. "If they are such miners as we see, do they account for the ice-wall too?"

"Yes indeed," Arwain assured him triumphantly. "If they've tunnelled in the high peaks, they could easily have caused a new water line. Caused the broken shelter too - or killed its occupants. I am vindicated!"

"You are," declared Hiraeth, "and long may you continue to so guide us."

Two days later, they found more desiccated vegetation in a shelter and stopped to give forage to the yaks. By this time, the dread lassitude had imperceptibly fallen from them, much as the Aelans had predicted. Once more there was time and breath for idle chatter, speculation and plotting for possible scenarios within the castle. As they moved onward, they could hear the doleful wail from a uniquely discordant wind sculpture, a weeping dirge that yet held echoes of unforgotten anger, unsleeping and unrelenting. Bathed in its bitter wash, the Aelans would not comment upon its disharmonious cry but hurried past it with eager feet.

They reached a time-mottled monolith, staunchly guarding the head of a steep-sided ravine. Behind it reared a huge barrow of round stones with a disquieting resemblance to petrified skulls. While the lowlanders stood awkwardly, dwarfed by this emblem of past glory and sacrifice, the girls both dropped to one knee and covered their faces with their hands. When they rose again, Hophni started to ask about the louring cairn but was cut short by Arwain.

"This is part of Aelan history, nothing to do with foreigners."

"Mighty as you are, you are yet foreigners," mumbled Tywy, transfixed by the towering stone.

At last the company turned and crept away from the standing stone. They processed in silence past the foreboding tumulus while the frost-cracked rocks grinned down at them in malicious spite and the grating moans of the sculpture rattled from wall to wall of the ravine.

The Rokepike

They stopped at a junction and, as one, their heads tilted back as they looked up to the Rokepike. High on a crag reared seven towers of pale stone linked by sheer battlements, the keep looming over them all. Flags and flickering pennants snapped hungrily at the empty air.

Though outer walls of the castle sloped outwards from the edge of the cliff, murder holes and bastions gave vantage over any position that might have been sheltered from the top of the high walls. The sloping design made the castle seem to lean threateningly towards them, black arrow-slitted eyes piercing them with a pitiless stare.

Ygyrd meticulously paid the Aelans their dues and thanked them for their care, shaking hands solemnly to mark the end of their contract.

Arwain said, "We are greatly honoured to have escorted you. Long have I dreamed of treading the High Hithrogael, yet without the strong arms of your guards, I, Arwain, a child of the peaks, would have failed in the crossing. I thank you."

"I hear you," replied Ygyrd. "You know how we'd have fared without your aid. However, when we depart from here on whatever the next leg of our travel might be, could we hope for your help a second time?"

"There's a village some three leagues down this road with a way station. We'll wait there awhile for new employment, although normally we would head back swiftly for Lana where there is the best chance of work with other foreign traders. The first deal is always the best." She had the grace to look embarrassed at their ability to extort money from foreigners who did not know their tricks as Ygyrd now did and continued swiftly. "For the return leg, most traders find guides unaccountably absent and only when they are desperate and the price is right do we reappear. However, if your business is soon concluded, you may reach us there. We would like that."

"But first," said Tywy, "it's customary for mountain guides to offer gifts to their charges commensurate with the mutual satisfaction obtained. Usually this is waived in all but form. However, you merit the greatest gifts we can offer. We wish we had more."

Arwain continued, "You, Ygyrd, as the leader, have been the solid rock upon which all else has been built. To you we give this rough map of western Ael. While it will not replace a guide, it will prevent a less scrupulous individual leading you on a circuitous route."

"My thanks for your noble generosity. A gift of rare value, for the problem is not unknown," said Ygyrd, accepting a folded parchment.

The two girls turned and knelt to the wrestlers. "Such puissance is beyond us. Upon you both we wish to bestow these emblems, asking only that you reveal not their significance outside Ael. The Levin of Ael is a badge of great honour. While they will not necessarily ensure you are accorded good treatment, they show that you have earned full respect and are not to be treated as mere foreigners."

The girls unpinned small brooches fashioned like milky-white lightning bolts from their own clothes and attached them to Bolan and Hophni, who murmured awkward thanks. The Aelans then both kissed Hiraeth, much to everyone's surprise, and asked, "What gift would you have of us, Song Master?"

"To have heard a few of the songs of Ael is reward enough for me but if I might ask a favour, tell me the tale of the barrow and the stone on the Hithrogael. I hunger for that tale like a starving man and beg to hear it."

They both stared at him, then turned to each other. "Sit then," said Arwain at length, "and you shall hear, though I am not the teller for this tale. I trust you to hear with the ears of imagination.

"During the long years of the Belmenian Empire, fierce Ael remained aloof and independent, raiding into the soft lowlands and fleeing, laughing, into the mountains when the Belmenian cavalry pursued in lumbering outrage. But either we tweaked the Imperial nose too often or some new campaign became politically expedient for them. The Imperial generals were ordered to reduce Ael into subjection.

"Ael comprises many tribes and their vendettas made co-operation impossible even in the face of a foreign threat. Such as the Condors would side with the Belmenians to further their own ends without a thought for the future of our land. But there were two heroes; the twin brothers Tarren and Siglo. When the mighty army of Belmenia stormed Lana and penetrated into Ael, Siglo pretended to defect to their cause, saying he wished to oust his brother who ruled their tribe in his stead. While Tarren raised what of the tribes he could, though they were pitifully few to face the invaders, Siglo convinced the foreigners to follow him onto the High Hithrogael, aided by rock-falls and ambushes laid by his brother Tarren.

"The Belmenian army was mighty and well supplied but the Hithrogael took its toll. Then Tarren met them with all his strength at the Nethangard. When they saw his position, the foreigners were aware that they had been tricked by Siglo and slew him cruelly. But they had just crossed the Hithrogael with a storm at their heels and dared not face it once more. They chose to meet Tarren, thinking to sweep his few warriors from their path. They were weakened with cold and the altitude but they outnumbered him twenty to one and the skills of war were theirs, they thought. They attacked but the Aelans gave not. They fought until the dead lay in heaps but they could not force a passage through the ravine. Tarren's sword broke in combat but he slew a Belmenian captain with his fist and took his sword. Peerless Tarren held them. But when he killed two, ten took their place; when he killed ten, twenty more surged forward. He would not yield and the dauntless Aelans battled with him. The Belmenians died but still they came onward with the dreadful Hithrogael at their backs. Then Tarren forged forward, striking right and left. He stood over the mutilated body of his brother Siglo and defied the whole host.

"It could not last. It did not last. A nameless foreigner hewed off his sword-hand. Another soldier Tarren felled and yet a second but the ebb of his hot blood could not stem the flood of the freezing Belmenian tide and he fell across the corpse of his brother.

"They thought we should break then, that the loss of our leader would be the end. It was not. Most of the Aelans lay dead or wounded but none yielded. Boys fought like mountain lions. Boys died as men. Any who could climb hurled rolling death from the sides of the ravine, once and again. The Belmenians now could hardly gasp for breath, much less fight and at last they turned. The cream of the Imperium dropped their weapons and staggered back to the cold heart of the mountains. They chose the ice before our knives. But they misjudged the Hithrogael and few survived to be driven from Ael.

"Our losses were more than grievous: there were no triumphant rejoicings. Siglo and Tarren were no more. Now the standing stone marks where they lie together, still holding the last ravine of the High Hithrogael. There lies the unsleeping spirit of Ael."

Arwain lapsed into silence with her head bent. Hiraeth leapt forward and kissed her hand. "How we are honoured," he cried. "A tale to cherish and well told. May it uphold the mountains for ever!"

Last of all, the girls bowed to Jebbin. "Exceeding rare it is to find a wizard upon a trading mission, we have heard of no such thing before. In your way, you too are puissant."

"Thank you, I think," returned Jebbin. "However, in truth I squandered my power in rash, ill-conceived and unintelligent spells in a manner that nearly cost my life and, without Hophni, would have done so. I shall not so err again."

The Aelans looked at his grim expression in surprise, then enquired warily what he might ask of them.

"As my boon, call us friends and not foreigners."

Ygyrd and Hiraeth smiled at this but the girls were surprised again.

"Small is the gift and yet great. It is given with pleasure. Farewell, our friends."

With a final bow, they turned and set off at a rapid pace for the village, packs hoisted high on their sturdy backs, Tywy's crampons clinking a fading tintinnabulation. Their departure cast a gloom upon the travellers. Not only did they miss the girls' company but their absence brought home with needle-pointed clarity that the end of their quest was in sight. And they were laughably few to enter such a castle with hope of working ill against it.

"We must use stealth," murmured Jebbin. "Get in and let Ygyrd sell the bibelots for the best price he can manage. While he's doing that, we must manufacture some opportunity for Bolan to spring Matico. I hope I'll find further clues to chase the treasure I seek and then we must all leave as swiftly as may be."

"That's the sum total of your plan?" Ygyrd cocked an eyebrow at him. "If so, then I have the easiest part."

They began to travel upwards once more on a zigzag trail, switchbacks defended by squat towers, door-less and superficially deserted. None felt that a closer inspection would have been in keeping with their role as traders.

The sun had rolled behind the high peaks before they trundled to a halt in front of the great barbican protecting the gates. Beneath it all was shadowy and dismal but Ygyrd strode forward underneath a weighty portcullis as though unconcerned and rapped sharply upon an iron-studded door in the gates. A small hatch swung open and the weathered face of an Aelan glared out. He wore a massive helmet.

Jebbin started as though struck and chanted audibly, "Behind morne infare and heaumed guards... By the lady, this is truly the place!"

"State your business," snapped the guard.

"Trading," Ygyrd replied civilly, as unperturbed as ever. "Goods specially selected to appeal to the lord of this castle; trinkets for his lady, little treasures from the world over."

The guard interrupted him with a nasty laugh. "We'll see about that in the morning. Be off with you."

"You must let us in," Ygyrd remonstrated but once again the guard cut in.

"Don't tell me what to do. I have my orders and now you have yours. Be quick about following them." He glanced significantly at holes and slits almost lost in the gloom beneath the bulk of the barbican. "I'll generously recommend you camp out of bowshot of the walls. We wouldn't want any accidents."

The hatch slammed shut, leaving Ygyrd to shrug and return to the wagon. There was nothing for it but to turn round and camp for the night in a gully off the winding approach road.

They formed a cross little group, facing another cold, uncomfortable night with only stale hard-tack and water for their supper. The yaks fared worse still and gazed mournfully about them with luminous eyes before settling down and chewing the cud with self-absorbed resignation. A light snow was floating down, keeping everything damp and slippery.

"I don't see why we shouldn't go back down to the main trail and follow the girls to this town they mentioned. There'd be an inn, no doubt; perhaps hot baths, hot food, company, beer, beds...." Hophni sighed gustily.

"Still have to guard the wagon," said Jebbin

"A murrain on the wagon!"

"Having brought it this far, I'm not going to lose everything in sight of the Rokepike - but the rest sounds good to me."

"Forget it," growled Ygyrd. "You're traders. We cannot take this wagon down an unknown trail in the dark and snow."

"Why not? I haven't been dry since Lana and I've forgotten what it's like not to be shivering. Probably die out here anyway if I have to eat one more mouthful of this frozen, dead donkey stuff," grumbled Hophni, waving a strip of dried meat.

At that moment there was a discreet cough from the trail up to the Rokepike and a voice edged through the drifting white, "My pardon, sirs, but might I be permitted to offer one or two conveniences for the evening?"

Bolan immediately sidled into the darkness, leaving Ygyrd to summon the newcomer towards the wagon. "Come forward and show yourself. We may have some minor interests."

A mule plodded carefully towards the meagre light that bulged past the huddled figures in the wagon. Behind it came a well-wrapped figure who threw back his hood in a flurry of snow and bowed to them. He had little need to speak for the mule's burden was spouting its message with incomparable eloquence.

"Balgrim!" cried Hophni, inhaling deeply and quivering all over like a mastiff on a spoor. "Speak up, man, what have you there?"

The seller pushed back a net of fodder for the draught animals and unpacked a stained, leather pannier from the mule. His face appeared demonic, lit from beneath by the orange glow of a small brazier. His eyes were lost in blackness while his beard sparkled as though afire, his cheeks and nose were daubed with garish light and teeth glinted as he spoke, his breath a copper cloud.

"Roast sweet potatoes, hot chestnuts, venison steaks stuffed with onions, garlic and mushrooms and wrapped in pastry, various sweetmeats and, in the other pannier, a modest pipkin of hot ale mulled with kumquats and spices."

"And how much for these unnecessary luxuries?" enquired Ygyrd, trying to ignore Hophni's ecstatic groans.

"I could not accept less than thirty ryals for the full load," declared the man resolutely.

"Thirty ryals! You jest," Ygyrd cried but it was too late. Hophni had already snatched and sunk his teeth into a pastry.

"Pay the man, pay him," he said indistinctly, rolling his eyes round his head in euphoric delight.

The seller smiled ingratiatingly at Ygyrd, wringing his hands, but Ygyrd was as bleak as the stone about him when he tossed a bag of coins at his feet.

"That's twenty ryals - which should include the mule, five times as much food and your worthless service for a year. You're a parasite preying on those trapped by the Rokepike's regulations. Go."

"As my lord says, I'm sure," said the man evilly after glancing at Hophni, who was calling to Jebbin to pour the ale. "I'll collect the panniers and heaters in the morning," he said and backed away into the night.

Shortly after he left, Bolan returned, shaking his head to indicate there was no sign of other interlopers. They collected food from wire baskets in the panniers, tossing pastries and potatoes from hand to hand until they were cool enough to devour but, before they had time to take more than a mouthful, Jebbin shivered away the memory of a minim of *sear* and declared, "The beer is polluted. Nobody drinks it."

"By the gods, it smells divine," croaked Hophni. "Are you sure? Perhaps it's just the spices?"

"The True Sight tells me there is some contamination. Not lethal, I think, but there may be herbs to induce a deeper sleep than is advisable."

"Truly, you have grown cautious. We must be doubly vigilant, for there would be little point in knavery with the beer if further devilment were not planned for tonight," said Ygyrd, regarding his pastry critically. "You're sure the food is pure?"

Jebbin nodded his answer over a mouthful of venison. He stared up through the darkness to where the invisible weight of the castle pressed upon them. Thanks to his spell, they knew trouble would come to them from that looming edifice tonight, but not why. Why did the wolf strike at them from his den? Did he know why there were there? Glaring upward, he chewed meat and thoughts together.

They catnapped with a double watch, weapons at the ready.

But the fresh snow deadened all sound and frozen night was wrapped closely about them. Nothing heralded the attack. Hiraeth and Bolan were alert, watching the swirling phantasms that danced their mesmerising pavane behind seven veils of white flakes, and both turned at the sudden sound of tearing canvas. A dark shape bulked visibly against the snow-paled side of the wagon. In an instant, both were shouting alarms and the defence was roused.

Bolan bounded forward and dealt a double-handed blow at the centre of the form but it shrank before him and his blade met no resistance. The apparition sprang back from the wagon and disappeared in the brotherly darkness ranged at its shoulders. Only razor white claws and a mewling, sucking mouth could be seen, driving towards him. Bolan gave ground uncertainly before this hidden attacker but then a shower of sparkling fire shot forward as Jebbin joined the fray and gleaming light spangled over a hulking form, rendering it visible. Bolan grunted in satisfaction but the apparition trumpeted thinly and floated towards the mage. At that moment, a flask of oil hurled by Hiraeth splattered over it, drenching its insubstantial body. A torch followed in short order and the apparition vanished in a sheet of stark flame.

Hophni's bull-like roaring carried from the main trail, punctuated by the heavy twanging of Ygyrd's crossbow; a brief scream spearing the belly of the night. Even as the apparition dissolved from sight, the three pelted through the snow towards the clangour from the trail; hoarse shouting and the mad cracking of a whip.

The first thing they saw was Ygyrd's solid frame, hunched over while he cranked his crossbow, then a glimpse of a rapidly retreating cart. Men slumped in the cart, one figure hanging to the back of it and being dragged helter-skelter across the icy trail. Then the snowy night swallowed them as though they had winked out of existence, only receding cries and crackings told of their continued flight towards the Rokepike. They stared after the diminishing racket, panting pale wraiths of nascent reprisals into the frosted air.

"I'd hoped this one might have told us what this was all about," said Hophni suddenly from behind them. "But he sort of died." He lowered a limp body into the snow with distaste. "Still," he added cheerfully, "I doubt we'll see any more of that lot tonight."

"Let's get back to the wagon before we freeze. We can sort this out in the morning when we can see further than our boots," suggested Ygyrd, as though the whole affray had been nothing more than a minor excursion to examine a mountain flower.

As they trudged back, Jebbin looked at the dim but solid form of the great wrestler beside him. "Hophni, why do you never use a blade? Bolan does, so it can't be against your code."

"Codes count for little when death grins too closely," chuckled Hophni. "But Bolan's handy with a sword. In fact, he's good with every weapon I've seen him use; good enough to be a weapons' master. Me, I was hopeless. Weapons just seemed to get in the way. Half the time I would hold a sword in one hand and hit opponents with the other. Caused havoc with the ratings! I was always getting disarmed and then winning the fight. My sword master tried and tried to teach me how to avoid disarmament; total failure. Eventually he became so annoyed, as my weapon flew over my shoulder yet again, that he threatened to give me a few scars to make me learn. So I took his sword away. Unfortunately, he was a sword master so I had to be a bit rough and his arm broke. Got me into all sorts of trouble. Now not having a weapon means I don't rely on something that I could lose. In fact, when I fight people who carry weapons, they tend to expect an easy victory and relax. So I find that not having a sword actually gives me an edge." He burst out laughing suddenly. "Hey, Bolan, did you hear that? Not having a sword gives me an edge!"

But then they reached the wagon and the lingering reek of the burnt oil and found they had not done as well as they thought. The apparition, not so easily dispelled, had only retreated before Hiraeth's assault and both sides of the canvas over the wagon were now ripped. After a rapid search, Ygyrd announced that all the trade goods were gone. While Bolan and Hophni looked vaguely at disappearing tracks in the snow, Jebbin cursed volubly and execrated his stupidity in leaving the wagon.

"Seems odd," mused Ygyrd. "That was a huge effort to steal a few trinkets. Cost more than their value. That offends me."

"It's my fault for only half solving that cursed riddle," shouted Jebbin testily. "Only now can I guess what "niffled" means. He gains his pleasure from the theft. But now is too late and the whole trading charade is destroyed."

At that moment, a new voice spoke through the darkness, telling them to remain stationary but drop their weapons. In the pause that followed, Jebbin looked up sharply, his brow furrowed.

"Lord Rallor?" he enquired of the seething night.

The wind blew quiet and cold before the voice continued, "Who is that?"

"Jebbin. We met at Farralei."

A moment more and the big southerner coalesced from the substance of the night with others of his entourage. Their boots scuffed up the soft snow which ran away, whispering in the rising breeze.

"I see you solved the riddle. I meant to leave a message that I was still working on it but forgot what your Narbez traded."

"Pearls," said Rallor distractedly, "but I left word for you.

No matter. I'm not here chasing your little enigma. Indeed, that would hardly be possible when some villain went to great lengths to steal it. He failed and died but the copy was destroyed. I told you I had other business at Lana. I'm amazed to find you here of all places. This, too, is the end of your quest? But who are these others? And what of the Gesgarian?"

Jebbin performed introductions, leaving Rallor still more surprised at the presence of Bolan and Hophni, both of whom were known to him. "I suppose," he continued to Rallor, "that it's the prospective union of Triva and the Snow Leopards while the latter are bound to Lykos that brings you here?"

"No. Lykos seeks to destroy the old structure of Ael and re-form it with himself at its head. He forges what tribes he can control into an army for war and conquest. I oppose him. But what union is this? That news is very bad."

"Come now," interrupted Hiraeth, "there are tales to be told all round here and we must hold a moot. You, Bolan and Jebbin are all here at one time on different affairs, if related, which is good news for me, for the best stories are ever begotten by coincidence. But perhaps guards should be posted before more visitors spoil the listening?"

Rallor had already delegated this to Hol, who later joined them in their discussions, where each told another part of the tale of Lykos and his machinations. After some reluctance, Rallor told how he came to be in Ael.

"Pattacus, the famed sage of Shekkem came to me with a tale of a Gesgarian stealing knowledge of the location of the Staff of Sumos. From another source, Pattacus also knew how the Staff was defended. I was to collect the Staff and deliver it to the Ravens in Ael. So we foil a thief and gain an honest excuse to get my knights to the Rokepike. Thus far, our local guides have kept us from Aelan raiders, though Yulin tells me that we have passed fresh battle sites. Blood was plain on the snow, suggesting others have been less fortunate. Now, standing before the castle of Lykos, the duty and honour that shone so brightly in the words of the sage seem less plain. What is left but to stop him? But Hophni, why are you here?"

Hophni jerked a thumb towards Bolan, who answered, "Matico will be released."

"I'm no wiser. Who?"

Jebbin cut in, "A prince of Ael. Lykos holds him and others prisoner as hostages to keep the tribes of Ael under his thumb."

"I see, but why are you the man for this?"

"More important, how?"

Then discussions in the gully became more vehement. As the night faded, the wind rose to a gale that forced them to huddle in the exiguous cover and turn their backs to the raging whorls of blown ice that coated them with white. The snow was no longer falling but gravid clouds threatened to spawn teeming children at any time.

Jebbin and Hophni approached the gate before the first hint of dawn and attempted to gain entry. The guard demanded to see samples of their wares and then sniggered when they could provide nothing. To all their offers, blandishments and threats the guard answered that as they had nothing to trade, they had no justifiable reason for coming in and he shut the door upon them.

Now Rallor was discussing storming the gates while another knight tightened the buckles of his armour.

"That enterprise is perilous to the point of foolhardy," remarked Hophni. "I've seen those gates and they are not for breaching with, what, forty men?"

"Perilous indeed but I trust we may baulk at the foolhardy," returned Rallor. "Nevertheless, we have crept to these gates under cover of snow and dark and it would be death to wait in this gully for imminent discovery. We must not lose our only advantage of surprise and this blasting cold draws the very life from our veins. Perhaps we can conceal ourselves until someone else enters or leaves and risk all on a charge."

"The military mind!" exclaimed Ygyrd in a derisive outburst. "When doors have a handle, it is folly to burst them open. Men have fought since the dawn of time but greed ever came before strife. I will open this gate for you, though at this last I think I should have returned to Gelavien. Or Jerondst. I really did want to see the place."

Jebbin moved to speak to the northerner but Ygyrd turned and busied himself with the traces for the yaks. For the first and only time since Jebbin had met him on the road to Lana, there was a weariness about him that made him look old. Then the moment was gone and Jebbin joined the wrestlers and Hiraeth on the wagon as Ygyrd drove it through the roaring wind back towards the Rokepike.

"Keep out of sight and keep watch," Ygyrd told Rallor. "You'll know when."

Ygyrd rapped on the door once more and the hatch opened to reveal the guard, munching away on a mouthful of bread. As Ygyrd drew breath to speak, the guard said, "Off." He was not a man for undue loquacity.

"Listen, you can't turn us away. We came over the High Hithrogael to get here."

"Sure. I go up there with my granny for tea every day."

"But we have no supplies left. If you refuse us entry, we die. You must help us."

"So you have a problem. But that's it: your problem. Get your supplies elsewhere, nobody asked you here trading."

"Look, you seem an intelligent and sympathetic sort of chap," said Ygyrd, stoutly flying in the face of all the available evidence, "and we do have money."

"So?" drawled the guard, his eyes narrowing with dawning interest.

"We cannot eat it. I understand that despite your personal wishes to help, you have no authority to let us in. But even if we have to pay double or treble costs for provisions, we must have them. We don't know where else to go. Unless guard's wages are a lot better here than anywhere else, we could help each other."

"Don't see how," frowned the guard obtusely, taking another bite at his loaf. "I ain't got stores of food, you know."

"No," agreed Ygyrd patiently, "but if you offered the quartermaster double what he paid for supplies and we paid you triple, who's going to lose?"

The guard paused, looking round furtively and licking his lips. "Lessee the money," he hissed.

Ygyrd obligingly spilled golden ryals into his own palm and waved them gently. "Just let me in to say what we need and a couple of lads to carry the stuff and it's all yours."

"I can charge you four times the price and you have to pay!" declared the guard in delight.

"You're a cunning fellow and no mistake," admitted Ygyrd sorrowfully, evidently considering the term capable of wide interpretation. "But as you have spotted, we have no choice."

"Deal!" the guard cried, checking behind him once more. "But you even think of trouble and Gerulf will freeze your eyes off a lance point."

Ygyrd turned and waved Hophni and Bolan forward but the guard took one look at the two wrestlers and refused. "No chance. I'm not letting those two thugs in here."

"But we're totally unarmed," said Hophni innocently, assaying a sweet smile.

"Well you surely don't look it. Back off. You two'll do," he pointed at Jebbin and Hiraeth. "And you can leave that stick behind too. Calwyn," he called over his shoulder. "Come and watch these characters. Any trouble, sound the alarm and Gerulf will battle the crows for these three; you got that out there? Now let's go - and bring that gold."

The three of them slipped inside after the guard had suspiciously raked the roadway with a searching stare. There was no sign of Rallor who evidently considered that the moment would be more propitious when the guard was busy counting gold and the provisions might conceal his early rush. Calwyn latched the door and stood by the hatch. Hophni kept him talking, telling him how cold it was outside and trying to wheedle him into letting them rest just inside the door, without any success at all.

Meanwhile, the guard led the others into a wide hallway with various doors, passages and a stair leading from it. It was paved with smooth yellow-ochre stone and roofed by a vaulted ceiling. Lances bearing pennons and insignia strutted stiffly over all the doorways. Two women idly ambled across the hall, mouthing vague speculations over the newcomers, whom they eyed coyly. A kitchen boy galloped from a passageway clutching an empty tray. He skidded past the women and was gone in a patter of bare feet. Over the moaning wind, the distant noises of habitation crowded back round them in a familiar buzz that seemed extraordinarily loud after the long silence since Lana. Hiraeth stopped in amazement.

"It's warm!" he exclaimed in astonishment.

"Of course, you foreign dolt. This is the Rokepike," said the guard as if that explained everything. "Now, what do you really need? I doubt your purse will buy you a wagon load at the prices I'll have to charge."

But now Jebbin had halted next to Hiraeth. He was staring

at a dark entrance in a corner of the hall. Unlike other openings, this was so lightless it might have been where night laired throughout the day, an inky curtain drawn across some lethal pit.

"That's it," he whispered, the words of the seer thudding in his mind. "We have to go that way, now, immediately."

"Why?"

"I don't know. I didn't understand."

"But we must get the others in first," Hiraeth urged.

"Come on lads!" Ygyrd called from the passage. "What's the matter with you? We're in a hurry."

Jebbin gazed at the black entrance, feeling the exhalation of warm air as though from a dragon's mouth. A soft vibration almost below hearing wriggled down his spine.

"Down there, Jebbin? Frighten me to death though it may, I will join you, but later. Now we must follow Ygyrd's lead. Come." He pulled Jebbin away from the weird blankness and after the guard, who was entering a room at the end of a passage, still discussing Ygyrd's requirements and making up new and higher prices as he went.

Just as they caught up, an alarm bell from a distant part of the castle began a furious clanking, rapidly joined by others. They all jerked round in a tableau of surprise, then the guard drew his sword and hacked wildly at Ygyrd, in a panic that his failings as a door-ward would be exposed. Instead of falling back, Ygyrd slipped a dagger from his boot top, drove inside the arc of the guard's clumsy swing and stabbed hard. The dagger skittered over the guard's armour and sliced into his ear. Yowling, the guard thrashed backward and struck again but the trader had the guard's sword-arm in his gnarled fist and thrust again with the dagger. As the guard slumped to the ground Ygyrd cried, "Get back to the others! This is real trouble."

But at that moment, a group of guards burst in from another

door on their way to the armoury. They were not yet armoured but most carried knives.

"They've killed Haern! Get them!"

Ygyrd brandished his own dagger and Haern's short sword but he could not hope to cow such a superior number and the guards closed with them. A thrown knife struck Ygyrd in the thigh, a second sliced into the top of Jebbin's shoulder. He cried out and dropped his ball of *sear*. He glimpsed Ygyrd thrusting his dagger into the guts of one man and slashing wildly with the sword. With a surge of adrenalin, Jebbin tore the knife from his shoulder and leapt on an Aelan about to throw a knife at Hiraeth. He discharged all the pain from his shoulder in a shocking jolt into the Aelan's chest. Then another guard cannoned into him and there was no chance of further spells as he was swept into a confused melee of stabbing and punching.

Hiraeth stepped back in horror. "I'm a bard!" he squeaked as one of the charging guards elbowed past the embattled Jebbin and reached out for him. Hands clasped round his throat and he was pushed back into the wall. Hiraeth began beating vainly at the throttling fingers but he was banged into the wall again and again. Blackness, shot through with red streaks, swept down over his sight and the strength evaporated from his legs.

The world drifted from Hiraeth as though it turned without him. He could no longer feel his burning throat and a pink warmth reached out to engulf him. For a timeless instant, Hiraeth hovered on the brink of death but he had no strength with which to fight and he accepted his fate. As he sank down towards that numbing embrace, the splotches before his eyes formed a sad, yearning face; a small face with bulging soft brown eyes that saw nothing beyond his shop.

"Poor bard," a voice seemed to murmur. "You said you would come back, come back, come back."

"I can't now. I can't fight. It's no use."

"I will give you my strength."

"Erridarch," cried Hiraeth, remembering the geographer dragging his slight body on lamed legs, "Your strength is too little, my small friend."

"It is all I have. I wanted you to sing to me so much. Now you must sing of me." The soft tones faded into nothing.

A tiny flare of vigour bloomed feebly in Hiraeth. Its very uselessness, the death of a hopeless dream, reached Hiraeth as nothing else could. That moment of doomed courage, futile as a lone farmer defending his last lamb from the entire Belmenian cavalry, ignited his draining shreds of life, and at last he fought. Not for himself; he fought for all like Erridarch, for all the little people and lost causes and overmatched people, all the downtrodden, bereft and forlorn. He jerked his knee into the guard's groin, then, half punching, half collapsing, he swung his fist with the last dregs of his might. By some miracle, he caught the retching man on the adam's apple and the guard toppled like a falling tower, Hiraeth dropping beside him.

Calwyn heard the frantic tolling of the alarm bell at a distant point in the castle and started round in surprise with a brief exclamation. Instantly, Hophni's fist burst through the hatchway and smashed into his chin. His head snapped back and the huge helmet flew off to sound its own alarm on the stone floor. Even before Calwyn landed in a clatter of armour, Hophni's arm was through the hatch and unfastening the door and Rallor was pounding through the drifts of snow in a mighty charge, his men close behind. The wind screamed a warning to the castle and buffeted the running men until they reeled and staggered like drunkards.

Bolan snatched up Jebbin's quarterstaff and followed Hophni into the warm hall. A guard leapt from a recess, lunging at

Hophni. Hophni sidestepped the blow, grabbed the man's wrist with his left hand and yanked him further on his line of attack, unbalancing him. Hophni twisted so the man crunched into his shoulder, then drove his right elbow into the unprotected solar plexus. Completing the move, he smacked his right fist back into the man's face. The guard crumpled as though pole-axed and probably thought he had been. Hophni did not bother to check on the Bear guard but darted left towards the sound of a fracas up one of the passages, Bolan at his side.

Rallor faced guards erupting from the right and hit them like a tornado, his great sword thrumming, ripping jagged rents through armour and shields while behind him his men struggled through the narrow door in the gates and into the fray. More defenders came racing from the dining halls but when the first of them saw the heavily armed knights battling in the hall, he hastily backtracked, shouting for the others to take a different route to the armoury.

The two wrestlers spurred on after their friends. As they rushed down the passage, one of the doors opened just ahead of them and the head of a pole-arm emerged. Hophni took off and hit the door full tilt with a flying dropkick. There was a choking cry as the door splintered backward, cracking under the impact. Hophni landing rolling and sprinted onward and into the fight. They strode through the guards as though amid children, Bolan first hurling the quarterstaff like a javelin to fell one of Jebbin's opponents. Hophni's full destructive abilities were unleashed in an awesome display of skill. Each attack against him seemed a clumsy parody of a move in slow motion. All the energies of his opponents were turned against themselves. It was as though he danced amongst them as he flung one into another, and all they could touch of him were booted feet and iron fists.

Bolan forged through them like a ram-ship. He methodically

avoided the knives and ignored punches and kicks. His sword or fist would flick out and on he went. It was Bolan who dragged the last guard from a melee with Jebbin. He lifted him bodily with his left hand and demolished him with a punch from his right that sent the guardsman flying back into the wall. The Aelan bounced off it with a bone-jarring thud and toppled forward without bending to land face down on the floor.

Hiraeth slowly crawled up from a guard finally incapacitated by Hophni, clutching his throat and rasping painfully for air. Jebbin rolled dazedly to a sitting position, one hand over his shoulder. It was numbed from his spell but the whole area ached with a hollow coldness. His arm still worked, so he tried to ignore the slowly oozing blood. Pok's carefully concealed poniard had never cleared his clothing.

Bolan collected the staff and tossed it to him, suggesting he kept his distance a little better in future. Jebbin caught the staff and gave the wrestler a wry grin but before he answered, he glanced up at Ygyrd. In trying to ward his unarmed companions the trader had borne the brunt of the fighting. His leg was drenched with blood, dark punctures showed on his arms and his face was cut; his white, stubbly beard beaded with red. The dagger was long gone and, as the battle finished, he dropped the sword with a groan. It pattered a knell on the floor while he stood, bent forward with both arms pressed to his left side, but as the sword quivered to a halt, he fell back to land in a sitting position. Bolan and Hophni helped him back against the wall. His face wrinkled with pain as they shifted him and a dark flood of fluid gushed past his pressing arm. But then his old inscrutability drew back over him and his face smoothed, ice-blue eyes opening once more. A fine sheen of sweat made him seem doubly pallid.

"Ygyrd!" cried Jebbin, hastening to his side.

"Go. I'm all right." The attempted firmness in his voice was hollow with huskiness, as though his normally gravelled tones were clogged with clotting blood.

"We cannot leave you here. You saved us both."

"You must hurry.... from here.... or I won't have." Each new breath Ygyrd took was delayed longer and longer and came in a rattling spasm. His eyes drifted from Jebbin to look over his shoulder. "Make him understand," he murmured in a low plea to Bolan.

"There are spells to aid healing..." Jebbin faltered, unable to keep his gaze from the widening puddle soaking into Ygyrd's clothes and spreading across the pale stone floor. He knelt and placed his quivering fingers over Ygyrd's own gnarled hand. It felt cold.

"Not to.... heal me, boy. Go now. Make it worthwhile." Ygyrd's voice was little more than a soft growl.

Jebbin felt Bolan's huge hands softly raising him but a great lump blocked his throat and tears coursed down his cheeks. Through a blur he saw Hophni reach out and gently squeeze the northerner's shoulder in farewell. Ygyrd turned his head fractionally and nodded at him. Hiraeth, too, stretched out and rested his lean hand lightly on Ygyrd's white hair. Then the trader's gaze grew blank and his head tilted forward to rest. His arms relaxed away from the hideous wound in his side and he was still.

Hiraeth touched his thumb to Ygyrd's forehead to make the sign of the teardrop. "Go with the Lady," he whispered.

As Bolan steered him back towards Rallor's company, Jebbin asked brokenly, "What did he mean? Make what worthwhile?"

"Dying," replied Bolan softly. "Has to be worth more than money. Be strong now and achieve your quest. Do not fail Ygyrd."

Bolan said no more but guided Jebbin swiftly back. When

they regained the first hall, Jebbin's grief had been kneaded with anger and leavened with a determination to succeed that burned more fiercely than ever. He felt it was his error in not acting upon the riddle at once that had denied the trader his sight of the grim, giant walls of Jerondst; a reflection of his own character. He would not fail Ygyrd again.

Rallor held the hall unopposed but in answer to Hophni's question, he replied, "They do but wait to arm the rest of the garrison properly. Our advantage of surprise evaporates momently - a curse on whatever caused that alarm to ring! We must make for the keep with all speed or be whelmed by numbers."

"This way," commanded Jebbin with a new authority and headed for his dark exit.

"We cannot dive down that lightless hole," exclaimed Hol. "It reeks of traps and delusions."

"We have flouted the words of the seer long enough and death has been our reward. There's no time for discussion or delay. Follow or fail." Immediately Jebbin turned and plunged into the blackness of the narrow entrance, Hiraeth and the wrestlers on his heels.

With swift decision, Rallor silenced Hol with a shake of his head. "Bring torches," he called, "and hasten where the mage leads. Hol, bring up the rear and brook no delays. None." Then Rallor was gone after the others and his disciplined knights filed rapidly after him. At the rear, Hol looked from side to side back into the hall, its grand beauty marred by blood and the scattered bodies of dead and unconscious soldiers. He shook his head sadly at the trials of following the southern lord and stepped into the warm dark.

Suddenly doors crashed open into the hall. Warriors streamed inwards, yelling battle cries, naked blades brazenly dancing. Hol found himself wedged against an invisible knight, unable to move further. Looking back, he could dimly see a magician with a hazel staff upraised, poised on the verge of magic. The magician gradually relaxed, initially ignoring the captain of the guards who came to report, entirely unnecessarily, that the attackers were gone.

"Thank you, Captain Addrach, I am not wholly blind," the magician said in a contemptuous voice. When the captain blanched and moved backward, the magician stalked forward until he stood barely a sword's length from Hol, gazing into the irredeemable blackness of the dark opening.

"If they've taken that way, then there's an end, lord Rhabdos."

"Perhaps," Rhabdos spoke slowly, making it obvious that he was trying to say something even the regrettably limited captain might comprehend. He closed his eyes and extended his hazel staff towards Hol, venting awkward syllables. His frown deepened but then he spoke decisively. "Ware the keep! I will call upon its..." he spared the captain a withering glance, "...effective defenders." He gathered his midnight blue robe about him and swept off at a great pace. Captain Addrach sighed in relief and called to his men to take to the battlements and repulse the other invaders.

Jebbin stopped suddenly and Hiraeth blundered straight into the back of him. Hophni sensed the presence before him and halted quietly with Bolan behind him.

"We're out of it," whispered Jebbin.

"What?"

"A torch, please."

In a moment, Rallor passed one forward and crowded after it himself. Just as Hophni was handing the light to Hiraeth, it suddenly brightened and illuminated the corridor they were in, showing where it divided just in front of them. Behind them, Rallor's knights were still lost in the blackness.

"Watch," said Jebbin, taking the torch. He moved it slowly towards the dark curtain that hid the knights. As it passed through, they were plunged into darkness once more. The torch was still visible as a dull glow but it shed no light. He drew it out again and its flickering rays washed down the walls about them.

"Sorcery," said Hophni dismissively. "What now? Which way?" He indicated the divergent passages ahead.

"Vital now is schetic docimasy," muttered Jebbin. "Quiet now."

Hophni raised his eyebrows and shrugged at Rallor, who grimaced back. "Wizards. They're all the same."

Jebbin paused at the junction with his head on one side, breathing softly through his mouth. Warm air moved from both entrances and waved the strands of his hair. Along one passage he could see an old chest at the limit of the torch's light, down the other he could occasionally hear a distant low grumbling, murmurous but heavy. He beckoned Rallor forward.

"There may be many lures or phantasms down here," he said, pointing to the chest, "Whatever your men see or feel, it is imperative that they stray not from my path. Should I fall, head for the chamber where this noise originates."

"What then?"

"Ah, what then indeed," mumbled Jebbin cryptically and not particularly helpfully. He turned into the right-hand tunnel and warily began to descend its steady slope. Behind him even the dour knights were exclaiming over the extraordinary blackness of the passage opening and whispering together until Jebbin had to call back for silence.

Jebbin stopped in a small chamber. A rusted weapons' rack sagged on one wall. Amidst the grimy and cobwebbed swords hung a silver mace, untarnished and flashing back the torchlight in alluring gleams. The gilded handle sparkled with tiny gems set in the semblance of great leaping cats. What magical properties it had to make its value in combat still higher than that on the market only its possessor might know.

"Touch nothing," Jebbin warned again.

Rallor noticed slots by each of the four entrances to the chamber and emphatically reinforced the prohibition. He called forward the only unarmoured knight, a dark, wiry man with an acid-pocked face and assigned him a place beside Jebbin.

"Yulin is the man for these traps and subtleties. If a man can keep our steps safe, he will," Rallor explained. Silently, Yulin took his place, black liquid eyes lambent in the torchlight.

Once more, Jebbin selected a downward path to another chamber; square this time, with three more exits. The floor was paved with large black and white tiles about a pace across. Yulin looked first up, then lay down before them with a torch and drifted his fingers over their surface like a blind man. He stood with a grunt of satisfaction.

"Tread only upon the white. It's good work," he said, looking over the deadly tiles with a strange pleasure.

"And the black?" queried a voice.

Yulin pointed at holes hidden in the patterned ceiling. "A bolt in the head, a hundred bolts, a purulent gas? I don't want to know."

On they went, through corridors and rooms. A half-empty barrel of spare torches sprawled drunkenly near one wall, bundles of reeds spewed incontinently about it. Hol suggested they should collect more torches. Yulin examined them briefly.

"They're laced with tiny spines. Probably poisoned."

"We brought few lights, little expecting to be clambering about in some cellar. We must not get caught by darkness down here amid myriad traps and what matter a few spines to a mailed hand?"

With a deft movement, Yulin drew a knife down a bundle, severing the cords that bound the reeds. They fell apart with a soft hiss to reveal a yellow powder concealed in the centre. It gleamed urgently.

"Have you not heard the mage? Touch nothing."

"Nevertheless," muttered Hol, "we must have light."

"Then we must husband what we have," put in Rallor. "Gifts from the master of the Rokepike must be taken with care."

At one junction, Jebbin had little difficulty in picking the left-hand passage, the din swelling ever louder, but a few strides down it, Yulin's arm brought him to an abrupt halt. Yulin bent to finger a fine wire stretching across the passage and indicated Jebbin should step over it.

"How in the name of the Lady did you see that?" asked Jebbin in wonderment.

"By looking for it," grunted Yulin laconically. He motioned the next man to guard the wire and rejoined Jebbin before allowing him to continue.

Another chamber, the exits partially blocked by the blowing tatters of false cobwebs, be-dewed with scintillating drops of poison. On one exit alone were the drops of water but without the throbbing noise to guide them, telling water from poison was impossible. Even with the knowledge that their way must be possible, they threaded their path through the webs disturbing them as little as possible.

The next chamber was throbbing with noise as though some glutinous surf pounded through it. Hot air beat against them in sudden pulses, an acrid tang gnawing steadily at noses and throats. Side by side, two dark passages yawned in poker-faced glee at the dilemma they posed, then sloped down into the glittering rock. Jebbin grimaced in perplexity, unable to tell where the noise was loudest. He took a few paces down the left passage,

returned and tried the right. He then chose the left passage, ignoring Yulin's grumbling over his indecision. Again, Yulin's arm
stopped him. The dark knight raised a cautionary finger and
moved a few more steps down the sharp incline. He called back
for a length of rope and wrapped it about his waist. Advancing
another couple of inching paces, he could see a glint of red. As
he stretched to see more, his feet whisked from beneath him and
he crashed to his side. With horrifying speed, he shot down the
passage on an almost frictionless surface until the rope brought
him up short with a twang, one of the precious torches hurtling
from sight.

Yulin offered no recriminations and scarcely bothered to
glance at Jebbin as he was dragged past. He did not respond
to Jebbin's suggestion that perhaps they might follow the right-
hand passage further than accepting another torch and taking
the lead once more. Behind him, the knights were almost engulfed in the creeping night of the passages and stumbled and
scuffed their way in near dark. Childish imaginings of looming
shapes and evil chitterings in the darkness took substance from
the oppressive catacomb about them and preyed on their minds
with vampiric insistence.

But after descending yet again in wide turns, the passage de-
bouched into a broad natural cavern, brilliantly lit with flaring
red light from a chasm. Directly above the chasm was a hole in
the rock wall. Had Yulin not roped himself back, he would have
issued from that opening and followed his torch down into the
molten rock that was the burning heart of the Rokepike.

A great stone tongue reached out over the glowing abyss, its
surface protected by inlaid runes and sigils of silver; the edge
graven with mythical beasts whose redly glittering eyes raked
the company through the unsteady air. About the walls, a heaving profusion of carved monsters reared in revulsion from their

captivity in wood and stone. Two dragons forever glared and gnashed ivory fangs either side of a narrow stair wrought of a midnight blue stone that looked black in the coloured light and only revealed itself where splotches of torchlight fell on it.

"Behold the Fireheart Chamber, centre of the Rokepike," roared Jebbin over the detonations of the bubbling, booming lava, gasping in the oxygen-stripped air. His mind swam with visions of wild rites and forbidden supplications performed on that unholy spur of smooth stone.

Hol was pointing upwards, bawling, "The keep, the keep!" Above them, no ceiling was discernable but an orange glow reflected back from the protuberances of layers of balconies, fading into the upper shadows.

"And yonder stair leads to our goal or nowhere," bellowed Rallor, nodding in recognition. He motioned Yulin forward even as Jebbin tugged at his sleeve.

"There is more here. You must wait."

But now Rallor shook his head vehemently. "No time. Pursue your own ends but our aim is different. If we strike not now nothing more will avail us. Now for an end," he cried, his strident tones ringing over the blatting bass of the lava. "Forward!"

Rallor drew his great sword and charged after Yulin up the shining stair of darkest blue. Jebbin was perforce drawn along amidst the knights as they pounded up the stairs and the mocking leer of the dragons throbbed behind his eyes.

The Wolf

Jebbin struggled along at the tail of elbowing, jostling knights on the stairway, unable to see the treads before him, orange light lashing at his back. However, it was soon plain that their almost unfaltering haste had enabled them to burst into the keep ahead of whatever defences Rhabdos sought to awaken. The blue stair had obviously been constructed to allow easy access to the Fireheart chamber for the masters of Rokepike and to provide an impressive entrance for the patriarch at rites after the laity had been guided to the chamber in the dark; walking down dismal and lightless passages following chanting initiates, where faith alone could persuade them that their next footfall would not be their last.

At the head of the stair they had faced an inviting door. Yulin had insisted they avoid it and demanded silence while he twisted flat silver dragons on either side of the door. A hidden entrance led them into a small library and a rushed defence from an adjoining robing room, whence issued a wild-eyed priest, laying about him with a ceremonial mace; a doughty guard and two nervously determined acolytes, clad in flapping robes and attacking with silver-tipped staves. The fight was long over by the time Jebbin blinked his way into the light of the library and Hol

306 ~ ACM PRIOR

was bundling captives into the robing room, their hands secured with silken sashes. The guard, somewhat dazed, was as quiet as the neophytes but the priest's vigorous writhings and thrashings had necessitated his being comprehensively bound and gagged. Hol locked the door with a convenient key and winked at Jebbin.

"They'll break out in time but it won't matter by then. Get moving."

"Where to?" asked Jebbin, tagging on to the knights filing rapidly out of the door.

"Find the gates of the keep and seal them. Rallor knows his way round any fortress ever built. A donjon this size alone may be too much for us but if it's reinforced from the castle, it'll go hard with us. Go, go!"

Jebbin squeezed through the door alongside Bolan; Hol and Hophni just behind him. Running down a short section of corridor flagged with polished marble, they turned through an iron-studded door into a courtyard.

Instantly the forgotten wind skewered them like a lance, stealing their breath and tripping their feet. The knights butted their way past a leafless tree before a mighty fountain frozen to towering ice. They stumbled by a stone bench beneath a statue of a maiden standing firm and defiant between the claws of a snarling dragon.

Then Rallor was bawling instructions, charging into the hall of the keep gates through a sally port. The forge-like clashing of arms told of fierce resistance.

While they were waiting for a chance to cram through the doorway, Bolan tapped Jebbin on the shoulder and pointed to a high section of crenellated wall between one of the four great corner towers of the keep and a lesser turret. "Explains the first alarm and the broken defence," he shouted. "But how they got there..." he shrugged stolidly.

Looking up, Jebbin recognised dark figures high above them. The Gesgarians were trapped on the battlements. As they limped along in the teeth of the gale, Jebbin could see several islanders being half-carried by their companions. Ahead of them, an iron door in the turret was sealed against them. Behind, helmeted warriors boiled from the tower and hastened towards them. Orrolui was bellowing inaudible instructions to his countrymen. A bald man nodded and formed a line of Gesgarians before the door. They produced a hum, slowly descending in pitch, while Ukanu stood with his palms pressed to the door. Suddenly he signalled to the others and backed away from the door into the semi-circle. The hum steadied in pitch, a low throbbing beat set at the harmonic frequency of the door.

Behind them, Orrolui stood alone to face the oncoming soldiers, the wind pressing at his back. He twirled his scimitar in a circle and summoned the Staffwhirl. The captain of the warriors braced himself against the sudden increase in the ripping wind and waved forward archers to shoot down the mage. But this allowed Orrolui to build the power of the spell, level by level, his sword an invisible spinning circle, until the blast of the tempest tossed the arrows aside like leaves. Jebbin could hear Orrolui's manic laugh crackling over the pounding pulse of the spell against the door, mingling with the shrieking wind. The colossal roar of the staffwhirl added to the gale stopped the charge of the soldiers as though they had hit a wall. The captain's feet were blown from beneath him and he bowled back into the others, one man tipping over the edge and plummeting down, his mouth forming a silent scream drowned by the wind as he curled away.

"Balgrim's beard, come on!" Bolan shouted at him. "At least they're drawing the Aelan's fire. We must go."

Jebbin started after him. Glancing back he saw the triumph in Orrolui's face as he hurled power forward, the Rokepike's soldiers toppling backward defeated. Behind Orrolui, his fellow Gesgarians were equally engrossed in their spell, the door now visibly resonating. But the master of the Rokepike had other forces at his call and above Orrolui a bloated shape drifted downwards, heedless of the wind. Lykos had not been idle.

For a second, Jebbin gaped at the taloned horror, then thumbed a grain of *sear* into his mouth with an automatic gesture. He swung his hands up and spat a knife of fire lancing into the segmented belly. The demon was little injured by such a tiny spell but howled in rage and sank more swiftly upon Orrolui. The Gesgarian leapt sideways, darting a glance of piercing intensity downwards at Jebbin's wild gesticulations before spinning to face his new foe. Jebbin hastened after Bolan, his last backward glance showed Orrolui fighting extravagantly, blasting power in a continuous rain of flashing might, his scimitar rippling under the strain; the demon careering wildly; the steel door sagging ajar with a lone warrior framed in its ruin and, at the end of the battlements, the soldiers freed by the lapse of Orrolui's staffwhirl reforming to attack.

Back inside the keep, Jebbin grabbed Bolan as he moved towards the melee on their left. "Leave that to Rallor. You're here for a different purpose and if he fails, you may yet succeed. Take Hophni and free Matico. Free all the prisoners. They may help us in turn."

"Rallor finds his way with ease. Lack this facility."

"The keep's full of non-combatants; kitchen boys, sweeps, chamber maids, anyone not waving a sword, for the Lady's sake! I'm sure one could be prevailed upon to tell you the way, if you asked nicely," retorted Jebbin.

"Sounds more fun to me. Let's go, Bolan," said Hophni, pulling at the shorter man's arm.

"What of you?" demanded Bolan.

"I go back to the Fireheart to solve the riddle. That is my task," said Jebbin softly.

Bolan fixed Jebbin with a steady gaze. Then he clapped him on the shoulder, saying "Go well," and the two wrestlers ran down the passage.

Jebbin turned and almost bumped into Hiraeth. "You should get out of the fight. You're a man for the word not the sword. I know Lykos is the wolf of the riddle. I must follow the seer." He clasped the bard by the hand and hurried away.

Hiraeth called after him. "Beware the Wolf, Jebbin. We've not seen all his teeth yet."

But the mage was hurrying back outside, arm raised in farewell. As he ran back across the courtyard, Jebbin looked up to the battlements again. There was now no sign of the Gesgarians.

* * *

The wrestlers were walking along a lamp-lit corridor some two levels below the ground. The passage looked poorly hewn; crevices stuffed with crude stonework. The walls glittered with dampness and droplets plinked steadily from the roof into wide puddles. The area seemed deserted.

Hophni and Bolan had been following corridors and taking stairs down according to the directions obtained from a terrified servant and sketchily confirmed by a cheerily impish scullion. But for some time now they had seen no one and they were beginning to suspect that they were on some forsaken escape route from the castle itself. They came to doors and opened them only to find more of the same passage beyond. After taking exaggerated care with the first, they became less alert as they progressed and discussed retracing their steps. So it was that they marched through the last door ill-prepared. There was no warning at all.

Hophni was the greatest wrestler of his age. Perhaps he had

a warrior's sixth sense of danger, perhaps it was the smell of an extinguished candle or even the whispering death of the blow itself, but before he was hit, he threw up an arm to ward the strike and rolled away from it.

Had it been an ordinary weapon, driven by an ordinary hand, all might yet have been well. But he was hit by a prodigious club of red iron that could pulverise rocks. And it was swung by a giant. Hophni saved his life but he could not avoid the massive club altogether and in a shattering impact, his mighty arm was splintered and ruined. Blood pulsed past crushed bones and flooded down his dangling hand.

Bolan jerked Hophni out of the way of a return stroke that cracked a flagstone and whirled to face their attacker.

"Ommak," said Bolan.

"Yes."

Here was a giant indeed and the rumours that had drifted from bleak Torl to Lana Fair spoke no less than the truth. Bolan was aware of Hophni clutching an oily cloth from beside a grindstone and attempting to tie a tourniquet round his mangled arm. He tried to stall the giant.

"You missed the bouts at Lana."

"Lucky for you. Lykos needed some non-Aelan to keep the locals under control. In charge of his dungeons, I have found work that pleased me." Ommak's glance flicked towards the grindstone where he had been sharpening an interesting array of instruments. He looked at Hophni's bowed figure. "I'm going to enjoy working on you two."

"How'd you know we were coming?"

The giant laughed. He flicked a little bell which tinkled with an incongruously jolly note. "You've been standing on pressure plates under the water and trampling alarms all over the place. See the candle in that niche? There's an air hole contrived behind it. No matter how cunning the thief that opens the previous door, that candle flame wavers. You fools blew it right out."

Bolan was out of conversation. Ommak was the keeper of the jail where Matico was imprisoned and for Rhesa, Bolan would brook no obstacle. He surged forward. Ommak swung the battering-ram club as though it weighed no more than a hammer but he was slow to react to a charge at a time when most fled. Bolan dodged beneath the blow, striking upwards against the wrist. The club's vast inertia snapped it from Ommak's grip and fired it across the dungeon like a slingshot, bouncing from the wall. Before Bolan could regain his position, Ommak's forearm scythed forward and smashed into his chest with such force that he was sent flying across the floor to land on his back. He completed the somersault onto his feet, drew his sword and attacked, determined to protect Hophni while the wounded man fought his own battle against pain and blood loss.

Ommak leaned forward into the attack as Bolan stabbed the blade into his belly but it jarred to a halt as though thrust into a wall, only a tiny cut opening in Ommak's skin. Laughing as Bolan staggered in amazement, Ommak booted the sword from Bolan's grasp and delivered a back-handed punch across Bolan's face that brought the blood trickling from his nose.

The wrestler recovered fast and they traded blows briefly. Ommak was staggered to cautiousness by Bolan's power but his own unnatural might was beyond even Bolan's mastering and the shorter man had to avoid being caught in a clinch. The kicks and punches that he was able to land rebounded as though from plate armour. Eventually Ommak delivered a titanic blow just beneath Bolan's ribs that stopped him in his tracks. In an instant, Ommak struck Bolan so hard that his head snapped back and he lost his balance. Ommak seized Bolan and threw him hurtling to land face down, the rough floor scoring bloody runes of defeat in his chest. Roaring with triumph, Ommak moved in for the kill.

Even though his vision had blurred and the dungeon was no more than a series of reds and greys shuddering into each other, Bolan could feel the giant's approach. "Hophni!" gasped Bolan in his extremity. "Help me!"

And Hophni came, leaping forward to lash blows with his feet and good arm, the other pressed to his chest. Deflected, Ommak turned and, dodge as Hophni might, eventually he grappled the wounded man. In his state, Hophni could not cope with Ommak's brute strength and found himself hurled backwards into the wall by a twisting throw on his crippled arm, the shattered bones slicing through flesh. Even as he slammed into the wall, Ommak followed and smashed into him, crushing the breath from him with his colossal bulk. Ommak stood back and raised both arms on high, fingers straightened like spades to chop at the sides of Hophni's bowed neck.

But Hophni's intervention had bought Bolan a precious recovery and at that moment he jumped and delivered a flying kick to Ommak's kidneys. The giant grunted and staggered forward as Hophni straightened up and crunched a clenched fist into his throat that should have crushed his larynx. The giant reeled backward and gave Bolan a chance to execute a leg trip from the ground. Ommak tumbled heavily but rolled back up to his feet and faced the two once more. His breath whistled strangely until he yanked at something at his neck that clicked sickeningly.

Again they closed and fought, the extraordinary force behind Bolan's punches at last eliciting wheezing pants from the giant. Then Ommak sent a sledgehammer clout of his own whistling past Bolan's guard to strike him on the side of the head and while he was momentarily dazed, the giant howled and darted forward to sweep his arms round Bolan, lifting him high in the air and crushing him in a bear-hug. Bolan flailed and struck repeatedly but had no leverage and his blows seemed ineffectual. Unable to draw breath, he swam in a clawing, cold blackness.

Then Hophni kicked the back of Ommak's legs so that the giant fell forward to his knees. The great wrestler climbed the giant in two bounds, leapt high above him and delivered a clean killing blow to Ommak's cranium with his boot. The giant fell forward, releasing Bolan, blood seeping into a hideous dent in his head. Sullen red sprouted in a strange line across his forehead.

Wearily, Bolan and Hophni hauled themselves to their feet. They were appalled to see the giant clambering up once more, shaking his misshapen head.

"Yield," gasped Hophni, his face white and streaming with sweat.

Ommak bared his teeth and shook his head in a spray of blood. "You minikin fools," he said contemptuously. "You don't understand. You cannot even hurt me! I am invincible, I am deathless!" He flung his arms over his head and roared in a monstrous bellow, "I am power!"

He lumbered forward again, his long arms spread wide as a net to catch Hophni. Hophni swayed under his hands with the subtlest timing, then side-stepped left and right as the giant clawed at him. While Ommak clutched at Hophni, Bolan had time to put all his strength into a spinning kick to the giant's side.

There was a metallic clank as Ommak fell sideways, receiving a slash across the throat from Hophni as he went. The skin split down his side where Bolan had kicked him and a bent plate of steel poked from the gaping slit. A thin trickle of blood spotted the floor.

"Balgrim! What are you?" said Hophni softly.

"I am your killer," Ommak answered equally quietly. With a

stunning shout he feinted towards Hophni, then turned to batter at Bolan, who dived backwards. But this too had been a ruse
and once again Ommak managed to grip Hophni's broken arm.
He threw the master of Lana over his shoulder to land flat on
the stone floor. Instantly the giant leapt high in the air after him
and came crashing down with all his gargantuan weight on his
knees, slamming like pile drivers into Hophni's solar plexus. Ommak raised his fists and brought them smashing down towards
Hophni's unprotected throat in an unnecessary completion of
the killing manoeuvre. The blow never landed as Bolan's desperate scything kick deflected the attack and the impact of his body
sent the giant rolling off Hophni.

Bolan turned to Hophni, whose face was locked in a rictus of
effort, striving for breath. Three times his mighty fist balled and
his head pulled forward but three times it relaxed again. Then the
ghastly contortion sagged from his face, his eyes rolled upward
and he was still. Bolan regained his feet as he heard Ommak approaching once more. They both looked at Hophni's limp body.

"So much for the master. Now for the boy," Ommak leered at
the squat man before him. He smeared away the blood trickling
down from the leaking trench in his head, then raised his arms
on high with a mighty shout.

Bolan only knew one way to fight the giant and charged headlong. Ducking under Ommak's hasty blows, he struck like an
avalanche. Even the massive Ommak was cannoned back into the
wall. Then Bolan blazed with power. Prepared to take any damage the giant could hand out, he hunched his head into his shoulders, planted his feet as firmly as oak trees and bludgeoned his
enemy with all of his enormous strength. Never for an instant
did Bolan slacken his assault, allowing no blow from Ommak to
slow him, no tiredness to weaken his attack. He powered forth
punch after punch with every vestige of his being, sledge-ham-

mering his fists into the giant's body until the steely plates guarding Ommak's chest ruptured and pink froth splattered over the
combat. For all Ommak's superhuman construction, Bolan denied him breath and the buckled plates of his chest failed him
as his pulverised heart shuddered to extinction in the force of
Bolan's onslaught. Bolan was still punching as Ommak's lifeless
hulk toppled sideways and thumped into the floor.

Bolan turned from the armoured carcase without another
glance and knelt by Hophni. He laid a gentle hand on the stilled
chest in silent homage. Reaching across him, he plucked the
tawdry rag, blood-drenched and useless, from Hophni's forearm
and threw it away. With solemn care he laid Hophni's arms by his
sides, realigning the gruesome hand with its elbow, trying to conceal the jagged shards of bone. Then rage clenched his features in
a grip of implacable ice. He stood, glaring round as through each
stone were an affront, then shouldered his way into the dungeon,
unstoppable as time.

* * *

Jebbin opened the door from the courtyard as softly as he
could, horribly aware of the rushing airs that must whistle down
the cloister, obvious as a horn blast in a chapel. Two green creatures were plodding awkwardly away from him, each swinging
a short stabbing spear, but they took no notice of the sudden
draught, if they were aware of it. Jebbin skidded nervously across
the passage and back to the library as soon as the coast was
clear. He eased the thick wooden door ajar, crept into its shelter
and listened carefully. There was no noise from the robing room,
so Jebbin edged further into the library and headed for the
wall where they had entered. He stared blankly at the unbroken
shelves of books; the doorway was hidden. He tapped at the
shelves in perplexity with his staff, wondering how to discover
the secret exit.

A contemptuous voice shattered his musings. "Well, well, what an unpleasant surprise."

Jebbin spun round with a jump to see a tall hazel staff emerging into a shaft of light, followed by a dark figure clad in a midnight blue robe as a man eased himself from a shadowy corner. A sneering visage measured Jebbin carefully and clearly found him wanting.

"Dreadfully sorry to disturb you, of course. Forgot to seal the door with a spell to deter the peasantry, did you? How terribly, fatally careless. I knew the second rabble was led by a mage. I did so want to meet you."

Rhabdos stalked forward towards him, venom oozing from his scornful tones, forcing Jebbin to retreat. He stopped scant steps from Jebbin and drew himself up to his full height, his eyes flashing.

"Now you shall pit your puny, dead-stick staff against the hazel of Rhabdos - and learn of pain!" Summoning power, Rhabdos held his staff horizontally before him in both hands. He clenched his fists, forcing splinters beneath his fingernails with the heels of his hands.

Without a moment's hesitation, Jebbin brought his staff scything down vertically and smashed it into Rhabdos' staff between his hands. With a crack like the first snap of thunder, the hazel staff shattered amid darting lights and the smell of chipped flint.

"What the..?" gasped Rhabdos in agonised disbelief. Then Jebbin lunged forward using his staff like a spear. He caught Rhabdos squarely in the middle of the throat and the combat was over.

"One up to the dead stick, I think," said Jebbin to the collapsed sorcerer. "And your hands are going to really sting until you get a new staff and cast a spell, so you can learn about pain all by yourself."

Although unable to find a catch or even any sign of the door, Jebbin could not bring himself to fling books around wholesale but began to pull them down at random; histories and biographies, liturgical tracts and studies of law. He flicked through a brilliantly illustrated copy of *A Herbalist's Jottings*, briefly admiring pictures perfect as pressed flowers and vivid as Spring, then dropped it idly on a book of Belmenian poetry. Remembering Orrolui mentioning the author, he plucked out *Essays on Ethics* by Clearmont, wondering who could read such a thing. It was far more scuffed and thumbed than he would have expected. On a whim, he opened it but instead of boring text he found the pages had been cut away to make a hollow. Nestling within, in a bed of brushed silken strands to prevent it rattling, was a silver key. Jebbin pocketed the key hastily, feeling deliciously guilty at such a fortuitous find, and returned to his search of the books.

He teased out a great leather book, hasped in brass, from a high shelf; Legends of Shekkem emblazoned in letters of gold upon its spine. The first verse of the paean to the glory of Shekkem's long and gory past of rising kingdoms on the ruins of older civilizations was printed on the first page in beautifully illuminated text.

The Land Of Shekkem
Where towers grown from ancient stones
Are raised and razed again.
Dreaming mists cloak schemes and fists
And shroud the priestly chants.
Great armies march on shifting paths
Carve names in History's bark
And kings arise, their treasures pile
In shadow-haunted dark.
Whole cityscapes of minarets

Are razed and raised anew.

He lowered the book with a yearning sigh, then dropped it in a wild flutter of pages when there was a gurgling cry and a loud crash from just behind him. A Bear soldier was slumping to the floor, a black knife slobbering blood in the side of his neck. Yulin was poised by the door, a second knife ready in his hand. Checking the passage, Yulin shut the door firmly.

"When you're engaged in sacking a fortress, it is not normal practice to stand with your back to a door and your nose in a book!"

"I ... I can't find the door."

"Of course not. I expect that's why Rallor sent me back."

"Rallor sent you? Doesn't he need you? How can he think of me at a time like this?"

"Why do you think we stick with the big fellow?" grinned Yulin. Then his eyes defocused as he began to run his fingers over the books, trusting to their tactile sense alone.

"What's happening out there?"

"They sealed the gates all right," replied Yulin in a dreamy tone, "but strange beings are marshalled against us. Green, faceless men. They do not ... die easily. Then Lord Rallor sent me back here - perhaps he hopes you will find something to aid him. I passed four Gesgarians, curse them. All dead. Still, their attack has confused the defenders mightily. Ah, here it is!"

While Jebbin watched with astonished admiration, Yulin opened the door, calmly pilfered and lit a small lamp from a reading desk and led the way back down the spangled steps, allowing the door to close behind them. A forlorn pile of books marked their passing and the Legends of Shekkem told its tales to the blank ceiling as a curious draught riffled softly through the pages.

At the foot of the stair they passed between the dragons, forever pawing with falcate claws, and out onto the broad ledge of rock. Yulin's lamp was reduced to a spark of white by the red glare of the lava light. Jebbin gestured upward at the high balconies above them and shouted that Yulin should extinguish the lamp. Yulin shook his head.

"Just hot air ducts," he yelled back. "Maybe used to view rites. Not now. Just the colour of this rock-light throws me off balance."

Jebbin shrugged and looked round. He was sure the doorway past the dragons had been wrong for him; if he hoped to find the blocked doorway, he could hope for no better company than Yulin. Jebbin studied the carven figures on the side of the tongue of rock, animals, demons and gods disporting themselves in fierce battle. Yulin tapped him on the shoulder and he turned to look into a face already sweat-streaked by the enervating heat of the chamber.

"What am I looking for?"

"A door." Jebbin's voice was hoarse in the sulphur-laden air. "A blocked-up doorway, camouflaged."

He knew they must hurry. Any rites conducted here were sure to be brief and probably very unpleasant, a blast of terror and splendour calculated to instil fear and obedience in the faithful. Already the gases from the molten rock far below were rasping in their lungs and leaching the strength from their muscles as they paced the walls. There seemed no hope of finding a concealed entrance in the tableau of writhing forms on all the vertical surfaces. Even splitting up and independently scrutinising the carvings on different sections of wall, they moved too slowly. Not even Yulin could discern any sign of a door and all the while the burning atmosphere etched its way through their resistance.

To search thoroughly enough to find anything was too slow

to survive for long enough to complete the search. Jebbin found himself muttering from the riddle, knowing he must be quicker, "Ere taigling causes labefactation, ere taigling causes labefaction." He straightened with a jerk, remembering the lilin.

"Yulin," he called, harsh as a corncrake, then he had to pause and shout again as an abnormally massive explosion from the lava submerged his voice in a rolling welter of booming sound. "Yulin. Find a niche. A niche with an ornamental little goddess. Under an arch."

Yulin bellowed something lost in the noise and gesticulated vehemently. When Jebbin shook his head uncomprehendingly, Yulin ran back with plodding steps unlike his usual lithe and sprightly movements. He was gasping for breath. Without wasting time trying to speak, he gripped Jebbin's arm and pulled him back to a shallow alcove. A stone cat fawned before a little wooden goddess seated cross-legged on a beam.

Jebbin nodded excitedly, wiping away sweat and tears provoked by the acidic gases. His vision remained blurry. He reached up and ran his fingers along the small beam until they came to an old cut in the woodwork.

"Here. Kerf. Must cut it off here," he panted.

Yulin wedged a knife in the cut to use as a lever and gave a sharp tug on the wooden figurine. A second harder pull snapped the goddess from her perch. Without a glance, Yulin tossed the desecrated figure down to lie blind and inert against the wall, never again to receive and ignore desperate prayers with aloof insouciance. Yulin's interest was centred on the spring-loaded steel rod that now projected from the hollowed beam.

"Some kind of lock," he rasped but Jebbin had fallen to his knees, clutching his cloak over his face while his brain filled with tormented visions in orange light.

Yulin coughed continually in the seeping poisons, his shaking fingers finding no crevice that seemed out of place. He held up his lamp and peered into the shallow alcove. Dashing the water from his streaming eyes, he looked again. There were now red lines, invisible in the red rock-light that pervaded the cavern but revealed by the whiter lamplight. He heaved on a projecting leaf of wooden ivy now limned in red and a door half the size of the alcove groaned slightly open. His chest heaving with racking shudders, Yulin stumbled through with Jebbin clawing after him.

Yulin slammed the door and the two fell back to sit against it, closing stinging eyes and dragging great draughts of the purer air into their lungs. The passage was warm but felt chilly after the scalding air of the cavern and they revived swiftly.

At length, Yulin spoke, "And now?"

"Yulin, you're a wonder-worker! Now there's only one way to go. I am not certain what we shall find but at least we know we have not been forestalled: the lilin seal was unbroken."

"Good enough," said Yulin, easing a knife in its sheath and re-gaining his feet with more of his accustomed agility.

The narrow passage struck straight away from the Fireheart chamber and gave the impression of being much older than the carven walls and stair of the chamber. Everything was thick with pale dust, scuffed by their steps and floating in their wake like white shadows. The diminutive reading lamp showed little more than their immediate surroundings and soon they could see nothing before or behind them but more passage, fading into darkness. Sound was muffled to death and all that invaded the pale quietude were scattered paintings of desiccated creeping moulds. The musty smell of distilled age replaced the blazing sul-phur of the Fireheart. As the dust swirled behind them before settling once more in the revenant darkness it was as though the passage consumed them, they were forced on without volition by a peristaltic constriction of dust, a bolus of light.

Then with a suddenness like a portent of violence, the walkers found themselves before a door, as though it had rushed upon them up the passage. A mighty iron door, rusty and pitted but built for strength. Huge bolts were hammered deep into rock and a great bar was wedged across it.

"Errela!" Yulin muttered. "What sort of monster was this designed to hold?"

"Time to find out," grunted Jebbin, heaving at the bar.

"I'm not sure I want to," said Yulin, helping him.

They then tackled the bolts which proved so stiff that only with much kicking, cursing and levering could they be persuaded to open. Bangs and clangings jolted sleeping echoes to life and sent them rolling down the passage.

"Of course," Yulin said caustically, hammering vigorously with the butt of a knife, "we will still have the inestimable advantage of surprise, won't we?"

It took their combined efforts, tugging and jerking, to pull open the door on its rusted hinges, their hands slippery from moisture beaded on its surface, a drift of dust forced up before it. Only then were they able to advance into the cell behind their little lamp, hard breathing only partly due to their exertions.

The cell was not large and the rays from the lamp poked inquisitively into every corner, the first glimmerings of light to do so for unknown years. The far left-hand corner glittered with moisture trickling down into a small hole. Fungi bulged obscenely with damp flabby wattles. Elsewhere the walls were dry and unadorned but for a cupboard on a ledge, the doors long since rotted off, so old that its final collapse into decay looked imminent.

In the middle of the room sat a cross-legged figure before what appeared to be a crumpled rug. They were just wondering how long had passed since the man had died when the head slowly rocked back and they saw the face, its eyes tight shut against the unbearable glare of their feeble lamp. Bony hands spasmodically straightened into daggers as the emaciated figure lurched to its feet. Then, movements swiftly becoming more fluid, the figure darted forward aggressively.

"Hanjar!" cried Jebbin.

The man halted, his head twisting slightly from side to side but the eyes still closed. Lips moved and Jebbin expected a voice as cracked and decayed as the crumbling aumbry but the tones were as mellifluous and perfectly modulated as those of a trained singer.

"Who is this? Who has come to gloat?"

"We've come to free you." Jebbin spoke quietly, aware of the poised destruction and just the glinting line of eyes being forced open to withstand the forgotten light.

"How kind. Come in, come in."

Uncertain how to react, Jebbin and Yulin edged forwards. Then a dart, a jump and with astonishing speed Hanjar was at the door and looking in at them, triumph blazing across his face as he prepared to slam the prison door. He paused, his head cocked. "There are none others?"

"We are alone."

"I am free? No tricks, no lies and treachery?"

"None."

"The blessed Sipahni be evermore praised! Who are you, then? You must surely be Sipahni's also."

"The followers of Saint Sipahni are long gone. You cannot be one of them," put in Yulin, as Jebbin stood bewildered, the name unknown to him.

"All gone?" breathed Hanjar bitterly. "My brethren! Did Remis slay every one? Does he now rule completely? What has happened?"

"Not all were killed but I heard that those who remained forswore violence and became the Searchers, the Forshen, for reasons they did not care to explain."

"Forshen!" exclaimed Jebbin. "What's this?"

"Wait! If you are not of the brethren, how come you are here, for Remis swore that none should find the entrance that hid my bones while he lived."

"We followed a riddle of the seer: a page from the Enchiridion of Echoheniel. We knew not what end it would have."

"Did she not die hundreds of years ago? Was I one of her visions? Ah, blessed Sipahni, your sight is long! I will tell you something of my past, then you must tell me what is afoot here. But we must be swift, for my incarceration has irked me.

"I am a monk of the holy order of Saint Sipahni. Some time ago - I cannot say how long, for here time has meant as little as light - the Order was held in high esteem and we revelled in our strength, using our skills as we thought best for the good of all, never seeking domination. Yet one came among us: Remis. Remis, steeped in magic and cunning, he talked in the words of the saint, but he turned them. He insinuated himself into our topmost counsels and sought to rule them. He preached that we should lead more vigorously; take up the mantles of kingship over all the lands and enforce that which was right and good. And many saw that in so doing we could eradicate much that was wrong and unjust.

"But we knew this method was contrary to Saint Sipahni's holy law, for did he not say that one must lead by example and not beat with a stick lest the stick become an iron bar? So we became aware that Remis sought power for himself.

"Then there was rebellion and strife. I led that revolt, declaring Remis wolf's head. He had great powers but we had prepared a magic of our own and the cauterising pain of his own uncast spell leached his power for a generation. I turned many monks of Saint Sipahni against him, yet we were whelmed. There were too many that fought on his side, too many who saw their way to power by growing in his shadow, even monks of the Fist who forsook Saint Sipahni for Remis's dream and Remis won the victory, though his own forces were reduced so greatly that he had nothing to celebrate. The faithful were destroyed and scattered.

"Remis had me dragged hither - wherever this is - and tossed me in this cell of forgotten usage he had found by his arts. He said I would remain here until his final victory, live if I could.

"And I have lived, by the intervention of the blessed Saint Siphani. He sustained me in immobile slumber through this longest night. And when my insufficient faith failed me, I nurtured my gross flesh licking filthy water from the wall and consuming vile filaments of fungi. Yet he forgave me and beckoned me to sleep once more.

"But now I wake. Not to find Remis come to show me his final triumph, nor to welcome, as I had prayed, a cabal of monks of Saint Sipahni, whom I thought would have pursued Remis throughout all the world, unrelenting. You say the brethren are no more. What of Remis? Why should Echoheniel and blessed Sipahni lead you to me now?"

Jebbin was silent, wondering over the miraculous survival of the monk and assimilating his information. But Yulin spoke,

"I know little more than I have said. The battle between the once noble monks of Sipahni and Remis is known history. But there has been no breath of news of Remis since that time and Saint Sipahni is all but forgotten. All that was long years ago. Twenty, thirty years back now. You cannot possibly..."

"Faith," Hanjar stated. "One needs but faith."

"Hanjar," said Jebbin, "you said Remis' power was leached for a generation. He may well have regained it now. To speculate, I

326 - ACM PRIOR

think Remis fled the vengeful wrath of the remnants of the Order, then too weak to defend himself. He changed his name and hid in a defensible bolthole while he recuperated and built anew with those that remained to him.

"Furthermore I guess that the Order, unable to find any trace of him or you and aware how they in their power had become a tool for others, surrendered their martial skills and immersed themselves in a new doctrine, developing different talents. They became the Forshen, searching ever for the lost Hanjar and Remis, to save one and damn the other.

"And I believe that as Hanjar is now found, so too is Remis. For there is a power in this castle that has arisen first by political machinations and latterly through magic and that power seeks dominion by force. I say that bolthole was the Rokepike; Remis is now Lykos and that the riddle of the seer is a plea to stop him before he accomplishes the plans that so nearly came to fruition when he suborned the monks of Saint Sipahni."

In the silence that followed, Hanjar walked back into the room to the mat on the floor. He bent and scratched it tenderly. Jebbin and Yulin were amazed when there was a movement and a long, gaunt head appeared, barely able to lift itself from the ground. Dull, yellow eyes opened and fixed their gaze on Hanjar before closing once more.

"My friend and final companion," whispered Hanjar, crouching beside the beast. "If you could only fight beside me this one last time. We are bound as one, sustained as one and now fate has decreed we shall die alone. We shall meet again at the foot of the blessed Sipahni. Farewell, until then."

He stroked the tangled fur, then spoke aloud, "All is clear to me now. Saint Sipahni, this is your last test of your humble servant." Hanjar dropped to his knees and bowed his head, covering his face with his bony hands.

"Saint Sipahni, give me the strength to fulfil this final quest. Guide me with your sure hand and with your might, let justice prevail. For my sins, spare me not. Let the end of your last worshipper be a fitting sacrifice to renew your name to glory in this world. Let Remis not hide from me, as he once hid the wolf in the man and to our shame, we saw it not." He regained his feet, the light of fanaticism soaring brightly within him. "I go on my last wolf hunt, for the wolf's head Remis is now Lykos the Wolf.

"I thank you for your part in my rescue, even if you did not recognise the blessed Sipahni's guiding hand upon your shoulders. Praise unto him. Let justice prevail!"

With that he was gone, running swiftly and easily up the passage in the darkness, leaving Yulin and Jebbin alone in the mouldering cell. Yulin looked glumly at the hideous place and the flaccid animal that remained.

"I hope it was worth it; to free one madman who has existed in a lightless cell for a quarter of a century and still thanks his patron saint for his release, then rushes off to commit suicide on the blade of the first guard he meets."

"Possibly. But I do not forget the riddle. We have not finished."

"If you're right about this riddle, then your seer did not foresee Rallor."

"Or Rallor fails," said Jebbin softly.

"He won't," maintained Yulin stoutly, doubts plain in his face.

While Yulin watched in alert curiosity, Jebbin selected a large bolt from outside the door and approached the cupboard. After a quick glance inside confirmed it was completely empty, he swung the heavy bolt into the end panel. It shattered into a brown dust. In a cloud of debris, Jebbin moved along, smashing all of it and brushing it from the ledge. He frowned at the bare wall behind it, then examined the ledge. With a cry of elation, he whirled the iron bolt once more into a hidden panel, despite Yulin suddenly leaping forward with a shout of warning.

But this time there was no trap. Jebbin uncovered a long niche in the ledge and reached in to pull out a small inlaid wooden box, perfectly preserved, and a fearsome-looking war flail, despite Yulin imploring him to check things first.

"There's no need. I have worked long to this end and will not fail now."

"That's a poor epitaph," said Yulin dolefully.

Jebbin opened the nacre and pearl embellished box and removed a golden necklace with a pendant shaped as a sword with a double curved blade. With shaking hands, he lifted it and placed it about his neck. His eyes shone.

Now he forgot none of the words of the seer and having donned the yataghan he approached the limp creature lying on the floor, its sunken flanks barely moving. The opinicus vented a tiny growl, which Jebbin ignored. He touched the blunt symbol to a bald patch of skin between clumps of dusty fur.

Immediately, life began to pulse back into the beast. Eyes of tawny gold snapped wide and blazed in the lamplight, slitted pupils like black lance points. Dried tissues filled, firmed and pulsed with vitality. Yellow fur sprouted and bristled, legs thickened and flashed claws of shining ebony. Suddenly the creature bounded to its feet and roared, a bone-quaking, awesome roar from a mouth as red as blood and lined with fangs. It shook its short leathery wings fiercely, churning the dust into a maelstrom. Yulin gaped at it as it reared on its hind legs, framed in a glowing halo of diffused light, the roar echoing and echoing round the cell. Then it burst through the door, trailing dust like smoke, and loped after its master for the wolf hunt.

"What in Errela's name...?"

"An opinicus. Half lion, half dragon. I believed it no more

than an emblem." Jebbin lifted the heavy blue steel of the flail, covered in waving traces of finest silver and proffered it to the wiry man beside him. "Yulin, I won't have Rallor fail if I can prevent it. Let his faith in me find due reward. He is the man to operate this flail. It can be used to Command. I charge you to get both flail and message to him. There's no time to lose!"

"I understand nothing of this. But if it can be done, I will do it."

Wing-footed, Yulin fled through the Fireheart as through demons snapped at his heels, Jebbin trailing in his wake as swiftly as he could; noisier and slower, though he carried no flapping flail to smack at his back. They sped through the library, ignoring two terrified servants cowering by the locked door to the robing room. Silent running occupying his thoughts, Jebbin did not notice that Rhabdos had gone, nor would he have cared if he had, for Rhabdos' power lay in shattered splinters of hazel on the floor.

It was not difficult to locate the fighting; the roar and clash of battle was audible the moment they reached the corridor. The tireless Yulin tracked the sound like a bloodhound on a spoor until he skidded to a halt at a corner and was forced to hastily backtrack into a window recess, clutching his awkward burden to his side. Men ran past in a clatter of boots and armour. When Jebbin pounded up to him, he whispered in breathy bursts,

"Rallor's in a hall to the left. We cannot reach him. He must be trapped or he wouldn't choose such a place to stand. The doors are very tall so I guess there'll be a balcony or minstrel's gallery. We must find it. There's a small flight of stairs up almost opposite us. When I go, run for it!"

Yulin poked his head out once more, then darted across the passage and upward. Jebbin charged desperately after him. The shouting and screaming to his left made him imagine the swift pursuit of stinging arrows and clutching hands close behind him. He gasped his way up two flights to another passage and turned right, nearly falling over a Bear guard sitting on the floor, cradling the last of Yulin's black knives in his chest. Without pause for a much-needed breath, he lumbered after Yulin.

They slid on the polished wooden floor, past dark doors of carved wood and one surprised matron who barely had time to draw disapproving breath before they were gone, leaving her in a fluster of outrage, clucking furiously to unseen wards.

Unable to hear anything over the howling racket of the battle, Yulin flung open the door blocking his path and found himself on a curving balcony over the fight. As a surprised Aelan turned to face him, Yulin beat him flat with the mighty flail, a crushing swing that was fortunate to miss the lintel.

"Fight from here," roared Yulin over his shoulder as Jebbin caught up, looking at the ferocious melee below; the southern lord struggling savagely at the head of a defensive cordon of knights, Hol at his left fighting in a flicker of steel with a blade in either hand. "Rallor!" Yulin bellowed, then with a screaming battle cry, he launched himself over the edge and down into the fray.

Jebbin leaned wheezing over the balustrade as Yulin smashed into castle guards and green warriors of the keep alike and rolled desperately towards the knights, lunging ferociously with the flail while he was too cramped to use it properly. Rallor was roaring commands and forging forward to aid the embattled Yulin as swiftly as possible.

Rolling *sear* between his fingers, Jebbin tried to think how to help the leaping, twisting Yulin. The Blast spell was too likely to hit the wrong person. Jebbin watched him parry a spear with the flail, even as he twisted away from a sword strike. Yulin's hand flicked to his belt but all the knives were gone. He leapt away from another

Bear guard but cannoned awkwardly into a warrior and a blow from a green monster sent him to the ground. The Bear stabbed downward but even as he did so, Rallor's armoured legs straddled Yulin and the Southerner's sword split the Bear's giant helmet down to his chin.

Jebbin was suddenly overcome by a fey sensation. It was as though the battle and all within it receded in a bubble, leaving him remote. Straightening slowly, he turned and looked right into the eyes of a man. He was not tall. His head was large with thin, pale lips, a small nose and no eyebrows, making him seem almost featureless. But power emanated from him like a foul smell. His fingers tightened about a nightwood staff, polished pale where he gripped it. There was no mistaking Lykos.

"Having engineered this precise ending point with stratagems and manoeuvres not susceptible of disarrangement by you, surely you did not suppose that we would overlook this vantage point? Now, if you lay your staff at your feet, we can avoid your receiving much unnecessary suffering and my expending a supererogatory modicum of energy."

Jebbin looked wild-eyed down into the hall but he could not hope to emulate Yulin's feats and he would receive short shrift in the writhing steel porcupine below. His hope lay neither in strength nor flight but in subterfuge. Jebbin shrugged regret at the scene beneath him, then deliberately slumped his shoulders in a mute acquiescence of defeat. He paused for a second, then despondently let his staff clatter to the floor. Out of the corner of his eye, he watched some of the tension ebb from Lykos when the expected confrontation receded. The Master of the Rokepike waved a bodyguard forward.

After his successes against Hamaga and Rhabdos and knowing that his hope lay in a rapid success, Jebbin concentrated on disrupting Lykos' staff. He rubbed his eyes as though in despondency, then suddenly snuffed the ball of *sear* into his nose. Without the slightest warning, he threw all his strength into the spell.

Before the magic was born, flaring worms of streaking violet seared his vision as he was enveloped in Lykos' riposte. He was plucked up and hurled backward into the doorjamb. Sliding down to finish prone upon the floor, he gazed listlessly at the ceiling, spinning and dancing above him, barely aware of the dull ache of a Numbing hammering over his body, replacing all the sharp pain he needed for power.

"That was a most interesting and innovative demonstration deserving immediate attention," murmured Lykos to his bodyguard. "Bring him to my workroom with all celerity. We can leave Rhabdos to eliminate the residue of this puling incursion. You there! Instruct the archers to line the balcony and fire immediately, whoever's in the way."

* * *

Bolan marched into the dungeon and glared about him. A wide area was lit by oil lamps, light gleaming slyly on chains and manacles bright with wear, keen knives, whips, and cleavers heavy as doom and sharp as failure. Racks with well-greased winches and meticulously ordered shelves lined the walls; tongs and hooks peeped hopefully from a bucket. Flies buzzed fatly near a sealed barrel of gristly remnants which still managed to leak a sour stink to clutch at the unaccustomed stomach. A glowing brazier standing beside a pair of pillars wrinkled the air above it.

A limp, naked and dark-stained form dangled between the pillars, tied there with rawhide ropes. To Bolan's surprise a snaggle-toothed man with wayward grey hair was releasing the victim. He lowered the body onto a leather-padded settle and began gently sponging him down while the injured man whimpered between clenched teeth.

Bolan was still charged with adrenalin, quivering for a fight. He frowned and demanded, "Who are you? What's going on here?"

"Faun, my lord. Dungeon factotum," replied the man, standing awkwardly and self-consciously brushing dirt from his grimy, coarse-weave shirt and trousers. Perhaps they had once been dark green. He scuffled hessian slippers and said, "I was just releasing Cark. He's been scourged, you see? Due for more. But I usually find that when there's a change this is the best thing to do. Of course, if that's wrong....?"

"No. Release the man," muttered Bolan as he wandered round, peering into iron-barred cells, stinking of rats and fusty straw. Foundering wrecks of humanity gibbered, spat or gaped at him with sickly grins. Defiance still stood alongside fear in some of the newest arrivals. Turning away in disgust, he spotted the trapdoor entrance to the oubliette and guessed that Matico would be there.

"Yes, I thought so," Faun was prattling on, cleaning black specks from the peeling wounds he had cut in Cark's back with impartial fingers. "I've worked through many changes, you see. Four, no, five now. You'll find me useful, my lord. It's not everyone's choice of a place to work but I know everything here. I make it as good for everyone as possible, you see. Everything neat and tidy.

"Faun," Bolan snapped. "Enough. Where's Matico? Down there?"

"Oh, not here, my lord. And certainly not in the oubliette!"

"Not here?" thundered Bolan, fuming with impatience. "Then where? Take me to him."

"At once, my lord," cried Faun, leaving Cark prostrate on the settle, shuddering with every breath. He led Bolan to a narrow spiral staircase, dark and steep, behind a door. "These are only criminals here, spies, agitators or robbers, but Matico is with the hostages, you see. Don't worry about Cark, my lord, he won't go anywhere."

Faun stopped by a large wooden door in an airier part of the dungeons. A small metal plate concealed a grille and through this a steady hubbub was audible.

"I have the keys, my lord," said Faun, holding out two large keys with thick wards. "I said I'd be useful. You see?"

Bolan impatiently waved for him to unlock and open the door, then strode into the entrance. The noise dribbled away as Bolan glared round, the residents shuffling until they could all silently assess their visitor; did he come to taunt or fraternize, to free or oppress?

Surrounded by abandoned chairs, a huge table was burdened with the crumbs, rinds and empty bottles of a noble meal. Other doors opened on different rooms where yellow light betokened lamps within but most of the inhabitants were crowded below the narrow, barred windows that crept along against the ceiling. Two were clinging to the bars, pressing their ears to the outer world. They slid back to the ground as Bolan entered and all eyes turned to him.

Bolan instantly recognised the menace exuding from them as they took sidling steps towards him, clearly according to a pre-arranged plan. He weighed their unarmed numbers against his strength and checked the door behind him. Then a confusion crept amongst them and he heard sibilant voices whispering,

"Wait. Don't rush him."

"He's no Aelan. A foreigner!"

"Yet he wears the White Levin of Ael!"

"Who?", "Who?"

Quietness fogged the uncertain group before him as their aggressive resolve petered out in the face of his battered but intransigent mien and unknown disposition. But these were haughty and imperious princes, unused to being baulked by those of lesser caste and they glared at him or adopted aloof poses, arrogance a mask for common fear.

Suddenly one of them spoke in a voice tense with emotion, "Who leads the assault?"

"What?" Bolan frowned deeper than ever, dumbfounded by the well-dressed group before him.

"He is mazed or witless, whoever he is," murmured the speaker before repeating the question in loud, over-enunciated tones, "Who Leads Attack?"

"Where's Matico," asked Bolan gruffly, ignoring his supercilious questioner.

"The Snow Leopards? Impossible!" exclaimed someone.

"The Hawks, perhaps?" queried another voice and with a rush, all were talking again in a riotous babble of speculation.

"Silence!" roared Bolan in a voice that blasted the words from their lips, the rage and barely suppressed violence steaming within him. He turned his head over his shoulder. "Faun! What are they on about?"

"Simple, my lord," replied Faun softly. "If, say, Varbrim, son of the Hares' chief, is released by the Fox, an allied tribe, he will rejoice. But were he delivered by the Ibex, a feuding tribe, then his would be an evil lot. He is thus keen to learn who attacks."

"Does he not hope the Hares will free their chief's son themselves?"

"Perhaps not, unless they do so with surpassing swiftness, for the moment the attacking Hares are recognised, Varbrim's life is instantly forfeit. Is he not a hostage? They were expecting Ommak and death for one of them, at least."

Bolan nodded and stamped down the three steps into the room. "Matico!" he barked. "Step you forward."

There was a pause and sidelong glances before a handsome, red-haired man elbowed himself from the wall with studied nonchalance and swaggered forward. He glanced ostentatiously down at his own garb; soft suede trousers and waistcoat in bright blue over a white silken shirt, and then at Bolan, bruised and sweaty, blood and dirt abraded across his chest.

"Well, who are you, dwarf?"

In an instant, Bolan gripped Matico's neck like a hangman's noose and wrenched him to his knees with unanswerable force. "Don't understand this alliance between Triva and the Leopards. Don't understand the riddle. Barely know why'm here." Bolan bit off his words as savagely as though his teeth were in Ommak's throat, his face almost touching Matico's. "But know that better men than you'll ever see have died to get you out of here. And we're not out. So get all these people out and armed and do it now." He flung Matico heedlessly to one side and turned back to the door.

"It's not possible," croaked Matico. "We are guarded by a giant of flesh and iron."

"Yes," said Bolan flatly. "He is dead."

It was as though a shiver ran through the very walls of the prison. There could be no denying the truth in Bolan's tone and for the first time, the nobles of Ael began to hope that they would indeed be free once more. As they began to surge forward, Bolan's voice broke upon them once more.

"There are weapons, of a sort, in the torture chamber. Follow Faun, get them and fight well. Free everyone there, too."

They ran past him in an eager jostle, Matico at the rear still rubbing his neck. Bolan caught him by the arm.

"Matico, do you intend to marry Lady Rhesa?"

"That matter can hardly concern you but this I will say. Were all the legions of the damned lined against me, were the alliance to fail, were I to spend the rest of my life in abject poverty, come what may, I shall marry Rhesa. For I love her and, as I live, she is all the good I have found in this place."

Matico pulled away roughly and hurried out, leaving Bolan immobile, staring emptily over the wasteland of their last meal, the weight of Rhesa's ring almost more than he could bear.

* * *

For the second time in his life, Jebbin found himself being carried about a castle while he watched with impotent detachment. If he tried to move or even think, diminishing aftershocks of violet power wriggled across him, dulling all his pain to the poisonous grey of Numbness until they crept over the little necklace and disappeared into the yataghan.

He dimly noted their passage through stone corridors to a hidden door and more stairs. The broad bodyguard who carried him slumped over one shoulder was little discommoded by his weight and tramped upward steadily, occasionally banging Jebbin's head or feet into unyielding obstructions with no more malice nor care than had he been carrying a carcase. Initially, Jebbin felt nothing but, as more of the Numbing spell was absorbed by the amulet, pain made its voice heard again. It had a lot to say.

As they rose through the tower of bibelots, Jebbin caught glimpses of endless shelves zealously stuffed with little curios from the world over. He became oddly concerned that he had seen nothing from the collection he had bought at Lana Fair and became pointlessly obsessed in his search.

It came as a surprise to be suddenly thrown on a low table and he realised that they had reached Lykos' workroom in a turret. His head lolled sideways and he started in amazement. Scant feet away, on a similar table, lay Orrolui, beaten at the last. His clothes and hair were matted with blood, one eye puffed beyond opening, a sword gash in his pallid cheek leaving a wide flap of skin dangling, the hole filled with semi-clotted blood. Jebbin could see neither breath nor least twitch of life. Orrolui had not surrendered as tamely as had he.

Lykos dismissed the bodyguard from the workroom. He collected something from a drawer and bent over Jebbin's supine form.

"You realise, of course, that you are the only two with the secret of freedom from the artefact? Naturally I intend to invest myself with this knowledge." He held up a device upon a thin rod; a golden circle sparkling about a ball of silver wires that whirled within the circle, first one way, then the other, emitting regular, low notes. Stationary within the turning spindle, a luminous gem winked rhythmically behind the bars.

Lykos swung the circle with a steady pendulum motion and Jebbin found his eyes drawn to it irresistibly. Lykos continued in his soft drone.

"I was indeed astounded when the Gesgarian contrived to slay Lentor: his scimitar sundered and himself exhausted beyond credibility. Were it not for this connection between you, even I would not have guessed that this was a coherent invasion and not merely a coincidentally contemporaneous squabbling by these Aelan curs buying outside help. The Gesgarian, I admit, resisted capture fiercely. In truth, the fury of his defence and his astonishing resilience were quite revelations. Certainly to Lentor. Even I must confess ignorance as to where he could possibly have found such reserves. Nevertheless, he succumbed.

"But your presence is fortuitous, even serendipitous. He has spent himself utterly and I doubt he'll survive. Even so, it would be a considerable labour to extract what I require from him and not a matter without considerable attendant danger. You are whole, currently, far more malleable and with a better control of the technique."

Jebbin tried to rail and hurl defiance but his rage was sucked into the spinning silver and the shape looming over him chuckled humourlessly at his feeble spark of protest.

"Pathetic. After that Gesgarian, you redefine the parameters of meekness. A new talent after all these years. It cannot be permitted to waste away in one so puling. A nobody."

Jebbin tried to deny him but it was futile. He could only watch the swaying gold and chiming silver while his mind was ruthlessly invaded and ransacked, his store of knowledge ravished while the flashing crystal illuminated every crevice. In a dim recess, he groped for the syllables of the mind shout spell but the light caught him and the words were ripped away to leave him mewling in the revenant darkness.

"Gesgarian spells? Hm, an unexpected bonus."

As Jebbin lay pinned and dissected upon the table, the sound of fighting drew closer and the hope grew that they might be interrupted, a rescue made. Then the sounds faded and took the hope and he was left more alone than ever.

At last his final barriers were neatly snipped and set aside and he lay mentally nude and prostrate before Lykos' minute inspection.

"So, and so. Yes, fascinating. Quite extraordinary."

Then, quite suddenly, Jebbin felt Lykos withdraw from the mined ruins of his brain as the spinning device was stilled and removed from his vacant gaze, leaving his mind floundering as though cast into a warm, black sea, churning with invisible currents.

"Unfortunately, that leaves you and your colleague quite redundant and I certainly do not propose to give him a chance to recover. Well, there are some jobs it is wise not to delegate."

Humming softly to himself, Lykos returned his device of gold and silver to its drawer and picked up an old steel dagger, the horn grip smoothed and whitened with use, the blade reduced to a stiletto by years of frequent honing. He tested its edge with an automatic gesture, then stood at the foot of Orrolui's table for a moment, mechanically tapping the knife against his fingernails while he muttered over the procedures and spells he had learnt, imagining aloud their uses and impacts. Bringing himself back to reality with an explosive sigh, he callously approached the recumbent forms, arranging buckets to catch the blood.

Abused and broken with neither effort nor compunction, Jebbin could only watch in despair, tossed as shattered flotsam on the black tide that had engulfed him. But beneath his feet was one last rock. Before his glazed eyes marched the phantoms of those he had failed. Tagg, left to work his land with a son the fewer. Sola, sweet Sola, kissed and abandoned. Blunt Rilkas frowning in perplexity. Ygyrd, as cold as stone on his account. Even Orrolui, whose secrets he had revealed without striking one single blow. And Dewlin, who fought beyond her strength to save him.

On they stalked, spectral markstones on his road to ruin. And he would not accept it. If this fight were beyond the paucity of his power, then he would join Ygyrd and Orrolui and Dewlin before him, but with honour, not abject humiliation, the victim of rapine. He had no *sear*. But he remembered his mother's words before he ever left home; 'There are many sources of pain.' And if this were not pain enough, no physical pain would ever suffice. Every iota of his pain and power must go into one spell. Now was the time.

Marshalling the tattered shards of his strength, he jerked up his arm with his open hand pointed at Lykos. The first syllable of the Gesgarian stasis spell shuddered between them. Lykos turned his head to look full at Jebbin and their eyes met with fierce intensity.

"No," said Lykos. "You are Numb."

But with a cry and with a mighty effort, Jebbin snapped his fingers closed, his grip clenched about Lykos' heart as he used the perfect harmonic of the spell, the full Hearthammer. Instantly, he was subjected to an appalling magical battering, black arms thrashing and pounding wildly, slivers of argent lightning lancing pain through him. But he was not Numb. The yataghan about his neck had swallowed the spell. He felt all the pain. His body rigid in agony, he held his grip though the very skin was flayed from his fingers. Knots of power exploded against his spell as Lykos smashed at his hold but Lykos could not attack directly lest he rip his own heart asunder. And Jebbin would not be broken. He channelled every iota of pain burning through him into reinforcing his spell even as it racked his body. The blood pounded in his head until it burst from his forehead in drops of red but he only gripped the tighter in a tetany of pain.

The Master of the Rokepike had spent a lifetime managing pain but the excruciating pain of the Hearthammer was throttling his heart and he could not attack it. Lykos' massive power rioted madly out of control in a spume of light and heat, thunderous noise and the rolling acrid reek of brimstone and flint. His face contorted into a hideous screaming mask, purple blotches appearing on the fur-grey skin round yellow eyes, mouth impossibly wide with red gums and brutal, white teeth. The pain seared through him and he was Numbed.

The wolf still fought. In a last struggle for life, the sorcerer abandoned his useless magic, staggered forward and fell over Jebbin with his lethal knife stabbing down directly for Jebbin's chest.

Jebbin never even saw the blade descend, he was unaware of all but his torturing pain and his relentless grip on Lykos' heart. He had no defence.

But even as Lykos tottered over Jebbin, Orrolui's blood-stained fingers twitched and straightened. His one good eye half opened and the black orb glittered with passion from the ruin of his face. Frothy blood trickled from his mouth as he fought for breath. One finger's width above Jebbin's chest, Lykos' knife sank into an Argen wall. The knife was thrust down with no great power and that least of spells was just sufficient. For a timeless instant, Lykos remained balanced over the knife, bloody saliva drooling, his face inches from Jebbin's - and agony found a mirror.

By any reckoning but his own, Orrolui's power was long exhausted and his rigid fingers quivered and shook, yet the spell held. Then Lykos' eyes rolled up in his head and he fell away to the floor, mouth gaping as his last breath left him in a deathly growl. Orrolui sank back into unconsciousness and the tiny Argen wall folded back in upon itself and vanished.

Jebbin remained unaware of the fall of his foe. His mental fingers long remained clutched about the dead meat of Lykos' heart before realisation crept in upon him.

Ustulation

Exhaustion finally dragged them to a halt halfway down the stairs. A splotched trail of blood from Orrolui marked every stabbing jolt of their progress. The Gesgarian lay curled on the stone, coughing weakly and drooling watery blood. Struggling to haul himself onward, his bloodied fingers still clawed forward in little pawing motions, like waves dragging over a rocky shore in endless failure. Beside him idly rocked a figurine with a huge protruding tongue and bulging eyes, giant splayed hands and oversized genitals. One leg had broken off in its long fall from a shelf they had blundered into and toppled higher up the tower.

Jebbin sat with his back against the wall, eyes open but vacant, mouth hanging wide heedless of the sweat and blood that trickled together down his face, pallid where not bruised dark during his apoplectic exertion against Lykos. He saw nothing, felt nothing more than a rising warm lassitude. With the blissful cessation of effort, the trials and vicissitudes of the last hour faded like a half-remembered nightmare.

A faraway part of him heard the voices when they finally came but they were no more than an annoying distraction from the dark rest that folded its all-embracing wings about him and crooned a lullaby.

344 - ACM PRIOR

"Looky here! It's that lad. Jebbin's here."

"What? Alive?"

"Dead. Fought that Gesgarian slime from the looks of things. Must've killed each other."

"Gesgarian's not dead."

"Yet. Soon fix that!"

"Quiet, all of you," cut in an authoritative voice. "Jebbin breathes. Swiftly now, Theriac, have a look at him. Can you do anything?"

"Swift is no use and less than swift is worse than useless for it could kill us all, Lord Rallor," said a new voice from much closer but there was no sting in the tone.

Jebbin heard a rattle as a mail glove was dropped, then firm hands probed gently at his neck, feeling for a pulse. His throat was checked for blockages and his forehead wiped in an attempt to locate the injury. There was a gruff muttering, the sound of a cork being drawn, a whiff of piercing smell, then fluid seeped into his mouth, trickled down his throat and exploded into searing life.

Jebbin's pupils contracted sharply as he was yanked back from his slide into the abyss of oblivion and he coughed violently. He heard a voice.

"The Gesgarian won't live anyway. Do it quickly."

"N...N..." retched Jebbin, frantically waving an arm, fighting madly to free himself from the treacly webs that festooned his trampled brain.

"Hold there!"

"Rallor, we don't have time for this. If we are caught here.... Finish the Gesgarian and I'll carry Jebbin if necessary."

"Hold, I say. We're like rats in a trap wherever we go. I must talk with the mage."

"Leave Orrolui. You cannot measure his survival," gasped Jebbin weakly. "Help him. By the Lady, help him."

"Why? He tried to kill you!"

"He has …. endured sufficient. In his view. I stole the parchment from him. And after all his strivings … there was no treasure at the end. Just a flail he could never use and a periapt that I wear now. I owe it to him to try to save him." He glared truculently at the doubting faces round him. "Without his Gesgarians taking the brunt of the fighting, what hope would we have had of getting to the keep? He deserves a chance of getting out."

"Theriac, do what you can for him," Rallor signalled resignedly. "Although whether any of us will get out is another matter."

"How … you here? Were trapped in hall." Jebbin squeezed his eyes shut as the savage roborant of the cordial surged within him.

Rallor squatted before Jebbin. "Yes, that's right. I thought we were to stay there too. We would have done but for the joint powers of the flail Yulin brought and Hanjar. That monk is awesome beyond crediting. He fights like an avatar of death, a mighty creature of legend by his side, then just vanishes. Where he is now, I don't know. He only said he was hunting the wolf." Rallor shrugged, then leaned forward, his voice taut in exhortation.

"But Jebbin, we cannot master Lykos' creatures, these green warrior minions. They are virtually immune to our weapons and strike like giants. Only the flail is able to disrupt them with a word and a blow. We have failed in my aims and must now concentrate on survival, fighting our way out if possible. Most of the castle's strength is massed outside the gates to the keep and bars our route. The Fireheart chamber is blocked against us with spouts of magma. We must have … something, magic, anything. Do you have power to aid us? Jebbin, help me!"

Jebbin looked into the earnest face of the lord, now creased in worry. At last Rallor had tackled a foe too great for him. His reckless over-optimism had doomed his loyal followers with him and he could not bear it. He was grasping at straws now. Pleading for strength from one who could not stand.

He looked down at the bruised and bleeding knights, their matchless armour dented and stained, silently leaning on walls or sitting on lower steps, heads in hands, making the most of their brief respite. Nearby, someone's breath was continuously snagging in bubbly, pierced lungs. Cursing the pain, they coughed weakly and spat. There were others amidst the knights, unarmoured men with fierce eyes, clutching pokers and skinning knives. Jebbin could read in their expressions that they expected to die but there was resolution in their grim faces and set shoulders: their motley weaponry was ready for use. They all reminded him of the battered Gesgarians on that high battlement; they too were being worn down by the unimpeachable might of the Rokepike.

Now Rallor besought aid of him. He thought of the indefatigable Orrolui, whose inner fire soared so unquenchably that even had his outer body died, it would be impossible to believe that such a flame could be stilled. His valiant extravagance would never have admitted defeat or incapability. None had plumbed the end of his vitality and yet he had been broken. Tossed on a bench as salvaged flotsam.

And Dewlin. She had not accepted her limits, had forced herself far beyond her abilities, shown power scarce shaped in dreams. It had destroyed her. All her magic cauterised, annihilated. Numbed.

So he, what would he do? Already he had stretched himself too far, used up all his luck in daring the perfect harmonic of the Hearthammer, never practised, never seen. Now he too had gone further than could have been predicted, further than should have been possible. He'd had to. Nothing else would have availed against one who so vastly over-matched him.

But now was the time to turn back. Now, before he shot the wild rapids of unharnessed power whence none returned, even as Lykos had finally released his wizardry in a mad unravelling of theurgical potential. There was another way. A way dependent on stout thews, human hearts and the cunning mind unstained by the pollutant spells of man's overweening efforts to be more than man. To be his own god. And where the true gods had touched lowly mankind, there was the seer.

And she had spoken.

"Pyrotic accablation," croaked Jebbin. "Ustulation."

"He rambles," someone groaned. "Let us away."

"No. Fire is the solution. Fire will destroy the minions. Burn the keep!"

"And ourselves with it. That would be a last resort indeed. They will spend some of their numbers in trying to put out the fire perhaps but there will still be far too many for us to break out through the gates. It would be suicide."

"Rallor, they store oil in the keep to defend the battlements at need. Could you not set barrels against the outer wall opposite the gates. Expediently arranged and exploded they should hole the wall where none expect an escape, give you a chance."

Just then came a cry from lower on the stairs. "'Ware the foe!" But now Rallor was alive with fresh energy, needing no time to assimilate the suggestion. He was already up and crying orders, leaping his way to the forefront, trailing a contagion of hope. The knights were rekindled with him and again they fought and ran. Now they had a goal once more.

Jebbin found himself draped between two injured members of Rallor's retinue, their faces haggard but determined. To his

348 - ACM PRIOR

left, a stolid knight he barely recognised tried to ignore a crushed helm that leaked blood down one side of his face. Stumbling along, his eyes crossing, he pretended it was Jebbin's weight each time he tripped and swore in mock vexation, his voice slurring more each time. On Jebbin's right, a criminal clad in sackcloth helped as much as he could, though he winced at every step, pressing his free arm to his side. Fingers were clearly missing from a hand wrapped in a reddened but neatly tied scrap of cloth.

Jebbin tried to assist them, but he remembered little of that spasmodic flight amidst the smoke and the greasy stench emitted from the green warriors as they burned in sputtering spouts of coloured flames; knights casting aside their notched swords to fight with torches, hurling lamps and oil. Though Rallor never faltered in finding his way, they had to branch and double back many times to avoid strong knots of warriors. Once Jebbin was unceremoniously dumped when Bear guards burst from a side door into the middle of the group, his helpers drawing weapons with aching arms and defending grimly before they were re-inforced. Jebbin fumbled automatically for *sear* but just the thought of using it nearly made him vomit. He let it trickle from his hand and tried to wrestle his poniard clear of his clothes. The knight knocked him over with his elbow and by the time he struggled up, the melee was finished.

He glimpsed Orrolui, likewise slung between two wounded Aelans, one wearing rags, the other clad in brocade apparel of carmine and gold. And they were not the only ones so supported: Rallor's force dwindled but still his presence bore them up and infused them with hope. For a while yet, flail and flame wrought ghastly carnage and kept their passage clear.

Everywhere they set fires until flames ran greedily along beams, roaring and bursting through open doors, illuminating tapestries and hangings with one final glorious light before they were scattered in drab flakes of floating grey.

Even after all the crashings of the rampant fire, the sudden boom of the detonating oil barrels was sufficient to rouse even Jebbin and he tottered through a smoking hole limned in flame, still locked between the stalwart knight and the unknown malefactor, and out over shattered masonry into the freezing evening light.

Almost the entire troop complement of the castle was ranged before the donjon gates, guarding against a sally and trying to break the gates down to succour their own men and save the keep from the flames. Rallor led a wild charge through the emptied halls and corridors of the castle and dominated a brief and brutal melee in the hall of the main gates. Willing hands threw down the great iron-girt bar and the whole of one of the huge doors was dragged wide. Others wound the belatedly lowered portcullis back into its slot, clanking and juddering. Then they fled together, knight and robber, lord and commoner, bounding in exultation away from the untenanted arrow slits and murder holes of the grim barbican.

Jebbin was recovered sufficiently to stagger from the gates and stand alone when they halted briefly on the roadway. With the flail between his hands, Rallor held up his arms, a mighty figure framed against the mountains of Ael, spicules of ice powered by the wind ringing on his armour. He called to the disparate group before him.

"Our baggage and beasts lie this way. All who come with us are welcome to share what food and medicines we have. To those who choose their own way, fare you well. Let none tarry here!"

But at that moment they were aware of a drumming, swelling rapidly from a subliminal vibration to a pounding roar as a phalanx of riders as broad as the road swept into view and came hurtling towards them. Their horses were black, black were their furs, like ice shone the steel of their bucklers and rounded helms. White steam from the horses' nostrils, foam from their lips and snow from their hooves streamed away on the wind like banners. They galloped like emissaries of the gods upon the clouds.

"'Ware!" bellowed Rallor. "We must not be caught between the hammer of the riders and the anvil of the castle." He prepared for a last and hopeless defence, the ashes of their momentary freedom almost choking him.

Then Jebbin pulled at his elbow. "Whatever happens here, your mission did not wholly fail. Lykos is dead. The hostages are freed. The tribes of Ael may find their own destiny, there is none now to impel them to war."

"Lykos dead? Good news indeed but I would not die to hear it. Flee if you can. My armoured knights have no escape here."

It was too late for any to flee. The thunder of the riders bore down upon them. Snorting breath and rolling eyes of the horses, hunched forms with bared teeth and eyes like slits against the icy wind, a vision of the spirit of Ael, too powerful for any force to quell.

Then Matico uttered a wild cry of jubilation. "The Leopards! Ya hee! Clear the road. They try for the Rokepike. Clear the road, I say."

Knights flung themselves right and left from the roadway, barely in time to avoid the charging cavalcade that spurred past, never checking, leaving them swathed in a whirlwind of snow laced with the pungent aroma of horses, sweat and leather. On a long black pennant, a snow leopard bunched and sprang in time with the wind. It leapt into the castle as the leaders of the clinking, grunting horde rode right into the hall itself; others bounded from their mounts and landing running for the gates. In a matter of moments, nearly three hundred men had entered the indomitable Rokepike and not an arrow fired to gainsay them.

In the relative quiet after their passage, Rallor commanded that the worst of the wounded should be taken back to their baggage train and treated immediately under Theriac. Any hale or slightly hurt should return to the main gates and hold them. Any who wished to strike further blows to aid the Leopards should follow him. Rallor turned and strode after Matico, who was already halfway to the gates, whirling a clumsy cleaver as though it were the finest blade of Felugan steel, sending horses skittering from his path.

The Bear troops of the Rokepike were totally disorganised in what they thought was the aftermath of their battle. They had successfully battered down the gates and, finding the swordplay done, as many as practicable had been dragooned into fire-fighting teams carrying water from the cisterns. A long line swung sagging leather buckets and slopped most of the water to freeze a treacherous path on the ground. Others were strung out in knots of the curious between the broken keep gates and the gaping hole blown in the wall by the oil barrels. Some were idly poking chunks of ruined stonework and speculating as to the cause and the fate of any escapers.

They were taken completely unawares and stood no chance against the screaming flood of the Leopards pouring into the yard from the castle. By the time Rallor reached the keep, the Bear defenders had either retreated inside it or were lying face down in the snow with Leopard archers ready to send arrows into any that moved. None did.

The Leopards were ranged before the irreparable keep gates. Rallor was surprised that they had not raced inside as quickly as they were able. The pause could only benefit the defenders and allow them to strengthen the grim and blackened force of Bear that already thronged the entrance - unless the fires defeated them. He supposed that the Leopards feared the magic of Lykos and with good reason. He headed towards them, intending to reveal that Lykos would be chanting no more spells.

Before he could speak to anyone, he looked through the gates into the Rokepike keep, where a sudden contagious hush had fallen upon the Bears. It spread outward, infecting the Leopards until they waited in expectant silence, nervously gripping their weapons. The quiet accentuated the crackling and grumbling booms of the fire. Above them, the keep vented trails of smoke from windows and turrets and the occasional tongue of flame flared across the darkling evening to lick the stationary warriors with orange light.

Slowly the Bears fell back to form a lane. Beside Rallor, a grizzled Aelan commander moistened dry lips, staring down the human corridor as a shape approached. Bolan appeared, grinding his way forward, tread by measured tread. In one hand he held Ommak's darkly glittering club, almost upright, like a flag. Bloodshot eyes blazing, his whole burly frame charred and bloody, covered with welts and blisters, he looked like a demon from a nightmare. Whether they feared Ommak's badge of office or its new owner more was unclear but the Bear guards glanced sidelong and edged further away. From the scorched and gristly remnants adhering to the club it was obvious that others had not done so. Neither the Bears nor the Leopards were certain on whose side he fought. Yet such was the aura of force emanating from him that the Leopards too found themselves unconsciously moving aside to leave a path. Ignoring them all, Bolan stamped down it undeviating and none dared a move against him.

"He wears the levin," whispered a Leopard warrior.

"You fool. He *is* the Levin of Ael. So are the Bear punished for yielding to the flat-lander."

Even as the Leopards turned back to face the keep, there was a great creaking groan followed by a crash and a mighty whoof of flame as the lowest floor of the keep fell in upon the defenders in a blaze of fire and sparks. Those Bear still able cast aside their weapons and ran pell-mell from the showering debris, joining their colleagues face down on the frozen ground.

* * *

With the permission of Bundobust, the new castellan, Rallor had organised a team to collect his wounded and baggage into the protection of the castle. He led them across the stone floor of the gate hall, through a second pair of enormous doors and out again into the great yard where he was greeted by Matico who was still afire, quivering with elation.

"Lord Rallor. The impregnable Rokepike is ours at a stroke and hardly a life lost! Tonight, as is fitting, my father, chief of the Leopards, sits in Lykos' seat. Bereft of its body, Lykos' head will face Gerulf, wolf-demon of the north wind, from the point of a lance atop the tower he defiled; and I doubt not the ravens will gorge on his eyeballs before Gerulf has time to freeze them solid. Thus Ael is reprieved from his odious subversions - and the status of the Snow Leopards much enhanced.

"We are not ungrateful for your role in these events. A great feast is ordained for tonight: all those who fought so hard to liberate the Rokepike should partake of its bounty. You, and those brave members of your party who are able, are invited to the green buttery. In the meantime, apply to Bundobust for anything you need; facilities for ablutions, more suitable vestments for your comfort or physics to 'suage your hurts. He will provide you with the best accommodation he can find under the circumstances and ensure you are alerted when all is in readiness for our festivities."

Matico, regal despite his torn and blackened finery, strode

confidently away before Rallor could venture any reply. The Southern lord ran fingers through his singed hair despondently, unable to share Matico's euphoria despite the nominal success of his mission. The Rokepike had been taken with hardly an Aelan life lost, maybe. Several of his friends would lie forever beneath the Rokepike and many others suffered crippling hurts. Nasty suspicions were tugging at his sleeves like hawking urchins in a bazaar and they were equally difficult to dislodge.

Jebbin joined those already forgathered in the green buttery, gratefully accepting a pewter mug of mulled wine steeped in oranges, cloves and cinnamon from a steward sporting a noble black eye. The walls were covered with green hessian stitched with vibrant scenes of battle in high corries, hawking and the chase in wooded valleys. As he looked round, Rallor caught his eye and waved him over to join a stout man with bandy legs. Pale brown eyes matched the chestnut colour of his hair and neatly trimmed beard, except where grey paled his temples.

"Jebbin, may I introduce Duke Withersteen, the Trivan envoy to the Leopards."

"Ah, the young firebrand! I am pleased to meet you!"

Jebbin's hand was enfolded in a grip of measured strength. As the Trivan's hand was extended, Jebbin noticed that the nails had long ago been ripped from his fingers and he could not repress a faint shudder. Withersteen's gaze never shifted, but the Duke continued smoothly,

"You have quick eyes. I'm afraid diplomatic life is not always as refined and courteous as one might like. But come now, why so late? Did old Bundobust forget to call you?"

"By no means. Indeed, as a result of his diligence I have been reminded about five times, in increasingly acerbic fashion. I wanted to have a chat with Orrolui but I can't find where he's been billeted. Have I missed anything?"

"A visit from the chief of the Leopards himself."

"What was he like?"

"A man with presence. But his face is as flat as an iron and gives about as much away. He's got hair like steel wool, says little and comes up to here," replied Withersteen, tapping his shoulder. "I think his eyes did open a bit when Rallor offered him the flail."

"You offered to give that flail away?" exclaimed Jebbin in amazement. "But why?"

"Part of the castle plunder," shrugged Rallor. "As I suspected, he showed little interest in it. Said it was useless on a horse and if I wanted to waste my time with an ungainly peasant's tool, I was welcome to it. I didn't mention its other properties."

"You mean he asked for no further information and who are you to gratuitously vouchsafe superfluous details?"

"Any advice on dealing with wizards, Duke? A stout cudgel, perhaps?"

Jebbin grinned hugely. "What did he want, though?"

"Just to give the foreigners a patronising pat on the back and ensure that we don't intend to stay or promulgate our gauche interference in affairs that do not concern us" said Withersteen. "You'll note that all the brutish foreigners are lumped in here while the unsullied host of the Leopards stamp their feet and bawl drunken songs in the Great Hall."

"But there are Aelans here."

"Aelans, yes; erstwhile prisoners from tribes unsympathetic to the Leopards. Other Aelans have probably fared even worse than being equated with foreigners. But Jebbin, I must say how you have surprised me. I never would have guessed that Rallor would use a magician to defeat the warlock Lykos."

Jebbin and Rallor exchanged uneasy glances, both wondering who had been used by whom.

"Come now," chuckled Withersteen to Rallor. "You didn't suppose that all this came about by accident? You knew that neither Triva nor the Leopards could take direct action against Lykos. Triva wasn't prepared to stand by while she put her head on a block with a marriage she couldn't repudiate with honour. You were our untraceable solution."

"So I've been cozened like a bull on a rope!"

"You should not view it so. You have an awesome reputation; money wouldn't sway you, so we tried other ways. You came of your own volition and so it must remain."

"Had you asked for my help, I would not have been stinting."

"And the rumours of Trivan emissaries talking to the great Lord Rallor would have winged their way to Lykos and made your task impossible. No, we needed an unwitting agent and you had the qualifications we required. If there is any reparation you want from us, you have but to ask. As a matter of fact, I now understand that, quite independently, the Lady Rhesa came to the same conclusions that we did and produced her own agent; Bolan of all people. A remarkable lady. I hope Matico appreciates what he's getting."

"I had no idea the world was so full of devious manipulators," grumbled Rallor, pulling disconsolately at a goblet of dark wine.

"The diplomatic service is not for you," returned Withersteen blandly.

"You've been used," Jebbin told Rallor. "We've all been used and to what end? I wonder if the seer would be proud if she could see what she has wrought."

At that moment Bundobust called them to table and Jebbin found himself at the end of the knights with Bolan and Hiraeth. Their armour and weapons laid by, the diminished band of knights mostly displayed the results of Theriac's ministrations. Lesser cuts and bruises had been rubbed with an analgesic salve but major hurts were everywhere in evidence, bandaged with poultices, strappings and slings. Many gulped the mulled concoction with a wincing edge of desperation.

The table was laden with platters carrying chunks of beef freshly cut from one of the spit-roast beasts in the great hall, the fat still bubbling. A cold smoked ham, baked fowls stuffed with dill and almonds, roasted gamecocks smothered in a cranberry sauce, pies and crusty loaves vied for attention and were not denied. Pitchers of mulled wine rested on frames over candles and were frequently replenished.

Hiraeth was cutting himself a generous wedge of pie. He breathed deep the aroma rising from the interior.

"Lute and flute, smell those truffles! Men would die to create a pie like this!"

"They probably did and were put into it," retorted Jebbin. He chuckled at a sudden recollection. "Hophni would like it. Remember him tackling those venison pastries before we got into the Rokepike, Ygyrd getting cross because he wouldn't bargain and ..." He stopped in the sudden realisation, however impossible it seemed, that both men were really dead, and looked guiltily at Bolan. The wrestler gazed back with eyes as hard as knuckles in his blistered face. He looked as though a laugh would kill him.

"You think either of them would wish you to go moping round with long faces? They'd want you to enjoy and share a joke. Remember them at their best."

Bolan rose from the table and shambled out of the buttery, leaving his meal untasted. Jebbin half rose to follow him but Hiraeth's light hand restrained him.

"He bears a load too heavy even for his shoulders. But he's not yet ready to share it."

"He is hardly to blame for Hophni's death."

"So I have told him," said Hiraeth sombrely. They returned to their meal with reduced appetites.

Jebbin was halfway though his plateful when someone tapped him on the back. He turned about and almost choked in amazement as he looked into a pair of bright blue eyes under a thatch of red hair and a grin as broad as the face.

"Nith! What in the name of the Lady are you doing here?"

"Other than sampling this excellent free meal, you mean? I suppose the short answer is that the Forshen, the Seekers, at last found what they sought."

"But you're not... I mean at Lana Fair... I thought..."

"Of course, the best thing about magicians is that they're so articulate," chortled Nith. "Come along, there's something I want you to see. We may even catch the end of the argument."

Puzzled, Jebbin followed Nith's bobbing form through the buttery and into a wide corridor. A short way along it sat the opinicus, glossy and vital, licking stained claws with a forked tongue. Hanjar was standing against one wall, poised yet relaxed, exuding calm assurance. A swarthy woman dressed in tan and ochre robes was evidently trying to convince him of some point. They were in time to hear Hanjar's response, which sounded like a well-worn refrain.

"I see evil."

"But times have changed. Things are different now."

"Evil remains."

"Of course there is wrong in the world. But you cannot fight it all, blow by blow. We must search for deeper knowledge. Hunt out the weaknesses of evil to exploit them - if you must call everything imperfect evil. Instead of being confrontational, we must show people how things can be better by example. Give them the ability to seek out their own truths and justices."

"Justice is justice and not for bending by individuals."

"By being slower than rushing in with fists, we can be surer. Our work should be teaching not fighting. Strike off the head of evil and it grows afresh. Shear off its roots of ignorance and entrenched apathy and evil withers."

"I will not be beguiled by words again. The blessed Saint Sipahni indeed taught that we should lead by example but also that we should smite evil where it thrives."

"Hanjar, you are the greatest of our order. We need your strength."

"To squander in fruitless blethering to deaf ears? No, I am the greatest of my order. You have forsaken the blessed Saint. I will not."

The woman before Hanjar sighed and shrugged her shoulders. "I have done my best. We will miss you sorely and this is a bad end to the search."

"You sought me for a generation and then used others to fight Remis. Is this what you will teach?"

"You are wrong to judge everything as black or white. The monks of Sipahni were overrun by pride before, how can you proof them again?"

"When one is called to battle, one must fight even if victory is not assured - better than tricking others into fighting for you. Hindsight will make my defence surer. Before, some lost sight of what was right, but not all. And we must remain judgemental. Evil does not proclaim itself but speaks fair words."

"That's too simple. You cannot just say that man is evil and appoint yourself his executioner. Your arch-rival Remis thought he was striving for the best, he thought he was fighting evil, his mistake was forcing people to conform to his will. Perhaps we might even have approved the result had he won a generation ago, if not the means. We must learn tolerance and understanding lest we all become obsessed."

Hanjar contemplated the Forshen woman for some time before replying curtly, "The Forshen have sought long. I am sure they have grown very wise - and blind. I shall pray to Saint Sipahni and he shall judge through me."

"I cannot move you and this discussion is clearly over. Come Nith, we have other matters to attend to."

"No, Cosla. I believe Hanjar is right. Remis is dead. It is now time that the Forshen bloomed once more into the warrior monks of Saint Sipahni and put virtuous steel behind our velvet teachings. In a generation the Forshen have changed nothing. Hanjar has consented to take me on as his pupil; a new and humble disciple of the blessed Saint Sipahni."

Cosla teetered on the edge of a biting retort and barely collected herself in time. "In that case, I have even more to do and must bid you both farewell."

Jebbin well remembered the imperturbability of the Forshen and felt a deliciously wicked sense of pleasure at seeing one of them rattled. He also noted the deep satisfaction in Hanjar's aged eyes, but the monk was looking at Nith. Turning to Nith, Jebbin said, "So you found yourself a vocation."

"I always had one."

"I sense you've had a lot more to do with all this than you have let on!"

"True," admitted Nith cheerily, grinning more widely than ever. "As soon as the Forshen knew for certain that Lykos was indeed Remis, the plotting of his downfall was swift as we took advantage of circumstances. I met up with Cosla at the fair with the token and she's been our guide through Ael. The Leopards are only here because Cosla and I took the message to them. We knew Rallor was going to try for it as soon as he bought the yaks. And we've had quite a time of it. The Leopards have fought several times to preserve Rallor's group as they blundered about in the mountains. Do you know, even his supplies outside the Rokepike were unplundered!"

"Does Rallor have any inkling of this?"

"Certainly not. Reveal nothing or the Leopards will lose their reputation!"

"Poor Rallor is just concluding that there are too many devious manipulators and he doesn't know the half of it."

"Anyway Jebbin, Hanjar has accepted me as his protégé and we will build anew the fame of Saint Sipahni with or without the Forshen. But he says that you have already felt the blessed hand guiding you and you may also wish to join us. Do you?"

Jebbin was astonished but did his best to conceal it. He looked first into the deep unruffled gaze of the aged monk and saw his uncluttered strength as hard as adamant, then at Nith's innocent and enthusiastic face.

"No," he said softly. "Were I to join any such sect it would be with you. But my road is not yet fixed. I shall remember the words of the saint that I have heard."

Nith clasped him briefly but warmly, then the two Sipahnites walked away down the corridor, the mighty opinicus beside Hanjar, its tail twitching to and fro. Jebbin watched them go with wonder in his heart, then returned to the buttery.

Most of the noise was leaking through from the great hall, where hoots and roars occasionally rose over the general cacophony. In the green buttery there was little more than a pervasive hum of conversation, though wines and beers were freely quaffed. Most fell silent when Matico made a strutting entrance, now dressed in a lustrous black doublet with scarlet trimmings and a black cape with a Snow Leopard emblazoned in scarlet and silver. There was an initially sporadic outburst of applause and cheering led with considerable enthusiasm by those Aelans whose tribes had the most nebulous relations with the Leopards.

After gracefully accepting these plaudits, Matico held up his hands for quiet.

"Friends all, we have today been witnesses to a momentous event. The vile ravager has been cast down and the mighty Rokepike, hoarder of a thousand secrets, is back in the hands of the true children of the mountains.

"It is a great day which could ask for no further ennoblement, yet I have today declared my nuptial vows before my people. With all that these vows entail in the fostering of understanding and alliance between two great peoples, I now do so again before you, who have all had your parts to play in the great triumph. I present to you that paradigm of beauty, the Lady Rhesa."

The girl walked slowly from the door to the great hall towards Matico. Honey-coloured hair flowed back from her face, her wide blue eyes locked upon Matico, perhaps a slight tremble in her full lips, she advanced steadily. Before Jebbin could do more than sit up in consternation, Withersteen was on his feet, his face almost white.

"What is this?" he demanded in a shocked hiss.

Matico looked round at him in amazement while the girl quickened her steps to reach his side, one hand pressed to her mouth, the other clutching Matico's arm.

"Who is this trollop?" roared Withersteen, fury shaking him and leaving white marks on his fists.

"Silence, you buffoon. Another word costs you your head, ambassador or not. How dare you?"

"How dare I?" spluttered Withersteen, rage foaming his lips. "You insult all Triva, you blatantly repudiate the treaty. You lecherous popinjay!"

"By the great god Rashen-Akru, you disgrace the lady. Your mind has gone - but I have a cure!" Matico pushed the girl protectively behind him where she collapsed back against the wall, biting her fingers. He danced lightly over the table, silvered steel leaping like a salmon from scabbard to hand, and faced the unarmed Withersteen, who snatched up a stool and charged like a buffalo.

The noise hit them like a sandbag, a blast like a thunderclap with rolling aftershocks as dishes crashed, flagons shattered and benches were overturned and, in the midst of it, Rallor's voice, magnified to the very stuff of thunder, crying, "Hold!"

Withersteen tripped mid-stride and sprawled heavily before Matico, who staggered backwards, his sword spilling from his hand to spiral down in a flicker of silver and ring on the floor. They gaped stupidly at Rallor through the silence that permeated even the great hall, where the drunken Leopards cringed and blinked owlishly towards the green buttery.

Rallor stood over the tilted wreckage of the table, snapped asunder by the impact of the arcane flail, his stare quelling any notions the antagonists might have had of renewing their hostilities. He turned to where the girl was now weeping on the floor, Hiraeth bending down by her side.

"Who are you?"

The girl trembled still but seemed to draw strength from the bard and choked back her sobs to answer in a broken and strangled voice. "If you please, I hardly know. Once I think I was Alyvette, then I was Rhesa. Now ... I am Alyvette. And soon nothing."

His perplexity plain, Rallor watched Matico easing Hiraeth aside and lacing his arms about the girl, helping her to a seat. Jebbin's voice spoke softly behind him.

"A spell. Lykos cast a glamour upon her so she believed she was Rhesa. With his death, the entrancement fades."

"But why?"

Jebbin amid shrugged away a thousand possibilities. "Who

knows? When Rhesa came here, Lykos would just have held her. Matico would believe he'd married the real Rhesa and the Trivans would have believed she had married Matico. All would have been bound as Lykos planned but he would still have had Rhesa in his power, perhaps to make some new union for his benefit, some other plot or something more personal and worse. His underhand tactics are beyond me."

Rallor made to speak again but Matico held up an imperious hand to forestall him, his eyes hot with passion. For a moment he stood straight and silent, one hand on Alyvette's shoulder, and never had he looked more fine and noble.

"Duke Withersteen, I apologise for these events. Your anger was justified in the circumstances you saw, perhaps it does you credit, and I forgive your words. I understand that this is not the Lady Rhesa of Triva and that I have been fooled by yet more of Lykos' wicked deceptions.

"But I say this. Lykos knew not what he wrought. I love Rh.... Alyvette and I have sworn my vows to her before my people. Never will I abandon her." He gave a lingering glance at Alyvette's transfigured face as she looked up at him, eyes wide, the tracks of redundant tears glistening brightly on her cheeks. Then he looked back to Withersteen. "Neither will I renege on a single one of my commitments. I cannot now marry the Lady Rhesa of Triva but I wish to dissolve the compact without slighting Triva. Let not Lykos win this last battle. Duke Withersteen, agree to this and I swear by the bones of my father's father and the children of my unborn sons alliance and fraternal union with Triva. Let there be this true bond even without the marriage to seal it."

All eyes turned to the Trivan emissary, standing before Matico. He hesitated. "Will the chief ratify...?"

"My son," came an iron voice from the doorway, accenting the second word with warm pride, "speaks with the honour of the Leopards on his lips. Doubt him never."

Matico seemed to grow taller where he stood but his eyes remained bent upon Withersteen. The Duke looked towards the short Aelan chief standing square and solid as an idol in the entrance from the great hall. He turned back to Matico and met his hot gaze steadily.

"The Leopards will not lack for statecraft for another generation. Neither will they lack the staunch allies of the Trivans. Let us be brothers."

He clasped hands with Matico and then suddenly they were pounding each other on the back and the whole buttery was resounding to whoops and cheering until they rivalled the great hall. Withersteen was begging to be introduced to the Lady Alyvette, who was now crying for joy and clinging fiercely to Matico. Fresh flagons were brought and broached, healths and undying friendships toasted, pledges made and boasts begun. Jebbin glanced to the chief but the doorway was empty once more. He saw Hiraeth and chuckled. The bard was drinking in the scene more quickly than the most bibulous was tackling the wine. He would indeed have a song to sing when he returned.

* * *

Jebbin woke in the greyed end of the night with a budding hangover and an urgent need to relieve himself. While Matico and Alyvette had soon returned to the Leopards in the great hall last night, he had stayed talking with Rallor and Hol, drinking too much rye beer after the mulled brew was gone. When they had finally limped to bed, burbling song and ragged cheers were still emanating from the great hall in raucous crescendos. Rallor had commented disparagingly that if anyone sympathetic to the Bear were to wrest the Rokepike back from the Leopards, that very dawn would be the time, when no defender would be conscious, let alone effective.

Creeping about in bare feet on the warm stones, Jebbin visited the draughty garderobe but when he returned to the little room he shared with two unknown Aelans who had fallen flat on the floor, fully dressed and snored ever since, the place smelt stuffy and his stomach churned uncomfortably. Hoping to clear his head, he blearily shrugged his way into a heavy fur robe and boots and climbed a spiral stair to the battlements for some fresh air. On his way, he met a tired but alert detachment of Aelans descending, having just been relieved of their watch. Apparently, the hard life of the mountains taught lessons even this victory would not erase.

Jebbin paced the battlements. The bitter crepuscular chill, considerably fresher than he required, pinched his skin and froze the muzziness from his head. As the light grew, he could discern the tops of black pines in distant valleys far below, pockets of fog concealing their trunks so the branches appeared to float like furry islands on a pale sea. He noticed a familiar broad figure hunched over the parapet further along and hurried to join him.

Bolan was staring moodily outward, watching the snows on the peaks blooming through pale rose to jasmine and pearl in the dawn light. His hands, resting on the stone, were blue and shrivelled with cold.

After standing next to him in awkward silence for a while, Jebbin turned and sat down, his knees tucked into his chest, looking back into the castle. The little black ball of Lykos' head floated on an invisible spike above a tower. Jebbin could not tell which way the head faced but had a clear vision in his mind of the gory, sightless face, the scheming over, the dream now forever unattainable. Lykos would hardly merit a footnote in the annals of the Belmenian historians, just a failed wolf of the mountains in the fastnesses of Ael. How would those annals have described him had he conquered as he desired and enforced his decrees: saviour or despot, hero or tyrant? All that was left now was the odd ramification of old lies and a plume of smoke and steam still rising from the gutted keep to stain the mountain air with a trail of dirty grey. Gangs of dismal figures were still tossing water on the heated stones.

"You heard about Matico and Rhesa?" Jebbin said at last, idly watching the antics below him.

Bolan nodded. "Hm. Hiraeth told me last night." He lapsed back into immobility, his eyes still fixed on the distant rocky spires.

"And now?" prompted Jebbin.

"Don't know."

"Won't you go to Rhesa. She will want to see you very much."

"Don't know," Bolan repeated in a low whisper.

"But she was the whole point, wasn't she? Why else did you come?"

He thought Bolan was not going to answer but eventually the wrestler continued in his soft monotone, talking to the mountains.

"Friendship. Look what's happened. Came for my love for an ideal. Not for gain. Came to give away what I love most. Now things have altered and don't know where that leaves me, if anywhere. Afraid to find out. At the rising of the sun and in the last quiet of the moonlight, her face is ever before me. When I walk alone in the darkness, her presence is always beside me. Still don't know what she thinks of me.

"But know what is lost. A true friend. Someone to count on. Dead because of me. I begged his help when he was hurt."

"Hophni wanted to come. He died because of Ommak, not you. It was a fight. A battle. People get hurt." Jebbin tailed off, not knowing how to help the wrestler. Bolan did not reply but his look was plain enough. People may die, but not Hophni. Not in a fair fight. Jebbin was left thinking that not all those hurt were injured.

Soon Jebbin could stand the cold no more. He led the frozen wrestler back into the warmth of the Rokepike and down to where a few hardy souls were taking breakfast in the small lower buttery.

Bolan ate frugally and soon departed but Jebbin stayed sipping a strangely flavoured black tea until others arrived, pondering Bolan's predicament. His idol had faced an arranged marriage. Not unusual for one in her position but more than that, she had faced being trapped by Lykos or dishonour for herself and her country. She was now free of both threats. Had she just used Bolan or would she truly wish to see him and perhaps more? Jebbin was certain it was the latter but ugly Bolan, caught in the vice of cynicism, suspected the worst. He did not wish to face up to the truth for fear of being right and his idol no better than a pretty strumpet, bartering with her favours, his worship of the years a hollow profanity.

A poorly-humoured Rallor was one of the first into the buttery. He informed Jebbin that they were being more or less politely asked to leave at noon that day.

"They cover it well: Withersteen will wish to hasten with the news to Triva and stop Rhesa coming; we won't want to linger in the deepening Aelan winter; the Rokepike commissariat cannot cope with the extra demands; they are unable to offer us the hospitality they deem appropriate until they have arranged their own affairs here and invite us all back at some unspecified point in the future. Actually, it's an embarrassing rush to cleanse the place of foreigners but I can't say I'll be sorry to get away. There will be funerary services held in the west chapel after normal devotions at tierce. Then we all travel together back to Lana with an honour guard.

"This tea is vile. Excuse me but there's little time and I must roust out Bundobust to arrange the rites. I'll see you at tierce."

Jebbin was about to seek out Orrolui when Hiraeth gingerly lowered himself into a chair next to him. The bard grimly refused all food and tackled the tea with more determination than zest. Looking at Hiraeth, Jebbin felt better and better.

"The buttered kippers are excellent," he offered maliciously, having studiously avoided them himself, and grinned when Hiraeth groaned queasily. "I suppose you know we're off at noon?"

"I hadn't heard the time but I expected it to be today. It won't take long to pack. Poor Bolan though."

"Why can't he just talk to Rhesa?"

"Easy for you to say. She's been his idol for so long - and you don't just talk to a goddess. This is Bolan - what would he say? I suspect Bolan is not exactly a serial heart-breaker, his amorous conquests might have owed more to his purse than his face. That would colour his judgement."

"I can't believe it's over," said Jebbin suddenly. "It will be difficult to believe any of this happened when we go separate ways. You and Rallor and Bolan are all such incredible people in your different ways. If only I..."

"You have talents enough of your own," interjected Hiraeth sharply. "Why must all men wish for gifts they do not have and undervalue their own abilities? And remember, it's my job that what happened here does not fade. If the bardic contest at Lana Fair were still to come, what a song I could sing of the Rokepike. But of course, it doesn't matter so much now."

It was a sad little service in the chapel. A short prayer of thanks for the lives of the deceased and a blessing upon their future. A mournful litany of names: Darcassi, Melgan of the forked beard, Corm who had helped support him, Feradil the poet, Ux-aboi from O-Ram and dark Yulin.

Jebbin wept for them all but most for Yulin of the quicksilver hands and eyes, without whose aid Hanjar would still wait immured in the darkness of the hidden cell. Ygyrd was placed in honour alongside the fallen knights and Jebbin joined the survivors with bowed heads and heavy hearts, taking what comfort they could from the soft-spoken obsequies uttered by a samite-clad priest.

Although his name was spoken on the roll, the absence of Hophni's body affected them all. The whole keep was his tomb, the dungeons having fallen in as the keep collapsed. Bolan stood with dry eyes open, staring over the catafalque where the bodies lay. He heard nothing of the service but obediently filed out after the knights when at last they took their leave of their old comrades.

Matico took the trouble to meet them all afterwards. Alone of the Leopards he was moved by genuine emotion and even apologised for their rapid departure. He was particularly solicitous over Bolan, whose discomfiture affected him greatly. It was almost time for them to depart when he drew Jebbin to one side.

"I mislike all this skulking but it must be so. These are valiant men, more ill-used by Lykos than ever was I. But the heroic Bolan is beyond my reach, Rallor would be insulted by money, how can I reward them, make concrete the honour of all Ael?"

"I don't know. Tell them they have it. They know you do not lie." Having just discovered where Orrolui had been put, Jebbin was trying to hurry away.

"It is not sufficient. I am humiliated by the treatment they have received. For you though, and forgive me, I do not imply that you are more venal, but I hope you will accept this pouch of gold. I beg you not to refuse, if only to help salve my conscience."

After the briefest hesitation, Jebbin smiled and accepted the heavy bag. "You have my grateful thanks, for in fact I have no money at all. I should like to give you a small gift too. A wedding present if you like, with my best wishes to Alyvette and yourself."

Matico looked on quizzically as Jebbin fished around in his pockets and then gasped as Jebbin produced the key he had found in the book in the little library and pressed it into his hand.

"It can't be! The silver key!" exclaimed Matico in amazement. "We bribed half the servants in the Rokepike to find where it was hidden, to no avail. We have searched every inch of the castle looking for this and found it not. Ah, this is fortune indeed. How can you accept my pittance of gold with such grace and then give such a gift."

They were interrupted by a thrice-winded horn blast and the knights, now stiff and sore, began their limping trudge towards the gate hall. Despite his intense curiosity, Jebbin could not ask what the key opened without devaluing his gift. He had the little yataghan about his neck; other treasures of the Rokepike were not for him. As he turned away, Matico grasped his arm and looked earnestly at him.

"If you are within reach of Ael, or Triva, and you are in need, a message to me will bring you all the aid at my disposal. By the Levin of Ael, I swear it!"

Then he was gone to join Rallor, leaving Jebbin staring after him. Reckless, arrogant, he was yet steadfast and noble. With Rhesa he would indeed have made a formidable pair and matters would have been simpler had he married as all intended, allowing Bolan to feel that he had martyred himself with purpose. Now Rhesa was free, Bolan was compromised and the alliance was bonded not with a marriage but with the firm cement of Matico's word. All those intrigues and connivings and then affairs had found their own solution quite apart from anyone's plan. Perhaps it was better that Love had taken a hand but then Love would never say for whom it was better.

Jebbin had only looked back once towards the grey bulk of the mighty castle, louring over the dark-swathed riders jingling behind him but those towers were indelibly stamped on his mind, where the great keep still stood, scornful and defiant.

He was thinking back to Lykos' death, that unreasoned scrabbling to loosen the knot of an unknown spell, and remembering the minuscule but unmistakeable feel of a tiny spell uttered after Lykos' power had vanished in its disastrous storm cloud.

It could only have been Orrolui. Lykos had pronounced Orrolui weakened beyond spelling, probably beyond resuscitation, but he must have under-estimated the vehement Gesgarian yet again, like many before him. But what did Orrolui do? Now he had gone, leaving more mystery behind him. Various arcane oddments were in his room: an earthenware pitcher split asunder beside the fire, white mandragora upon a bed of cypress sprinkled with traces of zimort and saltpetre. But of Orrolui there was no sign.

Sighing, Jebbin clapped his heels to the black and shaggy Aelan horse until it began to gain on Hiraeth, then set his face resolutely forward.

Epilogue

Jebbin hopped off the tinker's cart with a wave at the rascal driving it. They had been companions since Jebbin had left Hiraeth near Dadacombe. Jebbin's mouth had hung open as he had witnessed some of the tinker's outrageously dishonest haggling. In the end, however, those dealing with the rogue seemed to end up with their gates repaired or gutters patched and the tinker never seemed much better off than before.

Jebbin watched him rattle down the slope with a wry smile and turned up through an avenue of pear trees towards Bodd's cottage. He had thought of Sola so often during his travels: no other woman had seemed so attractive. She thought magic was something wonderful, the fabric of dreams; the same way Jebbin felt. Only she had looked at the end result and seen beauty. Others saw only the pain that was the means. They might shrink with fear, sneer with disbelief or blame him for the inequality that set them apart but they all saw the pain. Sola understood the beautiful child of magic could only be born from pain. Now he was back he felt apprehensive but there was an air of tranquillity beneath the falling blossom, thick with the snoring of bees.

The cadence of Bodd's voice was audible and Jebbin headed towards it, emerging from the orchard to find Bodd on a patch of fresh soil in the company of a tall man with a mop of hair like a rook's nest. The young man stood with a stoop, abashed at some criticism.

"No, no," Bodd said patiently. "Throw the grain upward, not at the ground. It'll come down all by itself. Just practise by yourself a moment, Thrundil, while I attend to this gentleman."

Bodd abandoned Thrundil to his sowing and ambled over to Jebbin. He recognised Jebbin with a sudden start and looked slightly alarmed.

"Yes, well, Jebbin, isn't it? And what might you be wanting?"

"I was hoping to have a word with Sola if that would be all right?"

"Yes, hm. Well, she's up at the house. But don't you go upsetting her, mind," said Bodd after an awkward pause. Then he plainly elected to wash his hands of the whole affair and turned back to stop Thrundil wasting his entire stock of barley in drifts of gold.

Marching up to the door, Jebbin was about to knock when a voice from the garden stopped him.

"Jebbin. I'm so glad to see you once more."

He looked round to see the familiar face so often imagined upon his journeying, the eyes warm on his, the lips smiling.

"Sola. I've thought of you so often."

"And I of you. I'm sorry you were called away so suddenly. But I'm glad to be able to thank you for the present you sent back. It's just what Thrundil and I need to set up home together."

Jebbin was on the point of speaking when the import of her words shocked him to silence. Sola smiled at him again and laid her hand on his arm.

"We are to be married in a few days. You were my dream, Jebbin. An exciting dream of impossible magic that can't really exist, like the stories old Yarl tells round the fire in winter. It was lovely to share together."

Jebbin looked at her in amazement. She was so warm but so confident and distant. "I thought..." he began plaintively but her fingers stilled his lips.

"You pay me a lovely compliment. But Thrundil is a good man and he will stay. You are a travelling man. You would not stay, would you?"

He gazed at her longingly but he could only reply in a hoarse whisper, "No." No, he had not thought it through before but he would return home, see Dewlin and the rest of his family, enjoy the peace and security for a while. But even if Sola were to be his, he would not be able to stay. There was still the power and the pain.

Sola reached up and kissed him lightly. "Goodbye, Jebbin. You must go now before folk start wondering what I'm doing with a strange man almost on the eve of my wedding. Wish us well. I will never forget you."

Then she was gone in a rustle of cotton, leaving the scents of pear and polished wood behind her.

"Goodbye," Jebbin whispered to the empty garden. "And a blessing on your marriage."

* * *

Bolan waited motionless in the centre of the sandy ring. Another wrestling contest, another series of bouts for another hollow victory or pointless bruises. Oblivious to the crowds about the arena, he stood in limbo, dependent on autonomic reflexes.

His opponent appeared as his name was called, parting the ranks of immaculate Algolian soldiery, tall and proud with their plumed helmets, ruby cloaks and long ceremonial spears of ash and steel. A serious contender for this championship, Abaniel was a favourite with the Algolian crowd. Bowing and waving, Abaniel clenched his fists to the stands until the soldiers, in response to some hidden signal, raised their spears and brought the butts crashing down in perfect unison, producing a thump that rolled over the cheers and announced the start of the combat.

Still Bolan gazed over the heads of the audience, his mind turned inwards. He could scarcely recall anything of his journey from the great fair to Tarada or anything in between. He had just lapsed back into the old life, seeking refuge, but as an old garment it was no longer comfortable.

The crowd watched in breathless disbelief as Abaniel, silent in the sand, raced across the arena to attack his mesmerised opponent. Bolan could not rid himself of visions of Hophni, leaping high to deliver a killing blow that merely dented an artificial cranium; thrown by his ruined arm; lying pale and flaccid on the ground. And he, Bolan, had called for help. In his unforgivable weakness he had called for help from the wounded Hophni. His was the fault. He still saw Ommak as though he stood before him, towering and powerful, overblown with strength. In the midst of the whirling images, a new idea came to him. He reached a decision with abrupt certainty.

Bolan whipped round, the heel of his hand smashing into the charging Abaniel's chest, stopping all his momentum. Ribs broke with a snap like a whip-crack and Abaniel thudded onto his back in the sand, too paralysed to start retching for air.

The spectators gasped as one and were silent, waiting for Bolan to follow up his move or accept victory but Bolan merely glanced down at Abaniel as an irksome interruption. Compared with Ommak, he was nothing. Bolan had defeated Ommak - if only he had done so without begging for Hophni's aid - what glory was there in this victory?

He squared his shoulders with a return of some of his old vitality and marched from the arena. Killing Ommak had not been enough: Hophni was yet unavenged. There was still Ommak's creator who might still be practising his abhorrent arts. The battle was not yet over and against that creator he might find his apotheosis.

All watched in wonder as Bolan left the arena, far more purposeful than when he had arrived. High above him, Biwa the meddler sat with his eyes gleaming, a frown of delicious puzzlement creasing his face. Then the buzz of incredulous chatter swelled loud and none heeded the grumpy marshal as he curtly announced the injured Abaniel as the winner by default.

* * *

Some fifty leagues beyond the last reaches of the Felugin Sea and three hundred more from the great Guild-run city of Tarass, there is a small town called Bes-Thiope, about a day's ride north of the Golden Road. The town is centred about a river where it widens into a reed-fringed lake where trout rise and carp roll heavy shoulders in the evening light. Unlike the fear-ridden villages further west and north, here the streets are broad and houses straggle away until the town fades into farmhouses and bothies. A small plaza boasts a fountain set amid flowering shrubs and a marble statue of a maiden riding a wide-winged gryphon. Set within a quiet garden of laburnum, box and honeysuckle for reflection an elegant fane faces a polished inn for prosperous merchants across the square.

Behind these civic glories, denser houses cast a gloom over darker streets and rough taverns cater for labourers at sensible prices. Tlima stood outside one of the poorest of these and approved the choice of meeting place. She pushed open the door, avoiding the natural impulse to glance furtively left and right up the street.

There were a few groups already settled about the tables in the dingy common room. Smoking candles were wedged in the mountainous guttered remains of previous candles on all the tables. Flames fluttered wildly in the draught from the door and added their contributory dribble to the tallow sculptures.

One man sat alone by a stained and rickety table which he evidently did not trust to bear the weight of his beer, nursed upon his knee. His hood was lifted over his head, concealing all his features. Tlima advanced to his table and spoke softly.

"I am Tlima. And you ...?"

"Names are but cloaks we put on as disguises and doff at our convenience. Sit."

"Gesgarian!"

"Does it matter?" A soft voice, all the more predatory for its mildness. A glimpse of hot black eyes beneath the rim of the hood.

"No! No, not at all. To each man, his own customs; that's what I say." Tlima wished her voice were steadier and sat down, cultivating an air of indifference.

"Really?" A smile was visible now, or a baring of teeth. It was difficult to be sure. Candlelight peeked under the hood, saw nasty scars and retreated once more.

"Anyway, if you have the money, I have news for you."

* * *

Dadacombe's easy life was much recovered from the affronts perpetrated upon it during Hiraeth's last visit but there were lasting memorials. The bard stopped for a moment beside the blackened foundations of a warehouse and ruefully resettled his pack on his shoulders, producing a dull plunk from the oilskin-wrapped lute.

Before making his way to the house of the minstrels, Hiraeth edged his way through the busy streets and thence to the less populous district where Erridarch had his shop. He passed the aromatic bakery, almost sold out for the day, and soon reached the geographer's familiar sign. He pushed on the be-grimed door but it was locked and the windows were as blind as Erridarch. He rubbed on the glass with his cuff and peered through but could see little.

"No good looking for the mappy," came a gruff voice behind him.

Hiraeth turned to see a moustached man with a belly that threatened the stitching of his smock eyeing him from the ironmongery opposite.

The monger heaved himself from his doorway and plodded across the street. "No, mappy died a while back, the little scrap of a man. Hey, are you a bard?" he asked, suddenly catching sight of the wrapped lute.

"Yes," sighed Hiraeth. Deep inside, he had known that Erridarch had died but the hope had lived on.

"Strange. He kept saying a bard would come. Do you want to go in? I've got the key somewhere."

"Yes," repeated Hiraeth woodenly and waited, staring into the faded building while the monger puffed off to get the key.

Inside everything was cold and damp and dead, corners curling on once treasured maps. Hiraeth stared down at the map spread on the counter, still pinned by the familiar assortment of Erridarch's paraphernalia; but now the inkwell was dry and crusty and the first dusting of white mould erupted over the meticulously drawn vellum. As gently as though he were tending a grave, Hiraeth wiped the surface of the map and looked again at the valleys and spires of Ael at the western edge of that high plain, at the roadway and the mighty castle, the Rokepike.

Hiraeth stood still with tears blurring his vision, the last words of Erridarch crying in his mind - Sing of me. Behind him, the monger was still prattling.

"Don't know what he spent his time doing with all this stuff. Silly little fellow."

"You know nothing," Hiraeth roared at him with sudden vehemence, sending the astonished monger staggering backwards. "The man outside was no fit vehicle for the man inside. He was as great a man as any I've met from the hovels of Shekkem to Lana fair. Go! Host the village! Tonight there will be such a singing as I have never given. All shall be in honour of Erridarch the Far-Sighted, Erridarch the Noble, Erridarch the self-sacrificing Hero of Marigor. GO!"

* * *

The grim bulwark city of Jerondst stands high on the plains of Northern Azria, vast, old and gaunt. Westward lie the untamed lands where savage and hardy tribesmen eke an existence from pockets of thin, stony soil. Occasionally they band together and attack eastwards, but always there is Jerondst. Jerondst, who walls of legendary thickness have repulsed the bloodiest assaults for century after century.

Jerondst is the last outpost of civilization before the barbarous emptiness. It is the start and the end of the Golden Road that runs for leagues and leagues to distant Marigor and along it creep colour and culture, merchants and goods; life-blood feeding the valiant heart that pulses behind those cyclopean walls.

A rocky outcrop faces the city, looking down on the first curls of the Golden Road and its steady traffic. Slabs of brown, grainy stone are dotted with black lichen and the palest green moss. There are only the uncaring razor-billed Azrian hawks to watch as, just for a moment, an oblique ray of sun slants across the surface and Ygyrd's stony face is visible. He looks down at the grim, unconquerable fortress and the suggestion of a smile tugs at the line of his lips. Then the ray fades and there is nothing but slabby rock and patches of pale moss.

The End of The Riddle of the Seer by ACM Prior.

The second book in the Power of Pain series is **The Maker of Warriors** and deals with the fate of Bolan and Rhesa.

"Someone is practising arts best left to rot..."
Seeking revenge on the creator of the giant who killed Hophni below Rokepike Castle, Bolan must once again call for aid from Jebbin, the Mage without a Staff.

Only the Thieves Guild have the network to find the sorcerer. Unfortunately, they have also sworn to kill Jebbin and they have paid the assassins to kill Bolan.

Bolan's failure to follow Algolian rules forces him to flee across the country with Jebbin and a renegade captain, pursued by the army, Rhabdos of the Hazel staff, and the thieves before he can even think of reaching the Maker himself on the island of Torl. Bolan and the Captain must both come to terms with the traumas of their past - but will any of them survive a meeting with the inhuman Maker of Warriors?

The third book in the Power of Pain series is **The Drouhin of Shaddimur,** a murder mystery set in far Shekkem.

Kalainen the Drouhin is a distrusted outsider in the sprawling port of Shaddimur, living by solving crimes that baffle the city watch.

As war looms between the Seven Cities, a killer has been assassinating high-ranking members of Shaddimur society. Aided by his apprentices, Yanni, a gutter urchin, and Mardenifol, a noble's son with a predilection for chemistry, Kalainen must use his wits to solve the puzzles left by a treacherous spy and prevent the war by finding conclusive proof of the identity of the killer. And he must do it before the xenophobic leaders of Shaddimur use him as a scapegoat.

Lightning Source UK Ltd.
Milton Keynes UK
UKHW020932150822
407319UK00011B/2167